The Trickster

The Dreamcatcher Chronicles

Jason Lee Willis

Lura Publications

Mapleton, Minnesota

Copyright © 2024 by **Jason Lee Willis**

Editor: Raven Eckman
Editor: Caryl Bunkowske
Cover Design: Lyka Marie Toledo
Interior Chapter Graphics: Ella Olson

All rights reserved. No part of this publication may be reproduced, distributed or transmitted in any form or by any means, without prior written permission.

Jason Lee Willis/Lura Publications, LLC
803 Silver Street E.
Mapleton, MN, 56065
lurapublications.wixsite.com/books

Publisher's Note: This is a work of fiction. Names, characters, places, and incidents are a product of the author's imagination. Locales and public names are sometimes used for atmospheric purposes. Any resemblance to actual people, living or dead, or to businesses, companies, events, institutions, or locales is completely coincidental.

Book Layout © 2017 BookDesignTemplates.com

The Trickster/ Jason Lee Willis -- 1st ed.
ISBN 979-8-9903790-3-9

Dedicated to "my" Lacy Morrisons

In 1986, I was fifteen.
Any upperclassman girl that gave me attention
made me feel like a superhero.
Granted, I never had a chance to prove my love
by battling the forces of darkness
with the fate of the world on the line,
but I'd like to think I'd try
in order to impress them.

I guess I'm still trying to impress them.

Important People from 1986

- Tom Dobie—The Face of Death
- Brian "Biff" Forsberg—The Guardian
- Ansel Nielson—The Warrior
- Chuck Luning—A Leader
- Lily Guerin—A Spider
- Father Gary McKenzie—A Spiritual Guide
- Migisi—A Spiritual Guide
- Earl "Wally" Crain—A Leader
- Karson Luning—The Intellectual
- Leonard White Elk—The Poet

For the rest of Hiawatha County, check out the back of the Dream Journal
Sincerely,
--Robin Berg

Contents

The Trickster 1
Sweet Treats 7
On Patrol 13
Armed and Dangerous 19
Private Investigations 23
Red-Blooded 30
Why Migisi? 35
The Longest Night 40
Nevermore 46
Where There's Smoke 55
And Through the Woods 59
More Thunderbird than Jeep 63
Over the River 70
The Sleep of Death 78
Fortress of Solitude 82
The Black Horse 86
Out of the Loop 97
The Flames of Prophecy 101
A Deal with the Devil 105
Along Came a Spider 110
Rebounds 117
Murder Most Fowl 122
Auld Lang Syne 126
Wobble? No. 134

Snow Day	140
The Caged Bird Sings	149
A Foundation of Murder	155
The Missionary	160
Sleep No More	167
Perihelion	171
Promposals	176
Jaga	181
The Only Way	185
Time to Process	189
Til Death Do Us Part	193
That is the Question	199
To Be, or Not to Be	205
Abode of the Dead	209
What's In a Name?	215
Wendigo Moon	219
Mandatum Novum Do Vobis	223
Good Friday	227
Sabbath	235
Divine Intervention	239
Closing a Loop	244
The River of Souls	249
The Destroyer of Worlds	255
Memory Care	262
Bear Traps	267
Hypothetically Ever After	271
Playing with Fire	275
Witenagemot	282

The Betrayal of Verðandi	287
Repeat After Me	292
Bowling with Balboa	297
Stained Red	306
Arson and Old Lace	311
In Seventy-Six Years	318
This Mortal Coil	322
Up the Water Spout	330
Pewabic Means Clay	335
Stormchaser	342
Shadow and Smoke	345
God of Thunder	348
A Hostile Witness	353
A Change is Gonna Come	361
Caught in the Net	366
Guardians of the Knife	371
Eye of the Hurricane	377
Part of the Job	381
Best Friends Forever (and Never)	386
Like Pulling Teeth	393
My Mind's Eye	399
The Keepers of Secret Knowledge	404
The Long Game	412
Like a Canary	418
Clay Means Vitriol	422
Evidence Discovery	425
Manu Scriptus	430
A Strong Man's House	438

A New Era 445
The Hour of Doom 450
The Face of Brotherhood 455
Farewell, Sweet Prince 461
Burying Joey 471
Operation: Red Thunderbird 476
Right Beside Her 481

Robin's Photoshop Maps to Help Picture Where Stuff Happens in 1985-86

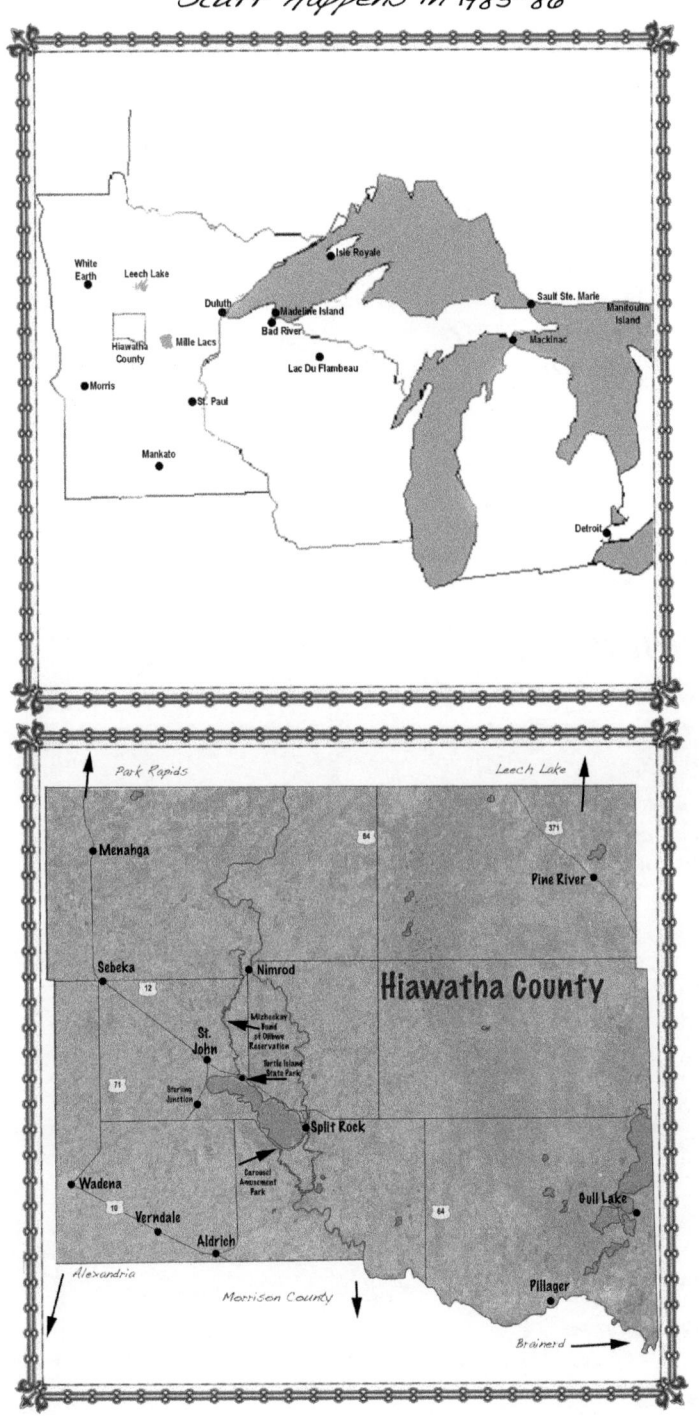

Robin's Photoshop Maps to Help Picture Where Stuff Happens in 1985-86

PRELUDE

The Trickster

Cass County, MN
July 2029

R agnarok, the epic Norse legend about the end of the world, began in the bedroom of Robin Berg. Instead of a triple winter, a ship of death, and the disappearance of the sun and moon, the harbingers of doom were a half-burned dream journal, a syringe of heroin, and a 23andMe DNA test.

A chill woke her, and her hand trembled as it searched for a blanket over the edge of her bed. Instead of the warmth of cotton, her fingers found a pool of cold vomit on the floor. Her other hand found a blanket between the wall and the bed, and she took control of her muscle spasms long enough to curl up with the blanket in the corner.

No one even checked on me, Robin realized. *How long have I been unconscious?*

Prior to receiving the DNA test results, Robin had been 85-90% certain that she wanted to kill herself. Her wrists were already covered in scars from previous attempts that went back to her sixth-grade year, but they'd been private experiments and the pain of blades on her flesh quickly changed her mind. The heroin had been a final coin flip to let whatever cruel god that ruled her fate (Odin, Manabozho, or Jesus) make the decision whether she lived or died.

Thus Robin 2.0 came to life with the stench of cold vomit in her nostrils.

She wiped her runny nose and stared up at the glow-in-the-dark stars pressed into her popcorn ceiling. Strangely, the stars in her imaginary worlds were the same as the ones in her own world, but the stories they told were different. Unfortunately, she couldn't be part of the world of Hiawatha County—since it didn't exist.

I'm just schizophrenic. She'd never seen a doctor for her mental illness. She was too poor for that, and her adoptive father believed that cellphones and "woke" culture were the reasons for mental illnesses. Robin knew that mental illnesses could be treated. *The voices are real only in my head.*

But if she wasn't mentally ill then…

Robin forced a deep breath and commanded her body to rise. Unlike the other girls in her class, she still had the body of a pudgy toddler; the magical wand of puberty failed to give her the right kind of curves. Her flawed body struggled to stand. Her room spun for a moment as her racing heart pounded in her chest. She saw the baggie, the spoon, and even the lighter before spotting the charred journal on her bedroom floor. *Thank God, I didn't destroy it.*

Her dream journal contained several years of strange dreams, and at the back, a chart of all the faces, places, and facts that had become as real to her as those in her real life.

I'm sorry, she told Lily. *I didn't mean it.*

Lily Guerin, like all the other people in her dream journal, was only a figment of her schizophrenic imagination, but to her, many were more dear than the people in the real world. Just a few weeks earlier, Robin had confirmed that neither Hiawatha County nor Lake Manitou even existed and that the reservation built along the banks of the Blue Knife River was only a potato field. Lily, the old Firehandler born to a Lakota mother and Ojibwe father, had been the first to visit Robin's dreams with dire warnings about the pending doom of the earth. Lily tasked Robin with a mission that would not only fix the problems caused by herself but also ultimately save the entire world.

But it turns out I'm just crazy.

Although Robin was relieved that her old friends—Lily and the others in the dream journal—had not been destroyed by her Bic lighter, she turned to her new nightmare instead. The 23andme DNA test had been purchased against her adopted father's wishes. Her adopted dad was one of Crow Wing County's notorious meth cooks, and while his lab reached Walter White levels of cleanliness, his home was a chaotic mess. Just like the filth, drugs and cash were left in the open. Rationalizing that her dad owed her, Robin stole big and paid big, but the results had almost killed her. She doubted he'd ever realize how much she even stole.

Despite the school social worker's and guidance counselor's promises about "being whatever you want to be," the results of the DNA test told her she had two X chromosomes—even though her eyes told her that she was different from the other girls in the locker room. Robin's recent downward spiral began with confirmation that her mind had been broken and ended with confirmation that her body was broken, too.

Robin's eyes looked to the empty plastic bag, and despite the tremors in her hands, she reached down to pick up the other pages of her packet on the floor. Everyone in her life said she was crazy, yet her broken mind had no problem with academic challenges, and the folks at 23andMe gave the result in a way that any idiot could understand.

Holy Shit!

Her colorized chart that showed the origin of her DNA lit up like a Christmas tree: yellow, dark blue, light blue, light green, and even purple—*I really am a Mut mutt*, Robin's inner voice bullied her with a bad Eygptian mythology pun.

Her first glance went right down the left column:

French and German—the light blue

British and Irish—the dark blue

Northwestern European—more blue

Central Africa—the purple

Native American—the yellow

Who am I?

Her whole body began to shake, forcing her to wrap herself tightly in her blanket. It was most likely a result of her purposeful heroin overdose, but fear and exhilaration also caused her body to shake. She tossed aside the easy-to-read chart and set the dense textual analysis between her knees for steadier reading.

The voices in her mind began to shout out interpretations.

Winnie Sweating Stone—Dakota, Lakota, and Pillager Ojibwe.

Big Squeak Weber—Anishinaabe, Potawatomi, and Cree.

Martin Nielson—Faroe Islands.

Bjorn Forsberg—Swedish Goth.

Jean Guerin—French.

Karson Luning—African.

Wally Crain—English.

Albert Fischer—German.

MacPherson, Campbell, Sinclair, Morrison—Scottish.

Larson and Berg—Norwegian.

Are they all part of me?

Am I the messed up final generation in their pathetic lineage?

Robin leaned her head back against her bedroom wall and closed her eyes. Her classmates hated her. She'd been ready to die only a few hours (or days) earlier, but that was only an attempt to stop the pain of her present torment—a torment of bullying, insecurity, isolation, hatred, and confusion.

The past, however...

Robin opened her eyes and held the results almost to her nose. Even though it was only a small percentage, her Indigenous DNA connected back to the story of Lily Guerin, the awful era of forced boarding schools, governmental theft of lands, and the eradication of customs and beliefs. Even before Lily, her DNA had walked the seven stopping places of the Seven Fires Prophecy migration from the Atlantic to the lands of the Sioux, the Oceti Sakowin. *Is Lily truly my ancestor? Is that why she called out to me from beyond the grave?*

Hell had also visited her dreams. The broken visage of a woman with half a face normal and the other side twisted and mangled—Hela from Norse mythology—called out to her in dreams, warning her just like Lily warned of a future of doom and destruction that would come in another thirty years.

A final appearance of Halley's comet before the darkness.

She bent down to pick up her dream journal, folded the DNA results, and slid them between the filled pages.

What the People believe is true, Robin repeated, words she'd received from old Migisi. But was accepting the premise of the saying a descent into madness?

Fuck it, Robin decided. The present wanted her dead for being a freak, but the past and the future called out for a champion. Even though her DNA had manifested in a mushy lump, she had the blood of warriors, guardians, prophets, poets, and leaders.

Like she did in school, Robin put on blinders, ignoring the details of the rental house where she'd almost died. Once in the kitchen, she found a pair of keys from one of the passed-out freeloaders her dad collected, and even though she didn't legally drive yet, she had no fear for the consequences. Soon, she found herself standing on the back steps facing the alley where several cars were packed in tightly.

A raven looked down at her from its perch in a silver maple tree.

Another raven sat atop the roof of a house across the alley.

Were they messengers from the past? The future? Or were they just schizophrenia manifestations of a broken brain?

What I believe is true!

Robin pushed the unlock button, and one of the cars mischievously winked at her. "Take me to the Roots of Lærad," Robin called out in the stillness of the present. Lærad—the old magical tree from mythology. The raven on the rooftop took flight. She had a general theory about the missing willow trees surrounding Lake Manitou and elsewhere in the world. Albert Fischer and Lily had stumbled across them almost by accident, but Robin's dreams had also shown her how the Order of Eos had used the timeless trees for ill purposes.

It's time I started fighting back, Robin decided as she committed grand theft by starting a stolen car. *It's time for me to send a few ravens of my own.*

CHAPTER ONE

Sweet Treats

Split Rock, MN
October 31, 1985

Levi MacPherson indulged Edna Forsberg when she opened the door. "Trick or treat." A beat later, ten-year-old Daniel MacPherson added, "Trick or Treat." Levi had to nudge his youngest brother Joey, to say the expected line, "Trick or Treat."

"Oh, my," Mrs. Forsberg said. The overweight widow clad in polyester clapped her hands together and then quickly retreated to the nearby table where a cookie sheet held a dozen popcorn balls, each wrapped in plastic. "I wasn't sure anyone would stop by tonight. Take two, Mr. Hamburglar."

Daniel boldly freed the first from its sticky status on the pan and dropped it into his empty ice cream bucket. "Thank you," he said without taking a second and bolting off the porch back to the idling car.

Joey was not so confident, and Mrs. Forsberg grabbed ahold of a sprinkled popcorn ball and offered it to him. "And who are you? Frankenstein?"

Joey nodded, extended his bucket, and darted away once he got the treat.

"And who are you supposed to be," Mrs. Forsberg inquired, turning to Levi. "Jim Morrison?"

Surprised the old farm wife even knew rock and roll, Levi chuckled, "I'm just me." He wore a canvas trenchcoat, snakeskin boots, a pair of leather pants, and a loose-fitting white cotton shirt, unbuttoned to show off his collection of pendants and necklaces "Thank you, Mrs. Forsberg. Have a nice night."

"Stay warm, boys," she called out.

Levi's black 1969 Mustang convertible purred in the Forsberg driveway. After a summer of baling hay, walking beanfields, tending chickens, and fattening livestock, he cashed-in all of his hard work for the coolest car at Split Rock High School. With his oldest brother Reuben crowned 1982 Homecoming King, and his sister Leah recently crowned 1983 Homecoming Queen, popularity was not a problem for the sophomore, but Levi wanted kids to know that he was different from his older "goodie-two shoes" siblings. They were Christian rock; he was heavy metal.

Levi handed his popcorn ball to Daniel, who was riding shotgun.

"I don't want it," Daniel said. "I didn't eat the one from last year.

Levi turned up the stereo, and "Tears are Falling" from Kiss drowned out his younger brother's complaints.

The trek into Split Rock took only a minute, and after pulling out of the Forsberg driveway, he followed Old Copper Road across the Doc Jenkins Bridge and into the downtown. From experience, Levi avoided the worn-down downtown neighborhood and instead drove to the north side of town, up the hill and past the high school. He parked at the top of the hill where all the newer houses were built overlooking the river valley.

As soon as they stopped, Daniel bolted ahead.

"Hey!" Levi shouted out. "Wait for your brother."

Just a kindergartner, Joey had already gone trick-or-treating twice, but this year, Mom had made a stink about Halloween being a pagan holiday and didn't want to bring her youngest sons into town despite having taken her four older children during their elementary years. So, Levi sat in the Mustang at the end of the block as he watched his brothers go door to door.

From numerous school fundraisers and a decade of Halloweens, Levi knew each and every house in Split Rock, a former logging town whose population had peaked in 1950 at 2,500 residents and was now down to 1,800 after the lumber mill, creamery, and half-a-dozen businesses closed along Market Street.

By the time he switched from the *Asylum* cassette to Mötley Crüe's *Theatre of Pain* cassette, his brothers had covered all seven blocks of the "new" avenues that were built along the upper parts of Split Rock.

"My bucket's full," Daniel proudly declared as he set it on the passenger seat and grabbed the second one he'd brought. Along with a ban on rock music and Halloween, his mother didn't buy sugary treats at the grocery store either, so Daniel planned to stock up for months.

Levi glanced at his Casio watch, which told him it was 7:43 PM. Standing at the car window, Joey's cheeks were bright red from the cold. "Joe, take a break for a bit, okay. Warm up in the back seat. Dan, you can do South Division street and then we're done, okay?"

Daniel shrugged and took off with his second bucket.

By the time Levi drove down to the hill, Joey was already half-asleep. Levi turned around in the parking lot of Telemark Bank so he didn't have to watch Daniel through the rearview mirror. He kept his lights off, but already, the throngs of trick-or-treaters had thinned.

A Hiawatha County Sheriff's Deputy cruised north on Market Street without urgency, a reminder that the adults still controlled the world around them. Meanwhile he saw Daniel running off up the hill with two other kids who were going up Tracy Street, a side street with about ten houses on it.

It'll be my fault when we're not back by 8:00 PM.

Although in park, Levi put his foot on the brake, thinking about driving down to intercept Daniel and putting an end to the holiday, but as he contemplated, he saw a distinctive sight in his rearview mirror—a woman's breast.

At first, he leaned forward to put his nose almost to the glass of the mirror, just to confirm what his eyes were showing him. Behind him, the Telemark Bank parking lot extended for about a dozen parking spots, and beyond that was a shared yard for about eight houses. In the space between Adam's Garage and the much smaller single garages of the residential neighborhood, a female figure stumbled unsteadily. His heart pitter-pattered when he confirmed the jiggle of a breast and an exposed nipple as the woman headed directly for his Mustang.

He turned around for a better look through the rear window. It was a young woman with a mane of curly blond hair. She stumbled in her white ankle boots, fashionable but clumsy on the grass. She wore a short mini-skirt also, but her tube top had been twisted into something that looked like a bandelier that crossed her torso.

This isn't a costume—this is bad.

His foot slipped off the brake pedal, and for a moment, the woman disappeared in the darkness.

When her hands fell against the trunk of the convertible, both Levi and Joey jumped. She found her way to the driver's door and all but fell into the open window.

"Oh, thank God," she said upon seeing Levi.

Besides the Penthouse magazine that Reuben kept in the hayloft, and one time that Leah left her bedroom door ajar, Levi had little experience with breasts and nipples, but there, less than a foot from him, he saw Lacy Morrison's left breast appear in his open window.

When she looked back to the garages in the distance, Levi noticed her face was streaked with rivulets of mascara, there was a swollen contusion on her cheek, and fresh blood trickled down from her broken lip.

"Get me out of here," she said as both a command and a plea. She nodded her head and Levi, his heart racing, nodded back. She went around the nose of the Mustang, her hands holding onto the hood for balance as she walked around to the empty passenger seat.

"What's wrong with her?" Joey asked from the backseat, now wide awake.

She's drunk, Levi observed as she fumbled with the big door.

The twelfth-grader flopped into his bucket seat with a stature not that much bigger than Daniel. She took one second to turn around, looking past a startled Joey, and twisted her face in anger to shout out, "Just go!"

Levi shifted and pulled out of the bank parking lot.

The deputy went north.

Levi kept his eyes on the road as he pulled onto Market Street, and Lacy's breathing filled the cab while "Raise your Hands to Rock" played in the background.

"Lights!" Lacy snapped.

Levi had pulled onto the main drag without turning on his lights. He nervously fumbled to find the knob, feeling the car drift as his attention shifted. "I saw a cop, um, just bit ago. He was—"

"No! No, no, no," Lacy said. She suddenly became aware of her exposed breast and pulled at the stretchy tube-top until it was covered. Drops of blood covered what remained over her shirt. "I'm…I'm…fuck. Just…just…take me home. I live just—"

Her shaky hands pointed ahead and slightly left.

Split Rock was a small town, so Levi already knew where Lacy Morrison lived, even though he'd never been invited to her house. He obeyed her command and turned onto Old Mill Road, which crossed over the Crow Wing River, past the public boat launch, and onto a short "private drive" for four newer lake homes. Lacy lived in the blue house.

Levi had barely put the car into park when both of her hands clamped onto his right arm. "Levi, right?"

He nodded.

"I don't want this to be, um, don't let…can you forget this ever happened? Seriously, I mean it. Promise me that you won't be one of those assholes that tells everybody what you saw tonight, okay? I made a mistake, and I don't want to make it bigger, okay? Okay?"

He just sat there like an idiot.

Her hand reached out and he flinched as she took hold of his chin. "Promise me, Levi," she said, forcing his chin to nod. "Promise me."

"I promise."

"Promise what?"

"I won't say anything to anybody."

Then Lacy turned to Joey. Her face tightened in painful contemplation. "I was at a Halloween Party and I fell down. My costume fell off and broke. Don't worry. I'm fine, honey."

The big door swung open, and she slipped out but stopped in the doorway. "Thank you, Levi. I won't forget how you helped me."

She gently closed the door, but instead of going in the main door, she walked around the side of the lake home and vanished in the darkness closer to the lake.

Levi watched the house for a few moments, but none of the lights turned on.

"What about Daniel?"

Shit. Levi turned the car around. "Look, Joe, I think that girl had been at a party where there was alcohol, and you know how much Mom hates drinking, right? If you say anything about her, Mom might think I'm lying and that I was at a party also. So can you promise me that you can keep a secret, too?"

"What happened to her?"

Lacy Morrison was raped. "I don't know. Like she said, she must've fallen down, and ruined her costume. Can you promise you won't tell Mom about this?"

"I promise."

Levi turned off the cassette player, and a few minutes later, he was driving up South Division Street. The parking lot of Telemark Bank was empty, so he continued half a block to turn up Washington, where he saw Daniel coming down the block toward him. Levi flashed the light and honked the horn twice, bringing Halloween 1985 to an end.

CHAPTER TWO

On Patrol

Wadena, MN
November 1, 1985

Brian Forsberg's belly gurgled at the thought of the Boondoggle. His 37-year-old bladder also demanded attention. He pulled into the town of Wadena a bit early, and at 5:50 AM, the little town of 4,500 continued to sleep. A block off the intersection of Highways 71 and 10, Forsberg parked in front of the Boondocks Cafe on Jefferson Street.

He picked up the dispatch radio. "Dispatch, this is Forsberg. Stopping at the Boondocks for a little breakfast."

"Roger that," Katie Lopez answered through the radio speaker. "Will you be coming in for the morning briefing?"

The lights inside of the cafe distracted him, and he saw Sherry unlock the door with a friendly wave. "Um, yeah, but tell Dave to do it, and, um, who's working records this morning?"

Katie Lopez, the low rung in the dispatch department, grew silent for a moment as she searched for her answer back in St. John. "Charlene."

Good. She knows what the hell she's doing. "Your shift ends at seven?"

"Roger that."

"I'll bring you a cinnamon roll. Over and out."

Stepping out of the SUV, Brian hiked up his gun belt and stretched his back after sitting for the past four hours. *Why do I feel like an old man?* As soon as he stepped through the doors, he was greeted by Sherry Lucas, who despite knowing him for a decade, still greeted him with, "Good morning, Sheriff Forsberg. The kitchen is still warming up, but can I get you a cinnamon roll?"

"Make it six," he said before turning to the bathroom.

WHEN HE SAT at his booth facing Jefferson Street, a box of cinnamon rolls greeted him. A moment later, Sherry came with a pot of coffee. He covered his cup with his hand, saying, "Orange juice today, I just worked an overnight shift and need to catch a nap by midmorning."

"Quiet Halloween?" Sherry Lucas, a mother of three grown children, now put her maternal instincts to use by tending to her regulars. For years, waitressing had helped her in hard times, and now she ran the restaurant and served as a surrogate mother of sorts.

"Night's not quite over," Brian said, knocking on the pine trim of the window frame for luck, "but nothing worse than some punks with eggs in Staples."

"Any company this morning?"

"Three," he said, glancing out to the street.

WALLY CRAIN WAS the first to join him at 6:02. At 58, Wally still looked as sturdy as he had been two decades earlier when he'd been Brian's Boy Scout Pack 88 leader. His dark hair had grayed, along with the hair in his mustache and eyebrows, but the oil delivery driver and World War Two Navy vet seemed a foot shorter than he'd once been.

Chuck Luning joined a few minutes later. Growing up, Chuck Luning had been Brian's hero after guiding the Split Rock Bulldogs to the 1956 Class A Football Championship. The former linebacker walked with a cane after a harrowing helicopter crash in the final days of the Vietnam War. Despite his gimpy leg, Chuck still had the shoulders and arms of a linebacker due to the fact that he regularly worked out with his disabled son, Karson, who lost the use of his legs in a hunting accident. Lifting weights was the only other socializing Brian had with the 47-year-old, and although he had a warm relationship with Chuck's 29-year-old son, Brian's relationship with Chuck remained frosty and was more complicated by the fact that he looked like his dead brother Chris, Brian's childhood friend.

Ten minutes later, Gary Mackenzie came rushing in and slid into the booth. "My apologies, gentlemen." Although a Vietnam veteran, Gary looked nothing like the three other vets at the table. First, he was a head taller than the other men and rail thin. The former high school phenom was also a hippy at heart, which manifested itself with an earring in his left ear and hair that was pulled back into a six-inch ponytail. Although three years older than Brian at 40, Gary was the closest thing he had to a true friend. Like himself, Gary was also single, and like Brian, it has been a deliberate choice, although for a completely different reason—Gary was a Catholic priest—a Jesuit, in fact, which was how his congregation in Split Rock rationalized his eccentricities.

After the four men finished their hearty breakfasts, their conversations became hushed as they found little privacy in a restaurant that was almost packed by seven o'clock.

"It appears as if all the kids in Hiawatha County came home safely last night," Brian began. "But we're heading into a weekend, so I have doubled patrols just to keep an eye out for weirdos."

"Like Troost," Wally muttered.

Brian saw Gary's eyes narrow. Although Gary knew the history of child abductions in Hiawatha County, he'd been in California in 1962 and had no connection to the name.

Hearing the name made Brian's stomach twist. Brian shrugged. "Like Troost. If the shit's gonna hit the fan six-months from now, it'll probably start quietly. Hell, we might not even know anything's happened." He was referring to any human sacrifices made by the sinister cult known as the Order of Eos. "So, I want to move forward as if something had happened last night."

"Full meeting?" Wally asked matter-of-factly.

"Everyone but Lily," Brian said in reference to the Isanti Lodge's founding member. "She needs to conserve her strength for the days to come, and if any of you visit her, keep things positive and light regardless of what's going on."

"If Lily's not coming, should we meet at City Hall?" Chuck asked. Since returning to Hiawatha County in 1972, he'd turned his football celebrity and war-hero status into political popularity as the mayor of Split Rock. In a way, both men were politicians, yet Chuck seemed more Hollywood than hick.

"Too conspicuous," Father Gary countered.

"You're all pillars of the community," Chuck explained.

"If it's a full meeting, folks in Split Rock might take notice."

"We'll meet at the MBO Rez like they did in the old days," Brian stated. They all knew about the Mizheekay Band of Ojibwe Reservation along the Blue Knife River at the heart of Hiawatha County. He turned to Wally to ask, "Can you make the arrangements with Migisi?"

"Absolutely. If it's a full meeting, we'll need to give Leonard enough time to fly out from Calgary—or drive."

The Isanti Lodge had been formed by Lily in 1898 after her encounter with the evil spirit known by her ancestors as the Wintermaker. Brian's Norse ancestors knew it as the evil fire demon Surtr. Father Gary theorized the spirit to be the sleeping demon known by early Christians as Apollyon and by the Jews as Abaddon. In 1898 and 1962, the Order of Eos had attempted to fulfill their dark prophecies by waking the spirit—only to be stopped by Lily. With the coming of Halley's Comet in April, a sign believed to be connected to the Seven Fires Prophecies of Lily's people, a battle brewed—if the tales were true.

"I'll, uh, stop by and speak with MacPherson," Chuck offered. "We need to keep him in the loop."

At this, Father Gary also took initiative by answering, "I'll try to say something to Nicki after choir practice. Don't expect any miracles, though."

"Keep setting the bar lower and lower," Brian joked. "Eventually we won't expect anything from you at all."

Father Gary rolled his eyes.

"What should we do about…" Wally suddenly grew hesitant and avoided Brian's gaze. He then looked up to finish, "about the Wa-bi-zha-shi situation?"

You had to bring up Jimmy, didn't you?

The Wa-bi-zha-shi was the Anishinaabeg word for the Marten, the symbol for the Warrior Clan within Ojibwe society, upon which Lily's Isanti Lodge was replicated.

Wally Crain represented the Ah-ji-jawk, the cautious leadership role.

Chuck Luning represented the Maang, the aggressive leadership role.

Forsberg represented the Guardians of society, the protective bear, Makwa.

Karson Luning took over the role from his great-grandfather Albert Fisher and despite his youth, served as the philosophical peacekeeper in the lodge.

When the Isanti Lodge formed, Migisi Asibikaashi assumed the role of the Bird Clan, the Binesi, which traditionally represented the spiritual, but since Lily had been baptized as a Christian, she insisted on dividing the role of spiritual adviser to the man who eventually became her husband, the defrocked Father Jean Guerin. When that role went empty, Brian filled it with a complete stranger to Hiawatha County, his former chaplain during the Vietnam War, Gary Mackenzie.

Ever the poet, Leonard White Elk took the original position held by Fawn Chevreuil, and despite living in the Canadian Rockies, the 60-year-old elder trained an entire generation of his family to serve as assistants, Fire Keepers, guards, and helpers for the sacred rituals that would be performed at the end of the Seventh Fire.

But when Jimmy Nielson took his life on January 6th, 1978, the role of the warrior, held by him after Martin Nielson and Ed Nielson, remained unfilled. Seven years after his best-friend's suicide, Brian still hadn't called Jimmy's widow or kids in Indiana. "Ansel's just a kid," Brian muttered.

A very damaged kid, too.

Wally had another layer of grit to his soul when he sighed. "So were you in 1962. It didn't stop you from picking up that pitchfork or jumping into the lake to save those kids. Do you want me to call?"

"And say what?" Brian grew even more bitter. "There's a reason they all left home."

CHAPTER THREE

Armed and Dangerous

Staten Island, NY
November 2, 1985

The monsters had found him.

Ansel Nielson hid in his bed wearing only his "tighty whities." A pillow shielded his head. Outside, on the roof of the building, he could hear the monsters clawing at the shingles of the house.

I need a weapon—I need to defend myself.

Ansel Nielson had recently turned fourteen, but puberty had done little to help him. Compared to other freshmen, he was short and thin. He'd grown out his hair into a mop that covered his forehead, brow, and eyes and then dyed it jet black to hide his optimistic blonde hair.

The scratching continued, and Ansel's fear of what lived under his bed was lost to the sounds coming from the roof. He swung his feet out, stood up, and glanced at his ceiling in case the claws ripped through the shingles. He'd always liked his upstairs bedroom since it was furthest from the basement. His dreams warned him that the monsters would crawl up from the moist floor drains, but now, this aerial attack caught him by surprise.

No use screaming—I'm all alone.

With six months of good behavior came the reward—trust. His mother and stepfather had gone into the city for a play and stayed in a hotel rather than returning late. Emily, the family's maid, stayed with him most of the day, cooking him lunch and supper, and all but tucked him in a few hours earlier. She lived in some shithole apartment at the center of Staten Island but with a push of a button, she could appear.

I'd rather face the monsters than be a coward.

First things first, Ansel dressed himself. He slipped on a pair of black Levi jeans, all-white Reeboks, and a Twisted Sister shirt with baseball cut sleeves.

How long have you been watching me? He asked the darkness. *When was the last time I was left alone?*

Most likely…seven years ago.

His father faced the monsters back then, and they took his life. A lightning bolt flashed across his brain, leaving him with a horrifying solution to his current situation.

The easier plan, if he chose it, meant going downstairs, where the call button could summon hope. *Is this me facing my fears or giving in to them?* The shrinks in Manhattan had helped him separate his monsters into two groups—the real monsters and those created by trauma. The real monsters were dead and buried in Churubusco, Indiana—thousands of miles from him. But the monsters of his mind shouldn't have been able to scratch on the roof with claws so real he could almost feel the vibrations.

Downstairs, Ansel found himself standing in the kitchen. Butcher knives waited in drawers. Steak knives waited in blocks. The phone. Pills. Hell, there was even alcohol in the top shelves of the cupboards.

He left the kitchen, pausing at the landing that separated the basement stairs and the garage. Over the past seven years, the monsters in the basement had been defeated through counseling, so he turned toward the garage.

His hand slowly turned the knob, and for almost a minute, he stood facing the darkness.

This time, there was no ladder.

Nor was the orange extension cord wrapped around the rafters.

Even in the darkness, he knew the Staten Island garage had a finished ceiling with a clean, gray floor that had never had a drop of blood upon it.

So, he boldly flipped on the light switch.

The bulging eyes of his father did not greet him, and Ansel let out a long sigh and went to work.

He found a ladder, centered it under the storage door, pushed the panel aside, and reached up into the hole. His arms were scrawny, but he had enough strength to pull the rest of his scrawny body up into the hole of the garage attic.

Thomas Archibald III, his stepfather, spared no expense. His stepfather had inherited millions, yet Tom didn't always waste it foolishly. He lived far below his means with the purchase of a modest cottage facing Hudson Bay; however, he had a yacht anchored in Greece that cost twice the price of the house. This cottage was meant to keep Ansel grounded, yet every corner of it had a certain extravagance, including the fact that the hidden garage attic was professionally finished and had wired lighting to illuminate the space.

It's where his mother Aurora hid the past.

Ansel had been in the attic half-a-dozen times but not in the past two years. Memory led him to a few boxes that contained the contents of his sister Tonya's room. Seven years ago, Tonya had been the one who first heard the disturbance in the garage, and even though she was five years older, she turned to her little brother to defend her.

The real monsters had already been killed by their father.

That's why their father had been covered in blood.

It wasn't Jimmy Nielson's blood that dripped onto the bare concrete floor in the Churubusco garage—it was the blood of human monsters.

Ansel found Tonya's stuffed bear and saw the dark blood stains upon its fur. He looked at his fingers that had no trace of blood, but the stains remained.

After finding his father hanging in the garage, some invisible force guided him to perform an inexplicable act. Not even his Manhattan shrinks had pried this detail from his traumatized mind: the head of the two-foot tall bear came off relatively easily to reveal a silver shaft extending down through the spine of the bear to where its hips held the mother-of-pearl handle of a Colt Python revolver.

One bullet, ready to be fired, remained in the chamber.

Dad left it for a reason—in case new monsters came back.

With the pistol he'd hidden seven years earlier in hand, Ansel found himself creeping outside the house. If it was time to battle monsters, he at least wasn't going down without a fight. The big .357 Magnum would likely knock him over but not until the monster paid the price.

Ansel chose a spot in deep shadow, where a tree provided cover to step away from the foundation of the house for a better view at the rooftop.

He held the pistol to his chest.

He took ten paces.

And then turned.

It wasn't a monster.

The inky, hairy creatures from his dream were nowhere to be found.

Instead, a single raven sat upon the roof, and before he could even move the pistol, it flew off into the darkness of the west.

CHAPTER FOUR

Private Investigations

Hiawatha County
November 3, 1985

The lights were still on when Brian Forsberg woke on his living room couch instead of his bed. The left tendon in his neck throbbed—an old football injury. Waking felt like a hangover, but it wasn't alcohol that caused him pain.

The coffee table in front of him—and its pile of evidence—still waited for him to solve the great mysteries of his life.

First, he packaged up the report from 1962 and put everything back into the file for Logan Troost.

Next, he packaged up the report belonging to the Whitley County Sheriff's department, which included the photographs of two crime scenes. The first was a double-homicide. The second was a suicide in a garage. The familiar faces of the dead no longer bothered him, but the photograph of the murder weapon made little sense—an ivory handled .357 Colt Python Magnum. *Can't these people count shell casings?*

Finally, he picked up his own .357 Colt Python Magnum, which he'd purchased at Ton Son Nhut as a Christmas present for the entire tank crew. 11th Armored Cavalry tank commander Jay Campbell's pistol had a wood-grained handle, loader Shane Lewis's pistol had an ivory handle, and for driver Jimmy Nielson, he purchased matching mother-of-pearl handles. If not for seven shells in evidence, Forsberg might've believed Nielson had pawned his own. Even though Jimmy's pistol was missing, the shell casings proved it'd been used the night of the murders.

After working three straight overnight shifts, he now had three days off, but in truth, he never had a day off as Sheriff. He found his shoulder holster on the floor and strapped the gaudy gun to his side. He slipped a red flannel shirt and hunting vest over his stained white t-shirt.

Brian Forsberg lived in one of the most remote corners of Hiawatha County—on purpose. His house was brand new, but the land was ancient. Outside his sliding glass doors, the river valley had dropped its leaves to reveal the confluence of Kanaranzi Creek and the Crow Wing River. A few miles up Kanaranzi Creek were the culverts that drained the wild rice fields of Lake Manitou. A few miles up the Crow Wing River was the town of Split Rock.

A few miles—that was as close as he wanted to be to either place.

SHORTLY AFTER LUNCH, Brian was on the move again, driving north to Leech Lake to visit an old woman who'd been dying for the better part of three decades. After almost dying from a house fire in 1961, Lily Guerin moved from Lake Manitou to her ancestral home at Leech Lake, leaving her Isanti Lodge to hold vigil over the *Place of Souls*. For better or worse, he'd done his part to protect the residents of Hiawatha County for most of his life.

A black car flew down Highway 64 just south of Akeley: Levi MacPherson.

Even though Brian had a removable cherry light he could put onto his roof, he let it go. The kid's speed didn't warrant a ticket. The greater mystery was why the teenager was visiting his great-grandmother when his mother Nicole refused to speak with the matriarch.

Leech Lake, besides being known as a premiere fishery, was the home of the Leech Lake Indian Reservation. In 1898, it witnessed the Battle of Bear Island, which is often referred to as "the Last Indian Uprising in the

United States." The Ojibwe community endured the conflict, and decades of hardship that followed; despite a majority of reservation land being possessed by white owners, several towns remained predominantly Ojibwe, including Onigum, a town that rested on a narrow isthmus at the heart of Leech Lake.

Over the past decade, Brian Forsberg had visited Lily Guerin regularly at the Wanakiwidee Retirement Home, one of the few modern structures in the community. Today, he found Lily hunched in a wheelchair that faced a glass window. At 102, Lily Guerin looked like a sudden sneeze could send her to the hereafter with her wispy white hair, sunken eyes, trembling hands, and skin like wrinkled tissue paper.

"Boozhoo, Tewapa," Brian greeted as he knelt beside her wheelchair. He didn't know more than a handful of Anishinaabe words, but his greeting meant to remind her that he'd done his homework and calling her by her Lakota birth name was even more intentional.

Lily slowly turned to study him, her hand settling on his shoulder. "My Teddy Bear. Your face does not seem troubled, so what news do you bring?"

Makwa—the guardian bear. It was a far better nickname than Biff. He summarized the uneventful weeks from the autumnal equinox through Halloween. "But we're six months from Easter and the return of Halley's comet, so a full meeting of the Isanti Lodge has been called. It will allow us to rehearse the rituals and also share information."

"Be careful with rehearsal," Lily began and then took a moment to gather her breath for another sentence. "This mess began when I rehearsed."

Brian was the third generation of Forsbergs to serve in Lily's Isanti Lodge, so he didn't need convincing that death was coming for more than their matriarch. Any day or hour, the secret society known as the Order of Eos could begin their own ritual meant to wake spirits and resurrect a buried god. For almost a century, the Isanti Lodge defended the people of Hiawatha County from the crazed cult, but in a few months, the defenders would go on the offensive.

Having served in Vietnam, Brian understood that even the best laid battle plans never went the way the generals expected. The Isanti Lodge members knew their parts, and their secret weapon remained hidden under the protection of Lily's brother, Migisi. He'd never seen the sacred Water Drum, but Wally Crain and a few others described its power to him. He also had never seen the relic known as the Ironwood Scrolls, but Lily insisted the ancestors who buried them in a cave centuries ago could somehow reach through time to give her the words.

Lily's plan involved ambushing the dark spirit known as the Wintermaker when the magical powers were heightened by the return of Halley's Comet, and in a strange exorcism of sorts, she would pluck the evil spirit from the depths of Lake Manitou and cast him down a literal and spiritual river so that his soul could descend to the depths where all must go.

"What was Levi doing here?" Brian finally asked after their discussion.

Lily did not respond immediately, a bad sign. "Levi?"

Now she's bullshitting me. "I saw your great-grandson Levi on the way here. What's a kid like Levi doing visiting his great-grandmother on a Sunday afternoon?"

Lily brought her arms back to her lap, clasping her forearms, before answering. "In the stories, the Horned Serpent is killed by a Great Thunderbird. I think Levi is the Great Thunderbird in the stories. Migisi once believed he was the Great Thunderbird, the one destined to defeat the Horned Serpent that swims in the deep, but I believed that role is reserved for a young man."

Horned Serpent, Manitou, Thunderbird—Brian knew all the names of his nemesis. "Is Levi a Firehandler like yourself?"

"These old hands will finish the fight, if that's what you're worried about. I will close the loop that began when I was just a girl and then finish the prophecies that began generations ago."

Is she being evasive or is it just her age? "You know his mother wouldn't want you meeting with him alone."

"Sometimes he brings young Clay also."

Young Clay? Levi's younger brothers were Daniel and Joseph. "Why does Levi come visit you?"

"With his hair grown out, he looks like my father," Lily added. "My father chose to reject the ways of the Wijigan Clan and turn his back on the Anishinaabe people in order to become a bootlegger. I used to despise him for selling alcohol to our people, but my sin—being a schoolteacher—was even worse. Now, life has come full circle, and instead of robbing my people of our language and stories, I am teaching the legends and lore that once brought me shame."

Ambushing the Wintermaker remained the plan, but the details were still too vague for his liking. *Keep her talking and she'll spill the beans.* "You're teaching Levi?"

"You've seen him. Tell me he doesn't look like my father."

"I've never met your father," Brian answered with a huff. "Should this training concern me? Or the Isanti Lodge?"

"Are you worried about me teaching him 'The Song of the Manitou' without proper supervision?"

The Song of the Manitou remained a troubling mystery to Brian. For generations, the Wijigan Clan passed on an oral account of the magical song needed to activate the Water Drum—the legendary Philosopher's Stone—and also wake the Wintermaker from the slumber of death.

Where did it come from?

Not even Lily knew the answer when he had first asked. According to Sakima Riel, a historical consultant and principal at Turtle Island Jesuit School, he believed that the Sacred Shell described in the Seven Fires Prophecy was a written account of the Song of the Manitou from which Lily learned her version. Riel believed the Sacred Shell was hidden in a cave somewhere in the east, and thus, he privately spent his efforts researching the migration of the Anishinaabe people. Even Lily believed she did not possess the entire song, and with only six months remaining until "the Sacred Fire" was lit by the arrival of Halley's Comet, she believed the full song would find its way to her lips.

That sentiment worried Brian Forsberg the most. From what he understood, Lily's partial song was recorded back in 1898, but in her hour of need, she received more of the song from mysterious figures that traveled back through time to come to her aid. As laughable as the premise seemed to Brian, it wasn't the supernatural aspects of the story that bothered him—it was the source. *Who was Lily's puppet master?* "If you want Levi to be trained, perhaps I should bring him to the Isanti Lodge."

"No," Lily answered quickly. "No, it's...he's just curious about his heritage. He's proud of his heritage, in fact. If I'm wrong about the coming battle, then I certainly won't live another seventy-fire years to see the comet arrive. If that is the case, perhaps Levi will need to take my place in the Isanti Lodge."

Wrong? Brian had studied Father Jean Guerin's journal as if it were a religious text. Even though Principal Riel and other scholars disagreed, Father Guerin believed that the Seven Fires were tied to Halley's Comet and that the first "fire" began as early as 1456 or 1532 when the Anishinaabe still lived in the east. "Lily, we're preparing for a battle with the Wintermaker in April. What makes you think you could be wrong?"

"We prepared to battle the Wintermaker the last time the Serpent Star appeared. We practiced our rituals during the winter of 1910 also, but when the time came, our plans fell apart. The Horned Serpent didn't rise, and the Thunderbird had nothing to strike. If our enemy hides, it doesn't matter how prepared we are. That is why I tutor my great-grandson independent of the Isanti Lodge—in case Fawn is right and I am wrong. But I am not wrong. Soon we will defeat the Wintermaker—with Levi's help."

What did Fawn think?

Brian Forsberg nodded in tacit agreement and became aware of the weight of the pistol along his ribs. "What should I do about the role of the Marten?"

"I had no idea how the Isanti Lodge would respond to the attacks of the Wintermaker back in 1962, but whether God or the Great Spirit, you were guided by the hand of fate to do your part. Put your trust in the plan, and we will find a way to victory."

She's as bad as the generals in Vietnam. I want details about the enemy.

Listening to Lily exhausted him. He'd never seen a Tak-Pei—the Little Men of the Forest—or a Horned Serpent, or a Thunderbird, or had a conversation with the Jiibay, the ghosts caught in Lake Manitou. Jimmy Nielson claimed to have spoken to the Wintermaker yet had taken his life in Indiana rather than joining the fight back in Minnesota. Brian Forsberg didn't know if any of the supernatural stories were real, but he did know the Order of Eos was real, and regardless of the twists and turns of prophecy, he meant to protect the people of Hiawatha County.

CHAPTER FIVE

Red-Blooded

Old Copper Road
November 4, 1985

Levi dreamed he killed them all. He didn't murder them in sprays of bloody carnage; in fact, he didn't even have a weapon in his hand during the dispensation of death. In his dream, he floated on a sheet of ice with the soaked, shivering Lacy Morrison huddled beside him. Lake Manitou held the rapists who frantically tried to claw their way out of the frigid water. Although rumors of the incident had spread, he didn't know the names of the assailants yet. Standing over the faceless monsters, Levi used the heel of his snakeskin boot to smash them in their pathetic faces and send them to the depths of the lake.

In his dream, he punished the guilty, but when his alarm clock rang, the identities of the rapists sank into his subconscious.

Levi wanted to be a hero for Lacy, but for now, he could only manage to be the hero his great-grandmother needed him to be. He groaned from the pressure of it all.

Monday mornings—the worst of the week.

Levi sat up in his bed and turned on his end table lamp. Living in the attic, he'd converted the space into a den of decadence worthy of any teenage boy. The bare rafters held posters of his favorite bands and babes. His entertainment center was a pile of boxes with a navy-blue sheet tossed over it. The only true extravagance was his Panasonic Stereo system, which he'd purchased the summer prior to buying his Mustang.

He slipped into a pair of black Levi jeans and grabbed a t-shirt from the top of the pile. He combed his fingers through his shoulder-length black hair to remove any snarls and then found his skull bandana used to keep his bangs out of his eyes.

Wijigan—the skull clan.

At the bottom of the stairs, Joey and Daniel shared a bunk bed in the bedroom that was originally built as an oversized landing. Both were already awake and likely downstairs since none of the MacPhersons ever overslept. Further down the hall, three of the four doors were also open. The first room on the left belonged to Reuben, his older brother. The next room was closed—Ben was away for his freshman year at St. Cloud State University. The room at the end of the hall belonged to Leah, who was still fixing her hair in the mirror in the bathroom as he entered.

She was a wonderful human and all that blah, blah, blah, but as the reigning homecoming queen, it mattered too much to her what people thought of her. Levi reached for his stick of Old Spice and quickly retreated a step. He tossed it back on the counter and reached for his toothbrush, Leah was applying her eyeliner and gave him little notice.

He scrubbed furiously and then inched in front of his sister to spit it all out in the sink.

"Aren't you even going to wash your face and comb your hair?"

He didn't answer as he left.

Downstairs, his family gathered around the kitchen table. Unlike the larger dining room table, the kitchen table acted more like a buffet. His father Gavin was flanked by Reuben and Daniel. The three of them woke around five A.M. to do chores, something Levi used to do prior to buying his stereo and Mustang. Farming was a good way to make a buck, but he was past all of that now. His mother Nicole was at the stove, transferring sausage links to a plate, which she then set in the middle of the table to join the French toast, scrambled eggs, and muffins. Several forks, including Levi's own, began stabbing sausage links.

He stood, plate full, and leaned against the counter.

The early bird got the worm, and at the MacPherson farm, the early bird got the choice spots at the table. When Joey got up from his spot at the end of the table, Levi slid in. By the time Leah finished polishing her veneer, Daniel would vacate his spot. It was orchestrated chaos, as his mother would say.

"Ben is coming down for practice on Wednesday," Mom told him, "so, I don't want any excuses about missing practice. Is that understood?"

He grunted as he chewed, and once he finished, he vocalized, "Understood."

Even though Levi had rejected the farming path of his father, he still walked the path of his mother, although to a much different beat.

A few years back, hoping to bring a dash of Holy Spirit to St. Marie's Catholic Church with a modern Christian Rock Band, his mother switched from being the church organist to being a musical director. The band featured her children. Levi played bass guitar, Ben and Reuben played electric guitar, Leah rocked vocals, and Daniel beat the drums. Even little Joey would pick up a tambourine and do his part while his bleached-blonde mother sat behind her electronic keyboard, reveling in it all.

They were the God-blessed Partridge Family of Split Rock—Rock of Ages.

Stylistically, they embarrassed him.

Music was the only thing that connected him to his mother, who trained him to be a damn good bass guitar player. She was vain, concerned only about social status, and from what he could tell—racist. Even though she was a quarter Indigenous, she openly despised "Indians," which is why she kept Gigi Lily tucked away like a skeleton in the closet.

After finishing breakfast and pecking his mother on the cheek, the first thing Levi did when he got into his Mustang was to put on his Megis Shell necklace, a sacred symbol to the Anishinaabe people. He'd pur-purchased it at the annual Powwow last September. Even though he was only an eighth Indigenous, the genetic wheel left him darker than his siblings—the black sheep in the family.

And Levi embraced his Anishinaabe blood.

HE DROPPED OFF his younger brothers at the elementary doors and listened to music in his car like the other rebels along the back row of the parking lot. When the tardy bell sounded, he and several of his "farm boy" friends shuffled off to the school. Forsaking the life of a Boy Scout and jock, yet still choosing to live a clean life without vice, Levi carved out an identity for himself in the Split Rock High School music program, signing up for both choir and band, where he could play six different instruments. To those kids, he was practically a rock star who'd soon be on tour with Mötley Crüe or Ormus, but he chose to play the part chill and low key.

Upon learning it was a lab day in science, he ducked out of the classroom to find a practice room between the band and choir rooms. In truth, it allowed him to tickle the ivory of a piano or to strum on one of the acoustic guitars.

When the door flew open suddenly, he expected a secretary had come to drag him back to class. Instead, Lacy Morrison stood in the doorway.

Looks like she's hiding, too.

The senior All-State alto who had never given him the time of day stared with a puzzled look on her face. Then she pushed the door shut behind her and sat down on the edge of the piano bench beside him.

"Hey," she began.

"Back atcha," he answered in her hesitation.

"Levi, right? You're Leah's brother."

He nodded. Her presence alone stunned him, but her change in hairstyle also caught him aback. Lacy's hair had gone from blonde curls and flow like Jennifer Jason Leigh in *Fast Times at Ridgemont High* to a short pixie haircut similar to Molly Ringwald in *The Breakfast Club*. There was nothing wrong with Molly Ringwald, but when all the girls at Split Rock High School had aqua net bangs, Lacy stood out even more. "I just wanted to thank you for helping me out the other night."

"Yeah, no problem," he said under his breath.

A crease formed on her forehead. "I just wanted to make sure we're cool."

"Yeah, I'm cool, but are you cool?"

She shrugged and looked down at her black and white Oxfords. Surprisingly, she shook her head. "I'll figure it out. The world keeps spinning, right. Can you keep it hush-hush?"

He nodded.

"I knew I could count on you," she said, leaning her head on his shoulder for a moment. Then, just as suddenly as she arrived, she got up and walked back to the door. "Open or closed?"

"Doesn't matter," he said with a shrug.

She left it open and vanished down the hall.

Her pain lingered in the room, finding its way onto his forehead, and for the next several minutes, a rage filled his soul even though he didn't know where to direct his anger. He chewed so hard on his bottom lip that he left a crease on the inside of his lip along his bottom teeth.

Finally, his fingers found their way to the piano, and he let Lacy Morrison drift away and the words of his Gigi Lily seep into his mind.

Focus on the big problems—not Lacy.

Even though the song Lily had been teaching him had no sheet music, he invented chords for it and filled the room with harmony. He cleared his throat but then remembered another promise he'd made: Don't ever sing it aloud until the day comes.

CHAPTER SIX

Why Migisi?

Turtle Island Jesuit School
November 10, 1985

The Isanti Lodge didn't know what they were doing now any more than when Brian Forsberg was just a kid gathered with others in an old deer stand. For most of the meeting, Forsberg sat with his arms crossed and his hand on his chin, hiding his mouth. Captain Chuck ran the meeting like a town council meeting.

This is bullshit.

But he wasn't going to say it around men he respected.

Ever the politician, "Mayor" Chuck moderated the meeting, cutting off frightened grown men who rambled for too long. The biggest rambling culprits were Principal Riel and Father Mackenzie, who debated the religious iconography of the Wijigan version of the Seven Fires Prophecy. By the time Karson added his two cents on a theory, things would spiral out of control.

Brian just kept his mouth shut and nodded along.

Old Migisi looked like a gremlin sitting in the big chair behind the superintendent's desk. The last link to the Wijigan priests of old had given them clarification of Lily's game plan, which was hatched the last time Halley's Comet visited. At the arrival of Halley's Comet in April, the Isanti Lodge, including Lily, would meet at Turtle Island in full force.

Armed with the sacred Water Drum, Lily would (somehow) invoke the magical words found in the Ironwood Scrolls to draw out the ancient sorcerer—the Wintermaker—and then cast this water spirit into the spiritual *River of Souls*, which would take him to the underworld where he belonged.

"If the plan works," Migisi added in closing. "Father Guerin died the last time we thought we were ready."

Both principal and priest agreed that this act would cause a chain reaction described in their religious texts. For Principal Riel, it would either usher in an era of rebirth known as the Eighth Fire or fail—and bring the earth's demise. For Father Mackenzie, casting the Wintermaker into the depths meant that the "delay" described in the Book of Revelation could now continue with a different kind of seven—seven trumpets. Either way, the End of the World loomed.

As the "Bear" representative, Brian sat back and let the leaders and spiritual guides figure out the meaning of the old rituals. When talk shifted, he, as Sheriff of Hiawatha County, jotted in his small pocket notebook a few questions that needed answering. While everyone else in the Isanti Lodge trusted in their Creator and boldly rushed forward, Forsberg's research produced questions.

During a lull in the debate, he cleared his throat to set up his first question. "Migisi, I was wondering: why did the Wijigan cultists that grabbed you back in 1898 fail?"

Suddenly, all eyes turned to him, and then to old Migisi. "They did not have the sacred Water Drum, which my forefathers possessed for generations."

"Exactly! So what made them think they could succeed? Why did they abduct you in the first place?"

Migisi's wrinkled face grew even tighter. "The Wijigan Clan existed for generations before my forefather came to Lake Manitou, and the ancient song was kept by the priests. Even though they did not possess the written version of the song described in the Ironwood Scrolls in the prophecy, they still had the Song of the Manitou, which had the power to summon the spirits."

"Lily knows the Song," Wally pointed out, prompting an inadvertent eye roll from Brian.

Brian knew all about the magic associated with the Song of the Manitou, but sorcery and spells were not part of an investigator's vocabulary. He looked down at his notepad, and the eyes of the dead stared back at him. "Why did these Wijigan Cultists grab you?"

Brian had done his homework. He knew all about the Battle of Sugar Point, as it was called, which was one of the last armed conflicts between a Native American tribe and the United States Government. The conflict took place on Leech Lake in 1898, and the newspaper articles mostly described its cause as a logging rights issue, but hidden between the lines, he'd found reference to the Wijigan Cult conducting a ritual on Bear Island, which was interrupted by American troops searching for rabble-rousers and bootleggers.

"The previous year," Migisi began, "my father Nanakonan invited three elders to come to Lake Manitou to test me for specialized training."

Brian also knew the different types of priests found in Anishinaabe culture, beginning with the Mide and advancing to the Jessakkid and Wabeno. "Did they grab you from the school here because of the training you were receiving?"

Migisi shook his head. "No, it was, um, because..." An answer did not follow his hesitation.

"Correct me if I'm wrong," Brian began with another way of getting to his point. He pictured the dead boy buried in a manure pile. "I grew up with Bleeding Rock in my backyard, so I've seen the grooves in the stone meant to collect the blood of human sacrifices, and how these channels collected and then drained into Lake Manitou. The Wijigan Cult sacrificed a dozen Dakota children to wake up the spirits that guarded Lake Manitou—only to be stopped. Again, in 1898, a dozen deaths can be attributed to waking the Tak-Pei around Lake Manitou.

THE TRICKSTER 37

When I was a kid, the same thing happened, which seems to indicate that the Tak-Pei didn't necessarily need the blood of a child. So, let's go back to your childhood. Why did the Wijigan Clan go through all the effort of abducting you and then hauling you to Leech Lake?"

Migisi's agitation began to melt. "The ancient prophecies indicated that the end of the Seven Fire migration would result in the discovery of an island. For generations, my people believed our sacred destination to be either Leech Lake or Mille Lacs since both which had an island and 'food that grew on the water,' wild rice. My family knew better. They knew the truth about Lake Manitou. When Joseph Little Toad's rituals failed at Leech Lake, he had no option but to risk bringing me to Lake Manitou to try again."

Principal Riel jumped into the conversation. He and Brian were of similar age, but while Brian went off to fight in the Vietnam War, Riel went to college and began the soft life of a scholar. "The term Omodai has its roots in the Anishinaabemowin word that means vessel or container. Usually, it is connected to words that mean cup, pot, or container. As I've said, I don't have any historical references to the use of the word Omodai in other accounts of the Seven Fires prophecies."

"You wouldn't," Migisi told his student. "Only the Wijigan Clan would have known the full prophecy."

"From what Lily has told me," Father Gary added, "Her grandfather Nanak told her about the Omodai."

"I'm not struggling with the concept of the Omodai," Brian told the group before turning back to Migisi. "The Order of Eos also failed in its attempts at unlocking the old prophecies, but even without the Philosopher's Stone, they had enough of their version of the Song to still give it a go. Why?" He looked to see if any of them could answer it. "That's a question for another day. I want to focus on the Wijigan Clan today. From what I can tell, the Omodai is not meant to be a final sacrifice, or else, Migisi would've been slain back at Leech Lake. Even at Lake Manitou, Joseph Little Toad and the Wijigan Cultists were in no hurry to open you up as a sacrifice, so perhaps—"

Father Gary interrupted. "Lily explained to me that the Wijigan ritual was violently stopped before it could be completed."

Brian glared at the Jesuit priest before focusing once again on Migisi. In the Vietnam War, Brian remembered a J-Company captain sending the FNGs ahead of his veterans. Now, Lily insisted on an Omodai being present at the ritual without explaining the purpose. "Why did the Wijigan go through all the efforts of grabbing you, Migisi? I need to understand that."

Migisi deflated. "It was a mistake. It was a sign that was misread. For generations, my Ojibwe people held strong in their faith, which was rewarded with the appearance of Megis shells. Since receiving the first prophecies along the Great Ocean, my people looked for the sign—the white cowry shell that is not indigenous to the land. From the First Stopping Place on Montreal Island to the Sixth Stopping Place on Madeline Island in Lake Superior, the mystical, unexplained appearance of megis shells has led the faithful on the path. Even though people believed Leech Lake fulfilled the prophecy, there were no shells found. Nor were there shells found at Mille Lacs."

"You found shells though," Wally Crain commented.

Migisi shook his head. "No, Lily found the shells. I told my grandfather that I'd found them, and then he told the Wijigan elders that I'd found them. They chose me to be the Omodai because I was the boy who found the shells."

The question had been answered; Brian nodded, and the meeting continued. Yet he still didn't understand what the Wijigan *expected*.

Ultimately, the ritual failed when Father Jean Guerin and the rest of the Isanti Lodge caught up to poor Migisi and his abductors at Deadwood Island just in the nick of time.

There's got to be more to it than we know.

CHAPTER SEVEN

The Longest Night

Haggard Bay
December 19, 1985

Lake Manitou quietly waited for another offering. In the red glow of the taillights, Tomas Dobie sucked smoke through the cap of his cigar, held the final draw in his lungs, and then flicked the butt onto the ice where its glowing ember slowly joined the darkness.

A few yards away, singing resumed inside of the wooden icehouse. Every once in a while, Dobie would hear a few foreign syllables that echoed familiarity deep inside of him, but the rest of the time, the vocalized phrases sounded like complete gibberish. Slivers of light found their way through the joints of the icehouse, and combined with the parking lights of the car, Dobie could clearly see the surface of the ice between the shore and the shack.

Too many eyes are watching, Dobie decided as he scanned the darkness of Haggard Bay. If the stories were true, the eyes watching him did not belong to the living. Unlike the main body of the lake, there were no houses built upon the shore of the old quarry. The only ambient light came from the nearby town of St. John, a mile to the north, but every once in a while, a car drove down the highway, spilling light onto the frozen bay.

Dobie knew he could find shelter and warmth inside the icehouse. Instead, he remained vigilant, a sentry in the dark as the car idled. Slipping his hands back into his coat pocket, he found the familiar shapes of his pistol in one and his knife in the other. Inside his insulated coat, he felt the shape of his Glock and several clips. Unlike his relatives, Tomas did not plan on dying in such a cursed place.

The singing stopped, and a moment later, the door of the icehouse opened, bathing the ice with light that could be seen all the way to the highway.

Douse the fucking lights, Tomas wanted to say, but instead, a morose voice called to him, "It's time."

Dobie turned back to the car, and before pulling on the door handle, looked around for any sign of activity. Hours earlier, he'd driven down an obscure access road to the southern shore of Haggard Bay where the icehouse had been placed for them.

Before arriving at Lake Manitou, the three travelers had stopped at a McDonalds in St. Cloud for supper. Dobie had handed Shamar Tietaja the boy's Happy Meal along with the rest of the order, and after a few moments of sorting out the order, Tietaja handed the boy his order—laced with sleeping pills. The boy had been sound asleep by the time they arrived in Hiawatha County, and around ten o'clock, while Tietaja prepared his strange rituals, he'd injected the boy with a dose that would see him to the end of their mission.

THE BOY SLEPT while Tietaja prepared the ritual. As soon as Dobie opened the door, the dome light revealed the sleeping figure covered in blankets. He slipped his hands under the child's body and lifted him into his arms. Quickly closing the door with a twist of his hips, Dobie paused beside the car for a moment.

Dobie kissed the boy on the forehead. *Goodnight, sweet prince. May flights of angels wing thee to thy rest.* A generation earlier, a civil war within Eos pitted Aleister Sinclair against Ross Delhut for control of the future. Believing the brash young Delhut would ruin everything, he sent his agents to Lake Manitou to test occult theories. Once of his agents had been Red Dobie, who first confirmed the evil spirits lurking within the lake and then sabotaged Delhut's excavation efforts in a dam catastrophe. Now, Tom Dobie carried another victim from the car to the icehouse for another test. He used his heel to open the door.

The interior looked like the closet of a deranged serial killer. Candles burned, talismans spun, and bowls collected strange concoctions. A set of blue runic dice had to be swept aside to make room for the boy's body.

"Set him down inside of the doorway," Tietaja said, scooting back on the plywood floor. On the opposite side of the icehouse, a 3'x3' hole gave Lake Manitou a personal view of the ceremony. Although Shamar Tietaja did not wear the ancestral robes of his forefathers, he accessorized his plain clothing with silver jewelry to heighten his powers during the longest night of the year.

Obviously, there was no room for himself in the icehouse, nor did Dobie want to see any more. While he owed his allegiance to the Sinclair family and didn't mind getting his hands dirty, the spells and sorcery bothered him. "This had better fucking work; I've grown fond of the kid."

Tietaja had no doubt in his eyes. When Dobie discovered him five years earlier, the man looked more like he belonged in a fantasy novel than in the modern world, and once he shaved his long beard and dressed in modern clothes, the Finnish shaman looked like a man who would hold a jigging rod in his hand rather than the slender knife he currently held. "Perhaps you should wait back in the car. I cannot guarantee your safety."

He nodded. "Stay in there until this works, priest. You've got a lot riding on this."

"*Until* it works?" Tietaja mocked. "I would not have had you bring the boy if my translation of *the song* was not already working. Now go. Leave me to my work."

Dobie stepped back, allowing the door to slam shut.

Although winter officially began with the night's solstice, the ice was already thick and cracked by expansion. Dobie looked around, unsure of what Tietaja had already woken. This time, he returned to the car, sitting in the driver's seat to warm up.

Even though it was the first time he'd ever been to Lake Manitou, Dobie knew all about the lake's sinister history. Two decades earlier, his uncle Red had been one of the victims of the Great Flood of 1962, which turned Haggard Quarry into another bay of the lake. Decades before that, his grandfather left Albany for Hiawatha County, only to witness wholesale carnage and death. Even though his blood gave him a key to his family heritage, it had taken years before he was shown the lock, and more years before he was allowed to open it. Now, as a fully invested member of the Order of Eos, he knew all about the purpose of the magic being used. The future of Eos still hung in the balance. In recent years, Ross Delhut strengthened his position with a philosophy of patience while old Aleister Sinclair turned to his granddaughter Maddy Sinclair, who believed spiritual victory could come in a matter of months.

Centuries of waiting have come down to a few months, Dobie observed. *I just need to make sure this mess is cleaned up when it's over.*

The ice boomed unnaturally, and Dobie again felt as if the world would wake from sleep to see what was happening upon the dark bay. On the east side, where a small bridge spanned the channel between the lake and bay, two hundred yards of breakwater formed a man made wall that rose ten yards from the edge of the ice. Dobie's hand went to his pistol when he saw movement come over the top of the road.

Son of a bitch.

The creature did not move like an animal or a human, even though it walked upon two legs. Its long arms hung low enough that it almost looked like it moved on all fours. At first, the thick torso resembled a sheep in need of shearing, but as it crossed the surface of the ice toward the icehouse, Dobie realized he saw quills covering the creature.

A Fossegrim.

Theory had turned from trial to verification. He crewed on his lip nervously.

Dobie's gun remained in his hand, but with his left, he pulled out a pendant hanging from his neck and let the copper medallion rest upon his chest along with a silver cross. For good measure, he pulled out a small dream catcher and secured it to a button on his jacket. Dobie knew the creature did not belong on earth and that his pistol was useless.

By the time he climbed out of the car, the creature had already reached the icehouse and vanished from sight.

Tietaja's voice belted out strange syllables, and the song resonated across the ice once more. As Dobie neared the door, he could see the creature had torn open the side, letting light and blood spill out onto the ice.

Only ten yards from the Fossegrim, Dobie could see black, lifeless eyes reminiscent of a shark glance up at him and hear music of the shaman like strings on a marionette. Although the creature had a hunched back and crouched legs, its shoulders were still level with a man, making it much larger than a man. Each elongated finger looked to be several inches in length, and taken prisoner in their grasp was the body of the boy, whose blood covered the floor of the icehouse as well as the arms, torso, and head of the creature.

"It worked," Dobie muttered. The blood summoned one of the demons.

The creature slid sideways and for a moment seemed to stand upon the surface of the hole as if the water were as rigid as the ice. With boy in arms, it slowly descended and vanished into the depths of Lake Manitou.

"It appears Miss Sinclair's theories were correct," Tietaja said after the water grew still. "The coming comet has made the spirits strong."

"Are there more out there?"

"Yes, many of them, but most are still sleeping. I found two, still awake, who'd been hiding all of these years, cast aside by some sorcerer. It took only a little coaxing to guide that one back home."

"Congratulations," Tomas Dobie said. "You've unlocked an ancient text that many believed had been lost." The test had been a success.

"Yes, well, this is only the beginning. The Manitoulin petroglyphs contained verses that do more than just summon mystical creatures. If these verses worked, then many of the others should also—"

In the still of the night, the silencer's blast sounded as loud as a regular gunshot. A spray of blood and brain matter covered the far wall of the icehouse, and Shamar Tietaja's body collapsed toward the large hole in the ice. Neither Ross Delhut nor Aleister Sinclair wanted Tietaja to hold power, and with the rediscovery of the ancient language confirmed, the shaman was no longer needed. Dobie advanced, reaching down to grab Tietaja's leg before his whole body fell into the hole.

The headshot had finished him quickly and painlessly, just as the boy had not suffered when he was sacrificed to Lake Manitou.

I meant the compliment, Dobie thought as he crouched next to the body. *Without all of your hard work, we never could have unlocked the meaning of the song.*

Dobie reached into his jacket and found a copy of the translated song, broken down into English syllables instead of exotic petroglyphs.

But you don't belong to the Order of Eos. My ancestors began this, and I will help finish it. When you learned our true purpose, you would have turned on us. Sorry about this.

Dobie cleared his throat and began singing the strange syllables, letting the offering of blood and the old magic lead the other creature back home.

CHAPTER EIGHT

Nevermore

Old Copper Road
December 20, 1985

Seven miles away, on the far side of Lake Manitou, Levi MacPherson dreamed of being a rock star after a strange song, a melody without lyrics, entered his dream. The creative impulses in his mind turned it into a new song, which he and his imaginary band instantly turned into another hit that made the arena go wild. His fingers plucked the strings of his white bass guitar, and the massive stage speakers shook the air. Instead of his siblings, the members of his favorite heavy metal band Ormus flanked him as the crowd roared.

Except for a small pocket at the center of the crowd.

A hunched, wrinkled old woman held the hand of a young girl on one side and an adult woman with a deformed face on the other.

Lily wouldn't be at a concert. This obviously is a dream. Levi put a foot on one of the front stage speakers and kept playing, and the crowd responded with thrashing and head banging.

Suddenly, a crackle of electricity came through the speakers, and the entire dream went silent. Levi and his band mates stood dumbfounded.

On the side of the stage, a shadowy figure stood holding the power cord that supplied the entire dream with electricity. The shadow spoke softly, "Sorry, but I had to stop you somehow. Do you see them?"

The crowd transformed into a ghoulish scene, an auditorium filled with the dead. Most he could not recognize, but several were faces of friends and family.

"I'll explain the rest to you under the willow tree," the shadow said before disappearing.

THE DREAM ENDED with the sound of shattering glass. Even in the darkness, Levi knew he wasn't alone in his bedroom. Glass shifted and fell, a strange sound...

"Levi?" His brother Joey called out, not from down at the bottom of his stairs but from beside his bed. "What was that?"

Although Levi's bedroom was larger and longer than any of his siblings' bedrooms, the biggest drawback became most obvious...a dearth of windows. At the end of the narrow room, one small circular window provided a small glimpse into the night sky and a sudden, cold draft.

The strange sound repeated, and Joey leapt into the bed and scooted between Levi and the wall. For a kindergartner, Joey remained quite composed. Levi sat up so his senses could understand what was happening. *If Joey's here it means I'm not dreaming. This is real.*

A piece of glass fell from the circular frame, causing the brothers to jump, followed by a violent eruption of sound from atop his dresser.

Wings?

Fifteen feet separated the dresser below the broken window and his bed.

A dark figure moved and spoke aloud, "Kraa, kraa."

Levi took a sudden breath: bravery chipped away at his fear. He found enough courage to lean out from his bed and feel for his lamp, but at the same time his fingers felt the knobby dial, the creature in the shadows moved again. The light came on, casting bright light into Levi's face that irritated the uninvited guest. *Lily was right—I shouldn't have been dabbling with the song.*

"It's enormous," Joey said, soft as a whisper.

For a moment, Levi couldn't believe his eyes either. A two-foot-tall crow, blinking and studying them, stood on his carpet. When it shook out its feathers and stretched its wings, the creature doubled in size, and its garble sounded like it came from an adult human. One of its wings did not fold back into its body right away; it quivered for a moment before the crow drew it back.

It hurt itself crashing through the window, Levi realized. Blood was on the glass, dresser, and carpet, a small trail followed the bird. Having grown up in Hiawatha County, it was not the first crow Levi had ever seen—only the first one in his bedroom.

It stood, stoically taking in the sights of Levi's room. Between the bed and the far wall, Levi had a stereo system with speakers and four crates full of records, eight-tracks, cassettes, and even a few CDs. On the other wall, he had his white bass guitar, amp, headphones, and a desk full of sheet music. The crow walked over to the stereo and inspected the technology with its three-inch beak for a moment before looking down at the open cassette boxes lying in front of the glass door of the stereo cabinet.

Its neck snapped back to look directly at Levi, and then its beak turned back to one of the cassettes and pecked it so hard that it came away with a foot of tape.

"Hey," Levi said, but not before the crow shook the cassette, bouncing it against the stereo and toward itself. Then with a powerful rap of its head, the cheap plastic of the cassette broke.

Levi leaned forward to do something, but before he could, the crow spoke the clearly discernible syllable, "*Stop.*"

What the hell, Levi thought, and if not for the presence of his little brother beside him, equally stunned, he would have thought he was still dreaming.

"*Stop, stop,*" the crow said, then let out a baritone gargle before adding another set of "*Kraa, kraa.*"

"It spoke," Joey said. "Can we keep him as a pet?"

Levi had to compose himself. Fear gripped his heart yet his little brother showed courage. "No, Joey, we just need to get him out of my room. He must've gotten disoriented and didn't seen the glass. Just move slow and steady."

"What we going to do?" Joey asked.

"We need to keep him from going into the rest of the house. Sneak behind me and go close the door at the bottom of the stairs, okay."

As they moved off the bed, the crow shifted but did not move. Levi stepped toward the stairwell, which led to Joey's bedroom on the second floor, allowing his brother to scoot behind him and run down the stairs. Levi took a few slow steps toward the injured bird before it again repeated, "*Stop.*"

Someone raised this crow as a pet. It's not a wild bird.

When Joey returned at the top of the stairs, Levi took another step. "We'll shoo it back to the window and see if it'll leave the way it came."

"But what about the glass? It's bleeding," Joey said, standing next to him to create a human wall across the narrow room.

Not answering, Levi stepped forward, and Joey followed. The crow finally turned, took two hops, flapped its wings with the dresser top as a target, but once its wings outstretched, one wing malfunctioned, causing the bird to crash sideways halfway up the dresser.

Levi approached gingerly. He stretched out his arms, but when his hands grew close enough, the bird defended itself with a quick peck at his fingers and darted low along the wall, heading right for Joey, who sidestepped out of the way, but with surprising deftness, swept his arms around the bird and penned its wings to its body in a hug.

The crow bit at Joey's forearm, catching a pinch of flesh in its beak, but Joey ignored the pain and began shushing it.

"*Fire,*" the crow said, just as distinctly as it had spoken earlier. Then it made a series of strange clicks.

THE TRICKSTER 49

Joey smiled proudly, the bird filling his arms. "He's just scared."

"He's also bleeding all over you," Levi said, seeing Joey's arm covered in blood. He crouched, staying low so as not to upset the bird. A couple of its wing feathers were bent, revealing a gash about two inches long. "I don't think he'd be able to fly right now even if we could get him outside."

"Let's keep him," Joey repeated.

"There is no way Mom will let that happen," Levi said, and then glanced over at the alarm clock, which read 5:27 a.m. *Wait…she must not have heard. Maybe we can keep him.*

"Change it all," the crow demanded. "Change. Change. Change."

Joey grinned widely. "He's awesome."

Levi felt terror but gathered himself. "He must've been raised by humans. I've heard crows are even smarter than parrots. If we're going to nurse him back to health, we can't let Mom know. She'll freak out and get Dad involved, and we'll end up ringing his neck or something. We need to keep it a secret."

The crow immediately mimicked the words, "*Secret, secret, ah…secret.*"

"He sounds like Fozzie Bear from the Muppets," Joey said. "Is your name Fozzie?"

The crow made a few strange gurgling noises while Joey petted its back.

A blanket rested next to his bed. "What were you doing in my room?" Levi asked.

Joey's face filled with puzzlement.

"Oh, I had a bad dream," Joey answered with a shrug.

What a strange morning. This has got to be related to Lily's stuff. Levi looked beside where he sat and saw the destroyed tape of his favorite band, Ormus. *I had a dream too.* Lily relentlessly asked about his younger brothers, especially Joey, who she mistakenly called Clay. *Joey's a part of this.* "You really want to keep him?

Joey nodded enthusiastically.

"Well, we can't keep him in my room, he'd destroy everything."

"We could keep him in the barn."

"Not with Dad around."

"We could put him in the loft. Dad doesn't go there."

"Too much space for him to fly around, and he'd probably wreck the equipment."

"What about the fort?"

That might work. "Now listen, we've both got to go to school today, but then we'll have all of Christmas vacation to help him heal up."

Joey nodded obediently.

"If Mom is down in the kitchen, we can't walk out holding it either."

"Fozzie."

"What?"

"His name is Fozzie."

"You need keep Mom distracted so I can get him out to the fort. Can I count on you to be cool?"

Wordlessly, Joey extended the crow, which thankfully found its calm.

"Let me put on some pants first," Levi said, slipping into his stonewashed jeans from the previous day. Joey extended the crow a second time, but Fozzie's black beak snapped at his fingers.

"*Ahhh,*" the crow screamed loudly enough for both boys to flinch. It then made a series of clicking sounds before finishing with "*brup, rup.*"

"Don't squeeze him," Joey said.

"I wasn't going to," Levi said, holding his fingers together as opposed to being spread out. This time, the crow watched as he slid his hands around Joey's.

"*You talking to me?*" the crow said, and Joey burst out laughing, stepping back.

"How does it know how to speak?"

"It doesn't," Levi said holding it the same manner as a rooster. "It's somebody's lost pet, and it just repeats phrases. That's from a movie. Now, give me your blanket so I can wrap him up in it. Then go change so we can get him out of here before Dad and Daniel get done with chores."

Using Joey's blanket, Levi dabbed at the blood along the cut, which dislocated more feathers, showed torn skin, but did not reveal bone. Leaving only an exposed beak, Levi draped the blanket over and swaddled the bird. As Joey returned wearing fresh pajamas, Levi slipped on a pair of untied Nikes. "Can you fake being sick?"

Joey nodded enthusiastically.

"You can't stay home, but you can complain about not feeling good. Tell her you had a bad dream and that you feel hot. She'll want to take your temperature, and when she does, I'll slip out of the house, okay?"

"I can do it," Joey said. "You'll be fine, Fozzie." Joey smiled at the bird.

At the bottom of the stairs, the brothers passed through Joey's bedroom strewn with toys. In the hall, Daniel's door was open, but the others were closed, and Levi continued down the second flight of stairs.

A light gurgle came from the crow, but it restrained itself as Levi passed through the dining room and nearer the kitchen. Levi nodded, and Joey, dragging a blanket, walked around the colonnade.

"I don't feel good," Joey whined to his mother who was making breakfast.

"Oh, sweetie, what's wrong?"

Sure, she immediately believes him.

"I feel hot, and I had a bad dream."

"You look a little flush. Let's check your temperature."

At that, Levi stepped out of hiding and peeked. His mother turned for the medicine cabinet on the far side of the kitchen, allowing him the opportunity to quickly cross through the edge of the kitchen and out into the mudroom. At the back door, he stopped and listened.

"So what was your bad dream about?" Mom asked.

"I had green hair and all of the kids in my class teased me and called me the wrong name. There was this girl with a smashed face who followed me around pointing at me, and when she spoke, blood came out of her mouth."

"Oh, how horrible," Mom said empathetically. "Now open up so I can get your temperature.

Can things get any weirder? Levi wondered, looking at his own reflection in the window of the door.

"Well, it doesn't seem as if you're running—"

Levi turned the knob and slipped into the darkness.

Dawn would not come for another two hours, so his secret mission would remain hidden as long as his brother and father didn't return unexpectedly from chores. The large red dairy barn was lit up for milking, and he saw both Daniel and his father pass by one of the windows.

So far so good.

The MacPherson dairy farm was built upon a rocky bluff that served as a watershed between the Crow Wing River and Lake Manitou. The front of the house faced Old Copper Road and the Crow Wing River Valley while the rear of the house sloped away toward Lake Manitou. A thick forest of oak, birch, and pines covered the rocky bluff that rose steadily for about a mile from north to south along the southeastern edge of the lake. The MacPherson boys had their own park-like playground just a few yards from the back door.

The fort, as Joey called it, was a three-level tree house built in the massive branches of a raggedy box elder tree. Several years ago, Ben had enlisted the help of his younger brothers to build his masterpiece. Built in the crook of the twisted tree, the first level was six feet off the ground, "Shh, it's okay," Levi told Fozzie as he cradled him like a football in his left arm and climbed with his right.

A series of strange clucks came from the crow as it studied its surroundings. *Why does it act so human?*

The second level followed at a lesser climb, allowing Levi to just use his fingertips to keep his balance. A 6'x6' platform with short railings had once allowed the brothers to play cards, but now, as a sixteen-year-old, Levi wondered if the aging boards would hold his weight.

The third level had been built with walls, a roof, and a trap door. As a child, he had to climb up the wooden steps, but now he could reach it from the platform, pushing the hinged door back into the tree house.

There wasn't enough room to stand, so he crouched on his knees as he looked over the small room. *This will work.* It was small enough to keep the crow from breaking into flight and hurting its wing, but it had enough space for it to hop around and explore while its wounded wing healed.

"Okay, Fozzie, we'll figure out what crows eat and bring you a big meal after school is done. Try not to make too much of a fuss. We're doing this for your own good."

Levi set the wrapped bird in the far corner and then quickly backed down, closing the trap door behind him. While the amateur construction had plenty of airflow, it lacked windows for covert meetings of the MacPherson boys. He glanced back to the barn, and then to the house just to make sure he hadn't been seen by his parents.

Standing on the platform again, he looked out across the ice of Lake Manitou. On the western shore of the lake, he saw the flashing lights of emergency vehicles.

"Fire, fire, fire," Fozzie called out, followed by a chorus of clucking noises, but with the fort surrounded by a grove of trees, Levi hoped Fozzie's croaks would not be noticed.

Levi found himself breathing heavily, and the December chill suddenly felt colder than normal.

Fire—this can't be a coincidence.

CHAPTER NINE

Where There's Smoke

Old Copper Road
December 20, 1985

Brian Forsberg stood at the cigar butt while the others scurried around the charred remains of the icehouse. Lights of ambulances and patrol cars parked along the highway illuminated the ice, but dawn brought a world of gray into view.

"Oh for Pete's sake," the sheriff mumbled to himself, realizing none of his deputies had noticed where he stood. He put two fingers in his mouth and whistled loudly enough for everyone in the small army on Haggard Bay to stop and turn.

He waved the crowd toward him, and luckily, a patrolman came jogging over to where Forsberg stood a few hundred yards away on the shore. "Is that Lieutenant Harper at the fishing shack?"

"Yes, sir," patrolman Gerber answered and glanced down at the dark object on the ground. "What did you find sir?"

"Go tell Harper to get everybody off the ice and back on the highway. Folks are going to be driving into town and wanting to see what's going on. I want things tight by the time the B.C.A. gets here."

"They found a second body. A kid."

The work of Eos? "Leave it alone," Forsberg said.

"Should we fish it out?"

"BCA will decide what to do. I want you to drive your patrol car back down to Sterling Junction and find this access road. I want to make sure nobody comes up that road for a better look at the murders."

"Murders?"

Forsberg didn't explain himself to patrolman Gerber, who took the hint and went back to the burned icehouse. When the fire had been called in, Forsberg had just finished his morning coffee and drove directly to Haggard Bay from his home, seven miles away on the east side of Lake Manitou. It had only taken a moment's glance to know the accident was arson, so he set out to discover the scope of the crime scene. The cigar butt told him more than the burned icehouse.

The patrolmen and EMTs vacated the ice as ordered and Lieutenant Griff "Bird Man" Harper came walking across the ice with "Disco" Ron Spears, the Emergency Management Director.

Forsberg's knee already ached, so he sat on his haunches until the two officers arrived.

"What do you got, Biff?" Harper asked. Only folks who knew Forsberg since childhood dared to still call him Biff, but Harper had worked at the Hiawatha Sheriff's Department prior to Forsberg and as a graduate from Wadena High School, still found inopportune times to tease his childhood rival.

Forsberg stared daggers at him for a moment before answering. "Do you remember the Troost case?"

"The child molester that almost got you."

Forsberg didn't quibble about the misrepresentation of fact. Harper remembered. "If not for a well-placed pitchfork, the guy's plan was to drop my body onto a sled, haul me out onto the ice, and drop me through a big hole in the ice, hidden by an icehouse."

Harper turned back around to the smoldering ruins of the icehouse while Spears studied the cigar butt and scanned for other clues on the shore.

Forsberg continued, "You and I both know that a bonfire on the ice would not burn a hole through the ice. A few pieces of plywood? Please. That hole was already there, and those bodies were already wet before that icehouse went up in flames."

"What? You think it's the same guy?"

"Of course not," Forsberg said with more than a bit of disdain. "That was 26 years ago. All I'm doing is drawing comparisons. Somebody stood right up on shore, undoubtedly near a parked car, smoking a cigar. When the B.C.A. arrives, I want tire track analysis and forensic examination of this cigar butt."

"You want me to hold off on getting those bodies out?" Spears asked. Like Harper, he was a middle-aged man comfortable around death. He wore a polyester windbreaker with a faux-fur collar, but unlike the others, he did not wear a hat, and allowed his thick silver hair to be moved like twigs of a tree. Forsberg met Spears in college. A decade later, Forsberg lured him to Hiawatha County to be his Emergency Management Director. His calm, discerning manner had yet to disappoint.

"Those bodies aren't going anywhere. No offense, but I'd like the B.C.A. to do all the heavy lifting on this one."

Harper and Spears solemnly nodded and left to gather up their respective teams.

Guarding the cigar butt, certainly key evidence, kept him from peering down at another dead kid in Lake Manitou.

When did death first arrive at Lake Manitou?

A Hiawatha County patrol car ended his silent vigil as it led a black B.C.A. van up the Sterling Junction road to the backside of Haggard Bay. A second van arrived moments later.

The men who came out of the first van looked more like scientists than law enforcement, acknowledging the elements with childish expressions. Some of the team guarded the scene at the ice house and others went to where Forsberg stood.

"What do you have there, Sheriff Forsberg?"

"You tell me," he said, stepping aside.

"A fresh cigar butt, smoked so recently that the wrapping has not absorbed any water from melting ice," one agent said following inspection.

"A jewel of information," another said. "Cigars can tell quite a story under a microscope."

"I'm going to want to hear some stories sooner rather than later." He released his breath, feeling the chill setting in. "I'll leave you to it."

Forsberg felt eyes upon him as he walked the two hundred yards across the bay to where he had parked his SUV along the side of the road. Once he was joined by Lieutenant Harper and Director Spears, a short woman in an oversized parka emerged from a white station wagon parked nearby—Mia Donaldson. His personal assistant held a thermos of coffee and a bag from the local bakery.

Twenty-six years ago, he and Jimmy Nielson snuck into Haggard Quarry near the same spot where Mia stood, and as all the duties of responsibility overwhelmed him, he couldn't help but remember a time before the flood.

Now Jimmy Nielson and Chris Luning were dead.

Neither could help him sort through the clues this time.

A flash caught his eye and he spotted a parked truck on a small hill overlooking the lake. *He knows I'm in over my head*, Forsberg decided, acknowledging the truck's owner, Wally Crain. *I think I agree with the old coot.*

CHAPTER TEN

And Through the Woods

Old Copper Road
December 24, 1985

Hiawatha County is located in central Minnesota in what once was known as "The Big Woods," which were mostly harvested by the turn of the century. Although it covers 1,300 square miles of lakes, rivers, fields, and forests, the population hovers around 20,000, with St. John being the largest town and county seat at 6,000. The county is framed by well-traveled highways: Highway 71 running north to south along the western side, Highway 371 flanking its eastern border, four-lane highway 210 along the bustling southern border, and Highway 64 proceeding through the center of the county north-to-south.

For the MacPherson family, who loaded up the Brown Beast, their fifteen-passenger Dodge van, it was a sixty-mile drive from their farm near Split Rock to Leech Lake in Cass County. Normally, the Brown Beast drove south to Sioux Falls for Christmas, but this year, Grandma Hannah and Aunt Charlotte showed up on Friday night to join them for the Christmas Eve morning trip north.

Great-Grandma Lily was dying of cancer and would not live to see another Christmas.

Levi sat in the back row against the window; Joey and Daniel slept across the large bench seat. In hierarchy by age, Ben (who'd returned from school) and Reuben sat in the seat in front of him, with Leah slumped against the window to sleep. Ben sat with his girlfriend of three years, Tammy, who would be taking him to her family the next day. In the forward bench, Aunt Charlotte and Levi's mother sat together. A bit of a recluse, who took it upon herself to tend to Grandma Hannah two decades ago, Aunt Charlotte would go from morose to jovial in a snap, and Levi's mother did her best to tap dance around issues that would provoke her. Grandma Hannah, an obese woman who gave incredible hugs, kept a running commentary of every house and farmstead along Highway 64 while Levi's father Gavin drove the van.

"So what is the deal with the double-murder I read about in the newspaper this morning?" Grandma Hannah asked abruptly when they turned at the town of Backus.

Levi perked up, and so did his older siblings.

"Forsberg told me they didn't think either of the victims were local," Dad hedged, "and it was most likely just a way to dump the bodies."

"Brian said the icehouse didn't have registration and was just put there a few days earlier," Mom added.

Mom's on a first name basis with the Sheriff? Levi wondered. No one at school on Friday knew anything about what had happened, and his obsession with crow care caused him to forget all about the news.

"That is why I had to get away from this place," Grandma Hannah said. "What is it about Lake Manitou that draws all of the crazies?"

"You can say that again," Aunt Charlotte added.

"It's nice that nothing like this ever happens in Sioux Falls," Mom said quickly.

Sensing Mom's snarkiness, Levi's father quickly threw out some more information. "It appears as if the killer set the icehouse on fire after leaving the bodies. Wally Crain told me he could see it burning from the edge of town."

"Mrs. Crain is retiring at the end of the year," Levi's mom commented as if to change the subject.

"I didn't get to go to public school," Aunt Charlotte complained. "I had to go to Turtle Island."

Grown women and still bitter, Levi observed.

"Is it true one of the victims was a child?" Leah asked.

"Apparently," Dad answered, "but Sheriff Forsberg didn't know the age since he didn't even know the identity of the victims."

"No missing child reports?" Ben asked.

"Apparently not."

"What is it, some sort of mob thing?" Reuben wondered.

"Can we *please* talk about something more pleasant?" Mom insisted, and everyone turned to their window views. Levi, worrying that the crow was a harbinger of bad things, agreed.

Outside of Levi's window, Agency Bay and Walker Bay were a sheet of white ice, equal to the size of Lake Manitou, yet only an arm of the massive lake. *I wonder if Lily had bad dreams, too.*

The Brown Beast soon stopped at Wanakiwidee Retirement Home, a modern, plain, care facility. All eleven of them piled out of the van and headed for the front door.

"Fozzie liked the dog food we bought him," Joey said to Levi as they moved through the lobby of the facility. "He ate the entire bowl."

"Was the water dish frozen?" Levi asked.

"Just the top. I broke it open for him."

"Is his wing any better?" Daniel asked, having learned about the crow by Tuesday morning.

"I think it was just a cut and not a break," Levi explained. Fozzie didn't speak a syllable in front of Daniel, who lost interest quickly. Plus, Levi had threatened him to not bother it.

On Saturday, after repairing the broken window and cleaning the blood, Levi revealed the bird's identity to his father, leaving out the details of how the crow hurt its wing, which would raise concerns from his parents. His father had recommended the dog food, which was far more practical than what the library books recommended.

If I'm lucky, he'll let me keep it in the barn once his wing is healed.

The family congested at Lily's doorway.

Lily Guerin sat in her chair and looked at the ice of Agency Bay.

Having met with Lily at least once a week for the past few months, Levi lingered in the back as his mother introduced everyone. When it was his turn, Levi approached sheepishly, and GiGi Lily rattled him with her offhand comment.

"This one reminds me of my father," she said. "My father was a criminal."

The whole family chuckled, prompting eye rolls from Levi, who bore the brunt of the joke as the black sheep of the family. Lily had explained much of her life prior to her encounter with the spirits of Lake Manitou, so Levi knew about Big Squeak Weber and his time as a bootlegger. She'd just told him about Big Squeak recently, which rattled him, yet GiGi managed to keep their visits and relationship hidden from the family.

When it came time for moving Lily to the family room, Levi volunteered to push her wheelchair down the hallway. During the slow moving parade, Lily reached a hand out and touched his hand. "The time approaches," she said cryptically.

Levi knew all about the Seven Fires, the coming comet, and even the Isanti Lodge, but he couldn't be certain what she meant. As they entered the large family room, he leaned in closer to ask, "Time for what?"

"It is time for you to close the first loop," she said and then looked up at the popcorn ceiling of the white room. "The dark spirits stir once again, but we are going to give them quite a surprise, aren't we?"

"I hope so," Levi answered, stepping away from her as their family packed the room and began chattering.

Softly, Lily gave him one last private comment, "Come visit me in a few days, and we will talk about the willow tree."

CHAPTER ELEVEN

More Thunderbird than Jeep

St. John, MN
December 26, 1985

Sheriff Brian Forsberg chewed on each fact for so long that by the time he spit it out, the members of the press looked bored and agitated.

He kept both hands on the side of the oak lectern, which held three microphones. In his five years as sheriff of Hiawatha County, he'd seen up to a dozen microphones clipped to the lectern and triple the number of people in the pressroom. The three XLR cables ran across the floor to the back of the room where three television cameras recorded his every word. The local CBS crew from Bemidji as well as two young crews from the Twin Cities had come. In the front row, he saw several familiar faces from local print and radio outlets.

An agent from the B.C.A. stood off to the side. *Andrew Ross*, Forsberg confirmed with a glance down at the notecard. It was the only piece of information he hadn't committed to memory.

Standing in front of the closed maroon blinds, Lieutenant Griff Harper crossed his arms and nodded along. If Forsberg botched any facts, his lead investigator would bail him out. Harper wore a suit with a name badge at his chest pocket while Forsberg wore his traditional white shirt, brown tie, and brown shoulder boards, which gave the impression that it was more than just fifteen minutes out of a normal day.

Unlike other press conferences, there were hardly any local citizens, so the room held a strangely apathetic tone than heightened meetings in the past.

No one wants to talk about murder a day after Christmas.

Brian had been to training sessions that warned of perpetrators attending a press conference under the anonymity of a crowd, but today would not be such a day.

Several friendly faces gathered for support—the Isanti Lodge. Earl "Wally" Crain, nodding along with each fact, sat behind the reporters in the second row. In front of the chalkboard along the back wall, Mayor Chuck Luning of Split Rock stood holding his chin, occasionally whispering to Chief Deputy Dave Ribbar, who readily ran the day-to-day operations of the department but would bolt out the door if the press asked him any questions. *Wally and Chuck are worried this is an Eos issue.*

The young district attorney sat at his own table beside the front row of reporters. Dressed in an expensive suit, the DA jotted down notes on a yellow legal pad, trying to justify his presence. Conversely, a young man wearing a Bemidji State Beavers hockey jersey under an insulated flannel shirt scribbled in a pocket notepad upon his lap.

All had come for their own reasons.

At the center of the room, where the black XLR cables spanned the ten feet of carpet between the lectern and crowd, his trusted secretary Mia Donaldson busily typed a transcript of every word he said to later be released in print form from the department. Occasionally, her face would wear a mask of abject horror when he spoke in medical or forensic terminology.

Twenty minutes after walking into the press room, Chief Deputy Ribbar cleared his throat for his only sentence of the press conference,

"On behalf of the Hiawatha Sheriff's Department, we'd like to thank you for coming. We will send out updates and press releases as they happen."

Ribbar then swung the door open and drew the blinds, flooding the room with reflective light from the wintry backyard.

Agent Ross shook his hand. "Do you need me to stay?"

Brian stepped back. "We've got it. Just call when those lab results come in."

"Of course, Sheriff Forsberg."

The television crews had already taken down their cameras and were out the door, while the local press rushed up to Lieutenant Harper for another perspective, which was standard procedure.

Wally Crain quietly passed through the crowd towards him, extended a leathery hand, and said, "We'll talk soon."

Chuck Luning also vanished with the reporters.

Although two nameless victims, including a young boy, had drawn the attention of the media, the lack of a local connection or even a cohesive dramatic narrative weakened interest. By the time New Years passed, Forsberg sadly suspected it would be wholly forgotten.

Except for the young reporter in the hockey jersey.

Percy Thorgard wore a mask of a perpetual crooked smile, as if he had headphones on and listened to a comedy routine while the rest of the world dealt with reality. His legs were kicked out and his water resistant boots crossed at the ankles. He still held his little flip pad and stayed in his own world until Forsberg took the bait and stopped on his way to the door.

"You watch the last Vikings game? I can't believe they blew that game," Thorgard said, blinking quickly as if nervous.

"I got my hopes up after the Tampa Bay game, but not even Bud Grant could turn around this franchise."

Thorgard winced, following Forsberg as they walked out of the press conference room. "A.C. is a heck of a receiver. If Wilson had time to throw, we might surprise folks."

The discussion continued as the two walked out the door, down the hallway, and all the way back to the main offices of the sheriff's department.

Percy, still a kid in Forsberg's eyes, worked for the North Stars News, a county paper out of St. John. A few years earlier, the high school hellion had found himself staring down the drawn service revolver of Deputy Forsberg. The incident stayed private and put young Thorgard on a new path that led him to a journalism degree at Bemidji State University. In 1982, Thorgard joined the North Star News as a sports reporter and, from time to time, covered more serious news.

He flitted about like a pilot fish around a shark as Brian dealt with a series of issues at the front desk. At one point, while Mia Donaldson went through a laundry list of questions, Thorgard sat down in the cushioned chair in the lobby corner and flipped through a magazine, but when Brian turned toward his office, Thorgard tossed the magazine aside and resumed a conversation about the University of Minnesota men's basketball team.

Thorgard kept talking even while Brian sat at his desk and flipped through his papers. The twenty-five year old reporter could talk sports for hours, so finally, Forsberg gave him what he wanted. "So, what do you want to know, Percy?"

The flip pad stayed in his pocket. The conversation was off the record—it was personal. "Do you have a suspect yet?"

"Yeah, Lake Manitou."

"Your department closed off the access road leading to the south side of the bay. Most folks who set up for ice fishing come off the highway or through the channel. Since there was no vehicle identified, I gotta assume you found something on the south side of the bay."

The kid would've been a great detective. "You assume correctly, but it is a dead end."

"What did you find?"

"Cigar butt, tire tracks, and footprints. The B.C.A. came to the same conclusion I did: whoever dumped those bodies in Lake Manitou left no clues or motives."

Thorgard grinned. "Yeah, they did."

"Enlighten me."

"Hypothetically, if I had to dispose of two bodies, I do like the ice fishing idea. Ice auger, sled, bulky equipment...they're a good cover, right? Plus, ice fishermen can be active day or night, so no one would take notice. But if I did kill two people and drove a day or two away from home, picking some random lake, why would I burn down the icehouse and draw attention to it?"

Sharp kid. Let's see where this goes. "Yeah, why would you?"

"I'll tell you why...a ritual. If you were just hiding a body, you wouldn't need the icehouse, but if you were doing something unnatural, then the icehouse would hide it and a fire would cover all traces of what you did inside. There was probably more evidence than just bodies, don'tcha think?"

Brian had already gone down this dark path. "Not bad, Percy," Forsberg said with a wry smile. "Do you want to know what the B.C.A. guy thought?"

"Sure."

"Psychological remorse. The person who dumped the bodies wanted them to be found because of a connection to the victims."

"So, you're looking for a housewife whose husband and son went fishing and never came back? Do you buy that?"

"I have a feeling that a year from now, we still won't know the identity of either of those bodies."

"Your suspect didn't leave any clues?"

"Oh, I've got tire tread and cigar type all figured out, but they're not going to give me any answers, are they? Do you think I'm going to make any arrests with this evidence? Even if I knew the name of a suspect?"

Thorgard did not debate as his eyes remained fixed on his lap. "So...this case is more Thunderbird than Jeep."

I should recruit him for the Isanti Lodge. He'd love the monster theories. Percy had crossed the line. "Are you—not today, Percy. Just...go away. I don't have time for this nonsense. Leave."

Thorgard looked up. "But—"

"Leave, Percy."

Thorgard stood up quickly, pushing his chair out of the way, but he stopped abruptly at the door of the office and turned to ask, "You'd tell me if this were...a Jeep situation?"

"Leave!" Brian fumed with a little more volume, but before Thorgard retreated, Brian added, "Next time you come here asking questions like that, bring a bottle of Absolut."

Brian did not watch him leave but sifted through the paperwork given to him by Mia Donaldson for a few more minutes. Then, alone in his office, he leaned back in his chair and let a quiver of emotion pass through before he grit his teeth.

I can't deal with the supernatural, but monsters don't smoke cigars. I can focus on cigars.

He pushed both his big leather chair away from his large desk and the pile of papers from his present attention. He spun around, glancing at a floor-to-ceiling bookcase filled with photos and memorabilia. On the adjacent wall, a metal organizer held dozens of binders, and next to it, a small three-drawer file cabinet stared at him with more speculation than Percy Thorgard offered.

More Thunderbird than Jeep? He shuddered. *I fucking hope so.*

Brian opened the bottom drawer, and his hand went right to the files seven inches from the front. His fingers hesitated when he saw the file for Wesley Thorgard.

Percy Thorgard's father had died in an accident involving Lake Manitou, thin ice, and a red Jeep. While tragic, it had an explanation rooted in reason.

"A Thunderbird Case" was an unsolved mystery involving sinister secret societies. Percy Thorgard had done his digging into old cases, and in a drunken stupor, confessed his theories to Brian, who met him halfway.

Acknowledging the Order of Eos shut up Thorgard and brought him back to the grim reality of life. "A Jeep Case" leaned toward the supernatural. Wesley Thorgard was likely killed by Tak-Pei.

Brian ended up rereading through the notes of his predecessor had left in the Troost file. Even though it had been an open-and-shut case for the press, Betzing privately had doubts. Brian's own eyewitness account, documented in the file, left the most paradoxical clue—a pitchfork wound. To save his buddy Chris, Brian had thrown a pitchfork, which not only struck Troost but also Luning. Sheriff Betzing compared the wound on Luning with the two puncture wounds on Troost, noting the healing on Luning compared to the fresh nature of the wound weeks later on Troost as well as the difference in height from a standing position.

Betzing knew it was a lie, but he couldn't prove it. He sat in this same office, unable to act. Chris Luning told Sheriff Betzing how he smelled smoke on the man's breath, and sure enough, when investigators found Troost, they also found a pack of Camels and a Bic lighter. Brian had not been close enough to smell the breath of the man with chloroform, but he'd been with Chris a few months earlier when a red Thunderbird stopped along Old Copper Road.

A gruff man smoking a cigar rolled down the window, and an exotic looking fellow in a white suit called out from the passenger seat, looking for directions to Lily Guerin's house, which burned down a short time later. Investigators ruled it an accidental fire, and no arson investigation was filed.

But us kids knew.

After Logan Troost hanged himself, things went back to normal until the day a bus drove into the floodwaters of Lake Manitou, and Brian Forsberg again smelled the same sweet cigar smoke he'd smelled pour out of the red Thunderbird.

Like his predecessor, Brian had a collection of facts but none of the puzzle pieces fit each other.

Yeah, Percy, I think this one is more Thunderbird than Jeep.

CHAPTER TWELVE

Over the River

Old Copper Road
December 28, 1985

The final Christmas celebration filled the house with smells that drifted all the way up to the attic. Levi set his presents on his bed and sorted through the CDs, books, clothing, and musical equipment in privacy. After unwrapping presents in the dining room, things had gotten way too loud and congested for him. Grandma Hannah, Aunt Charlotte, and Uncle Cameron (another Guerin) arrived after breakfast, and Great-Uncle Dale (MacPherson) brought his wife and Grandma Ida (MacPherson) just before lunch. Even though Joey's sleeping bag remained on his floor, he and Daniel played with their new toys downstairs.

Ormus played in the background, a renewed obsession since the night of the crow. Along with Metallica and Iron Maiden, Ormus ranked as one of Levi's favorite metal bands due to their reliance on mythology and occult themes, something his mother despised. The ruined cassette had already been replaced by a CD, yet he still searched for meaning in the act, so he fixated on the British band. The song "Longest Night" played in the background, and the lyrics gave him pause.

Winter demons scratching at my door.

Drag in the Yule tree, a sacrifice to Thor.

Levi tried to tell his mother once that decorating a Christmas Tree was an ancient pagan ritual, but she refused to listen to his point. The song referenced the Winter Solstice, the longest night of the year, which happened a few days earlier.

What a weird week it's been.

Levi walked over to his window, which had been repaired with duct tape and Plexiglas. The attic always was the warmest room in the house, so his repair job more than did the trick. Dad still didn't know about it yet.

Although the front of the house faced the Crow Wing River valley, the rear, including his window, faced the wooded slope that led to Lake Manitou. The roof of the fort could be seen just twenty feet from the window, which allowed him to look down on Fozzie. Beyond that, the barren woods descended to the frozen ice of Lake Manitou.

The brush of Carousel Island obstructed much of the lake, but he could see the distant western shore where the Ice House Murders happened. He wished he knew more than gossip. Newspapers weren't delivered on holidays, and the family did not turn on the television with company over. Three bizarre events—the murders, the crow, and Lily—all drove Levi to solitude to sort through it all.

He picked up the Ormus CD and studied the lyrics and liner notes. He'd already read all the biographies of the band members, so he turned to the production team. The band was signed to Atlas Records, owned by Aleister Sinclair, one of Europe's most powerful media moguls. His granddaughter Maddy Sinclair served as the band's promoter and—

"Boys! Time to eat!" Leah called up the stairs. With three Guerins and nine MacPhersons gathered for lunch, Levi had to sit at the "kids" table in the kitchen with Reuben, Daniel, and Joey while Ben and Leah joined the adults.

As mysterious as Great-Grandma Lily proved to be, Uncle Cameron creeped him out even more. While the rest of the adults exchanged pleasant (if not shallow) conversation, the "Can Man" fixed his dead eye on Joey.

A servant of light? Or a servant of darkness?

Cameron Guerin appeared harmless and was a bit embarrassing. Due to some sort of accident or illness, the fifty-year-old had a dead eye, white hair, and a pronounced limp. He worked as the custodian at St. Marie's Catholic Church, and when he wasn't lurking there, he prowled the streets of Split Rock on his blue bicycle, collecting stray cans and bottles for recycling.

Why the hell is he looking at Joey?

Just then the eye focused on him and Levi looked down at his plate. Feeling his uncle's gaze, he shoveled in his food quickly, dropped his plate in the sink, and darted for the mud room to once again escape.

Outside, he took in a few deep breaths. *It's Christmas break. If I'm ever going to be guarded from evil, it will be this week.* So he stepped into the old forest and opened himself to answers.

Although trees fringed most of the seven mile long lake, a dense swathe of oaks grew along its southern side, beginning midway at Turtle Island and continuing along the southern shore where the shore turned back north at Buffalo Creek. From there, the granite bluffs thinned the oaks, but those that took root were some of the oldest and largest along the lake.

According to Lily, Lake Manitou held powerful magic for good and evil in its foundations. For the past several weeks, she had chattered away about occult matters as if discussing *Wheel of Fortune* or *Jeopardy!*

"Sessile oaks," Great Uncle Donnie, just six years older than his father, debated with his father one day while they were working in the back feedlot. Levi's father tried to make a point about Lake Manitou's indigenous history, but Uncle Donnie countered with a strange theory about the trees. "The Ojibwe people were still in Michigan when the first explorers came to the Great Lakes region, but there were towering oaks all along the shores of Lake Manitou when white settlers came here in the early 1800s. A white oak can live 400 years."

"How's that prove anything? A forest doesn't get planted. It just grows," his father responded.

Uncle Donnie kept arguing. "These are sessile oaks. Sessile oaks are from Scotland. I'm telling you...these oaks are some sort of land claim. Scots were here a hundred years before the Ojibwe arrived."

But what does it mean? Does Lily know about the oaks?

He headed north.

Although a pine could take root in a crack of solid rock, an oak tree needed root space, which is why the top of the granite bluff had pines and almost no oaks. As the highest point along the shore, the wind kept any snow from collecting along the top of the ridge, making Levi's walk quite easy.

But no willows.

Both Lily and the shadowy figure from his dream mentioned willows, but in the dead of winter, most deciduous trees looked the same.

Although the MacPherson family owned hundreds of acres above the eastern side of the Crow Wing River valley, those acres were purchased years after Donald MacPherson built his dairy farm along the scenic but agriculturally worthless plot of land. Yet according to his father, dairy farming only needed a solid foundation for a barn with good drainage and clean water.

Gustaf Forsberg also realized the value of the property for dairy farming and purchased the plot of land north of the MacPherson property. There was no marker, fence, or wall that divided the two neighbors, except for the fact that the highest part of the bluff divided the property. When Levi found himself going downhill, he knew he was on Forsberg land.

Although Edna Forsberg still lived in the house, the barn had been retired for a decade, a relic of the past. There were cars in the driveway, including the Sheriff's SUV.

Another Christmas party hanging out with a grandma, Levi realized, and did his part to stay as close to the lake as he could so he could sneak past the house. The MacPherson kids had run wild over the entire end of the lake, so his presence would likely be ignored if seen.

Even before GiGi Lily told him about the place, Levi already knew about the existence of Bleeding Rock. According to legend, during the Dakota-Ojibwe wars of the 1700s, vengeful Ojibwe zealots took a dozen children to the granite cliff as sacrifices. Another variation of the legend said it was twelve Dakota women. A third variation claimed it was called Bleeding Rock because the fissures in the granite bled blue vitriol.

Reuben once went there with a bunch of the other preppy kids to drink and returned unaffected by the stories of folks who fell from the forty-foot cliffs to their deaths.

If Lake Manitou was the lake of souls, then Bleeding Rock was the epicenter of evil.

Even in winter, Levi had no problem finding the location. Stacks of flat stones, inuksuks, stood as silent sentries around the perimeter of the bald opening in the forest. Knocking one over was a bad omen, one that the recent teen drinkers respected, leaving behind plenty of Busch beer cans without knocking over a single pile.

Levi knelt down at the center of the opening and with his fingers felt the carved channel in the stone—a channel meant to collect and funnel blood.

With cold sobriety, Levi waited for answers.

What is the meaning of all of it? Jesus? Dreams? Murders? Strange rituals? A talking crow? The Manitou? Is any of this real?

"Is it?" Levi asked aloud, yet the lake, rocks, and trees remained silent. *Bullshit.*

Frustrated and cold, Levi turned to head towards home.

Then, at the top of the ridge, Joey stood, scanning the trees.

"Did you lose it?" Levi shouted out, helping his brother find his location.

Joey flinched with fright until he spotted Levi. Then he shouted, "Dad is looking for you."

Oh no. Why do I have a feeling Joey stirred up trouble with the crow?

Joey was halfway home when both boys turned. Once back at the house, Levi saw his father heading into the enclosure of the fort. *What did Joey do?*

Luckily, he heard garbles and clucks, indicating the bird was still alive and well. Once he reached the foot of the tree house, Levi called out, "Need something, Dad?"

His father remained in the opening for a moment, and then stepped down, pulling the trap door closed. "You can't keep it in a tree house. It's gonna shit all over and make a total mess."

"But...we're just keeping it until its wing heals."

"And how exactly did it hurt itself?"

Levi glanced at Joey, who shook his head defensively. "Like we said, we just found it flopping around on the ground."

"Really?" Dad started skeptically. "So, what were you out in the woods doing just now? Looking for another bird to rescue?"

"No, I needed to get some fresh air. We'll do a better job cleaning up after it. I promise. Let us keep it at least until the end of Christmas break."

Dad looked out toward the lake for a moment.

"A walk?" Dad doubled back. "You've been acting strangely this whole week. Is there something, you know, you need to talk about?"

What the hell? Does he know something? This isn't like him. "Um, no, I'm fine. Um...the crow can speak. Did Joey tell you that?"

"Yeah," Dad said, rolling his eyes a bit. "I heard it when I was in the garage. Your mom would lose it if she heard that thing calling out like it did." Dad turned to the barn. "This is what's going to happen: you and Joey are going to repurpose the old pigpen under the loft. You'll need to put some chicken wire along the front and a bunch of straw on the floor. Give it some perches to jump around on, too."

Really? He's helping us?

"We can keep Fozzie?" Joey asked with a broad smile.

"Yes, you can keep Fozzie until it is healed," Dad said to Joey, and then turned to Levi below him. "When it gets stronger, you can bring it

THE TRICKSTER　75

up into the loft for it to strengthen its wing until it's ready to fly off." Once down, he lingered a bit, looking at the woods, his sons, the tree house, and then back to the woods again. He stood with his hands on his hips.

Levi struggled not to fidget. *What does he want to say?* "Fozzie's not a crow, by the way," he said.

"He's not?" Levi countered.

Dad shook his head, and winced, still measuring his words. "He's a raven. Crows go *caw, caw* while ravens scream bloody murder. That was my first clue. Ravens are a few inches larger than a crow and have different looking tails."

"Cool," Levi said, and his father took a few steps toward the backdoor of the garage. "I don't want you or your brothers out wandering around until they find out what happened over at Haggard Bay, okay?"

"What happened at Haggard Bay?" Joey asked.

Yeah, Dad, what happened exactly? "Okay," Levi said, waiting in vain once again for his father to say more.

"You know…uh…Noah used a raven to find out if the flood waters receded."

"I thought it was a dove with an olive branch in its beak?"

"Nope," Dad said confidently. "Noah sent out a raven first, but it didn't come back, which meant it must've found somewhere to land, huh? Jesus seemed to like ravens. He said 'Look at the ravens—they neither sow nor reap, they have neither storeroom nor barn; yet God feeds them. Of how much more value are you than they!' Keep it as long as it stays, boys."

Strange. It was as sappy as his father had ever been.

When his father was in the garage, Levi asked Joey, "What did Fozzie say?"

"I don't know. Dad just came inside, called me with his index finger, and walked right back out. I heard Fozzie making noises when I got out in the garage. Dad told me to go find you and then climbed up into the tree house."

Jason Lee Willis

"Well, go change into some jeans and we'll start working on the old pig pen."

"Awesome," Joey said and darted to the garage.

Alone, Levi stood looking up at the fort, only to hear Fozzie cry out, *"Under the willow. Under the willow."*

You gotta be kidding me, Levi dropped his head. *This is nuts.*

CHAPTER THIRTEEN

The Sleep of Death

Staten Island, New York
December 29, 1985

A narrow spotlight filled the darkness with the radiance of the sun—a familiar nightmare for Ansel. "Okay, my little movie stars...in three...two...one...action!"

Then the details slowly began to change. Instead of shag carpet and a musty basement, Ansel Nielson found himself sitting alone on a massive slab of stone overlooking a lake.

Lake Manitou—my father's home.

Floating two inches above the surface of the water, fog covered the calm air above the lake. Looking down at his lap, Ansel examined his hands, one of which was covered in gruesome pink scars around his wrist and up his forearm. In the other hand, he held a .357 Colt Python revolver with one bullet remaining in the chamber.

My father's pistol.

He'd taken the pistol out of hiding enough times over the past decade to know the gun felt real, but the bright studio lights above his head felt unnatural. With the pistol aiding his hand as a shield, he looked up into the light and the metal ring surrounding it.

"Ready when you are," the man's voice said from the darkness on the other side of the bulb. Shane and Cindy had become faceless monsters in his nightmares. Ansel aimed the pistol at the center of the light, cocking the firing hammer back.

"Oh, there you are!"

The new dream defeated the old nightmare.

The sound of a young woman's voice dissipated the old scene in a puff of smoke, and when he turned, he realized he was sitting on a rocky point covered with cedars that grew larger the farther away from the lake they got. Just inside the protection of the woods stood a simple hunting cabin, stripped of paint, covered with a mossy roof. Standing at one of the corners, a young woman in a tank top and shorts folded her arms as if agitated.

I've seen her in my dreams before.

"What are you doing out here?" she asked. "We've got work to do."

Work? For a moment, she stood her ground, but then she marched across the rocks right to where he sat. Behind him, his black backpack remained unzipped, and without hesitation, she grabbed it as she knelt. "Give it to me. We don't have time for that."

Ansel glanced past her hand to her chest and then quietly down at the gun, guilty for even a glance at her breasts. She wore a WWJD necklace.

She snapped her fingers and pointed at the pistol.

He handed it over, and she stuffed it back into the depths of his backpack. "If this bag is indeed a metaphor for your soul, we've got a lot of cleaning out and throwing away to do," she scolded, her hands digging through it. She pulled out two plastic wrapped porn magazines and held out as evidence. *This is a new dream. Tonya's in those magazines.*

The dream girl did not shame him with the magazines. "I suppose we're going to have to deal with these sometime this summer, but everything else is going to have to wait." The girl was a few years older than him, but she was not as old as Tonya. She stood and pulled the pack over her shoulder. "Now let's go; we don't have much time."

By the time he stood in the doorway of the cabin, the fog had been replaced by another raging storm. "It's ironic that we met in a storm and now are going to die in a storm," the dream girl said as she sat down on the dry boards of the cabin floor.

"What are we doing here? What is this place?"

"This is your father's old hunting cabin. It's where you first kissed me. Don't you remember talking about *Nightmare on Elm Street* and ax-murderers using the cabin as a hiding place? This is our happy place, Ansel."

Ansel hadn't let anyone touch him in seven years let alone a kiss. "I'm dreaming, aren't I?"

"No, this isn't a dream. It's a choice. It's the price you paid for a single kiss."

"I don't understand," he admitted.

"You dropped right into the middle of a war, and no one told you how to fight. By the time you figured out what you were doing, the war was lost. Would you like another kiss?"

His dream girl giggled and leaned forward, taunting him with a slight lick of her parting lips.

Ansel leaned away.

With a nod of approval, she reached down and picked up his backpack with both hands, holding it at the top and bottom. Like hurling a shot put, she launched it across the small cabin until it crashed into the wall.

"Hey! That's my stuff," Ansel protested angrily.

She reached over and grabbed hold of his chin. "Who are you?"

"I'm Ansel Nielson."

"That's right. You are the Cloud Champion, so start acting like it."

"What's that supposed to mean?"

"Well, if you'd stop wandering off, then we could finish the song."

"What song?"

"Focus! You're going to ruin it all again, and everything that has been sacrificed will be washed away. We need to work on the song."

An acoustic guitar, sheets of paper, and an envelope appeared on the floor between them. "I'll give you a kiss if that gets you past it. I'll rip off my clothes and run around this cabin naked if that helps, but I need you to help me with the song. Big picture, Ansel! Big picture."

The envelope had writing upon it that read "Open at Home."

Then the writing evaporated.

A moment later, so did the envelope.

The sheets of white paper, covered in musical notes, all turned yellow, and the tablatures morphed into some strange pictographs.

"I'm focused. I'll do it right."

"You better," she said. She took his hand, pulling it toward her, revealing his scars. With her other hand, she wiped away the scar tissue as if a crust of mud. "That black bag and these scars—that's old Ansel. I need my Cloud Champion."

The young woman turned into a shadow, and behind the nebulous form stood a raven. "If you're ready this time," she said to him, "the raven will show you the way. Don't mess this up, Ansel. Everyone is counting on you."

Ansel squeezed his eyes closed, took a few deep breaths, and then slowly began counting to ten. When he opened his eyes again, his dream girl vanished along with the lake.

Well, that was different, Ansel thought as his eyes opened from sleep to see his alarm clock. He took a moment to make sure he was truly awake, and then his hand reached for his lamp.

A Shane and Cindy dream, he wrote down as requested by his headshrinker. *No Jimmy.*

He discreetly ignored the pistol and then pondered the other part of the dream.

Hot girl—not Tonya.

Lake Manitou?

Something about a song.

He was about to write down a note about the raven when he heard a familiar gurgle outside in the tree.

THE TRICKSTER 81

CHAPTER FOURTEEN

Fortress of Solitude

Split Rock, MN
December 29, 1985

Father Gary Mackenzie smiled and shook hands as the parishioners filed out of St. Marie's Catholic Church. Today, most of the emotional trauma seemed centered on people experiencing a holiday without a loved one—or being triggered by holiday memories. Even though the exchanges were brief, Father Gary made mental notes on whom to visit during the next week. His wounded flock slowly departed the church.

At forty, he'd reached a crossroads in his life and three generations of Hiawatha County saw him differently. To the elder generation, they greeted him with the title Father Mackenzie. Those from his generation, the baby-boomers, chose to call him Father Gary since the Beatles had ruined his identity with the song "Eleanor Rigby" during his seminary training back in California. The kids, known as Generation X, barely knew the Beatles and had dubbed him after the burger, Big Mack.

He'd always been tall, and coming out of high school, he'd been tempted by scholarship offers to play basketball, but his faith led him into the ministry. Near the end of his seminary school training, he enlisted as a chaplain to serve soldiers serving in the Vietnam War, which is how he crossed paths with Brian Forsberg.

Because of Forsberg, he found himself assigned to Hiawatha County, but after spending several months going down the rabbit hole, he returned to the surface fully committed to Lily Guerin's Isanti Lodge. Although he couldn't find a specific beginning, the Jesuit Order quickly fixated on the Anishinaabe people in North America, following their migration from Nova Scotia all the way to where they found the Ojibwe tribe camped along the Great Lakes.

When Halley's Comet—the Serpent Star—came in 1910, a suspicious accident took the life of the Isanti Lodge's religious leader. Since Lily's brother represented the Benisi Clan, he took the symbol of the Eagle, leaving the "black-robed" Jesuit Jean Guerin to adopt the symbol of a different bird—the black raven.

Now, Gary also stood as the Benisi—the bird clan. His role was to know all the legends and lore from the Catholic perspective.

Although the service had ended, a new song suddenly began. Back in the sanctuary, Nicole MacPherson's family rehearsed a new song. As usual, Father Gary had shaken the hand of Gavin MacPherson as he left the church ahead of his family. Once gathered, Nicole would keep her children together to practice a new song or two before they'd end practice for lunch. But today, Levi MacPherson avoided both the handshake and practice and slipped out of the church.

I need to say something to Forsberg about Levi, Gary decided and headed to his office to quickly schedule his coming week.

Since the Ice House Murder, Gary had been unable to rid himself of the chill that ran down his spine. While there had been horrible crimes and strange occurrences over the past decade of his time in Minnesota, the return of Halley's Comet brought a foreboding sense of doom with it.

With the names of the wounded flock written down, Gary ducked out of his office for home. Past the parking lot that was shared with the Lutheran Church, a small cottage house served as his fortress of solitude.

He had a small, detached garage for his silver Chevette and a modest kitchen, bathroom, living room, and bedroom for himself. His rigorous holiday schedule was now complete, and before he even left the kitchen, he'd poured himself a glass of Starka and unbuttoned his black shirt in anticipation of a few days without his priestly garb.

By the time he stood in the living room, he'd tossed his black shirt into the open doorway to his bedroom and kicked off his glossy shoes onto the carpet. Above his white tank top, his dog tags dangled as a reminder of those he'd helped cross over to the realm of death.

His head snapped back to the kitchen as the sound of Ann Wilson came up through the floorboards of his basement.

He had company.

Often, his youth groups frequently hung out together in the basement to watch movies, play games, or to listen to music when they weren't studying scripture or sharing life experiences. When one of the curious teens discovered his aging record collection, they'd brought him a new release by the pop rock group Heart, which now played on his turntable.

But those meetings were carefully scheduled.

He ducked as he descended his own basement stairs, and sitting on the floor in front of the circle of chairs and couches was Lacy Morrison, daughter of Gary Morrison.

His heart stopped for two reasons.

First, he saw fresh bandages wrapped with white athletic tape on both of her forearms. Dark bloodstains told him what had been done to her wrists. She'd come close to telling him what had really been bothering her over the past few weeks, but instead, she'd used the trauma of her Uncle Charlie's battle with cancer as the source of her melancholy. Instead of being dressed for church, she wore clothes more fitting for a night out on the town, a sign she hadn't even gone home from her Saturday night.

"What is this?" she asked when he filled the doorway of the basement.

The other reason his heart stopped was that she'd sat down in the middle of his occult research into the history of Lake Manitou. She surrounded herself with old police records, death certificates, newspaper clippings, books, charts, maps, and diagrams. Knowing he'd have vacation days coming in January, he'd turned his basement floor into a large table for his research. He'd stepped out of his house by seven o'clock to practice his homily, which meant Lacy had access to his material for several hours.

He ignored the question, knelt on some of his most precious records, and gently took hold of her hands. "Tell me what happened."

Today, she was finally ready to talk about it.

She told him about the sexual assault that'd happened several weeks ago during a Halloween party as well as what she'd done to her arms with broken glass the previous night, but twenty minutes later, after all the tears had been wiped away, she turned back to the floor of the living room to ask, "What is this stuff?"

Gary hesitated as he tried to find words that weren't a lie.

CHAPTER FIFTEEN

The Black Horse

Split Rock, MN
December 29, 1985

Driving his Mustang still made Levi a bit nervous. He purchased it just a few months ago, and despite its official designation as a "muscle car," he kept the speedometer bouncing a line below the 60 mph mark. His buddy Garrett Johnson mocked his driving, claiming he drove the car like an old woman. Garrett invested his own farming dividends into a full-size truck.

"It's a chick-magnet," Levi had told him back in October. "Can't pick up girls driving a truck."

The 1969 convertible was quite impractical during the winter. Aside from its thin top causing the heater to work twice as hard, the Mustang also had rear-wheel drive, making it twice as easy to spin out and end up in a ditch. Luckily, the roads to Leech Lake were well-traveled and free from snow. Instead of blaring Ormus, Metallica, or Iron Maiden, he went with some softer metal in his cassette deck, ZZ Top's *Afterburner*. Outside his window, Hiawatha County flew by as he took the same route to Onigum his family took on Christmas Eve.

Okay, I should've written down my questions, Levi realized as he grew nearer and nearer the nursing home. *What do I need answered?*

Hours earlier, he'd had a strange dream that couldn't be ignored.

Instead of a small congregation at St. Marie's Catholic church, an arena full of hypnotized fans shouted his lyrics right back to him as he put one foot on a speaker and pointed the head of his white bass guitar at them, plucking the four strings and vibrating the entire building.

Surrounding him, the members of Ormus moved just like they did in their videos, with Maleus Johannsen smashing cymbals, Reece Collins and Murray Smith dueling on guitar, and Ian Wilkinson emerging from a circle of fire at the center of the stage.

His dream continued even after the concert ended, as if an MTV backstage documentary allowed him to see the intimate moments of the band, which treated him as a friend and peer. Groupies waited for him, but a stately redhead took his hand and led him to a sports car, and soon he sped away at unbelievable speeds.

The third stage of the dream took him to a mansion in the deserts of California, where the beautiful redhead led him through a home and into a steamy bathroom. Instead of ending the dream with her in the shower, a hideous old woman emerged from the mist, muttering strange syllables to him.

"Vainamoinen," the toothless hag said with a smile.

"Aron Miku," the redhead responded with another nonsensical phrase to him, smiling.

Then the mist that surrounded them turned into a bloody cloud that buffeted and battered him, sweeping him into a whirlwind. Levi tried to grasp reality, and his grip tightened as the wind blew harder and harder. Suddenly, the old hag's voice ended, the whirlwind subsided, and his clenched fingered released, only to reveal the bulging green eyes of the redhead whom he had strangled in his grasp.

Levi had woken from the dream sweating and panting.

Now, he needed answers from Lily.

Obviously, I need to ask her about the significance of dreams, he prioritized. *All the omens, in fact. Ravens, willows, the strange women.*

THE TRICKSTER 87

His right snakeskin boot pushed the accelerator at Backus. He wore the boots just for her after she'd taught him about the Horned Serpent.

What else do I need to ask her about?

What's the Wintermaker?

What is the Song of the Manitou?

Levi already understood the basic concept of a manitou. With Lake Manitou's mythical namesake, also known as Nessie in Loch Ness, he'd grown up with tales of a horned water serpent that lived in an underwater den below the lake, but after his trip to the library, he learned the Horned Serpent was not only a prevalent Ojibwe legend but a universal myth as well.

Oh yeah, and who are the servants of the Manitou?

He rapped on the door of Lily Guerin's room. "Hello," he called out as he swung the door open.

"You've come back," she said sternly, quickly looking at his boots then past him. "Your little brother is not with you. Good. I will not die today."

Levi didn't know what to say about the reference to Joey, so he started with, "I've been having strange dreams."

"Have you seen the Tak-Pei yet? The Little Porcupine Men?"

"Porcupine men? No. I haven't seen any Porcupine Men. I wanted to—"

"Good, the recent deaths will certainly wake them, and I must protect you from them before they do you any harm, which they will. You are too old to serve the Wintermaker, but your death could be used to strengthen them. Stay away from the water. That is where they are bound."

She'd said so much it took him a moment to response. "I live next to Lake Manitou, Nokomis."

"Yes, so did I. If you are to be a warrior in the fight to come, you will need to stay near Lake Manitou to save your family and many others from certain death." Lily dismissed him with a wave of her wrinkled old hands when he went to speak. "This is all you need to know: the Wintermaker is coming. There will be at least eleven more deaths, ten for his servants, the Tak-Pei, and one for himself. When we last fought him, you and I, he almost claimed my brother Migisi, so he will want to claim your younger brothers. We are not going to let him do that, are we?"

"Hell no," Levi said with confidence, yet Lily's hand struck his cheek. His flinch was greater than any pain from her soft hand.

"No blasphemy," she scolded. "Your great-grandfather was a priest and would not approve of such profanity. You are going to perform a sacred duty and must be holy to do this. I failed because of my sins, and now, as an old woman, I must fight once again and finish the loop. The Wintermaker is an old enemy of God, and when I die, the spell I cast over him will be released."

"What does the Wintermaker want?"

"To defy God. He once was a powerful sorcerer who obsessed with death and dying. He grew more and more powerful until one day he devised an evil plan meant to shatter the plans of the Creator. When he heard prophecies of a great flood and a great fire, the Wintermaker fought against the plan meant to reconcile the Creator and his creation. Instead of worshiping the life-giving Creator, he worshiped Death and learned black magic that controls the other world, and in doing so, learned how to trap souls. At first, he experimented on his own family, and then he went out snatching innocents, bringing them back to his lair, until he perfected his evil plan and trapped the souls of the dead within the magical web he wove. When his own death came, he did not look away, for he saw it as a chance to destroy God's plan."

"How would dying stop God's plan?"

"When Christ died upon the cross, how long did he remain dead?" Lily countered.

"Three days."

"Yes, for it takes three days for the soul to descend to the Underworld, which my father's people called the Land of the Midnight Sun. All those who die are carried upon the River of Souls, except for one."

"Jesus?"

"No, remember, Jesus chose to follow the will of the Creator, and his death was part of the plan. The Wintermaker has lain in his tomb since the days of the dawn and has not descended to where all men must go. As long as his soul remains trapped at Lake Manitou, the Terrible Summer will never arrive nor will any other prophecies about the End Times. That is the Wintermaker's victory over God, but together, we will throw his soul into the pit where it belongs."

Levi grinned, enjoying her grandiose style of storytelling. *If true, I have a pretty epic destiny.* "How do we start?"

"We must first finish the loop, and to do that, you must be trained properly."

"What does that mean? Finish the loop?"

"It means many things. First, we must make dreamcatchers if we are to prepare you before the coming of summer. You must bring me branches from a willow tree so that—

Levi perked up. "A willow tree?"

"Yes, have you never seen a dreamcatcher before?"

"Yes, I just never knew they were made of willow. I had a dream about a willow tree. You were in that dream."

"Of course I was in your dream. You've been in my dreams since I was your age. I am the old end of the loop, and you are the young, new growth. We are both part of the same branch and when you stand at the cave and call out for me, the loop will be complete."

"I don't know anything about a cave," Levi confessed.

"You will. It is an unwavering fate. You came to me in my most desperate hour, and now that I am an old woman, you have returned so I can aid you in your desperate hour. The woman with the mark of the thunderbird—have you seen her?"

Thunderbird? Could she be talking about a raven? "I don't know who you're…wait…in my dream, you stood with two others, a young girl with blonde hair, and a woman with a scarred face."

Lily nodded. "She is the one who taught me the missing verses from the Song of the Manitou."

The toothless hag Aaron Miku? "Who is she?"

"Time will tell. There is very powerful magic at the cave, and when you sit there, you will meet her also. Before I can teach you the full song, we *must* make dreamcatchers."

"Can you tell me about—"

"No more questions. We don't have enough time for questions. Cancer is in my bones and the pain will continue to grow until it clouds my mind. And I won't take their pills, either. You must hurry. Bring me willow branches so my work can begin. Go."

Levi rose, even if he didn't want to leave. "Where am I supposed to get willow branches?"

"My grandfather paddled across Lake Manitou to a place called Jiibay Hollow, but that is too close to the lake. Albert used to bring them to me here, but now he is dead. There was a big willow tree in the old convent at the top of the hill. That is where I made my first dreamcatcher. You can find your willow at the Fisher Mansion."

Levi still didn't know what she talked about. She must have seen his confusion for she added, "It is at the end of Maine Street. Trust me, it is there. Bring me back only the new growth. A lot of it, you obviously need training."

He chuckled at her backhanded insult. "That's it? Cut some branches?"

"I'll be watching you…from the past. You'll also meet an ally who will be waiting under the willow. Albert Fisher helped me in my time of need, and I helped him when he was a boy. The Albert Fisher you will meet will be an old man. You need to bring him a warning for me."

"What kind of warning?" Levi asked.

Lily didn't answer but instead turned to a dresser drawer. She returned with a black slouch hat. She looked at his boots and then placed the hat on his head. "Now you are also ready to fight the Wintermaker."

"The Wintermaker is going to be under the willow?"

"No, only Albert. In two days, you will close one of the remaining loops."

AN HOUR LATER, Levi returned home.

Clouds hung low in the sky, and the air was still and frigid. The big red dairy barn was about a hundred yards from the back door of the house, slightly downhill by design. His father kept the large lot plowed, which provided access to the house and side garage, barn, and the big machine shed where Levi parked his prized Mustang. Deep piles of snow were pushed between the machine shed and barn, creating a small wall that blocked the gravel road and river valley.

The cows were milling around in the open yard, fed and oblivious to the mild winter weather. At one point, Levi almost knew them all by name, but once he had his wardrobe, bass guitar, and 1969 black convertible Mustang all purchased in cash, he let Daniel take his share of the livestock profits.

Levi walked through the outer skirt of the barn, which housed the dairy operation. The storage and containment facility was closest to the house, allowing easy transportation and access. The stainless steel equipment looked more like a science lab than like the interior of the barn, and a walkway separated the area where the cows were milked. Levi used this walkway to cut through the outer skirt and into the main part of the barn. Once, Willem MacPherson used the big barn as a diverse livestock rearing station, but now, most of the large facility was used as storage. The upper level still had a hayloft but also a practice stage, wired for the entire family band, *Rock of Ages,* to practice for church performances across Minnesota. Levi took a hard left, passing the loft for the old pig pen.

As expected, Joey sat on the fresh straw and watched Fozzie jump from platform to platform.

"I taught him a new trick," Joey said proudly as Levi entered the pen. "What's a muppet say, Fozzie? What's a muppet say?"

"Waka, Waka, Waka," Fozzie boldly cried out. "Waka, Waka, Waka."

"Oh, you've ruined him, haven't you?" Levi teased, tussling his brother's hair and sitting down beside him.

"He's not ruined: he's funny."

Along with the strange clicks, warbles, and croaks, the raven now threw out the phrase whenever it looked up, bringing grins from both boys.

"I read those books we picked up the other day," Levi said. "The books on raven lore."

"What'd they say?"

"Some stories are good, and some are bad. The bad ones talk about how ravens are servants of death, kinda like an angel that carries souls to the underworld. I guess it's because in nature, ravens can find a fresh carcass before any animal in the woods."

"Because they're so smart."

"Right. Obviously. Even the science books talked about how they are the smartest of any birds, which is why the myths thought they were supernatural."

"Supernatural?"

"Yeah, more than meets the eyes."

"Robots in disguise."

Levi chuckled at the *Transformers* reference. "In Norse mythology, Odin used a pair of ravens to spy on the world, and a famous Viking named Ragnar Lothbrok used one on his banner to let his enemies know death was coming for them."

"Cool."

"The Celts and the Welsh thought they were servants of war gods on the battlefield."

"Waka, waka, waka," Fozzie croaked, causing Joey to double over in laughter. "Can you imagine being a Viking warrior and Fozzie flies down and says, 'Waka, waka, waka,' right before you die?"

"No, Joe, it's hard to picture Fozzie on a battlefield," Levi admitted and pulled a handful of walnuts from his jacket.

Fozzie's feathers quivered, and his slender pink tongue flexed. Noticing this, Levi tossed the walnut halves onto the straw and watched as the bird hopped down the obstacle course of PVC pipe, boards, and cables to get his favorite treat. Even though Fozzie refused to let them close enough to pet, his hesitation on the floor was a step closer to trust. Snatching the walnut shell in its powerful beak, it hopped back up to one of the many shelves Levi had built for it.

"Dad was right about the raven being on Noah's ark and just flying off when Noah released him."

"Do you think he's the same raven?" Joey asked.

"Well, he'd be pretty old, wouldn't he? Some Indian myths say the raven was the creator of the world."

"How would a raven create the world?" Joey protested.

"I don't know, but there are a lot of Indian tribes. Many of them saw the raven as a trickster."

"Silly rabbit, tricks are for kids," Joey said unprompted.

"You really watch too much TV, Joe," Levi said with a playful eye roll.

"*Clay!*" Fozzie shouted out after shaking out the empty walnut shell. "*Clay! Clay!*"

Lily accidentally called him Clay, too. "I guess that means he wants more," Levi said, tossing a walnut up to its perch, which it caught on the rebound before it could fall to the straw.

"Do our people have any stories about ravens?"

"The Scots?"

"No, the Ojibwe."

Levi chuckled. "Do you remember what Donnie calls his dog?"

"Charlie?"

"No, what *kind* of dog."

"A mutt?"

"No, the other word. The one with ketchup."

"Oh, a Heinz-57."

"Right, fifty-seven varieties, which means—"

"Which!" Fozzie called out. "Which! Which!"

"Which means the dog has a little bit of everything. You're a mutt, with a bit of everything in you. Great-grandma Lily was part Dakota and part Ojibwe, so we're only...a sixteenth Ojibwe."

"Never mind," Joey said with disinterest and began to stand up.

"Okay, there was one story I came across about a *white* raven."

"Are you making this up?"

"No. It was an Ojibwe tale about how we got freshwater. In the tale, humans were poor and sickly, without sunlight or freshwater, so this raven named the-raven-who-sets-things-right decided he would help humanity. There was this man named Ganook who horded the only freshwater in the world for himself, so the-raven-who-sets-things-right flew down to his smoky wigwam to steal the water for the rest of the world, but he ended up staying for so long that his white feathers were turned black."

"Did he steal the water?"

"Do we have freshwater?"

Joey took a minute to figure it out. "Oh, so he did." He held a smile for a few seconds before adding, "I'm going back in. I'm hungry."

"I'll be in in a few minutes also. I'm just going to hang with Fozzie for a few minutes."

Fozzie watched the operation of the door closely, and Levi realized the bird was figuring things out, but even if he did manage to break out of the pen, he'd still have to contend with escaping the barn.

Levi held another walnut in his fingertips, getting the bird's attention. "Fire?"

Fozzie nodded his head a bit, letting out a loud scream.

"Did you see the fire, Fozzie? Is that what upset you? Fire?"

Fozzie nodded and let out a loud, "Fire! Fire!"

Why, though, did you crash through my window on the night of the Ice House Murders? Ravens are too smart to do something so stupid. Levi tossed the walnut to Fozzie, who missed it and had to climb down to retrieve it. It still didn't use its wing.

"Tell me about the willow, Fozzie? What's under the willow?"

"Which?" Fozzie said between stabs at the walnut.

Right. Which willow? Levi had not found any along the granite ridge, but Lily gave him new choices. "Which willow?"

The bird fixated on the walnut, stabbing and cracking until pieces came free from the thick shell.

"Willow, Fozzie? What's important about the willow? Tell me about the willow."

"Willow," Fozzie repeated, and Levi held another walnut.

"Yes, tell me more about the willow."

"Willow," Fozzie said, bobbing its head. Levi put the walnut back in his pocket and the bird flexed its wing muscles as if ready to dive down. Then, instead of bold syllables full of volume, it attempted a whisper, "Close the loop."

The loop of the dreamcatcher.

Levi had no other choice now.

CHAPTER SIXTEEN

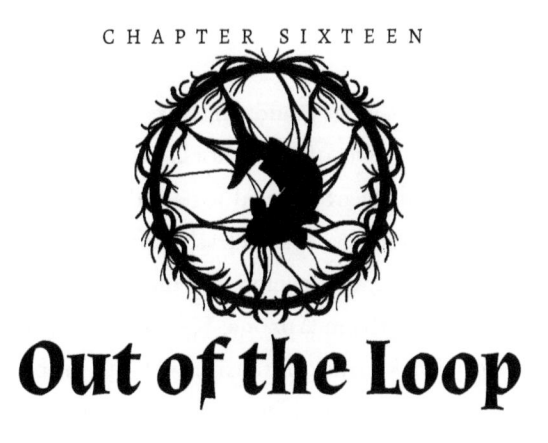

Out of the Loop

Split Rock, MN
December 31, 1985

The town of Split Rock earned its name when settlers noticed that the granite outcropping that formed the eastern shore of Lake Manitou literally cracked, allowing a small but steady flow of water to pass a hundred yards. Although the lake's primary outlet was in the wild rice fields of Buffalo Slough south of town, George Fisher saw the potential of the rocky creek, erecting a mill over the creek, and in the process, became Hiawatha County's first lumber baron. As his business grew, so did his wealth, and by the turn of the century, he gifted his home near the lumber mill to his plant manager Farrell Luning and purchased the brick convent at the top of the hill, which then became known as the Fisher Mansion to those born afterwards.

For decades, the Fisher family literally looked down on the people of Split Rock, but by the fifties, the town filled the river valley and came spilling up the hill. Thanks to a massive financial donation from Albert Fisher, a new state-of-the-art school for the Split Rock Bulldogs was built. Unlike the old school, which had been built near the river, the new facility was placed on the northern edge of town, near Highways 34 and 19. The isolation of the Fisher Mansion ended with the construction of

Seventh Avenue, which connected Highway 34 to Maine Avenue and South Division Street.

George Fisher's great-great grandson, Karson Luning, positioned his wheelchair to face the town of Split Rock. At 29, Karson's wild days were behind him, but his heart yearned for another night on the town. A hunting accident rendered his legs useless, leaving the former jock with the cruel irony of having to develop his mind. With Grandma Betsy spending the winter months in Arizona, Karson became the house-sitter and the single-story brick mansion transformed into his bachelor pad.

Dumbbells, videotapes, magazines, a massive television, a new Nintendo game system, and bottles of all varieties littered the living room floor. Once a week, his grandmother's maid would tidy things up with the magical force of the changing of the seasons.

Tonight, though, Karson had no interest in traditional entertainment. Instead, he found his way to his great-grandfather's dark office and peered down at the world through a pair of high-powered binoculars.

Just like in the comic books, tragedy had robbed him of his legs yet technology gave him a new power—the power of observation. Now in the midst of winter, the trees had dropped their leaves giving him an almost unlimited view of the Crow Wing River Valley. From the south edge of town along Market Street to the park where Fisher Saw Mill once stood, Karson watched the flow of traffic coming and going on New Year's Eve.

Although his voyeurism did provide an innate thrill, this time he used his superpower to be the eyes and ears for the Isanti Lodge—he was a Guardian of the Knife.

His binocular lens kept an eye on the distant MacPherson farm, Edna Forsberg, Father Mackenzie, and even his parent's home at the old Fisher Mansion along the Crow Wing River.

So when a figure walked across his lawn, less than a hundred yards from the dark window, he almost dropped the binoculars.

Son of a bitch.

The intruder came from the northeast, which meant the intruder jumped over the four-foot tall brick wall that encircled the property. Karson wheeled himself to the central desk, opening the drawer that held the Beretta 92 pistol.

By the time Karson returned to the glass, he could see the intruder did not get any closer to the house; instead the figure was in the middle of the yard—approaching the old willow tree.

Even in winter, the curtains of the old willow tree partially remained, and after a moment of hesitation, the figure stepped under the canopy.

This could be a supernatural trick. Halley's Comet grew closer by the day, and with it, the ancient magic grew stronger. Both Lily and Sheriff Forsberg warned of different types of monsters coming.

Karson quickly swapped the pistol for the binoculars, but by the time he got them refocused, the figure emerged from under the dark canopy.

Confirm it. I gotta confirm it.

The figure hustled away on the same path he'd come, forcing Karson to leave the window and roll back to the main part of the house.

His wheelchair stopped at the bottom of a steep staircase.

Hurry before the guy vanishes.

The three-story tower with a 360-degree glass enclosure meant Karson had to use a rope to ascend the narrow stairs. There were no stronger arms in the whole of Hiawatha County, and as soon as Karson took hold of the thick rope, his powerful muscles had little problem taking his lower body up the winding staircase. When he reached the top and the more powerful telescope, he was breathing heavily, not because of exertion but because of the unexpected action.

Most of the telescopes pointed toward the heavens, but a few, including his favorite night vision scope, pointed toward town. From his perch at the top of the hill, he could look down upon most of the town. He spotted the intruder jumping over the brick wall, and a moment later, a lone vehicle drove south on Market Street and turned at Old Copper Road.

Oh, shit.

Karson found the rope, descended down the tower, and wheeled back to his great-grandfather's desk. He picked up the old journal and thumbed to the entries made the final year of Albert's life.

Tonight I closed a loop, Albert wrote. *Just as Lily described, I became an old man who waited under the willow. She was still just a young woman. I assured her of the path she was taking. For a few moments, we existed in a timeless space before she went off to fulfill her destiny. We closed one loop but another opened. Moments before Lily arrived, a young man appeared, also sent by Lily. He warned me about the Wintermaker, so I told him about the Omodai.*

Karson set the journal down and quickly found the cordless phone in the pockets hanging off of his wheelchair. His fingers punched out the familiar phone number, and it wasn't until the phone was ringing that he noticed it was past eleven o'clock.

Sorry about that.

"Hello?" a gruff voice answered, followed by throat clearing.

"Wally, it's Karson. I just saw one of those loops close."

CHAPTER SEVENTEEN

The Flames of Prophecy

Sterling Junction, MN
December 31, 1985

The house went up in flames moments after Wally Crain picked up the telephone to speak with Karson Luning. He'd been so engrossed in the conversation that he hadn't noticed the situation until it was too late.

Now, Wally's arms wrapped tightly around his wife Nancy as the two stayed in the paradoxical void between the frozen snow bank they sat on and the heat coming from the flames in the window.

In the distance, a fire truck from St. John came down the road with its sirens blaring, and Wally, in the light of the flame, watched as his world turned to ash.

When the lights of the new fire truck came around the corner, Nancy's sobbing ceased, and for a moment, she returned to him. "What's happening?"

Unbelievable. "We're fine. Help has arrived."

A command van arrived first and three men jumped from the cab. Two rushed to the burning house while another rushed to where Wally and Nancy sat.

"Is there anybody else in the house?" the fireman asked, kneeling.

Wally shook his head. His girls were all married with their own families now. In the distance, the sound of sirens signaled more trucks.

"Let's move you out of the way. Come with me."

Even though he'd been on the phone with Karson Luning when smoke filled the kitchen, the flames spread faster than he could have imagined. *How did this happen?*

When the pumper truck arrived, the fire fighters attacked the house in unison, and by the moment, more and more firemen arrived. EMTs wrapped Nancy and Wally in blankets and set them on the open tailgate of a truck.

Wally put his arm around Nancy when she shuddered. The light from the fire illuminated her face, which had been washed free of makeup after their five o'clock dinner in Wadena, and by eight o'clock, she'd slipped into comfortable flannel pajamas. He remembered her coming into the living room during the Army vs. Illinois Bowl game and then ducking back into the dining room to work on her newest manuscript.

Fuel for the fire.

For most of Christmas Break, he heard her fingers clanking on the typewriter as page after page gathered onto the dining room table. The newest book was the sixth book in her novel series—*Livinia's Sacrifice?* Something to that effect. He'd asked her about it in November, and she told him the new title had something to do with the daughter of Titus Andronicus, who died a collateral death in order for her father to have vengeance against his enemies.

She was writing when the phone rang.

Wasn't she?

Karson Luning's phone call stole his attention away from his wife and the football game when he began spouting off hysterical theories. "It's the loop. It's Great-Grandpa Albert's time loop." Lily Guerin long ago explained to the lodge the time-traveling by demonstrating with her willow dream catchers. Although time was linear, growing out from a trunk like a branch, it could intersect with the past in the same way the thick end of a willow branch could overlap with the thin end.

Lily had experienced several of these "time loops," including the one that happened at Good Counsel Convent. Under the big willow that grew in the yard, she'd seen herself at two different moments in time (1897 and 1898), an old man that turned out to be Albert Fisher in 1962, and a young man, which Karson Luning claimed trespassed on his yard just a few moments earlier. "I'm almost 100% certain it was Levi Mac-Pherson."

That was the moment Nancy's muttering turned into angry shouts of accusation. At first, Wally thought he was being berated for interfering with some household system involving dishes, laundry, or the pantry.

Her voice filled the dining room: "They're gone. He took them! He took them away!"

With Karson in his other ear, and the phone cord tethering him to the kitchen wall, he simply ignored the unprovoked rant. In recent months, her mental health allowed her to be easily rattled.

"He's ruined everything," Nancy continued shouting and then her voice softened. "Oh my God. How? How could he do it?"

Wally had the audacity to cover his free ear so he could listen to Karson's rant about Levi closing the loop. A few moments later, he saw the smoke rolling across the kitchen ceiling.

Now beside him, the arsonist sat under the same blanket, covering her mouth in horror—but not in the horror of seeing their home in flames. Her eyes seemed to be witnessing a completely different horror altogether. As water blasted into the dining room windows, Wally squeezed her in a hug and then turned to ask, "What did...he...do?"

"He's going to destroy them all," Nancy muttered, her eyes fixed on the fire.

Which question do I ask? "Destroy who?"

"All of them. Jude, Vega, Maddy Sinclair, even the fat little girl at the end of it all. He just...he just...he's not the hero. He's not. He's tricking everybody into thinking that...that..." With a blink, Nancy flinched and returned to him, her eyes in a panic. "The fire!"

Years earlier, when Wally told his father Kermit about his intention to marry Nancy Anderson, his father, who'd claimed he stabbed the Horned Serpent with a Barlow pocketknife, responded with, "That girl's a bit touched, isn't she?"

Now, Wally understood his father's apprehensions. All he could do was pull her closer to him as they watched the battle between fire and water. A thousand gallons of water pumped into their house, extinguishing the fire that was greedily consuming the dining room.

"I think we saved the house," one of the firefighters said while hustling back to the pumper.

Wally hopped off the tailgate to inspect the damage. He knew they'd be spending the next few weeks in a hotel room or with one of his daughters, but he wanted to see the garage full of tools, the bedrooms, and even the living room to assess what had been spared. Yes, there would be plenty of water damage, but the bones of the house looked to be intact—a fortunate blessing.

The hairs on his neck suddenly stood on end, and he pivoted from where he stood by the front door.

The tailgate was empty, and a blanket crumpled on the ground.

"Nancy?" Wally spotted her silhouette standing in front of the big willow tree. For eighty years, the tree had stood in the spot where Kermit Crain planted it from a transplanted shoot. For the past forty years, Nancy spent her summers reading and writing under the canopy of the tree.

Like a marionette with its strings cut, Nancy fell to the ground in a heap.

CHAPTER EIGHTEEN

A Deal with the Devil

Indian Head Mountain
January 1, 1986

Leonard White Elk glanced to the east to see the sun peeking over the eastern coast of the continent his people called the Great Turtle. The sixty-year-old man, despite his athletic physique, felt every ache and pain in his body after his overnight vigil on the mountain.

Thankfully, the rising sun warmed his face even if it did little to soothe the pain in his back, neck, or legs. He'd spent the night staring up at the skies, hoping to see the omen known as the Serpent Star but instead his heart was filled with an overwhelming sense of despair and hopelessness.

I worry they are about to make a terrible mistake.

The last time the Serpent Star appeared, his mother had still been living along the shores of Lake Manitou. Fawn Chevreuil descended from the Wijigan Clan, which according to the lore, had been counting the appearances of the Serpent Star since they lived along the east coast in Nova Scotia.

Seven Fires, Seven Comets, Seven Stopping Places.

His maternal line was Anishinaabe—although the Wijigan Clan was considered a heretical cult within Ojibwe society. His paternal line was Lakota, who'd once stood in opposition to the Anishinaabe People.

In 1910, when the Serpent Star appeared over Lake Manitou, everyone assumed they stood at the Seventh Stopping Place of the Seven Fires Migration. Father Jean Guerin prepared the Isanti Lodge for battle against the Wintermaker with a plan to use the magic of Philosopher's Stone and Haley's Comet to cast the evil spirit living in the waters into the depths of the underworld.

The plan failed miserably.

Leonard's mother Fawn then realized it was because of Lily Guerin.

"Do not trust her," Fawn told him years later. "She is willing to destroy our world for her own selfish desires. For all I know, she has become a servant of the Wintermaker."

Fawn left Lake Manitou in 1910, moving to the Turtle Mountain Chippewa Reservation in North Dakota before coming all the way to the Canadian Rockies, which she believed was the *true* Seventh Stopping Place of the ancient prophecies.

Leonard reached a calloused hand to his neck and rubbed his sore tendons, which had spent the night staring up at the sky in anticipation of the return of Halley's Comet. Even though scientists said the comet was near, it was not yet visible to the naked eye. Prior to his vigil, he felt an unease, so he went to the mountain to seek clarity. His prayers were not answered, and he woke as troubled as when he'd gone to sleep.

If Lily's Wijigan accounts were correct, 1986 would be the end of the Seventh Fire and the beginning of the final battle. If his mother was correct, it'd be another generation before the end came. *Will the world come to an end when the Serpent Star returns in 2060?*

Long ago, his People still lived along the Atlantic Ocean, and after receiving the warnings from prophets, the Seven Fires Migration began. Although Leonard's nephew, Ben LaBiche, disagreed with the oral tradition, the account claimed that after each subsequent appearance of the Serpent Star (1456, 1532, 1607), the Anishinaabe (and the Wijigan Clan) discovered the next Stopping Place. In 1682, his ancestor Chief Bakinis lived in the woods of Wisconsin when the sacred Water Drum was found.

Within a generation, the Water Drum had been brought to Lake Manitou by Chief Wiyipisiw, where it was hidden in a cave along the Blue Knife River for generations until the children of Big Squeak and Winnie Weber discovered it. Even though Fawn Chevreuil was a descendant of Chief Wiyipisiw, Lily Weber was chosen by fate to be the Firehandler capable of wielding the magical stone.

Then the schism came between the cousins.

At the time, it appeared as if Lily had been a hero. She silenced the evil spirits, saved the life of Jean Guerin, and rescued Migisi from certain doom. A decade later, when Jean Guerin died, the truth about her victory came to the surface. In exchange for the soul of Jean Guerin and a life of "happily ever after," Lily became an ally of the Wintermaker, Fawn claimed.

To the Isanti Lodge, Lily remained a tragic hero whose goal in life was to destroy her enemy. With the Water Drum, "Song of the Manitou," and her guardians at her side, Lily boasted a desire to defeat the evil spirit, but Fawn discovered the method—the Omodai.

No one in the Isanti Lodge ever questioned her, the lore surrounding the ancient Horned Serpent, or the magic she invoked, so when she tossed around a ritual using the word Omodai, even Migisi softened to her plans.

Of course, Lily never fathomed the possibility of defeat. Following the death of her beloved Jean, her vengeance only sharpened her desire for victory. At the time, Lily only had a single child, Louis. Fawn's distrust of Lily led her to flee rather than raise her own children near Lake Manitou.

Fawn protected her family while Lily left hers at the edge of the fire.

For the Wintermaker to win, he needed a host—the Omodai. Like a demon or wendigo, he'd take possession of a fresh human body and rise from his own death, with the tool of his victory—the Water Drum—in his grasp.

Leonard thought of his own grandchildren and the possibility of offering them as bait. He understood the stark difference between Lily and

Fawn. Lily represented the concept of free will. Fawn represented the concept of grace.

Lily's desire to be the hero was about to turn her into the villain.

Fawn waited decades for the path to present itself, and now, two decades after she passed, Leonard sat alone on top of the world waiting for everything to burn around him. The Isanti Lodge called for him to return for help.

If I return to Lake Manitou and join in the fight, I'll forsake what my mother believed. He stood up, collected his belongings, and began his hike down the mountain. *If I remain, does that make me a coward? Am I dooming the world by not doing anything?*

Instead of taking the obvious path back down the mountain to his cabin, he took another route and opened his heart to guidance from the Great Creator.

For the next few hours, the only answer he received was the crunch of snow under his boot. His choice of path took him further down the mountain from his cabin, forcing him on a lateral path almost a mile from what he'd intended.

Looking back up the slope of the mountain, he spied the remnants of an avalanche that had come down the mountain and into the valley and left a tangle of trees, rock, and the frozen corpses of animals left for the carrion birds. The symbolism of a dead deer was not lost on him; his family represented the deer in the Isanti Lodge.

In a sea of white snow, the color of red flesh and brown hide could not be ignored, and a splash of black night also stood out as the same stark contrast.

Leonard paused on a bluff of exposed rock to study a dark object below him. Had it been summer, the full color of the season would have hidden the object from him, but the desolation of winter brought an acute focus to the foreigner.

The avalanche had broken on the bluff, sending the white wash to the east and into the valley below, making the snowpack soft and the passage slow.

Finally, he stood above an angular piece of stone that had not been shaped by nature. Darker than ink, a corner of the ebony stone emerged several inches from the snow. Leonard reached a hand out to brush away more snow but paused.

There was writing upon the stone.

CHAPTER NINETEEN

Along Came a Spider

Leech Lake, MN
January 1, 1986

Levi MacPherson watched as Lily held the switches of willow across her lap, yet she seemed more concerned with the comings and goings of the Rose Parade happening on her television. Levi began to watch the television also, but quickly losing interest, he scanned her room for clues about his great-grandmother.

There was a framed picture of Pope John Paul I on her wall as well as a simple crucifix hanging on a braid. There were some Ojibwe talismans: a four-colored circle and a string of shells. Between the two religious paradoxes, some cheap, mass-produced art hung, giving little insight or backstory. All of the photos on the shelf were in color, with no indication of her life prior to the 1960s. After a few moments of watching the floats, Lily turned back to him, almost appearing surprised to see him sitting on the edge of her bed.

"So?" Levi asked after her prolonged inspection of the willow.

Lily glanced down to the willow. "You have done well. Very well. There is great magic in willow trees, especially this one. By collecting these willow branches for me, you've completed the loop. Did you speak the words to Albert?"

Levi nodded. He'd done everything exactly as Lily insisted.

"Then the past is secure, but the future is not yet set. It is time you and I begin preparations for the final loop."

Do I tell her what he said to me? "Shouldn't we be speaking to the Isanti Lodge about these preparations?"

"No," Lily retorted bluntly. "Some parts of my plan are meant only for you."

Like the Omodai? Albert claimed he once thought he was the Omodai, hunted by the Porcupine Men. Back in 1898, evil was mistakenly drawn to young Migisi. Upon seeing Levi, Albert cautioned him about evil being drawn to him. "Obviously, Lily found the real Omodai," Albert had finished, "so my prayers go with you, young man."

Lily lifted a hand to point to the closet. "Last Easter, your mother brought me a ridiculous Easter hat and pants the color of grass. I refused to wear that ugly outfit."

Levi chuckled.

"It is because I'd seen that hat in a vision. Another loop must be closed before we can battle the Wintermaker. When I battled the Wintermaker back in 1898, I sat upon the edge of the Blue Knife River and saw myself as an old woman drifting down the river. My old self wore green pants and a large Easter hat."

Four months from now.

"I also saw you and your brother, traveling down the river in my canoe when the water was much lower. You and your brother are destined to find the sacred stone in the cave, and in that moment, when the ancient magic is released, you'll create another time loop. The past, present, and future will again intersect. From 1986, you will reach back through time to help me in my hour of need. You will help me find the Philosopher's Stone so that I can travel to Deadwood Island to fight for the lives of my brother and—"

"You've told me this." Levi knew the story about rescuing the man destined to be her husband.

THE TRICKSTER 111

Lily hummed and continued. "But you will also open a window into the future. A woman from the future gives me the words to the 'Song of the Manitou' in order to protect the loop, for if my precious Jean had died, the loom would have collapsed, and you would have only been a strange dream in my broken mind."

Levi thought of his recent dreams. "Who is she? This woman from the future?"

"An ally. She wore the symbol of the Thunderbird upon her chest and commanded the Water Drum as only a Firehandler could do. Her face had received a grievous wound, which affected her speech; nevertheless, she knew the full "Song of the Manitou," which meant she'd been guided by God to find the "Sacred Shell" lost centuries ago along the Seven Fires Migration. This woman is the key, and when you close your part of the loop after I pass, you must listen to what she says to you. She will guide you."

Pass? Is she talking about dying? Or just floating down the river?

"But *you'll* be commanding the Water Drum. *You're* the Firehandler."

Lily's wrinkled face wrinkled even more. "Bah, I can't think in this cage. Find my jacket. I need some fresh air."

Her request shook Levi's concern. "Can you do that?"

"Breathe? Of course I can."

"No, I mean, just leave."

"Do you see the walking path outside my window? What do you suppose it is there for?"

"Um, walking?"

"Yes, now fetch my yellow jacket from the closet," Lily demanded, setting all of the switches on her bed except for one. Then, with surprising virility, she shuffled right over to the closet to get the jacket herself.

She's as bossy as my mother. "You don't want your wheelchair?"

"Today, I feel strong enough for a walk; now hold this," she said, handing him a willow switch as she put on her coat. At room temperature, the willow branch regained its flexibility.

Levi's concerns about Lily alluding to her impending death and another taking her place quickly dissipated. Lily had lived at Wanakiwidee Retirement Home since 1962 when she was in her eighties. Levi realized she'd remained relatively healthy and active for her age. Her large down coat made her look like Big Bird as he walked her down the hall, but at least she would not be cold.

"She wants to go for a walk," Levi said and shrugged to one of the nurses who stopped to question them by the exit doors.

Even though the path was cleared, icy patches remained where the snow melted on the asphalt surface. Lily seemed to understand and kept a firm grip on his arm.

"Leech Lake has been a gathering place for our people for almost three centuries. One of my grandfathers had a home on Bear Island, but they would not let me stay there, so I stay here at Onigum. They tried to assassinate my husband here, just a bit up the road. He was trying to rescue my brother Migisi. How does the saying go? Out of the frying pan and into the fire. Ah, it seems like it happened yesterday. For a few days of my life, I thought the Battle of Sugar Point was the most terrifying thing I'd ever seen. Then I fought the Wintermaker."

"Is it really a Horned Serpent?" Levi asked about the enemy he'd soon face.

"Not today, boy. You asked me about dreams, so I will teach you about the legend of the dreamcatcher."

It's a start.

The snow upon the yard tapered away toward the shore, making it impossible to see where the lake actually began, and the lawn ended. Decorative trees were planted along the walkway, some barren and others evergreen. After several moments of silence, Lily began her explanation.

"When I was your age, I hated my grandfather Nanakonan for being an ignorant pagan, but he insisted on teaching me nevertheless. My brother had been taken to boarding school, and my grandfather grew old. My father rejected his training, so I was his only choice. Do you know the meaning of Asibikaashi?"

"It's your family name, isn't it? A Clan name."

"In a way. Asibikaashi is our word for spider. Our clan was the Wijigan, the Skull Clan, feared by the others the same way Puritans were afraid of witches. In the time of the dawn, sometime after the great flood, Grandmother Spider spoke to Manabozho about the sad plight of the Ojibwe people, who were spreading across the back of the Turtle in search of megis shells. Do you know the Seven Fires?"

Levi nodded. Anishinaabe history had become his obsession.

"When our people lived along the Atlantic Ocean, prophets from the future came to guide our people on a sacred journey."

"From the future?"

"Like you came from the future to guide my path to the cave," Lily agreed and took the willow switch, bending it into a teardrop loop. "Prophecy is a strange thing and can only occur at a crossing of the loop. Only at the end of a prophecy can one reach back to the beginning. The prophets from the future sent those in the past on a quest: find the sacred megis shells at the seven stopping places. Those who believed and left became the Anishinaabe—those who came from nothing. Those who arrived at the Seventh Stopping Place and found Turtle Island were the Ojibwe."

"Turtle Island State Park," Levi repeated. "So, Lake Manitou was the end of the journey."

Lily avoided answering that. "Grandmother Spider knew the journey would be challenging once her people spread out across the lands, so she invented the dreamcatcher to protect the children from...bad dreams."

The Omodai will be a kid like young Albert, young Migisi, or...Joey.

"Did you bring the webbing?" Lily asked.

Levi had options, but he'd stuffed them in his pockets. After brushing off the melting snow, he led Lily to sit.

"I have feathers in this envelope, and leather in this bag, but I wasn't sure what you'd want for string, so I brought some nylon line, some craft thread, and some yarn."

"Have you seen a real dreamcatcher before? It is made of sinew not string."

Levi had one hanging from his rearview mirror, but he'd purchased it at a museum at Mille Lacs. "Sinew?"

"Animal tendons. There is no magic in string," Lily grumbled. "What about the gems?"

"No problem there. I have beads, stones, and even those funny little shells."

"Megis shells."

"They're called cowrie shells on the bag."

"This is good."

Finally did something right. But the moment vanished when Lily turned to the envelope of feathers. "What are these? I asked for bald eagle feathers."

He didn't want to tell her about Fozzie. Not yet, at least. "I think it's against the law to collect them, but I did find owl feathers."

"These are not owl feathers," Lily said, holding up one of Fozzie's raven feathers. "They are from a raven. The raven is a trickster, so how can his dreams be trusted? Migisi told me that a raven once followed my father all the way to Lake Manitou. One morning, he woke up and shot it with his pistol. He ripped the raven's wings off and stuffed them into his black hat like a mad man."

The hell with that. I'm not hurting Fozzie. "What happened then?"

"My father was killed a few weeks later in prison. Perhaps he should have listened to the raven."

"Should I go find another feathers?"

"No, we don't have time. I will make a dreamcatcher with these feathers, but next time, bring me eagle feathers and sinew, even if it is deer sinew."

What other kind of sinew would she want?

THE TRICKSTER 115

"When assembled, the shells are placed at seven crossings in the web to represent the seven fires of prophecy. The hole at the center is left for good dreams to pass through, and the bad dreams collect upon the sinew. Day after day, and year after year, the sinews dry until the willow branch cracks, a sign the child has become an adult in the eyes of Manabozho. With the proper materials, a dreamcatcher will do far more than protect from bad dreams."

"Like what?"

"Bring me better materials, and I will show you wonders," Lily said. "But for now, your raven feathers will suffice."

CHAPTER TWENTY

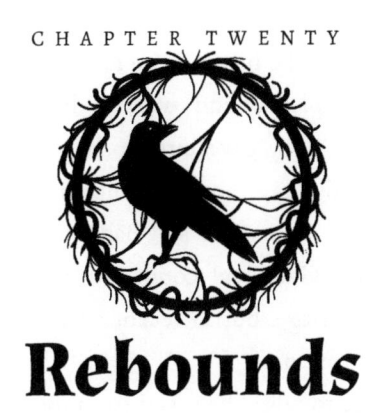

Rebounds

St. John, MN
January 3, 1986

Father Gary Mackenzie parked his Chevette, stepped out of the car, and took a dozen paces across the parking lot to stare out at the frozen waters of Lake Manitou.

What are you? Who are you?

The Manitou did not answer.

During the Vietnam War, Gary would often wake up early and observe the beauty of nature; he knew that by noon, his world would transform into a living hell. The current vast horizon of white also hid a horror that was slowly waking up.

Gary's shiver caused him to pivot for the warmth of the Golden Shores Nursing Home.

Death and tragedy frequently filled his days in unexpected ways; nevertheless, he had a routine and pace with his weekly schedule, which included visits to the hospitals and nursing homes.

As soon as he stepped through the glass sliding doors, the familiar sound of a live piano greeted him. Karson Luning, playing songs written decades before he was born, sat behind the keys. The paraplegic entertainment director would be his final meeting of the stop.

First Gary found his way to the business office and knocked on the door of Molly Chauvin. Like many at the nursing home, Molly had started as a part-time employee and worked her way into a full-time management position. Molly gave birth to her firstborn daughter just a few months after graduating, and her unplanned pregnancy kept her from going to college. At 30, she still had obvious beauty despite the weariness in her eyes. Gary had counseled Molly and Mark Chauvin through a difficult marriage, but in recent years, the couple had settled into a more amicable routine.

"Do you have time to talk?" he asked from the doorway.

"I'm just working on a new schedule," she said. "It's so nice to have the holidays behind me. I suppose you're exhausted, too."

"The shepherd never truly has a day off from tending to his flock," he answered honestly. "I saw Wally Crain's truck in the parking lot."

"His wife was admitted last night. The doctors have her on medications to prevent another stroke, but it's going to be a long road to recovery for her."

Father Gary reached into his front pocket for his spiral notepad. "What room is Nancy's?"

As Molly looked up the room number, Gary reflected on his hospital visit to Brainerd the afternoon after the house fire. The earliest rumors claimed that Nancy had been hospitalized due to the fire, but neither smoke inhalation or flame had been the culprit. Once doctors diagnosed the stroke, her erratic behavior made sense to everyone but Wally. He could not get past his grief over both tragic events.

"It's so sad," Molly said after giving him the information. "They are supposed to be enjoying their retirement together."

Another casualty in the coming war? Wally Crain was the glue that bound the Isanti Lodge together, and Nancy's stroke effectively removed him. "I've got a favor to ask. I've got a young lady who's looking for a fresh start. She's had some tough times lately, and I think a change of pace might help her get back up on the horse, so to speak. She's from Split Rock, but I think you might know her. She's Charlie Morrison's niece."

The gasp was unexpected until Gary remembered that Lacy Morrison's uncle was close in age to Molly. His two-year battle with lung cancer ended in early fall. "Of course. What are you thinking?"

"I know you probably don't have the budget for it, but I was hoping you could make her an assistant to Karson Luning."

"I barely have the budget for Karson."

"Lacy's just a pixie, so I don't think she'd be good for either the kitchen or direct care, but she's a musical prodigy, and she'll charm the residents, I'm sure. Her rough times are more than just the loss of her uncle, though. She needs to be away from her peers over at Split Rock. She needs to see the bigger picture, and I think playing cards with residents could be as good for her as it would be good for them. Just a few shifts to start with. What do you say?"

"I'll figure something out. Tell her she can start next Saturday."

AFTER MEETING WITH Molly, Gary visited with the residents on his notepad. A few of them were old enough to remember the last Jesuit priest to come to Hiawatha County and the comet that followed, but most were in too poor of health to care about such things. When he found Nancy's room, it shocked him how much younger the Crains were than the other residents.

Near sixty, both were healthy and bronzed, but instead of hiking the deserts of Arizona or walking the beaches of Florida, Wally and Nancy were huddled in a small room overlooking a frozen lake.

After an exchange of pleasantries, Wally was swallowed by silence, prompting Gary to ask him, "What's going through your head?"

"Revenge."

"How so?"

"The doctors say that a blood vessel in her brain plugged up and then, like a balloon, expanded until it just popped. They don't know if the damage it caused her brain will ever get better. She's young and strong, so they try to fill me with hope. But what if it was more than just a blood vessel?"

"Why do you say that?"

"Right before it happened—or, heck, right as it was happening, she went into this...manic rant. Now, I'm reasonable enough to blame the stroke for any strange behavior she was having, but she got angry—the kind of anger usually reserved for me when I track in mud, blood, or grease. I don't think she ever said a name, but she acted as if an intruder had walked in through the back door. She started ranting about "him" ruining everything."

"Who was she talking about?"

Wally shook his head. "Him? I thought she was revising her manuscript and that it was just a character she was imagining. She acts like her characters are real people some days. Again, it could just be her broken brain, but in the middle of her ranting about him ruining everything, she set a pile of papers on fire, which spread to the curtains and lit up the whole damn house. Reality and fantasy came crashing together when she lit that match, and now, that broken blood vessel in her brain has become my enemy. I blame it for starting the fire. I blame it for destroying everything. I should have asked her his name, but now...now I'll get no answers."

Both men looked to Nancy, whose closed eyes might never open again. Gary knew what to say when despairing people blamed God, but he didn't know how to respond to Wally's accusations. "Do you need anything?"

"The girls are at the old house, packing up what can be saved. They found a small cottage in St. John and are transferring all of the belongings. You could stop by and bring them lunch. Other than that, I don't know what I need." Wally shook his head. "Thanks for stopping by. I just need some rest."

Gary patted Wally on the shoulder before leaving the room.

A few minutes later, he stood beside a piano.

Karson Luning paused when he saw Gary, who updated him on both Lacy Morrison and Nancy Crain. He nodded along as if he was listening to every word, but when Father Gary finished, Karson nodded a few more beats before asking, "You don't suppose she was talking about the Wintermaker?"

"Excuse me?"

Karson leaned forward to whisper. "Mrs. Crain—the night of the fire. I could hear her on the phone ranting about how he changed everything. What if she was talking about the Wintermaker?"

"From what I know, the Wintermaker is asleep and will remain asleep until the Song of the Manitou is sung."

"It's just that…"

"What?"

"I'm pretty sure at the exact time Nancy Crain was having her stroke that I saw Levi MacPherson walk into my yard to steal willow branches. If it's not the Wintermaker she was talking about, you don't suppose she was talking about Levi?"

The Crains have a willow in their yard also. "Do your best to keep Wally from fixating on this. We need him to think rationally in the days to come. I'll speak to Forsberg about all this and see what he thinks."

As Gary left the nursing home, he almost felt himself stagger back to his car.

Is this what I've been called to do?

He stopped again to look out at the frozen lake and wondered who Nancy saw in her final moments of clarity.

THE TRICKSTER 121

CHAPTER TWENTY-ONE

Murder Most Fowl

Staten Island, NY
January 5, 1986

Ansel Nielson had everything he needed for the anniversary of his father's death: the .357 Magnum, polaroids, porn magazines, guitar picks, a couple cassettes, a book of poetry, some snacks, and enough heroin to kill a horse.

Tomorrow, instead of going to school, Prince Hamlet would confront the ghost of his dead father.

Ansel propped the backpack between his nightstand and bed before leaving his room to go brush his teeth. He passed the closed door of Tonya's vacant room and stepped into the little bathroom. With his mother and stepfather downstairs, he didn't even bother closing the door to empty his bladder before brushing his teeth.

At fourteen, his skin was the only thing that had gone through puberty: acne speckled on his back, chest, and nose. He brushed so hard his gums bled, and after spitting toothpaste out, he stared at himself.

Something is different.

He stared at himself for several minutes until only the eyes of his father remained in the mirror. In truth, he didn't remember much of his father. His nightmares of childhood held the faces of Shane and Cindy, and his father only passed through those memories like a shadow. The old house in Indiana had also become just a shadow, with the only details of the nightmares belonging to the basement of the Lewis house.

He squinted and then opened his eyes wider. He lifted his mop of hair from his forehead to reveal the landscape of Mars. He splashed hot water on his face, scrubbing his skin until it was as red as the acne.

When he stopped scrubbing, he spotted the difference as he removed his hands from his face. At first, his focus remained on the lines in his palms, and then he flipped over his hands to study his knuckles, but two feet away, in the inverted world of the mirror, he saw jagged scars running down from his palms all the way to his elbow.

The scars existed only in the mirror.

When he looked down, his arms were unmolested. When he looked up, his arms belonged to Frankenstein.

What the fuck?

Having faced plenty of horror in his life, Ansel knew the answer—*I'm dreaming.*

He turned from the open doorway to see his bedroom, where he still slept and his backpack rested beside the bed. His jaw clenched at the subtle manipulation. He had a new bully in his dreams, one he meant to confront within the dream.

With one step, he was outside of his house yet still in the same dream.

The fowl with fiery eyes perched atop one of the trees in the backyard. For the past three months, the raven had been haunting him, prompting his mother to send him back to Dr. Jacobs. Ansel fed his shrink the regular stuff about his childhood trauma as he sorted out the newest twist in his personal melodrama. When he spotted the raven during waking hours, the bird all but ignored him, which brought up concerns about schizophrenia. In his dreams, the black bird behaved far more aggressively.

"What do you want?"

"A loop has been closed," the raven said, speaking in the voice of a female, most likely a teenage girl. It wasn't the cute blonde from his dreams or his sister; nevertheless, the voice resonated with him.

"So?"

"The Firehandler will need your help."

"I don't care," Ansel said, and no sooner had his voice echoed in the darkness than his arms fell limp, wrist bones exposed and hands dangling awkwardly from tendons still attached to his forearms.

"Yes, you do," the raven squawked. "Tomorrow your choice will either lead to destruction or to a rekindling of the fire. You must be able to join in the song."

"What song?"

The ground under his feet began to shake, and he scrambled backwards just as a fissure formed. The crack in the world devoured the ground, until he saw another figure being drawn to him. Like himself, the figure was a teenager, dressed in tattered jeans, snakeskin boots, and a felt hat. He stood under a large willow tree, which became the new perch for Ansel's ebony tormenter.

"If I'm going to do this," the figure said, "We'll need your help."

"Help!" the raven repeated. "Help, help, help."

Between himself and the figure under the raven, the dark waters began to swirl with the passage of a dark serpentine leviathan. As the monster turned in the channel between them, its reptilian back surfaced briefly.

Oh, shit. Ansel felt something clamp down on his arm, and he tried to spin free, to no avail.

It shook him.

The dream flickered.

His eyes opened.

The tentacle latched to his arm became his mother's hand.

"Ansel?" she said. "Wake up. You're having a dream."

The dream was over, and he found himself back in his bed without the Horned Serpent, the raven, or the boy under the willow.

"I'm here, Ansel."

Disoriented, Ansel looked around his room, the light came from the hallway, where his stepfather stood in the doorway. "We heard you calling for help."

It wasn't me; it was the raven.

His mom placed a hand on his cheek, ever briefly, before her hands withdrew and her back stiffened. "You're safe."

Ansel could see in their eyes what they assumed. *They think this is about Dad.* He took a deep breath and both the past and the future crept back into the shadows, leaving him in the present.

"I'll change my plans for the day," his stepfather said and slipped back into the hallway. His heavy steps could be heard descending the stairs.

"Do you want to talk?" his mother asked, a typical passive-aggressive question for her. He knew she didn't want to talk about her dead husband any more than Ansel wanted to bring up what happened to him and Tonya. Yet his subconscious mind had apparently called out for help.

That fucking raven.

It tricked me into making this moment happen.

Ansel's heart paused when he realized his mother's legs were practically touching his black backpack beside the bed. If she discovered it, his freshman year would come to an end, and he'd spend the next five months in counseling.

So he reached out and hugged her.

He didn't blubber or cry. He just held her and put his head onto her shoulder.

She'd come to the rescue eight years too late.

For now, Ansel put aside his plans to confront his father's ghost.

But in his mother's arms, he knew the inevitable was coming.

He needed to go to Lake Manitou.

THE TRICKSTER 125

CHAPTER TWENTY-TWO

Auld Lang Syne

St. John, MN
January 6, 1986

A blizzard buried Hiawatha County in a foot of snow, making the day even more intolerable than Sheriff Brian Forsberg expected when he woke up. It snowed heaviest in the morning hours, causing schools to be canceled and most businesses to close. Rather than sulking in his office, Forsberg spent most of the day patrolling the roads.

Eventually, the snow relented, and Forsberg returned to the department. He sat for a few minutes in his Suburban before turning off the engine. The lights of the building created a mirror effect on his windshield, and for a few fleeting moments, he stared at the reflection of the stranger looking back at him.

When he stepped inside of the front doors, he stomped his boots on the doormat to knock the snow off of his boots but then noticed multiple wet, muddy trails heading in all directions of the station.

"How are the roads, Sheriff?" Mia Donaldson asked as she looked up from her typewriter.

"It's fine out there now. Plows had it cleared by mid-afternoon."

"Good, because I have to drive into Brainerd with Dean tonight, and I hate driving on bad roads."

"Highways 10 and 210 will be clear," Forsberg promised as he stepped behind the front counter where Mia was stationed. Several of his office staff greeted him but only received a token nod from him in return.

"You have any plans tonight, Sheriff?"

"Yeah, I've got a date tonight," Forsberg answered, eyeing his office. He noticed two of the twenty-something dispatchers suddenly looked up at him in interest, and he glowered back.

"Oh really?"

"Yep. Got a date with some walleyes. My ole buddy Wally Crain told me the walleyes are biting on Lake Manitou. If I hurry, I might get there before it gets too late. He tells me they bite at dusk and about midnight. I sure don't want to have to wait until midnight."

All those eavesdropping immediately went back to work after he disappointed them with his solitary plans for the evening. Satisfied, he walked back to his office and closed his door.

He stripped off his heavy sheriff's jacket and hung it on his coat rack. Next, he unbuttoned his white work shirt and also hung it on the coat rack in the corner. He picked up his favorite red plaid shirt from where he'd hung it in the morning and put it on over his insulated long johns. Finally, he removed his gun belt from around his waist, opened his wall safe, and swapped his county-issued gun with his personal weapon—a 1965 Colt Python .357 Magnum. Forsberg quickly slipped the gun into his shoulder harness and sat down at his desk.

Since being elected as sheriff of Hiawatha County in 1980, Forsberg followed a daily routine of looking at unsolved cases. But today, he only needed to look at one file.

Nielson, James Allen. 10/16/1948-1/6/1978

He flipped through all of the reports he'd received from the Whitley County Sheriff's department in Indiana. He read over the details of the two homicides before reading through Jimmy's suicide report, again. Then he looked over the evidence files including the photo of the murder weapon—a 1965 Colt Python .357 Magnum.

While on leave in December of 1968, four soldiers from J Company of the 11th Armored Cavalry Regiment had purchased .357 Magnums while waiting for their flights in Saigon. Forsberg and his lifelong friend Jimmy Nielson had both bought pistols with mother-of-pearl handles while Shane Lewis had chosen ivory and Jay Thompson had chosen wood.

The pistol that the Whitley Sheriff's Department held in evidence had an ivory handle. Something wasn't right, and he knew one day, he was going to have to test all six bullets they also had in evidence. Forsberg was willing to bet that they weren't all fired from the same gun.

But it didn't really matter anymore.

Jimmy was dead.

A tap rapped on his door. Detective Ray Irvin stood in the doorway and peeked around the corner. Irvin had earned the nickname "the reaper" for obvious reasons. A slender man with a quiet personality, he often startled people who didn't realize he'd been there for some time. Although only 34, his high brow, thin neck, and taut cheeks made him look like an old man as he quietly peered at situations through his small glasses. Forsberg had hired the gentle soul from the Sioux Falls Police Department as a death investigator. Irvin investigated natural deaths and accidents, but occasionally, he worked homicides.

"I thought I heard you," the Reaper said, his eyes flitting around the office. "Do you have a moment?"

"Sure," Forsberg said, sliding the Nielson file aside. "What's up?"

"I spent the day making phone calls."

"And?" It had been weeks without even learning the names of the two victims.

"The hardware used to build the icehouse indicated that it was custom built and not manufactured. The hinges, support pipes, type of wood, even the tarp material—all sold individually. None of the companies I contacted had anything close to ours."

"Well...if that don't beat all."

"It certainly aligns with your theory, Sheriff. With all of the trinkets Disco pulled out of the lake, that Subaru would have had a pretty full rear hatch."

"Roof rack?" Forsberg speculated.

"Possibly, but it would have been quite a sight. The bottom of the icehouse was built with an eight-foot piece of plywood."

"You'd need a truck."

"And with the testimony of our witnesses…"

"The icehouse was set up days before Mr. Cigar parked the Subaru at Haggard Bay," Forsberg reviewed. Without names, Forsberg dubbed the primary suspect Mr. Cigar; the bodies found in the lake were Mr. Dice and Sleepy. Ron Spears and his local dive team found ritualistic paraphernalia, including runic dice. The B.C.A. autopsy results indicated the boy had been drugged and that both had eaten fast food prior to death. "So is Mr. Cigar local, or does he have an accomplice?"

The Reaper shrugged, taking one more glance at Forsberg's desk, cataloging every little detail into his brain for possible use later. Without prompting, the secrets would remain unspoken.

Forsberg knew the Reaper would not even speculate about the files unless asked. "Nice work, Ray. Keep it up."

Once he left, Forsberg looked at the Polaroid he'd put into the file a few years ago. In the picture, four young men posed while holding their new pistols while showing off the 11th ACR "Blackhorse" tattoos they'd just put on their upper arms.

Unwilling to cry, Forsberg just grit his teeth together as he tried to understand what had happened to his best friend eight years earlier. Everyone that knew Jimmy assumed something terrible had happened to him during the Vietnam War, but Forsberg knew the truth. He'd lost Jimmy to something far worse than war when they were just boys. He'd made a promise to Jimmy never to speak of it again, so he swallowed back his emotions and put the file away. There was only one person he could talk to about his feelings.

HALF AN HOUR later, Forsberg stopped at the edge of the highway and shifted his Suburban into four-wheel-drive. Unlike most of the other ice-fishermen who drove to either Turtle Island State Park or to Chippewa Beach, he knew a shortcut to the frozen lake. He drove off the road, through the cattails, and onto the two feet of ice on Lake Manitou.

Forsberg parked his Suburban next to the man-made icehouse with a tight blue tarp stretched over a pole frame connected to a wooden base. The lantern inside illuminated the shadow of a solitary figure sitting on a chair.

"Anything biting, you old coot?" Forsberg called out to his friend as he closed the door. A 40" northern pike stretched out across the ice like a frozen baseball bat.

"Of course not!" Wally Crain yelled out. "I haven't had a cotton-pickin' bite all evening."

Forsberg turned the wooden handle of the icehouse and quickly stepped inside to keep the warm air from escaping. Earl "Wally" Crain sat with a small jigging pole in his hand with his stocking-feet propped up on a bucket. He leaned over to the insulated metal milk box to see several walleyes already inside.

"Damn," Forsberg muttered and sat down on the seat Wally had prepared for him. "Did you save any for me?"

"I just got that snot-rocket earlier today, but I caught those walleyes as soon as the sun went down. You better wet your line, boy."

For the next three hours, the fishing was good enough to keep Forsberg's mind occupied. When fishing finally slowed around nine o'clock, he shared a late supper with the man who'd once been his boss. Forsberg drove a propane truck for Wally before getting his law enforcement degree at Central Lakes College. Wally had even been his Scoutmaster when he and Jimmy were just kids. If there was anyone who understood what January 6th meant, it was Wally.

Instead of Forsberg unburdening his heart, it was Wally who suddenly covered his eyes and began to sob. Wally's hand only stayed at his brow for a few seconds before he quickly wiped his eyes and acted as if nothing had happened. He reached up his line, pulled off the limp minnow, and replaced it with a fresh one. After dropping his line back to the bobber-stop, he finally looked up.

"I woke up this morning and I didn't know where I was," Wally explained. "Just like that, everything changed. My wife is gone, my house is gone, and...this icehouse is the only thing familiar."

Forsberg knew all the details about Nancy's stroke and the fire, but he also knew Nancy was an unofficial part of the Isanti Lodge. Despite the medical reports, it still felt like an attack. "Golden Shores is the best facility in the area. She'll get round the clock care there."

Wally was fishing just a few hundred yards from the nursing home. "Yeah, that's what I tell myself. But in the back of my mind, I think back to our wedding vows. I promised her I'd take care of her in sickness and in health. I just feel like I let her down."

"But you are taking care of her. I know you, Wally. I can't imagine you cooking and cleaning. Bringing her to the professionals is the best bet until she recovers." Forsberg reached into his thick fur-lined bomber jacket and pulled out a flask. He poured a little whiskey into his coffee and then handed it to Wally. Wally poured some in his own thermos cup.

"So, what do we drink to?" Wally asked.

"How about to Jimmy?" Forsberg finally brought up the other subject they'd been avoiding all night.

Wally raised three girls, and without a son, he took to the boys in Troop 88. Rory Stewart, Chris Luning, and Jimmy Nielson all met tragic deaths, leaving only Brian as Wally's adopted son.

"A few days ago, Tonya Nielson's name came across the wire. She's in Chicago."

"Do I want to know what kind of trouble she's in?"

Forsberg shook his head.

"To Jimmy..." Wally nodded. "And to Nancy."

"To auld lang syne," Forsberg put both pains together into one toast. They both smiled.

"To memories forgotten," Wally added and drank, smacking his lips and clearing his throat. "Did you have a chance to check out Levi MacPherson?"

Forsberg nodded. "Against his mother's wishes, Levi has embraced his Indian heritage, which is why he's been visiting Lily on a weekly basis. She's teaching him some of the old ways. When Karson spotted him, the kid was on an errand to collect some branches for a dreamcatcher."

A different heaviness fell between them.

Back in 1962, Forsberg and Jimmy Nielson had been in the hospital recovering from hypothermia when the shit hit the fan back at Lake Manitou. Lily Guerin, Gavin MacPherson, Nicole Guerin, Cameron Guerin, Ed Nielson, and Wally Crain had all seen evil rise from the lake, and it was their claim that Albert Fisher and Chris Luning had been killed by the dark spirits.

Forsberg stewed for several minutes. He'd accumulated too many secrets over the years, but Jimmy Nielson's secrets weighed most heavily upon him.

"I know why he ran away," Forsberg began then totally lost his nerve. They'd only been boys looking for an adventure, but somewhere in the depths of Haggard Bay, the truth waited for him.

"Huh?"

"I can't be certain why he took his own life. After what he learned and what he did, I don't know how I'd react. But I know why he ran away from Lake Manitou. I was thinking of the flood of '62."

"I've been doing the same. You and Jimmy were heroes that day."

Forsberg shrugged. "We both did what we could do to save folks, and if we have to do it again, we'll do it again, right? Some days I feel like a real hypocrite. I swore an oath to protect the citizens of this county, but in reality, I'm just a janitor."

"What do you mean?"

"I just clean up the messes left behind. I lie to myself that I can help these people from the evils in our world, but what if I can't protect them?"

"If you can't, I don't know who can," Wally took a sip of hot chocolate and handed the thermos over to Brian. "I'm sure you'll do your part. Just keep a close eye on those kids."

CHAPTER TWENTY-THREE

Wobble? No.

St. John, MN
January 11, 1986

After another visit to Gigi Lily, Levi parked his Mustang next to the barn rather than his normal spot in the big machine shed. The lights were on, and he could hear his family's instruments warming up.

I'm late.

Levi jogged up the carpeted staircase to what had once been a hayloft. Plush carpet panels now acted as sound dampeners. A few years ago, the place was a haven where Levi spent hours learning his craft. Now it was a hell that kept him from musically evolving.

"Well," Mom declared loudly when Levi appeared, "Look what the cat dragged in."

Levi kept his head down and quickly walked over to his place beside the drum set and quickly slipped the bass guitar around his neck.

His mother wore her turtleneck and sequined vest, which meant she intended for a serious practice.

And it was.

With the Christmas season over, Mom had a dozen songs for the band to learn for the next few months. Some were new and contemporary and others more traditional. Levi plucked away on the four strings of his guitar, totally focused.

Joey, however, flitted around the room, playing tambourine beside Daniel for one song and cowbell by Levi for another, strumming an acoustic guitar by Reuben, and singing background vocals on a stool beside Leah. Each time Levi looked at him, Joey gave a nod.

Something's happened.

After two hours, his mother ended practice, sending Reuben with fifty bucks to go pick up pizza from Split Rock for the family. Joey immediately came walking up to him, wanting to talk.

"Hey bud, can you bring my bass up to my bedroom, I've gotta go move my car and bring in some stuff I bought in Brainerd."

"But I thought—" Joey began but Levi rudely cut him off by walking down the stairs. He also purposely avoided visiting the Fozzie in its pen to keep the bird out of his mother's radar.

After moving the Mustang, Levi tucked his contraband under his arm and made small talk with his family, which meant a bit of lying about a trip into Brainerd. After running the gauntlet of the kitchen, Levi jogged upstairs.

"The police were here," Joey said full volume when Levi reached his room.

"Shit," Levi said, dropping a Sam Goody bag which held a couple cassettes, a magazine, and a dreamcatcher. Levi had been so focused on smuggling Lily's dreamcatcher inside that he had not seen Joey waiting on the beanbag chair. "You scared me." He quickly picked up his mess and asked, "Did he want to see me? What did he look like?"

"He was big with red hair."

Forsberg. An ally. "And he wanted to see me?"

"He wanted to see Mom, but I heard him talking about you."

"What did he say?"

Joey shrugged. "What did Grandma Lily say?"

The Omodai is a vessel. "She said too much."

"About the Water Drum?"

THE TRICKSTER 135

"What?" Levi rushed over to Joey. "What did you say? How did you know about the Water Drum?"

"Fozzie, um, he…well, he told me. He called me Clay, and then kept saying the word wobble, wobble, wobble."

"Instead of Waka, Waka Waka?" Since speaking with Albert about the Omodai, Levi began to fear for his younger brother. "How did Fozzie tell you about the Water Drum?"

"Well…he spoke, and then he had others come and talk to me."

"Other ravens?"

"No," Joey chuckled. "Other kids, but they weren't real kids."

"What do you mean they weren't real kids? Tell me what you saw, Joey?"

"They were the kids from the lake."

Son of a bitch. "You didn't go to the lake, did you?"

"No. They came out of the lake. I stayed on one side of the fence, and they talked to me from the woods."

Levi felt his heart racing. He thought of Regan from the *Exorcist* and Damian from the *Omen*. Both horror movies featured creepy little kids. "Okay, let's get things straight. Don't talk to Fozzie when I'm not around, and definitely don't talk to kids from the lake. It's dangerous, Joey. They want to hurt you."

"Fozzie says they are friends."

"Well, don't trust ravens or kids from the lake. Did you tell Mom or Dad about this?"

Joey shook his head.

"Well, don't. Okay? Lily says if Mom and Dad find out, they'll only make matters worse."

"What did Lily tell you today?"

"She told me all about the coming fight with the Manitou. She talked about how she had a dream about you and I paddling down the river to help find something."

"Clay," Joey inserted.

No, the Philosopher's Stone, her Water Drum. "Did Fozzie call you Clay?"

Joey shook his head. "The little girl who looked like Sommer?"

"Summer?"

"She looked like a girl in my class. Sommer Chauvin."

"Oh, so Fozzie called a ghost to speak to you?"

Joey nodded. "She told me a secret."

"What secret?"

"I can't talk about it until you go to the right willow tree."

The right willow? Between Lily and Joey, Levi had crazy coming at him from two directions now. Levi looked over at his clock and took Joey by the shoulder, leading him to the bookcase along the wall to the unfinished portion of the attic. "Sit down."

How do I get him to trust me more than the raven?

Levi grabbed his "Rambo Knife" that he purchased at the state fair lying horizontally on the top shelf of the short bookcase. He picked it up and took it out of its sheath. "You know I love you more than anything else in this world, right Joey?"

Joey nodded, suddenly filled with fear.

Levi held the black blade to his thumb, and quickly slid the edge against it. Blood immediately trickled down into his palm. "I would rather hurt myself than let anything happen to you. You believe that, right?"

Joey nodded again.

"Do you feel the same way about me?" Levi asked, followed by another nod. "Say it, Joey."

"I can keep a secret. Give me the knife and I'll prove it."

Levi shook his head. "I'll keep the knife. Just give me your thumb."

Joey bravely stuck out his hand. Levi took his thumb in one hand, and with the big military knife, he pressed the point into Joey's thumb until the skin depressed, and then with a quick flick, cut his thumb, leaving a scratch that slowly filled with blood.

"This is a blood pact, making us even stronger than regular brothers, right?"

"Right."

They held their thumbs together, smearing the blood before releasing. Levi grabbed a sock and handed his brother another. "Lily said that when she dies, a monster called the Wintermaker will wake and look for a young person to possess. Before he wakes, twelve lives must be sacrificed."

"That's what the girl in the red boots said."

"See, Joe, I worry that they're trying to lure you to the water because our family has special blood. Lily said evil will be drawn to us, so I need to prepare to defeat the Manitou. Lily has a plan for me to learn something called the Song of the Manitou."

"The wobble song," Joey stated.

"The what?"

"The wobble song. Fozzie told me."

Why would the raven tell all this to Joey? He must be the Omodai. I have to protect him from all this. "After supper, you're going to have to tell me everything that bird told you. We need to find both the song and something called the Water Drum."

"Right, the clay and the rock."

"No, Joe, a drum. It is some sort of ancient weapon created by the Wintermaker, but if we learn the Song of the Manitou, we'll use it against him."

"And then stab him with the spear."

"No, there is no spear."

"What about the turtle shield?" Joey pressed.

"No shield, either. The Water Drum is a magical weapon, and Lily said you'd help me find it, but first, I have to learn the song. She said she's going to summon the Children of the Dawn, contact a woman with a smashed face called the Future Spider, and when the time is right, summon the Great Thunderbird."

"Fozzie?"

"No, Fozzie is just a weird raven," Levi admitted with frustration. "The Great Thunderbird is the enemy of the Wintermaker, and after I sing the song, it will come down from the clouds to destroy the Manitou and send it to the Land of the Midnight Sun."

"Alaska?"

"No, Joey. Hell. Just listen." He took a deep breath. "Now, according to Lily, a lot of people will die if I don't take this seriously and do things exactly as she says. A lot of people are going to die even if we do it right, but I need you to keep all of this secret. Can you do that? Don't talk to anybody about Fozzie, Children of the Lake, or anything I share about Lily, okay?"

"A blood pact," Joey repeated and licked the blood from his thumb.

CHAPTER TWENTY-FOUR

Snow Day

Old Copper Road
January 15, 1986

A second blizzard buried Hiawatha County in a foot of snow, making the highways all but impassable and prompting the Split Rock High School superintendent to cancel school.

By midmorning, Levi climbed on his Polaris snowmobile and followed the railroad tracks that passed through his farm all the way through town and north toward Nimrod.

I'll be safe with Garrett.

Garrett Johnson lived on a small farm north of Lake Manitou that had once belonged to the Apple family, original settlers and homesteaders. Like himself, Garrett had little interest in farming and dreamed of leaving for bigger and better things upon graduating.

Through the whipping winds, Levi spotted a single headlight coming toward him, and when he saw the red of Garrett's Yamaha Snoscoot, he stopped on the tracks.

Hidden behind his black helmet, Garrett slowed and circled once around him until he pulled up beside him. "Ready?"

Levi extended his thumb on his gloved hand, and Garrett took off in a plume of snow.

Just like Levi's father, Garrett Johnson spoke few words during work or play, which was fine by Levi. He chased after his friend, following the old railroad tracks that had been abandoned several years earlier. With the old logging fields in northern Hiawatha County now depleted, the railroad tracks served as a snowmobile trail that extended for miles.

After paralleling the Blue Knife River for an hour, the two cut across the bridge at Nimrod and headed west through the ditches to the town of Sebeka. The western side of Hiawatha County was flat and open, allowing the wind to create drifts that exploded as the noses of their snowmobiles broke through.

The boys reached the small city of Wadena in the southwest corner of the county while the blizzard raged around them, having put on nearly fifty miles. Both filled up with gas in Wadena and followed Highway 10 back toward the east.

At Staples, the two farm boys turned their sleds back north on the railroad tracks that led to the second largest town in the county, St. John.

After almost three hours of muted silence, Garrett lifted his visor at the intersection. With the wind limiting visibility to less than a hundred feet, Levi could see only a wall of white in front of them, but Garrett said, "I want to show you something."

The two followed a drift high enough to allow them to pass right over a fence as they entered a field. A dark shadow turned into a cluster of trees and four dilapidated buildings that had turned gray from the elements.

"House fire," Garrett explained, stating the obvious. "They're going to tear it down come spring. This used to be Sterling Junction. My great-great-grandfather was the county's blacksmith."

"So?"

"What do you mean, 'so'?" Garrett asked indignantly. "These are the remains of the first buildings in the whole county. It's history."

Boring history. Instead of arguing, Levi just cranked the throttle on his Polaris and shot back into the teeth of the blizzard, leaving Garrett behind. He glanced over his shoulder to make sure the red snowmobile followed as he cut across fields.

Blinded by the storm, he had to turn his sled sharply to let momentum and friction aid him from going over a ten-foot drop. A few moments later, Garrett joined him at the edge of the little cliff.

"Assinikande," Levi countered Garrett's previous claim several minutes later.

"What?"

"Assinikande, it's an Anishinaabeg word that means Flat Rock."

"This is Haggard Bay," Garrett insisted.

"Before it was a bay, it was a quarry, and before it was a quarry, it was a field of flat rock. My family came all the way from Nova Scotia to settle here almost two centuries before your family came here. The Weber family was the first settler family in Hiawatha County."

"But they were Indians."

"So?"

"So, you're from here."

"No, we weren't. We were from Nova Scotia, along the Atlantic Ocean."

"Okay, then, dumbass, we were the first white family to settle Hiawatha County."

"Somehow I doubt that, also," Levi jibed just to push Garrett's buttons.

Then Levi watched as a cartoon exclamation point all but formed above Garrett's head. "Okay, I'll prove it to you then."

"How?"

Garrett slammed down his visor and turned his snowmobile around, following the shore to the west a bit until the rocky ridge flattened at a place where the snow hid the boundary of land and lake.

The two entered the deep snow on the extreme western edge of Lake Manitou and then raced across the frozen waters of Haggard Bay. Shaped like an arrowhead, Haggard Bay was a flooded quarry that had joined with Lake Manitou during a flood in the sixties. Only a narrow channel kept it connected to the main lake, and as soon as they passed under the bridge, the vast white expanse of Lake Manitou stretched before them.

Let's see if Frankie is an honest ghost.

Garrett's Snoscoot opened up full throttle as he made a beeline across the lake. From Haggard Bay, it was a mile to the next prominent landmark, Chippewa Point. He stopped in front of a plywood icehouse where a green GMC truck, half buried in the drift, was parked beside it.

"Grandpa?" Garrett called out as he stood on his slowing snowmobile.

Wally Crain flung open the door of the icehouse. Levi knew the toughened piece of leather from his childhood as the propane man who delivered fuel weekly to the farm. Despite living his entire life with both Garrett and Wally, he never connected the two.

"Hey, look who it is! I thought I'd be the only one foolish enough to be out in this blizzard. I guess the apple doesn't fall far from the ole tree, does it?"

"Catching anything, Grandpa?" Garrett asked as he pulled off his helmet. Levi followed suit.

"Catching anything?" Wally Crain playfully mocked. Dressed in a long john shirt and denim overalls, Wally turned back into his fish house, bent over, and tossed out a big northern pike. "I thought I hooked the Manitou for a few minutes until I saw this toothy snot rocket coming up the hole."

"Wow, that's gotta weigh fifteen pounds, Grandpa."

While Garrett stood over the pike, Wally glanced over at Levi as if trying to remember his name. "You boys enjoying your day off of school, I see. I've got some chicken soup on the propane stove if you'd like some."

"That's okay. We ate in Wadena."

"Wadena? You boys have put on a lot of miles. Well come on in for a minute and at least warm up."

Garrett and Levi were given buckets to sit on that overlooked a hole in the plywood above a hole in the ice that descended more than two feet down. A little red and yellow bobber shook as the minnow far below it tried to escape.

"You're one of the MacPherson boys, aren't you?"

"Levi."

"My grandpa knows everybody in Hiawatha County, don't you, Grandpa?"

"I wouldn't go that far. There's a lot more people coming and going these days, as well as a whole lot more people that have moved in since I retired, but I do know a good number of folks, including your dad. How's he been?"

"Good," Levi added but found himself for a loss for words since he knew Wally was part of Lily's Isanti Lodge. *Does Garrett even know about it?*

"Gavin MacPherson's a good man. I miss seeing him on my route."

"Yeah, my dad's still a good guy."

The wrinkled corners of Wally's eyes tightened as he evaluated Levi like a prized bull at an auction, causing Levi to look down at the bobber drifting around the hole.

"Me and Levi went by Sterling Junction a bit ago, and I tried telling him that the Crain family was the first to settle in Hiawatha County, but he didn't believe me."

"I didn't say I didn't believe you," Levi corrected. "I said that my mom's side came first."

"But Indians don't count because they already lived here."

Unlike most of the other old-timers, Wally seemed to recoil at his grandson's crude use of the word Indians. "Your friend Levi has a point. My father, your great-grandfather Kermit, told me that the Mound Builders lived here thousands of years ago, even before the Dakota. Levi's family, the Mizheekay Band of Ojibwe, settled here more than a hundred years before the first White Man put up stakes. Although, if I'm not mistaken, you have a little Dakota in your blood also."

Levi grinned, a bit perplexed. "That's right, but technically, it's Lakota. My maternal side is from the Black Hills area."

Garrett sighed. "Okay, then. My point is that we, the Crain family, were the first White settlers here. What's not clear about that?"

Wally raised an eyebrow. "Technically, that might not be true either. While there were fur traders around here as early as the late 1600's, I think the Berg family put up the first permanent home almost ten years before the Crains came with a handful of others from the East. Levi, you should ask your great-grandmother Lily about this."

Garrett sighed and surrendered.

Levi felt better about meeting the Isanti Lodge in the days to come, yet a founder of the Isanti Lodge, Albert Fisher, gave him worry about Lily. "How well do you know her?"

"I've known her my whole life. She's well over a hundred now."

"Yep." Levi wanted to press Wally about the role of the Isanti Lodge and added, "She's convinced she won't see another winter, so she's been teaching me the ways of her ancestors." As soon as he said it, he felt a slight betrayal to Lily. "I should probably get going home, actually, or my folks are gonna skin me alive."

"I suppose," Garrett grumbled.

The two stood up from the buckets, and when they opened the plywood door, the diffused light of the blizzard blinded them, even though it was obvious the afternoon was almost spent.

"Levi," Wally called out from the door of the fish house. "If you're going to head home straight across the lake, be sure to avoid Carousel Island. You might not think so, but there is current around that island that sometimes keeps the ice thin even in the coldest winters."

"Sure," Levi said with a shrug as he climbed back onto his snowmobile. With a nod, Garrett cut a path to the north shore while Levi aimed to the southeast.

With six miles of ice in front of him, Levi managed to get his Polaris up to sixty miles per hour, making Turtle Island Bible Camp and empty ice houses pass by in a blur. But the tangle of dead trees and rusting steel that was Carousel Island proved the fastest and most direct route back home to his farm.

All along the southern shore, a thick forest of oak trees along Old Copper Road would have forced him into a ponderously slow end to his trip. Racing around Deadwood Island and then past the reeds of Buffalo Slough would allow him to pop right onto the gravel road that went right by his farm.

Levi thought of the two-to-three feet of ice below the bobber and ignored Wally Crain's warning.

Even two decades after the catastrophic flood, the old roller coaster tracks could still be seen leaving the lake shore and again appearing on the southern shore of the island, where trees hid the rest of the old skeleton.

Levi slowed.

In the dimming light of early evening, his headlight caught an irregularity in the ice.

Slowing to a halt, he spotted a buckle in the ice a dozen yards from the edge of the shore. The blowing snow had almost covered it, but he could see a two-foot ridge where two sheets of ice cracked and shattered like a fault line.

But the old man had been wrong about the thin ice.

From what Levi could see, the jagged fault had been formed by broken pieces of ice well over a foot thick. It only took several inches of ice to support his sled.

Even though Carousel Island was less than a quarter of a mile from his farm, he'd never been near the island before. He knew some of the upperclassmen partied on the island despite the futile warnings of the numerous "no trespassing" signs. Levi also never enjoyed fishing or boating, so until now, he'd never been so close to the abandoned amusement park.

If not for the ridge of ice that acted like a defensive wall, he would have taken a quick tour along the shore. The backside of the island, however, nearer Buffalo Slough, would have much shallower water, so he reckoned if he went around the buckle, he might still be able to get a peek.

The blizzard strengthened, and a gust of wind stole his curiosity.

As his hand gripped the throttle, the ridge of ice seemed to move in the blowing snow. The snow that whipped around the frozen upheaval spun into strange funnels that almost took shape.

And then a gray figure took a step out of the ice.

At first, Levi thought he was staring at a pack of wolves instead of a ridge of ice. He'd heard stories about buffalo and cows that would line up with their tails to a blizzard, and as the ridge of ice came to life, he thought he might have driven up to some sort of similar situation.

The creatures did not move like dogs or wolves, nor did they have slender bodies. They moved like ice encrusted raccoons or porcupines, but instead of walking on four legs, they seemed to waddle like bushy gnomes.

Beady eyes penetrated the blizzard.

Levi had seen enough.

He gunned the Polaris, which lurched and stalled.

In a panic, he turned the key. As soon as the engine turned over and started, he gunned it.

Again, the sled lurched and stalled.

The eyes advanced.

"Son-of-a-bitch," Levi muttered as he turned the key again. His faithful motor started again, but before he gunned it, he noticed the tracks of his Polaris had been swallowed by ice.

He'd only been parked for a minute at the most, but the ice had climbed up and over the track to freeze his sled to the surface of the lake. This time, instead of gunning it, he gently twisted the throttle allowing the RPM's to steadily climb and build strength.

The engine died again.

"Shit," Levi glanced up. The strange creatures, blanketed in the blizzard, now stood less than ten yards away.

"You cannot cross the threshold," the creatures spoke in unison. "It was agreed."

"And you cannot leave the island!"

Levi jumped as a young girl shouted from beside him. He almost fell from the sled as he saw a school girl dressed in a yellow rain jacket, plaid skirt, white socks that climbed up to her knees, and red galoshes. Despite the fact that a blizzard surrounded Levi, the little girl seemed to feel no effect.

The gray creatures paused.

The little girl stepped forward. "Leave him alone, or I will call for Grandmother Spider to come and cast you into the abyss. Go back to your home."

With a swirl of snow, the gray creatures vanished, taking even the ridge of ice with them.

The little girl turned back around to look at Levi before she also vanished into the wind.

Levi turned the key and the tracks effortlessly pushed his sled forward. He turned back toward the southern shore, choosing Old Copper Road over the uncertainty of continuing near Carousel Island.

Frankie Auerbach spoke truth.

CHAPTER TWENTY-FIVE

The Caged Bird Sings

Old Copper Road
January 15, 1986

It's real. Everything Lily has told me is real. Levi tried to ignore what he'd seen but couldn't, so he immediately went to the machine shed when he returned home.

"Something wrong?" his dad called out from the doorway. Metallica blared from the speakers in the Mustang, limiting Levi's response to a small flinch at the unexpected voice.

A lot is wrong, Dad. I'm either insane or cursed, Levi thought from the nose of the Mustang. Levi sat on the rolling stool—feet propped up on the bumper. "I'm just changing oil and draining the radiator fluid."

"I hope you're not planning on going anywhere tomorrow; it's supposed to stop snowing but start blowing."

"No, I was just making sure the old girl is ready for winter. I might go visit Grandma Lily on Sunday after church."

"Really? Well, that would be nice of you," Gavin said, beginning to tidy up his workbench. "There's a lot of history you don't know about between your mom and Lily. Don't say anything about it to your Mother, okay?"

A lot of history. What isn't he telling me?

"How'd the sled run today?"

"It, um...ran great for most of the day, but when I stopped once, it, um...stalled and wouldn't get going."

You know, because Tak-Pei came up out of the ice to kill me. Lily talked about the "Little Men of the Forest," which her clan called Tak-Pei. Levi tried to look up information on it, but he only found references to Pukwudgies and Memegwesi in a few books.

"Stalled?" Suddenly his father had a challenge, and like a knight of the Round Table, took up arms to vanquish his foe for the honor of the realm.

The machine shed held more toys than farm equipment. There were a few tractors and mowers on the far side nearer the barn, but it also held the Brown Beast, an RV, and a fleet of snowmobiles, including a few old ones that were now collector's items. Levi had already parked his Polaris in its proper spot.

Gavin had the hood up in seconds. "So would it not start, or did it sputter?"

You see, Pop, while I was checking out Carousel Island to see if Lily's stories were true, the gray demons ambushed me, and they used their magic to melt the ice so that the tracks got stuck. "It was more of a stalling issue. It started just fine."

There had been twelve creatures, just like in the tales, but only three of them came out onto the ice. The other nine seemed bound to the island.

"It could just be old gas or the fuel filter," Gavin muttered from behind the hood.

Or black magic. If it had not been for the spirit of the little girl with red galoshes, he might have been killed by the three gray monsters. Three deaths...three grown strong. "I don't think it's bad fuel. We filled up in Wadena when we had lunch."

"Wadena. You boys put on some miles today. Did you turn off the engine at all after you filled up?"

"Yes, we stopped by Wally Crain's icehouse and warmed up for a few minutes. Wally caught a big northern."

"Only Wally Crain would be fishing in a blizzard. How was the old coot?" Gavin asked.

How does Dad know Wally? "Fine," Levi said, closing the hood of his Mustang. "And said he thought he'd hooked the Manitou. Why don't you talk about the Manitou, Dad?"

Levi turned the key off, and silence filled the shed. He put everything away while his father continued to work on the snowmobile.

I was attacked, Dad, and the only one that came to my aid was a dead girl. Where were you? Or Mom? Why is Lily the only one helping me?

"Well, your spark plugs were a bit fouled, so that might have caused it. Next time you take it out, keep it local—at least until we put new ones in."

Yeah, right. Like I'm going out again after what happened. "Okay."

"Things going okay at school? You seem quiet lately."

"Of course. School is cool."

"Girl troubles?"

Levi chuckled. "Thankfully, no."

"No more problems with Kristy?"

"No. We just look the other way when we see each other. The hostility is over."

Their conversation was enough to put Levi at ease, and even though Levi felt trapped between a rock and a hard place, he felt a bit more relaxed, so he helped his father put the Polaris back together and then walked with him back into the house.

He sat on the couch with his family as they watched *Mr. Belvedere,* but when *Falcon Crest* came on, Levi used it as an excuse to leave.

"Make sure Joey has brushed his teeth for bed," Mom said. "I'll come up next commercial break and tuck him in."

Joey was playing on the floor of his room yet immediately stopped and turned to look at Levi when he entered. "You okay?"

"I had a bad day," Levi admitted, but gave him a thumbs up, which took on a whole new meaning with their shared blood brother scars. "I'll talk about it tomorrow. Mom says you need to go brush your teeth for bed."

Without waiting for a response, Levi walked past and jogged up the stairs to his room.

On the other side of the room, the raven-feathered dream catcher was silent.

Lily warned me about it, just like Wally warned me about Carousel Island. Why didn't I listen?

Now the web of the dreamcatcher was empty, but during the snowstorm, it'd been full.

He walked over to the plexiglass window and ripped the dream catcher down, twisting the willow branch until it snapped and cracked. He doubled it up again, snapping all the branches in half, even if the thin part held the branches together. He ripped the feathers from their leather bands and carried the mangled mess over to his garbage bag, where the Sam Goody bag still rested.

Lily's magic worked with mixed results. As she had warned, her magic would do more than just ward off bad dreams. As a Firehandler, her dreamcatchers would catch the spirits of the dead that lingered around Lake Manitou, trapped by the Wintermaker. Just like fishing, it took a while before anything took the bait, but the moisture of the snowstorm drew out a soul by the name of Frankie Auerbach.

"Would you like to hear how the Manitou killed me?" Frankie had asked, just the night before, and then the spirit of the school boy told a harrowing tale of how he'd been lured into the tall grass of the wild rice fields by frogs, only to be drowned by the water spirits, the Tak-Pei.

Through the web of the dreamcatcher, Frankie confirmed the Tak-Pei needed death to bring them back to full strength, and that once the twelve spirits were ready, they would aid in the resurrection of their master.

Young Frankie Auerbach had even known Lily as his Sunday school teacher, vouching for her from beyond the grave. In death, he'd been a witness to her confrontation with the Manitou back in 1898.

"The island," Frankie explained. "The Tak-Pei are trapped on the island. Go see for yourself. It's all true."

Levi had listened, using the snow day as a passive excuse to go investigate, yet it had almost cost him his life.

Everything started the night that damn raven flew through my window, Levi decided and shoved the dream catcher into the Sam Goody bag. *It's like Frankie knew what would happen.*

He picked up his whole trashcan and walked down the stairs. In the hallway, there was suddenly a traffic jam. Joey stood in the doorway of the bathroom, brushing his teeth, and his mother had just reached the second floor.

"Could you take out the trash in the kitchen too?" she requested, glancing at the contents of the can as he walked by.

Gladly, Levi decided. Taking out the trash meant a trip to the burn barrel, set just a few yards from the floodlight in the middle of the gravel lot. Normally, any of the MacPherson boys would grumble when given the task, but Levi was on a mission, so he grabbed the kerosene can and matches, and took both bags of trash out to the 55 gallon drum.

"Fire!" Fozzie screamed from the barn. "Fire! Fire!"

A bad omen indeed.

Soon, the kitchen garbage, along with the other trash already in the can, blazed until flames danced above the top of the barrel. The Sam Goody bag was tossed on the pyre and quickly vanished.

Just one last thing to make things right.

"Which old witch? The wicked witch," Fozzie sang out as Levi neared the barn. The supernatural qualities of the bird could not be denied. Levi had long ago given up on the idea the bird had just been trained to repeat words, and he wondered if the raven could be trusted.

Sorry, Fozzie. I don't think I have a choice.

It's either you or Lily.

Once inside of the main barn, he did not walk over to the pen, but instead turned to the hayloft, opened a door to the cattle area, and then climbed up onto the hay, opening a wooden window that overlooked the roof of the skirting.

We all have choices, Fozzie.

"Under the willow," Fozzie shouted out, as if desperate. "Willow, willow."

Yeah, I know all about the fire and the willow, and the only one I'm listening to from now on are real people. No more ghost boys, dead girls, or talking ravens.

Fozzie eyed him suspiciously and did not move.

For a moment, Levi felt a bit intimidated by the black creature in the dim light of the barn. "Shoo," he said, and flapped his arms. He stepped forward toward the bird, and it jumped sideways.

With Levi following it, the bird crashed into the wire and then fell to the floor, but when it saw the open door of the pen, it quickly hopped toward the opportunity.

"Shoo," Levi repeated, and rushed at the bird.

This time, Fozzie took a few strides before its wings flapped in the hallway, and once it came out from under the wooden roof to the open side of the loft, it launched itself in the air, landing atop the haystack.

"Go on," Levi said. "You're free. Go back to where you came from."

"Willow," Fozzie croaked, and when Levi climbed up the bales, the raven spread its wings and crossed the loft to the far wall, perching at the open window. One last time, it called out "fire" and then flew out the barn window.

By the time Levi reached the window, the raven had vanished into the night sky. He left the window slightly ajar, and then went down to close the door to the cows. Going back to the pen, he left the door a few inches ajar and walked back to the house.

Crying is better than dying, Levi told himself as he thought of what Joey's reaction would likely be the next morning.

CHAPTER TWENTY-SIX

A Foundation of Murder

St. John, MN
January 20, 1986

As Sheriff Brian Forsberg drove by Haggard Bay, he saw the yellow police tape fluttering in the wind. He parked along the highway and looked over the ice-covered bay. Almost three months had passed since the murders, and the identities of Mr. Dice, Sleepy, or Mr. Cigar were still not known.

The only lead was a dead end. On the other side of the police tape, a dozen custom built icehouses dotted the main body of Lake Manitou. The police tape had been meant to keep folks out of an active crime scene, but either the wind or passerbys had left the perimeter looking like tassels on a bike handlebar.

He swallowed down his last bit of coffee and began buttoning up his heavy jacket. He grabbed his trapper cap from the passenger seat, lowered the fur-lined earflaps, and snapped them under his chin.

One more look.

At the bridge, Forsberg jerked the poles used to secure the police tape from the frozen ground. One of his deputies had been assigned the duty back in November. Some poles teetering and others sunk into six inches of ice. With just a little prying back and forth, poles were freed and carried under his left arm.

The dark legacy of Haggard Bay only grew in reputation with the unsolved murders.

Even before the settlers arrived, foul tales were told.

And now it has become my problem.

The comet will return in just three months.

Forsberg found himself at the extreme western side of the bay, where Mr. Cigar had parked his Subaru. Spring would soon destroy any surviving evidence, just like it had twenty-six years ago.

On Labor Day of 1961, he, Jimmy Nielson, and Rory Stewart snuck into an active and operational Haggard Quarry. With only a fence protecting its secrets, the trio managed to reach all the way to the quarry floor before the flood lights turned on and armed security guards came looking for them. At the time, it seemed fortunate that Brian's Uncle Ewan owned the quarry, which allowed them to be released without any consequence.

Why the fuck would a quarry have armed guards? Forsberg wondered again as he began retrieving poles along the western side of the bay. Jimmy had a theory, but it was one he'd only spoken once. Although the security guards had easily caught Forsberg and Stewart, Jimmy hid himself in a side tunnel, where he claimed to feel something beyond.

While child-molester and serial killer Logan Troost resided in St. Louis at the time, Forsberg stood in the tin office of Red Dobie, manager of Haggard Quarry, who took note of the two adolescent intruders. A few months later, Rory Stewart became Logan Troost's second confirmed victim, and against all odds, Troost chose Forsberg as his third.

Sheriff Don Betzing noticed the discrepancies, but when the flood of 1962 came, bringing the collapse of the Nicollet Dam, Lake Manitou reached out and covered up multiple crimes.

Forsberg found himself staring at a house where the quarry office had been. Instead of a crushed quartz ramp, gate, and a cheap modular home, the shorefront property had an asphalt driveway, a dozen planted pines, a boat house, garage, and a ranch house with a southern wall built mostly of windows, replete with a figure staring back at him.

Forsberg jerked the northernmost pole from the ground and dropped his armful of other poles onto the ground so he could rearrange the heavy stack. By the time he finished getting all the poles turned around in an easy to carry bundle, the figure in the window stood on his patio, still holding a large mug.

"No longer a crime scene?" the property owner called out.

It will always be a crime scene. I should just erect permanent poles along the shore.

In 1972, a decade after the flood, Forsberg and Wally Crain had been duck hunting along the cattails of Haggard Bay when they discovered an oil slick upon the water. A local teen drove his car off the road and right into the bay. Divers recovered his body a few days later.

Forsberg, a servant of the people, walked to the edge of the shore where a snow bank blurred the edge of the water. "Sorry for the inconvenience, but we had to let the investigation run its course."

"So we can drive snowmobiles through the channel and into the main part of the lake?"

Lieutenant Harper and Detective Irvin both interviewed Myles Stewart, the sole property owner who could have witnessed anything suspicious. Forsberg glanced at the large boathouse along the shore. "Yes, you can."

"Have you had any breaks in the case? Do they know any more about the victims or who did this?" Myles Stewart had good reason for his interest, which everyone else dismissed, since it was his older brother Rory who was killed by Logan Troost.

"We've collected all of the evidence; now we just need to follow where it takes us."

"Let's have coffee sometime before hunting season sneaks up on us again."

Forsberg nodded and turned. Even though Sheriff Don Betzing never reconciled the differences in the pitchfork wounds between Chris

Luning and Logan Troost, thirteen-year-old Biff knew the face behind the mask even before he threw the pitchfork and saved his friend's life.

Red Dobie.

The quarryman had worked his whole life for Triton Corporation. Red was a manager of the Haggard Quarry, and his father Halvar Dobie worked at the Nicollet Dam, which regulated water flow for the logging companies owned by Triton. While the world gobbled up the story of a young homosexual killing three local boys, Biff Forsberg knew Red Dobie targeted him for trespassing into the quarry. The odds of both witnesses becoming victims of the same serial killer was astronomical.

Plus, Jimmy Nielson warned him of certain doom.

If not for Jimmy, Chris Luning would not have stayed overnight with Biff, who would have been alone in the barn when the killer came to abduct him.

What had Jimmy found in that tunnel?

Forsberg turned back to Stewart. "Call the office sometime." He bent over and picked up the poles, carrying them under his left arm. He gave Myles Stewart a friendly wave before heading back to his prowler.

He couldn't fight Horned Serpents, Tak-Pei, ghosts, or anything else that went bump in the night. He could, however, fight the Order of Eos, which predated the settlement of Hiawatha County. With roots in the same mythology that led Hitler to seek out pure Aryan blood, the Order of Eos remained invisible puppet masters trying to bring a fulfillment of their prophecies. Every death in and around Lake Manitou needed proper investigation, even the damn nursing home, which allowed souls to be fed to the lake without question.

But Myles isn't in the Order of Eos. The Stewart, Haggard, and Marquette forefathers might've once been part of the secret society, but their strings had been cut for quite a while. Mr. Dice and Sleepy came from outside of Hiawatha County. Framing poor Myles would help eliminate loose ends.

After tossing the poles in the back end, Forsberg sat in his seat for a moment, studying the lesser Stewart estate for a few minutes longer, picturing a man opening the boathouse and dragging it out onto the ice where Mr. Dice and Sleepy were killed.

Or...it could be the phantom in the red Thunderbird, Brian thought and shrugged. After all, Red Dobie had been one of the flood victims too, killed while trying to save the Nicollet Dam from collapse—if any of it could be believed.

CHAPTER TWENTY-SEVEN

The Missionary

Wadena, MN
January 21, 1986

Father Gary Mackenzie withheld one detail from the breakfast briefing with Wally Crain, Chuck Luning, and Sheriff Forsberg—a private confession from Levi MacPherson. He chewed on his conscience as Forsberg finished his breakfast. Wally had given an update on his wife Nancy, whose stroke changed Wally as quickly as it had changed her. Forsberg spoke about private investigators at Mount Shasta, California and Nova Scotia, but his point didn't make sense. Mayor Chuck Luning talked about his concerns with spring flooding affecting the town of Split Rock.

With a full meeting of the Isanti Lodge in February, Gary kept his concerns to himself, choosing instead to talk about the little victories in his life. He left the Boondocks Cafe without making any confessions himself. *I can only make this confession to one man.*

Half-an-hour later, he parked his small Chevette beside the snow pile at the T-intersection of the Mizheekay Band of Ojibwe Reservation. The paved road from the highway turned north at the intersection toward the reservation, and the plow drivers simply pushed their way as far into the ditch as they could, creating a way between the road and the ravine of the Blue Knife River. Although there was a gravel road leading south, it had not been plowed like the other two roads, and his Chevette had the official clearance of a bare ankle.

So he walked.

Despite the depth of the snow around him and the ill-treated gravel road, it felt as if spring had arrived as Father Gary delicately plodded down the road.

I should have brought snowshoes instead of boots. Over the past fourteen years, he'd only been to the reservation a handful of times, yet he had taken youth groups to do service projects at Pine Ridge, White Earth, Red Lake, and Turtle Mountain. Wally's memory and directions served him well; the detail about looking for chimney smoke helped when the road seemed to vanish on a few occasions.

Oh, dear Lord, he chooses to live like this?

In a clearing, an old structure no larger than a garden shed or chicken coop sent smoke up from a simple tin pipe into the air. A covered deck as large as the home itself extended outward toward the river, holding suspended relics, artifacts, and knick-knacks like a man-made spider web. After hundreds of yards of untouched snow, the area around the shack was cleared and had signs of recent activity. In the front yard, a small rock fire pit, fed with bark and shavings, smoked.

Migisi Asibikaashi stood in front of the pit, ax in hand. Wiry white hair twisted in opposition to order, creating three patterns of tufts. He wore a tan jacket with fur lining appearing at the hood, hands, and along the bottom, which almost reached his knees. *Wait, he's wearing a buffalo hide flipped inside out.* Under it, he had a red and black flannel shirt, denim overalls, and a bright blue pair of moon boots.

Father Gary watched as the old Ojibwe elder picked up a quartered log, set it on a flat stump, and then lifted the ax to his shoulder and swung with no greater force than what gravity provided. A thin splinter came off the log before it toppled off the stump and Migisi prepared for another swing.

"Good morning," Father Gary said. "Mino gigizheb"

Migisi turned, ax still in hand. Father Gary knew what the old man saw: his universal calling card, his priestly collar, revealed under his long jacket.

Wally and Forsberg debated if Migisi had yet turned one hundred, but seeing him face to face, Father Gary wondered if he might be two hundred. With enough wrinkles, dark splotches, and growths upon his bulbous nose to make a dermatologist faint, Migisi was the human equivalent to a leather farm glove.

"You've finally returned," Migisi said. "...even though you now wear another face. Finish chopping this wood into kindling and then we can talk."

Still an athlete, Father Gary tore into the pile of wood, first sending splinters everywhere but after several logs developing an efficient strategy for quartering the timber.

Migisi returned from his shack with two mugs of steaming beverage and called out, "Come."

He joined Migisi on the porch, accepted the warm cup, and sat down. The beverage was neither coffee nor cocoa, and flecks of pink and purple floated in the dark brew.

"Just so you know, the young boy in my heart would have filled your cup with poison, but luckily, I have learned to tolerate my enemies in my old age."

"I am not your enemy, Migisi," Father Gary said. "I am your ally."

"What does a white man, especially a Christian, know of my conflict? Who do you think I am?"

This certainly isn't going well. "I am here to learn. I am hopeful we can be allies, for what little I do understand, I know we'll need each other in the days to come, especially with the coming of the comet."

"They tell me my sister will die soon."

"Yes, which will make you our last link to the past. I've come to learn."

"Yet you presume to be my ally already, coming to me with your collar and black clothes. You will mock my beliefs and twist their meanings to become what you want them to mean. You are not the first priest wanting to be my friend."

"You refer to Father Guerin?"

"I saw him die," Migisi said and turned to look at him. "He was not much further away than you are to me now. The lawman called Bushy Bill Morrison shot him in the back, killed two more men, and then shot him a second time through the heart. Your Christian God did not save him; my brother-in-law died in the sand, He also left me to my fate. Why should I want a weaker version of Father Guerin as an ally?"

"Oh, I am not a warrior like Father Guerin. From what I've read, he fueled three armed uprisings during his life, resulting in many, many deaths. Like Guerin, I have seen war, but never have I lifted a weapon, nor do I come to you with a weapon or ever plan to carry one. I am not a warrior. The only thing I can offer is the cup of life."

"Blasphemy," Migisi muttered. "Heretic. When I was a boy, the nuns used those words whenever I would try to defend myself. Do you know what the Church of Christ did to Indian boys like me? They would tear us from our homes and bring us hundreds of miles from home, cut our hair, force us to wear strange clothes, and forbid us from speaking our own language. When I see priests, I want to throw up. Yet you offer the cup of life?"

Gary remained calm. "I cannot answer for what happened in the past."

"Then why are you here now, if not to apologize?"

"I need your help in the days to come."

"My sister was taken to one of the schools, and she returned as a Christian, rejecting everything about who she was. I refused and stayed in the woods to remain in the ways of my ancestors. Then one day, with the promise of candy, she led me into town, where white men grabbed me from the streets and sent me away—stealing my destiny."

"What was your destiny?"

"I unearthed the megis shells in the mud and brought them to my grandfather Nanakonan. It was a sign, and I was to be trained as not just a Mide but as a Wabeno, a Firehandler. It was my destiny to fight the Horned Serpent and to call down the Great Thunderbird to destroy it. My sister stole all of this from me when she led me into town like a lamb to slaughter. Beware of my sister's plans, for they serve no one but herself."

"I want to talk about your sister. With the return of the Serpent Star in April, we've been busy preparing ourselves for the rituals. Now, I've reconciled myself to the idea that reality will fall somewhere between the Catholic Rite of Exorcism and the Juggler Ceremony of the Jessakkid—it doesn't matter the names we use for our enemy. I am ready to do my part."

"So am I."

"Everyone is preparing, but it seems Lily has her own agenda. She's recently fostered a relationship with her great-grandson Levi and has gone through great lengths to teach him the ancient ways. Recently, she's opened his eyes to the evil that sleeps under Lake Manitou."

Migisi's eyes narrowed with anger. "It was supposed to be me. When the Wijigan elders learned that I had found the sacred megis shells here at Lake Manitou, they believed I was the one to fulfill the prophecy."

"And what prophecy is that?"

"You won't find it written in books. In his battle with the Creator, the Wintermaker shaped the Water Drum, wrote the Song of the Manitou, and crafted the prophecy that he placed inside of the Sacred Shell. When the Wintermaker learned of the doom of mankind, he both embraced the prophecy and made plans to destroy it. He submitted to the fate of his own death, allowing himself to be killed and buried here at Lake Manitou. By the time his heart stopped beating, his plan was already underway."

"His soul remained trapped here," Gary added. "How do you know this?"

"The Wijigan Clan can trace itself back to the reception of the Seven Fires Prophecy given to us when we lived along the shores of the Atlantic. Even though the People tried to cast us out from society, our old legends did not die. In his excitement, Nanakonan reached out to the remnants of the Wijigan Clan to tell them about the discovery of Megis shells here at Lake Manitou, not understanding how they intended to fulfill the prophecy—the Omodai."

"Albert Fisher wrote of the Omodai," Gary commented.

"For the Wintermaker to win, he must cheat death. He's partially achieved his victory over the creator by creating a place that does not allow souls to journey to the next world. His ultimate victory, though, is to rise from his own death and walk the earth once again in human form. Father Guerin said your religious texts speak of such a figure."

"The Antichrist," Gary said softly. The Bible verse from Revelation 13 came to mind: *I saw one of his heads as if it had been fatally wounded, and his fatal wound was healed. And the whole earth was amazed and followed after the beast.*

"My life was not in danger, for the Wijigan did not intend to harm a hair on my head. No, it was my soul that was in danger. Omodai is a word for vessel, and that is what I almost became: an empty container for the Wintermaker to possess. The Black Robes sent Father Guerin as a spy among us, and when the moment happened, he saved my life—or did he crush the prophecy like an egg? You come to me with the face of friendship, but when the moment comes around again, will you squash the prophecy?"

"If this prophecy indeed involves the ascension of the Antichrist then—"

"Don't answer. Put it to prayer, Father Mackenzie. Unlike the Predestination found in your Christian prophecy, the Seven Fires Prophecy is not so…absolute. One choice will result in destruction; the other choice will result in a renewal of life. When Father Guerin squeezed the trigger to save my life, was he hero or villain? That answer remains to be seen."

Gary had read about many of these concepts, but he knew little about the Omodai. "Does Lily believe Levi is the Omodai?"

"Lily made a choice decades ago, and now we must pray it was the right choice. There is a reason I did not take a wife and produce children. If it came down to it, could I give up my own child to save the world?"

Give up a child? "Hold on, what did you mean by that?"

"Bah, Lily's plan is not to sacrifice her own family, but there is a reason why Fawn Chevreuil took her family as far away from Lake Manitou as she could. Lily is not afraid of the Wintermaker, and if her path is righteous, she will use her family as bait for the Wintermaker. She'll draw up the Horned Serpent from the depths, and when the moment is right, the Great Thunderbird will strike him from on high and cast his soul into Jiibay Ziibi, the River of Souls."

Levi is bait for a trap.

"Does that put your mind at ease?" Migisi asked.

Not really. "She's preparing him for his part in the coming ritual," Gary recapped. "For his role as the Omodai."

Migisi shook his head. "The fewer people who know—the better. The boy's parents were witnesses to what happened in 1962, so they must have their suspicions. It is best to keep them ignorant about the plans of the Isanti Lodge. Despite my misgivings, I've learned it is the easier option to trust in the plan even if it puts the boy at risk."

"What's the other option?"

"My sister has doomed us all."

CHAPTER TWENTY-EIGHT

Sleep No More

Old Copper Road
January 21, 1986

Levi MacPherson pulled the covers over his head and scooted to the crease between the bed and the wall. Something climbed onto the roof outside. The noises continued in a steady crunch of compressed snow.

It's getting closer.

Squeezing his eyes shut, he tried not to think of the beady eyes of the porcupine men or their long fingers, but instead, a green, slimy tentacle materialized in his mind. It reached up from the lake, through the woods, and now pried at the weak Plexiglas of the repaired window.

If I scream, will it kill my family? Or will it just snatch me from my bed and drag me to the lake?

Something now moved across his floor.

Did the Horned Serpent blindly feel around for him? He pictured the suction cups of an octopus individually feeling the contents of his room, sweeping aside his old cars or G.I. Joe action figures. If the Wintermaker sent only a tentacle to claim him, then it was blind, and Levi kept so still that he did not even take a breath.

His stereo and alarm clock created just enough modern illumination to show the truth: Joey. His little brother had crawled up the stairs still wearing his blanket. "Are you awake?"

"Yes, Joe. I'm awake."

In full scamper, Joey threw himself onto the outer edge of the bed, and for a few minutes, the two brothers sat quietly together. His brother held onto a plastic action-figure of He Man.

I owe him the truth of what happened last night. "I've seen the little girl," Levi admitted. "The one who spoke to you."

"You have? What did she want?"

"She said she couldn't sleep because her soul was trapped in the waters of Lake Manitou. She said I have an important part to play to help free the souls stuck here. She called me the Trickster."

"Silly rabbit, tricks are for kids," Joey said and looked to Levi for approval. When he didn't laugh, he asked, "What's wrong?"

"I think I might have made a big mistake. Do you know how Fozzie managed to escape his pen?"

"Cause he's smart?"

"No, Joe. I opened the doors and chased him out of the barn. I watched him fly off."

Joey's face wrinkled with anger. "Why would you do that?"

"Something bad is going to happen. I wanted to do everything I could to keep you safe."

"But Fozzie was our friend."

"I thought he was trying to lure you down to the lake to...join the others. When I heard you talking about ghosts by the lake, I panicked. I'm sorry, Joe, I shouldn't have done it or let you think it was your fault somehow."

"It's okay," Joey's glare softened. "What are you going to do?"

"Gigi Lily's plan is to use the Wintermaker's magic against it. She's teaching me the Song of the Manitou so I can use the magic against it when it's vulnerable."

"Like a sneak attack."

"Exactly. The Wintermaker thinks that when Gigi Lily dies, it will be free to do whatever it wants, but by that time, I'm going to know how to use the Water Drum. The servants of the Wintermaker can't fully wake their master without it, and only I'm going to know how to use it."

"What's a Water Drum?"

"Some sort of secret weapon. You're going to help me find it, apparently. Lily had a dream about it, and she says, you'll find it for certain."

"But I don't know where it is?"

Will Joey become a victim like Migisi? Do I have to put him in danger to win? "I guess that doesn't matter. You *will* find it. The destiny of the Wintermaker is to be destroyed by a boy who tricks it. You and I...we're going to trick it. It's going to wake up and find the two of us holding its favorite toy."

"Is the Water Drum an actual drum?" Joey asked.

"No, when it is inert, it is—"

"What's inert mean?"

"When it's off. When it's off, it is cold and shrinks up like a big rock, but when the Song of the Manitou is sung, it transforms into something like liquid fire."

"Like a lightsaber," Joey said, a little awed. "I heard you sneak in last night. Where were you?"

Do I tell him about Lacy? "I was at a party. You're not the only one I'm worried about protecting, Joe. There's a lot of folks, especially young people, who are in danger from the servants of the Wintermaker. The last two times someone tried to wake the Wintermaker, a bunch of folks died."

"Why would someone want to wake the Wintermaker?"

"I don't know, Joe. I'm trying to figure that part out as well, but I'm running out of time."

"Because Gigi Lily is dying?"

"Yes, that, and it's getting warmer. Lily says they will try to wake the Wintermaker during Midsummer's Eve."

"When's that?"

THE TRICKSTER 169

Before I tell him more, I need to find that willow tree. "June 20th, but remember, I'm the Trickster, so we're going to catch them off guard before they are ready."

"While they're sleeping."

"Right, while they are sleeping. Go watch cartoons or something and let me sleep. Don't tell Mom I snuck in, okay?"

Joey still held tight onto Levi's old He-Man action figure. "I promise."

CHAPTER TWENTY-NINE

Perihelion

Old Copper Road
February 7, 1986

Karson Luning began his long goodbye at 3 PM. His afternoons were spent in the main hall. Today, it'd been cards, which he gathered up and put away. He talked shit with the old-timers, promising rematches on Monday.

First, he rolled into a private room and pushed the "nurse" button. After a shift where he pretended to be charming and vibrant, his mood darkened when confronted with his reality: paraplegia. A deer slug destroyed his L1 vertebra, leaving him without control of his legs, bowel, and bladder. Pearl Smith, the oldest and ugliest of all the nurses, earned the honors of helping him through the humiliation of digital rectal stimulation and changing his catheter for the weekend. Even though little was said between the two during the half-hour ordeal, she received floral arrangements for her birthday, anniversary, and major holidays.

His second stop meant visiting the main office, where Molly Chauvin played the game of "What Coulda Been" with him. At a Halloween party hosted by Myles Stewart in the fall of 1972, Karson lost his virginity to Molly in the boathouse. Nine months later, Molly had married her college boyfriend Mark Chauvin, Karson was paralyzed, and newborn Penelope Chauvin was none the wiser.

C'est la vie, Karson thought with a shrug.

"Do you know what I was thinking of?" Molly Chauvin asked him after pausing from her paperwork when he entered the office. "I had a dream about Leah Kauffman."

"Oh, shit. Wow. What prompted that?" Karson asked.

"A fox ran across the road on my way home the other day."

"The dead fox in the instrument locker."

"I tried to get you expelled," Molly said. "What a psycho bitch."

"Are you talking about Leah now?"

Molly laughed, which had not been the case years ago. A dead fox stuffed inside of her instrument case. Karson developed a kinship with the eccentric daughter of Pastor Kauffman, and as the only non-Caucasians, the two outsiders formed a bond in junior high. But when sports transformed Karson into a football star worthy of asking out Molly Knutson, Leah Kauffman grew dangerously jealous. At the time, the acts of vandalism and desecration were attributed to him, but in hindsight, it was much more obvious. "What do you think she's up to these days?"

"I heard she's a scientist."

"Get outta town! A scientist?"

"She was always smart. Crazy, but smart. I think Forsberg told me she was some kind of genetic engineer living in California."

"I thought she was in a mental institution."

"Oh, she was for a while, but then, you know, if they had to let out Norman Bates, they certainly had to let out Leah Kauffman."

Molly's face grew solemn. "I had a dream that she tried to burn down my house with me in it. I was running around, looking for Sommer, but I couldn't find her anywhere. All I could hear was her crying out to me."

What about Penelope? Unlike Penelope, who had dark hair, Sommer Rae Chauvin had vibrant blonde hair like her mother.

Karson changed the subject. "Any plans for the weekend?"

"Dinner and a movie, most likely. You?"

"Stargazing. My new telescope has arrived."

AFTER VISITING WITH Molly, Karson made a purposeful trip to visit Nancy Crain. Like most of Split Rock, he'd had Mrs. Crain as his English teacher back in the day. Wally Crain and Brian Forsberg had been instrumental in his recovery following the accident and went beyond building ramps at the house. While Brian helped him physically rehab, Wally helped him emotionally cope with his loss. Now, Karson meant to return the favor.

Nancy slept most of the time, but during her physical therapy sessions, he saw some of the spark still in her eyes. Her breathing tube had been removed a few weeks ago, but paralysis on her right side kept her from being able to communicate. As soon as he rolled into her room, he saw a stranger—a typewriter.

Wally came for breakfast each day and read the news to her, but today, he'd left a typewriter on a small table. Besides a few of her favorite novels, a bound stack of 8 ½ by 11 pages were on the shelf.

"Hey Mrs. Crain, I just wanted to say goodbye for the weekend. My new telescope arrived, so I'm going to spend the weekend gazing up at the stars. I'll tell you what I see on Monday."

Before he left, he rolled closer to the shelf and took the bound manuscript down from the shelf. *Walking Through Shadows*—by Nancy Crain. Taking the manuscript down, he noticed the date for the chapters: 1988.

Apparently, Nancy believes we'll survive the coming battle with the Wintermaker.

After just a few pages, Karson caught the location—Ayers' Rock, Australia—and the main character, a boy named Conner Wallace. Another 50 pages into the book, the location shifted to Mankato, Minnesota and so did the central character, a college kid named Jude Kauffman.

Kauffman? What are the odds?

Of course, Mrs. Crain had once taught Leah Kauffman, so it didn't surprise him that she'd borrow a local name for a character. He set the manuscript back on the shelf. Mrs. Crain didn't react at all.

WHEN HE RETURNED to the commons, the music had already started. Lacy Morrison, his new entertainment assistant, brought a ragtime song to life. While Karson could play piano only, Lacy also could sing, and she belted out the lyrics for the residents.

When the song ended, he rolled up beside her. "You cut your hair?"

"Do you like it?" Lacy asked with enthusiasm. "I like it this short, but the kids at school think I'm a lesbian now."

"No, it's um," Karson withheld the flattery, afraid of it spoiling things between them. Despite being a kid, Lacy Morrison fearlessly wore revealing shirts and short skirts in contrast to the cotton uniforms of the nurses. She was beautiful in a sporty sort of way—and also a Morrison. "It reminds me of Molly Ringwald."

"The girl from the *Breakfast Club?*" Lacy recoiled. "Thanks, I think."

"She's a Hollywood movie star."

"Well, I'm too short and flat to be a movie star." Lacy shrugged and started in with the next song.

Well done, creepy old man. Karson rolled away to the front doors, where his van service waited to bring him home.

IN THE OBSERVATION tower, Karson studied the sky. Somewhere behind the sun, Halley's Comet hid after returning from the nether regions. In a few weeks, it would come out from behind its spin behind the sun and pass right by the earth. In its wake, it would bathe the earth in magic.

Magic!

Years earlier, Leah Kauffman had sparked his interest in magic. As the adopted daughter of Pastor Kauffman, she rebelled against her Lutheran upbringing. Convinced she was a gypsy left on their doorstep, she studied eastern religions before getting a fixation on Chippewa culture during her freshman year. Many kids thought she was Native, so Leah embraced the fallacy.

Now, looking up at the stars, he could remember bits and pieces of her stories.

The Pleiades, Leah taught him, represented "Hole-in-the-Day," and had spiritual connections to the sweat lodge purification ceremony. "It is through the hole in space that human souls both enter and leave our universe," Leah added. "The entrance is guarded by a being called Grandmother Spider."

He also remembered the story about the Big Dipper. Instead of a bear, Ursa Major, the Ojibwe saw a smaller creature, the fisher cat. "The fisher cats are fierce warriors, unafraid of danger. Because of this, Ojiig the Fisher Cat volunteered to fight against the evil sorcerer who captured the summer birds in an attempt to keep the seasons from changing. During the battle, they climbed into the stars, where the fisher cat was pierced with an arrow in his tail."

Karson had asked who would try to stop the seasons.

Leah pointed to Orion. "Some call him Missabay, the Giant, but most call him Biboonike, the Wintermaker. Just as winter brings death, Biboonike tried to bring death to the whole world by trapping the summerbirds and bringing eternal winter to the earth."

"I'm glad someone stopped him," Karson had said as the two sat out on the Doc Jones Bridge late at night.

Now, years later, Karson remember the conversation in his telescope tower. With the final approach of Halley's Comet, he worried the duty might fall to him.

And he'd never been good with tests.

THE TRICKSTER   175

CHAPTER THIRTY

Promposals

Split Rock High School
February 13, 1986

Love was in the air at Split Rock High School, so Levi MacPherson kept his head down and simply hid behind his long hair as he went about his day. After lunch, he was able to hide even better when he signed out from study hall to go to the library.

Thank you, Albert Fisher. Levi MacPherson leaned back from the microfiche machine, stunned by the technology he held at his fingertips. He looked around the Split Rock High School media center to see who else lingered.

While the spirit of Albert Fisher warned him about the Omodai, a Fisher grant had given him the state-of-the-art facility that was Split Rock High School, which now allowed him to research the truth of what'd happened in Hiawatha County over the past ninety years. The media center was the central hub of the high school, with access doors on all four sides of the spacious library. It was Levi's fifth year of using the Media Center, but he'd never stepped into the small room with the big machines. Levi rolled back a few feet from the machine to a cabinet that held decades of scanned newspapers on thin plastic photographic sheets. He could read accounts from the Little Falls Herald, the St. Paul

Globe, or the St. John North Star News. He no longer needed Lily to tell him what happened in 1898.

Or another ghost.

Despite the assurances of both Lily and Wally, Levi now had unbiased, unfiltered accounts, and after a half-hour, his notebook was filled with names, dates, and anecdotes.

He researched villains—Azero Gunn, Halvar Dobie, Ozias Haggard, Phillip Marquette, and the Pater Familias, Scott Sinclair. He couldn't find any mention of archfiends Joseph Little Toad or Bushy Bill Morrison, but he did find a short obituary about Constable Gordon Graham being killed "in the line of duty" during the Indian uprising at Leech Lake.

A lie.

Lily was right about the Order of Eos.

He also researched heroes—Farrell Luning, Arne Forsberg, Liev Nielson, Kermit Crain, Albert Fisher, and his great-grandfather, Jean Guerin, all members of Lily's "lodge" of guardians, the Men of the Knife—the Isanti.

All of the deaths Wally Crain spoke of were also confirmed, both in 1898 and 1962. The newspaper articles confirmed the facts but not the circumstances.

"Are you standing me up?" The voice had been so unexpected that Levi jumped, causing Lacy Morrison to chuckle at the doorway to the microfiche room. "Sorry, I didn't mean to startle you."

Levi hastily closed the notebook and shrugged. *Oh shit, it's Thursday.* "Oh, man, I lost track of things. I'm really sorry. How long did you wait for me?"

"I didn't wait. I found Garrett instead. Do you still want to practice?"

Levi looked at his watch. There were ten minutes remaining in the period, leaving him almost no time to get back down to the choir room and still have a meaningful practice with his accompanist. "Sorry, Lacy. We can run through it a few times next week. We've still got a lot of time before the competition."

"That's what everybody says," Lacy said as she stepped into the room and sat down on the chair in front of the other machine. "You should've seen poor Garrett. I don't think he'd practiced it once."

"Yeah, he gets a bit flustered around girls, though."

"Not like you, loverboy. How are things working out with you and Jill O'Brien?"

How can I focus on a girlfriend when I'm about to battle monsters? "Jill? Oh, please, once she left the couch, that was over. Did you see what she did to my neck? I had to wear my sister's makeup to cover up the hickey."

"Yes, I saw. I saw her giving you those hickeys."

Levi felt a flutter go down his spine. Jill O'Brien had latched onto him at Lacy's party and didn't let go until she passed out watching a movie, but while he'd made out with her on the couch, he had caught a glimpse of Lacy, curled up in her boyfriend's arms glancing over at him with a wry smile. "I heard you broke up with Shane."

"Good riddance, too. Have you ever seen his teeth up close? Two words: plaque buildup."

"Did you dump him for that older guy?"

"What older guy?"

"I visited the nursing home in St. John on Tuesday and saw you cozied up with the piano player while you put on a show for the residents."

"Karson? Ew, he's like thirty-something. I suppose you didn't see that—oh, never mind. What were you doing at the nursing home? Why didn't you say hello?"

"Oh, it's complicated."

"And?"

"With my great-grandmother nearing the end, I've been doing a lot of family research. I met with an old friend of the family, Wally Crain."

"Oh, he's such a sweetheart. He reads to Nancy every morning. Have you heard how they met? It is so romantic. Nancy found a gentleman like Wally, but I get creeps like Shane asking me to prom. So are you doing anything fun this weekend? Got a hot date?"

Levi glanced down at her knees and noticed a slight rise in the fabric as if she had kneepads under the denim. Then he saw a scab on her elbow and scrapes on her right palm. "Ah, no. I'm going to avoid parties for a while. I almost got caught sneaking back into my house last time."

"I wish I was that wise when I was a sophomore. I'm just starting to learn that lesson."

Levi felt like throwing up. He thought back to their encounter on Halloween, and how she'd likely been sexually assaulted moments earlier. *Lacy Morrison has her secrets.* He cleared his throat and threw out fodder for conversation. "While I was reading, I came across some Morrisons."

"You don't say. Do you have a secret crush on me?" Lacy flirted.

"Um, no. I...think Morrison County was named after your family."

"You don't say."

"Well, I looked into Morrison County history, which was named after William and Allan Morrison, fur traders and explorers. William was the first white man to ever visit the headwaters of the Mississippi, apparently, but here is where it gets complicated. After visiting Minnesota, he went to Calgary, which is where a local lawman named Bushy Bill Morrison came from."

"Bushy Bill?"

"Big eyebrows," Levi explained remembering them from the microfiche picture he's seen earlier. "Bushy Bill had an affair with a local woman named Adrianna Sinclair, but before they could get married, he just vanished in 1898. But they had a kid, whom she named Jack Morrison, who moved to Colorado."

"Great-grandpa Jack. Wow, you really do have a thing for me, don't you?" Lacy ignored all the facts and went right to the core of the matter. "So is this how you flirt with girls? Bring up their family trees?"

Levi shook his head. *Why am I telling her this?* "Sorry."

"Here I thought Reuben was the honor student and you were the dumb and handsome loverboy. You've got a lot going on upstairs, don't you?" She studied him for a few moments, making him look down at his own knees. "I've noticed how your fashion has been evolving from L.A.

Glam to Precolumbian. It's a cool look. I dig your shell necklace. Is that your way of connecting to your great-grandmother?"

"I suppose it is."

"I like the hat you wore to the party. Okay, I've got a hypothetical situation for you, okay, Levi? Let's say there is this senior girl who just broke up with her boyfriend right before prom, and she pretty much hates the rest of the guys in her class. And the junior class. Unfortunately, she already bought the dress, but she kinda hates the whole idea of prom. Should she sell the dress and skip prom, or should she stoop so low as to ask an underclassman to prom."

Oh, shit. Is she asking me to prom? "Hypothetically?"

"Hypothetically. What should she do?"

"It depends."

"On what?" Lacy toyed.

"If this hypothetical senior girl is hot. If she's hot, then she'll have no problem finding a new guy that's as cool as she is instead of one that would make all of her friends roll their eyes."

"I don't care about my friends."

"Okay, yes, I think she should have no problem asking an underclassmen to prom, but make sure it is the right one. Most sophomore guys would kill to be the date of this super hot hypothetical senior girl, but there might be one who is struggling with stuff right now. Stuff he can't talk about. If she asked this guy, he would want to say yes but would tell her no for reasons she couldn't understand."

"Oh, really? Well, I guess that tells me all I need. Guess I'm selling the dress." Lacy stood up. "Next week, you're going to be on time for your solo practice. There's a lot more than prom that you and I need to talk about." Lacy paused to look down at her scuffed palm. "I've also got a lot of stuff I'm struggling with right now."

His supposed mortal enemy, the descendant of Bushy Bill Morrison, gave a forced smile through eye glossed with tears.

What the hell was that?

CHAPTER THIRTY-ONE

Jaga

Kanaranzi Creek
February 15, 1986

The odds are in my favor, Brian Forsberg reminded himself as he strapped his pistol to his torso prior to his daily fight against the Darkness. His two German Shepherds, sensing he was leaving the cabin for the day, nuzzled his palms. They followed him to the garage door. He'd installed doggie-doors leaving both the kitchen and garage to give them free patrol of the property while he was away.

Climbing into his HCSD SUV, Forsberg sat for a moment in silent reflection.

It was 3:30 AM.

Hiawatha County had 1,300 square miles to patrol, running 39 miles east to west and 30 miles north to south. Brian made a point to know each and every square mile since he returned to the county in the summer of 1972. As Sheriff, he had an annual system of "getting to know" each and every square mile by driving different routes to work. For both political and protective reasons, he wanted each and every citizen to know that he knew where they lived.

Brian turned the key and fired up the cold engine block.

For the next three hours, he would not be sheriff—he would be Makwa, the bear. Geri and Freki escorted him as if he was Odin himself from the garage and up the narrow driveway. Geri and Freki were trained to patrol the property, and Brian's driveway made it nearly impossible for anyone to travel. Plus, the cattle gate at the end of the driveway kept vehicles at a formidable distance.

Climbing out to unlock the gate, his shepherds waited attentively for the command. He pulled his SUV forward and reversed the process, but this time he barked out the words they wanted to hear: "Jaga."

Both dogs took off through the pines.

The descendant of Viking Goths, Brian managed to learn new Swedish words each night. Including the word Jaga—the command to hunt.

He drove south.

A few minutes later, he approached Lake Manitou from the Aldrich Road, which still had old billboards advertising Carousel Park. He paused at the intersection of Old Copper Road. Straight ahead would take him to Chippewa Beach. A right hand turn would take him to the familiar ruins of the old park. A left hand turn would take him toward Sterling Junction.

He took the path less traveled—right.

Three generations earlier, Martin Nielson had cleared rocks from his fields to make a makeshift road between his two wheat fields. Each spring, after the frost had come out of the ground, Brian and Jimmy Nielson filled a truckbed full of rocks that rose to the surface. Now, his SUV followed the secret road between the Berg homestead and the Nielson homestead.

The Nielsons were all gone but the road remained.

His eyes were so focused on the vacant homestead that he almost didn't see the fresh tracks descending to the shore opposite of Turtle Island.

He put the SUV into park and stepped out.

Teens looking for a private place to party traveled in packs.

He walked down the track of a single, large vehicle.

Even though it remained a possibility that a kid took his girlfriend to a secluded location for a night of sex, Brian reached inside of his jacket to draw out his Colt. Unlike his service pistol, the Colt had the kill impact of a Scottish broadsword.

In 1980, the Nielson children leased the entire property of the island to the Mizheekay Island Lutheran Ministries of the Wisconsin Evangelical Lutheran Synod, who hastily erected a bunch of cabins and a large building for worship. Six years into the project, the Bible Camp had become a growing presence on the lake during the summers.

But no one went there during the winter.

After cautiously crossing the bridge, which left him quite visible, Brian stepped out of the ruts and took to the protection of the pines.

His grip on the pistol tightened when he spotted a large passenger van in front of the Mess Hall. He watched for a few minutes.

The power had not been turned on; the lights came from portable lanterns that were set on the table. At the van, he saw a set of footprints coming from the driver door and the passenger door, and then a convergence of prints at the rear door.

They carried something into the hall together.

Or someone...

He circled the hall, which had been boarded up tightly against a cruel winter and trespassers, leaving only slivers of light between the plywood and the windows.

When he returned to the front of the hall, he saw the two-by-four that had been screwed into the door and frame leaning against the wall. He slipped the revolver back into its holster and took hold of the 2x4 and, standing aside, used it to gently push open the door. After a moment, he set the board down and drew his pistol.

And brazenly took several steps into the room.

It certainly wasn't textbook procedure, but his plans had nothing to do with protocols.

Brian ignored the fact that a child was hanging by a rope from the ceiling.

His eyes looked for motion. One predator stood still, while the other—also wearing an ancient wooden mask—made a quick motion for a nearby table.

Brian adjusted his aim, struck his target just above the knee, and sent him tumbling to the cement floor in sprays of blood as only a few tendons kept the lower leg attached to the rest of him. The echo of the Colt still reverberated in the empty hall by the time the metal site focused on the center of the second mask.

"Kneel," Brian commanded and saw the dragon-like exhalations coming from his own lungs in the frigid air.

The first man began to holler in agony, and with his pistol still drawn on the second masked man, Forsberg moved swiftly to his victim. With his heavy leather boot, he stomped the man's face so hard that his head hit the frozen concrete with equal force, knocking him out.

He followed the barrel of his pistol until he stood directly in front of the kneeling man. He didn't need to see the man's face yet—that would come later.

Nor did he need to appraise the condition of the child. It'd only taken a glance to know the vessels below the pale child collected almost every drop of blood from the ritualistic spear wound to his torso.

A sacrifice to Odin, Forsberg knew, even if the gods the men served had names far more ancient than those the Vikings used. Along with the child, several other animals hung from the rafters of the mess hall, most likely brought to the scene in the storage van.

"Face first on the ground," Brian next commanded, and the startled Eos priest obeyed. Brian almost read him his Miranda rights, but he knew neither man was going to walk in with him to the Hiawatha County Sheriff's Department today. Once the man was on the ground, Brian looked at his watch.

4:37 A.M.

Plenty of time.

CHAPTER THIRTY-TWO

The Only Way

Old Copper Road
February 15, 1986

Levi MacPherson's dreams of a beautiful redheaded groupie waiting for him backstage of an imagined concert turned to ash when he heard the angry cry of a raven.

Fozzie's back. Perhaps I'll get another chance to listen to him.

He pulled his pillow up over his head but the sound of clawed feet upon the ridge of the roof made it impossible to ignore the agitated bird.

So much for sleeping in on a Saturday.

Slipping out of bed, he picked his clothes carefully for his date. No, it wasn't with the imaginary redhead (Maddy Sinclair?) or even with Lacy Morrison—it was with Lily. She promised to teach him the last of what'd been handed down to her by her own grandfather, Nanakonan. After that, they would go to prepare with the Isanti Lodge.

At the bottom of the first flight of stairs, Joey's window was tossed wide open, and the fresh snow on the roof had raven footprints on it.

Is he feeding it through the window?

Joey hadn't crawled onto the roof, so Levi shut the window. He freshened up before following the smell of bacon and eggs downstairs to the kitchen, where his mother lingered with her apron still on.

"I was about to throw this out," Mom said after setting a full plate in front of him at the small kitchen table.

He just started shoveling in the eggs to avoid talking, but then she slid into the chair opposite of him. She had a full cup of coffee, which meant she wasn't going anywhere anytime soon.

"Plans for the day?"

"I might run to Brainerd to pick up some new tapes."

"Not Leech Lake?"

Levi kept chewing, trying not to miss a beat. Instead of lying or avoiding, he twisted the conversation to, "Do you think the roads are good enough to get to Leech Lake?"

She sighed. "I talked to Biff the other day, and he was under the impression that you've been visiting Grandma Lily quite often."

He ignored the comment since there wasn't a question.

"Sheriff Forsberg and I go way back, and even if you weren't driving around in that hot rod of yours, he'd still let me know where my son was. Why are you spending so much time with her suddenly?"

Levi took a bite of toast just so he could answer with his mouth full. "She's interesting."

"Oh, I know how interesting Tewapa Asibikaashi can be. I grew up forty yards away from her. You might not know this, but I also attended Turtle Island Jesuit School before I graduated from Split Rock High School, so I understand your obsession with your Indian culture."

We're not from India, mother. It wasn't until Lily celebrated her 100th birthday that Levi even became aware that he had a great-grandmother and great-uncle, Migisi. He knew Grandma Hannah as well as all of his MacPherson relatives but his mom's heritage had caught him off guard.

"You're almost the same age I was when I got pulled into this," she continued. "Now, if you're half as clever as I think you are, you already think you know everything there is to know. As a mother, I've done my best to shelter you from…things, but I'm not going to be able to do that for much longer and I wanted you to know that—"

"What sort of things, Mom?" Levi didn't mean to ask it so bitterly. If anything, it felt good that she was protecting him.

"Good and evil are not just concepts. I've seen evil. I've seen magic. I've seen the things other people only whisper about. Your Grandmother Lily held fire in her hands as she battled real monsters. Your father and I both witnessed what happened at Carousel Island, and even back then, we knew the truce was only temporary. We thought about running away—selling the farm and never looking back at Lake Manitou, but I found my strength in Christ."

Levi almost shivered at the sudden paradox within his mother.

"Your Great-Grandmother Lily is a complicated woman, but I don't know if I can trust her. Do you remember the stories about King Solomon?"

"The guy who asked God for wisdom."

His mom nodded grimly. "In his later years, with all of his accumulated wisdom, he turned away from God and began worshiping the gods of his wives. I worry that Lily has also lost her way. Instead of putting her faith in Jesus, she's turned to the false gods of her ancestors. She spends her waking days searching for answers in other places than the Bible. Remind me, Levi, what is the only way to Heaven?"

"No one gets to the Father except with Jesus," he repeated.

"Exactly. This is a battle of Good versus Evil, but your only shield in the days to come will be by putting your trust and salvation in Jesus Christ. Perhaps I've assumed too much. I raised you in a Christian household and surrounded you with songs, but do you believe, Levi?"

Levi recoiled. "Well, yeah."

"Father Gary said the Isanti Lodge will be meeting soon with Lily in preparation of...whatever. You'll be surrounded by people I love, but that doesn't mean you won't be tested by Satan. All of you will be tested. I'll be tested. I can't stop it from happening, so just remember what I've tried to teach you."

How does my mom know more about this than I do?

She reached into her pocket and handed him a cross pendant made out of barn nails. "Wear this. Your Uncle Cameron made it for you. When we faced our demons back in 1962, they almost killed my big brother. He's never been the same. So go ahead, wear your shell necklaces and listen to your heavy metal music, but when the darkness comes, know where your salvation lies."

When he didn't respond, she got up and went over to the dirty dishes at the sink, leaving Levi holding the cold metal of the cross pendant.

CHAPTER THIRTY-THREE

Time to Process

Staples, MN
February 16, 1986

Karson Luning heard a vehicle approach and looked up from his lifeless knees. He spun his wheelchair on the cold cement floor of the meat processing facility and rolled over to the black canvas tarp that hung from the ceiling.

"I'll check it out," Karson said to the brutal inquisitor standing between the sink and the metal tables of Western Locker.

As soon as he parted the seam of the tarp, the cold, dry air bitterly greeted him. Dusk had already arrived, but the lights of the SUV were easily recognized. Forsberg had returned.

Karson broke down into sobs for about ten seconds before wiping away his tears. He didn't want to give the macho veteran another reason to judge him.

The Beretta M9 pistol still rested above his crotch, still holding all 15 bullets. A yellow notepad was shoved between the side of the wheelchair and his left thigh.

A chain rattled as Forsberg unlocked the doors.

"Honey, I'm home," Forsberg cruelly jibed as the door opened a crack.

"Fuck you," Karson answered, but then found enough callousness to play along. "How was work, dear?"

"Fairly quiet for a weekend," Forsberg said, stepping through the heavy front door of the meat locker. Karson spun around again, returning to the larger processing room.

The captive, Terry, hung from hooks normally used for deer while two corpses rested on metal tables meant for processing the venison. Karson knew he'd likely become a vegetarian after the past two days, and it royally pissed him off. "What's going to happen to the kid?"

"Now that I've got the boy's fingerprints, dental measurements, blood, and a hair sample, I've privately arranged for him to be buried in a nice little cemetery in St. Paul."

"Are you serious?"

"Well there's not going to be a public service, but the poor kid deserves a proper burial, unlike these two pieces of shit. Did we get our answers?"

Karson handed Forsberg the yellow notepad.

For most of his thirty years of life, Karson had lived in ignorance; he didn't want to acknowledge the existence of the supernatural Wintermaker or the sinister Order of Eos. On Saturday afternoon, that all changed when a wheelchair transportation service showed up at his front door with paperwork ordered by Brian Forsberg. Seeing the transportation vans drive to his estate was a normal occurrence, but the private driver didn't bring him to the Hiawatha County Sheriff's Department. Instead, it brought him south to the small town of Staples. A mile north of town, the driver turned onto a rural gravel road, and in a small tree break, two vehicles were parked in front of Western Locker, a private meat processing facility used mostly by deer hunters. In February, it was all but abandoned.

The Inquisitor, who'd already been torturing a gunshot victim on Saturday afternoon, never bothered to give Karson his first name, nor did Karson ask. The Inquisitor had short, thinning black hair and a wiry body. What he lacked in physical strength, his tools more than made up for. In a different nightmare, Forsberg and the Inquisitor would have made formidable monsters, and Karson had to quickly remind himself that the men they held were the real monsters.

"Save your moral outrage," Forsberg had said once Karson arrived on the scene. "I caught these guys red handed moments after they killed that poor kid. Neither had anything to do with the Ice House Murders, but they're still Eos men. I can't stay here without raising suspicions about my absence, so I'm going to need you to babysit these two. Listen. Keep notes. Ask a few questions. On Monday, I'm burying these two bastards where they'll never be found."

In 1975, after a physical therapy session at Karson's old house, Forsberg first told him about the Isanti Lodge and its mission to protect Hiawatha County from the evil Order of Eos. It had done the trick. Karson came out of his depression from losing the use of his legs and became the scholar for the Isanti Lodge, something that would've made his Great-Grandpa Albert pleased.

Seeing the Inquisitor take hold of nerve endings with his surgical forceps once again changed everything for him.

When Forsberg finished looking over the yellow notepad, he looked up and gave a cold nod of approval. "I suppose you'd like to get home and take a shower."

"I don't think a shower is going to wash this away."

"You needed this. I've never seen any of the supernatural shit the others talk about, but I've known for a long time about Eos. Just like the Viet Cong sent infiltrators into villages all over South Vietnam, Eos has been sending folks out into the world as agents and spies. Lily was right about them cooking up something," Brian said, glancing down again at the pages of notes. "You understand now why I couldn't just haul them into jail."

Karson had to wince to keep from sobbing. As a member of the Isanti Lodge, he stood in for Forsberg while he was tending to his duties as Sheriff. Karson nodded, cleared his throat, and said, "I understand. So now what?"

"I'll call your shuttle service to come pick you up. I know the guy. He'll be discreet. I'll deal with the rest of this mess. We'll process all this information and talk to the others about it on Tuesday."

Forsberg didn't answer the question. Thanks to a bit of torture, Karson knew what the enemy planned. He even had dates. On Saturday, June 21—at the summer solstice—the Order of Eos planned to resurrect a fallen god.

CHAPTER THIRTY-FOUR

Til Death Do Us Part

Split Rock, MN
February 20, 1986

Captain Chuck Luning woke from his nightmare with such ferocity that his wife Helen clenched a pillow in each hand to create a defensive shield. In his nightmare, he was the one being tortured from the rafters at Western Locker, and the faces of Cambodian tormentors transformed into the inky forms of the Tak-Pei, whose hands peeled away patches of skin from his body.

Chuck lifted his hands, acknowledging the reality of the moment.

Helen, still wide-eyed, nodded and tossed the pillows aside, saying with a sigh, "I'll go make some coffee."

At forty-eight, Chuck was still in great shape despite the deep aches in his scarred body. Burn marks, bullet wounds, and scars from open fractures decorated his body from his service during the Vietnam War. His brother-in-law, former Viking Craig Redding, dealt with obesity and diabetes, which is why Chuck kept himself in such good shape. A chance encounter with Craig Redding's younger sister Helen during an All-American High School football camp stole Chuck's football career, sending him to the Air Force to pay for his indiscretions. Following his harrowing experience as a MIA pilot shot down in the last days of the war, Chuck returned to Split Rock in 1973 a shell of a man.

Self-pity took a back seat after finding his sixteen-year-old son Karson in the hospital with a spinal injury after a tragic hunting accident. For the past thirteen years, he and Karson rebuilt their broken bodies and relationship.

His relationship with Helen was still a work in progress.

He put his hands on her hips and kissed her right cheek as she stood in front of the stove brewing the coffee. She leaned her head into the kiss but then began reaching for the cups and spoons, spinning away from him in a flurry of activity. In just his boxers and robe, he retreated to the kitchen table and sat on a cold chair.

Helen moved with the precision of a chemist as she prepared two cups of coffee before finally sitting in a chair opposite of him. At forty-six, Helen had little need for working out. Her belly had a little pouch, her ass rolled a bit above her thighs, and without a bra, her breasts hung a few inches lower, but even at 5:22 AM, she was stunning. She blew gently onto the surface of her coffee, which she cradled with both hands. Unlike the dark complexion of her older brother Craig, hers had more cream, and her paternal genetics remained a mystery to this day. *Mama Redding had her secrets just like her daughter did.*

But Chuck didn't keep anything from Helen.

"There's some stuff that went down this past week that you're not going to read about in the newspaper," Chuck began. "A war has started and the shit's about to hit the fan."

"Is Karson in danger?"

Chuck shrugged. "Probably, but we're not putting him in any obvious danger. He's more…strategic. We had a meeting the other day to go over the new information we learned. Karson got his hands dirty."

Helen's back arched like a cat about to hiss. "What is that supposed to mean?"

"Human sacrifices—that's the sort of people we're facing."

"Like the Ice House Murders?"

Chuck nodded. "Forsberg kept it out of the news this time, and even managed to catch them red-handed, so to speak. Karson saw one of them die, and the other one, well, tortured. He's pretty shaken up, but he doesn't have anyone to talk to but Father Gary, so...I don't know, bring him some food or something."

"Food?" Helen recoiled.

"He knows which end is up. Hell, he asked for more responsibility."

"I'll be bringing him a plate of Gozinaki this afternoon," Helen said and then did something that surprised Chuck. "How are you doing with all of this?"

Chuck retreated to his coffee cup for a moment, taking a few sips before looking back up at her. "I had a nightmare about monsters," he began with a chuckle and a crooked grin before ending with a grimace. *Killed in a flood*—that's how the conversation began thirteen years ago when Chuck had to explain to Helen what had happened to his grandfather and little brother. Instead of stepping up in 1962, he ran from his duties and left for Vietnam. When he returned, his son was crippled, and his wife was pregnant.

"Monsters," Helen repeated without judgment. "What kind of monsters?"

"The Lake Manitou kind," Chuck said, thinking of the Tak-Pei peeling away his skin to reveal raw muscle underneath. "Father Gary and Migisi both agreed that our enemies are making human sacrifices in order to wake the ancient evil that slumbers in the lake. Lily described twelve Tak-Pei that guarded over the Wintermaker. When the time comes, they will obey the song of their master. Until then, they are like wild dogs prowling the streets. Heck, I know what to do with rabid dogs. How do I protect Split Rock from monsters?"

"That's a good question. What's the plan?"

"The Order of Eos plans to act at Midsummer—the summer solstice. The magic created by the arrival of Halley's Comet will still be powerful, and they plan to take the Philosopher's Stone by force and perform their own version of the "Song of the Manitou" ceremony."

"How would they know where it is?"

"Do you remember Leonard White Elk?" He'd visited them several times in the past decade but rarely participated in conversation.

"The guy from the Canadian Rockies?"

"Yeah, him. Well, he thinks whenever the Water Drum is used, it creates some sort of window in time. He thinks when Lily used it in 1898 and 1962, she never really closed those windows and that they're still open."

"Honey, I didn't understand any of that."

"I don't know if I'm even explaining it right," Chuck sighed with frustration. "Leonard thinks that just like the windows of the past are still open, some windows in the future are also open. His theory is that the Order of Eos knows where to find the Stone because they've found it in the future and then communicated back to the past."

"Our present?" Helen clarified and then chuckled, taking a few gulps of her coffee. "Oh, it is much too early to hear all this hocus pocus talk. So, what are you going to do between now and June?"

Chuck hesitated for just a moment, knowing that Helen wasn't officially a member of the Isanti Lodge, just like Nancy Crain hadn't been an active member either. Teen pregnancy, a shotgun wedding, alcohol abuse, domestic violence, adultery, death, and tragedy had left their marriage a complete and utter mess by 1973, but since he returned home, the fractures had become stronger bonds than what had originally held them together. Brian Forsberg, ironically, kept their family together, physically rehabbing Chuck and Karson while also counseling Helen through her relationship with her husband.

The four had been sitting at the same kitchen table when Biff told them his theory about what happened to Albert and Chris in the flood as well as the truth about the Order of Eos. It was the craziest shit any of them had ever heard, and when Forsberg finished, Helen became his partner again "in sickness" and now "til Death do us part."

"What are we going to do now?" Chuck repeated to give himself a bit of time. He trusted Helen with his life even if he couldn't trust her fidelity. "We're going to do a dress rehearsal of the "Song of the Manitou" ceremony on March 21st, which is a full moon. Apparently, even without Lily, magic is heightened on a full moon."

"Is it wise to do it without her?"

"She's convinced that she's going to live until Halley's Comet passes. She talked about closing a loop around Easter. She said that once the loop is closed, she'll be able to take on the Wintermaker."

"On Midsummer's Eve?"

Chuck nodded. "It's a bold plan. Migisi is going to place a placebo, a fake, in place of the Philosopher's Stone, which we will allow them to think they've found. On game day, Lily will have the real deal. She's going to let them begin the ritual to wake Wintermaker. If they can lure him up from the depths, Lily will use the real Philosopher's Stone to take hold of him, and then Migisi will play the part of the Thunderbird, will rip the old sorcerer from the waters, and cast him into the River of Souls, which literally is the Crow Wing River." *Quite the plan, huh?*

"Where is all of this taking place?"

"We'll keep Lily at Turtle Island; Migisi and the Isanti Lodge will be at Bleeding Rock, which is the border of the old magic. It'll be a spiritual ambush—one the Order of Eos won't see coming. By the time the dust settles, the Wintermaker will be halfway down the Highway to Hell, so to speak."

"And you think these zealots will just pout and shuffle their feet back home?"

"Forsberg has tactical plans for the physical side of things—trust me. The only way any of this happens is if the Order of Eos thinks it'll work. We're going to have to lay low and look away for the next few weeks, which is hard for any of us to take."

Helen's eyes showed a bit of understanding as to why he'd been having nightmares again. "Where will Karson be during all of this insanity?"

"He'll be with me. I'm in charge of the Bleeding Rock location, where we'll be letting Migisi perform his exorcism ritual, for lack of a better term. It's Lily and Father Gary that will be vulnerable on Turtle

Island, where it'll just be the two of them. Forsberg has his official net and also a network of mercenaries that will be backing up both locations. He also has a tactical assault unit ready for Eos."

"I'm beginning to understand why you want me to speak to Karson. Perhaps you should call your mother also—just to talk."

"Any good ideas on how to keep her from coming home this summer?"

"Kitchen fire? Let her precious Karson take the heat. We'll blame it on him and tell her she won't be able to return until after the Fourth of July."

"Good plan," Chuck said, finishing his cup of coffee. "Any advice on how to kill an immortal sorcerer?"

Both laughed at the absurdity.

"Perhaps after breakfast," Helen said, standing to collect the coffee cups. "Any requests?"

"I don't deserve you," Chuck said as she walked by him.

"Just keep our children safe," Helen said. "Do that and we'll talk about worth."

CHAPTER THIRTY-FIVE

That is the Question

Golden Shores Nursing Home
February 22, 1986

Wally Crain only wanted to make her laugh again. Nancy's broken brain allowed her heart to beat, her lungs to breath, eyes to blink, and in recent weeks, allowed her mouth to open and close for food. Her throat even managed a bit of vocalization, which two months after a stroke, gave the doctors hope.

As his wife sat across from him in the dining hall, it'd been two months since he'd last heard her laugh. A simple laugh would prove she was still inside.

Instead, a laugh came from across the hall.

Lacy Morrison stripped off her bright yellow down jacket and hung it on the rack near the entryway, chatting pleasantly with Molly Chauvin as their conversation grew farther and farther apart.

Wally looked down as he remembered seeing Molly's dead sister pulled from Lake Manitou. When he looked back up, Molly was in her office and Lacy was standing beside a table where Karson played cards. The residents perked up with each syllable she uttered, and when she smiled, they smiled. When she giggled, it was like a shot of penicillin to the infection known as old age.

Wally looked down again.

Like joyous thunder, the piano came to life under Lacy's fingertips, and music suddenly filled the hall. Nancy's eyes lit up.

Two songs later, Karson rolled away from the table and went to where Wally sat with his back to the frozen lake.

"Good morning, Mrs. Crain," Karson began, taking hold of her hand for just a minute. "Do any fishing since we last spoke, Wally?"

Wally nodded. "This is my life now. Morning visits, afternoons out on the lake."

"Don't you have to remove your icehouse soon?"

"Another couple of weeks, but yes. Spring will be here before we know it." At Karson's nod, Wally continued, "The Morrison girl seems to be working out."

"Yeah," Karson said apprehensively. "She's quite a charmer."

"Jailbait," Wally joked, bringing a smile to Karson. "That's what we called girls like that."

"Oh, I wish, Wally, I really wish I had those sort of problems still."

"Do we need to talk about problems?"

Karson shook his head. "Naw." A moment went by. "Am I really the weakest link? Everyone keeps checking in on me like I'm going to let folks down in the moment of crisis."

"It's not like that," Wally said. "Some of us have walked this road already and some of us haven't. To be honest with you, it might be better *not* to know what's coming."

How could I forget what happened in 1962?

He'd seen Lily Guerin wield the Philosopher's Stone in a battle with the Tak-Pei. Wally understood why it was called the Philosopher's Stone by Europeans (it was a football sized rock), the White Egg by the Dakota (it was smooth and white), and the Water Drum by the Ojibwe (it pulsed like a beating heart). When Lily Guerin placed her hands upon it, the dormant stone came to life in a swirl of earth, air, fire, water—and also spirit. In his fishing boat, he'd ferried Lily, Nicole and Gavin to where monsters were trying to murder Cameron, Lily's grandson. He'd also seen Ed Nielson wrestling with Tak-Pei trying to drown him. Then and now, the fabric of the universe felt like it was about to tear apart.

Minutes—that's how long the battle at Carousel Island lasted.

The next day, he helped search for the body of Chris Luning after the sawmill disaster that also left his good friend Albert Fisher dead.

Then Glen Forsberg showed him where a couple of anonymous corpses were buried—the Order of Eos had almost won a victory.

Even though the body of Red Dobie was never discovered, Lily and Migisi knew how Dobie had tried to wake the Wintermaker on his own. To do it, Red Dobie had been willing to wipe out the entire community in a dam disaster.

Now, the Order of Eos planned to try again.

Thinking of 1962 made Wally remember those who'd been with him.

"Do you know if anyone has bothered checking on Cameron lately?"

"Can Man? Is there a reason why we should be worried about him?"

Wally shook his head. "You're probably right. It's always been the young people in danger." Wally could still hear the screams from Nicole, Gavin, and Cameron as they tried to survive long enough for Lily to put the Tak-Pei back to sleep with the stone.

Now, Wally and Karson watched Lacy Morrison until the towering figure of Father Gary filled the door. After dropping off his long black jacket, he strode through the hall directly to where Wally sat with his wife and Karson.

"Gentlemen," he said. "Good morning, Mrs. Crain."

Nancy only trembled in acknowledgement.

Father Gary continued. "I met with Levi after speaking with Nicole, and I'm going to start prepping him prior to us meeting with Migisi. Despite appearances, he's a sweet kid."

"Yeah, we were just talking about kids," Karson muttered. "We've got two schools full of potential victims we need to be protecting."

"But only a handful have connections to the old families of Lake Manitou," Wally added. "You remember Forsberg's theories about bloodlines?"

"I guess I should be thankful for my Ashanti blood," Karson mused. "I hope I taste bad or something."

Apparently, Crain blood interested the Horned Serpent, according to his father. With Kermit Crain's Barlow stuffed in his pocket, Wally pictured the Isanti Lodge and how it would be filled in the coming ceremonies:

Ah-ja-jawk—a chieftain…his role, the son of Kermit Crain.

Mang—a chieftain…Captain Chuck Luning, Grandson of Farrell Luning.

Gi-Goon—the intellectuals…Karson Luning, Great-Grandson of Albert Fisher

Mu-kwa—the guardian…Brian Forsberg, Grandson of Bjorn Forsberg

Wa-bi-zha-shi—the warriors…Sakima Riel, descendent of Chippewa warriors.

Benisi—the spiritual Leaders.

Representing the Midewiwin…Migisi, grandson of Chagobay.

Representing the Jesuits…Father Gary, filling the role of Father Guerin.

Wa-wa-shesh-she—the Gentle People…Leonard White Elk, son of Fawn Chevreuil.

Wabeno—the Firehandler…filled by Lily herself.

Others were lined up as Helpers, Fire Keepers, Guards, and Assistants, and it was indeed an amicable mixture of two cultures. Although there were several MacPherson kids, Levi was the obvious choice; he filled several roles, including the most important one—Omodai, the bait for the Wintermaker.

Before the music even stopped, Lacy Morrison skipped on over, pulling out a chair to join the men. "Guess what?" she asked Wally but didn't even wait. "I got Nancy to speak a whole sentence the other day."

The others warmed to the news faster than he did. "What do you mean?"

"You know how you brought in all those books and such to read to her? Well, I saw her Hamlet book, and since we were reading it for my World Literature class, I took it out. She had all sorts of notes in it, and I tried reading it, and then, pow, her teacher instincts just took over and she mumbled out a correction. I said something wrong and she tried to correct me. Isn't that great?"

Wally nodded, and Lacy took hold of his wife's hand to speak directly to her. "We're going to beat this stroke and get you talking again by summer, aren't we Nancy? I think she's just trying too hard and getting frustrated. But it'll come."

"What did she say?" Wally asked.

"Oh, um, I opened up to the 'To Be, or Not to Be' section since I know we'll get asked about it next week, and I just started reading. Well, I've known a few jerks in my life, so I was having fun reading the parts of Hamlet and Ophelia, and then, out of the blue, Nancy just blurted out 'Get thee to a Nunnery.' It was a bit slurred, of course, but there it was, right on the page a few lines ahead of where I was reading."

Father Gary chuckled, "One of my favorite lines, but it's used for different reasons in my profession."

"That's the time where Hamlet gives his girlfriend the cold shoulder because everybody is spying on him. They think he's crazy," Karson remarked.

"You told me you got bad grades in school," Lacy countered playfully.

"She said that to you?" Wally interrupted.

"Yeah, clear as can be. Does it mean something more?"

It did, even though Wally's mind was now unclear. Being married to an English teacher meant getting a lecture at the drop of a hat. He knew *Hamlet* had a part of her curriculum but his wife also penned a manuscript she titled *Hamlet's Ghost,* the story of a troubled teen trying to escape from the shadow of his tortured father.

Son of a biscuit. "Yeah, I think it does mean something."

Wally looked into Nancy's eyes and could hear her chuckling in the past. He remembered what she'd once said to him. *"Did you know that Shakespeare had a son named Amleth, and that he just flipped the H to create the name Hamlet? I'm thinking about naming the main character in* Hamlet's Ghost *Amleth. What do you think?"*

"Stupid name," Wally had muttered in the moment and stood up, alarming the group with his unexplained action. He paused and turned back. "Before I can explain myself, I need to check something. Lacy, can I get you to bring Nancy back to the room? If you've got time, keep reading *Hamlet*. Karson, I'll stop by your place tonight. You do know your home was built with bricks from a nunnery."

Karson wrinkled his brow. "I do now."

Wally walked with Father Gary. "Get ready for a bit of weirdness." Wally took hold of Father Gary's arm and began leading him to the door.

CHAPTER THIRTY-SIX

To Be, or Not to Be

Staten Island, New York
February 28, 1986

Ansel Nielson held the bullet in his palm for so long it was warm by the time he finished his silent prayer.
What did he save the bullet for?
 The puzzle was spread out over his bed, and it needed to be solved before his mother and stepfather returned from their most recent trip to Greece. The most obvious piece of the puzzle was Jimmy Nielson's Colt Python .357 Magnum. Ansel's second favorite clue was the Polaroid of the four men standing in front of a Saigon tattoo parlor in January of 1969. They posed in olive-drab fatigues while posing like frat boys around a keg, or in this case, their new instruments of death. More recently, however, Ansel focused on his father's sketches in the bound notebook. There were several of his mother Aurora as well as the guys in his unit, but the most intriguing picture to him now was the drawing of a tunnel.
 Where the hell is this?
 Ansel's dreams led him to the New York City public library's periodical room, and on microfiche, he went through the *North Star News* for the better part of a week, looking for clues from his father's birth in 1948

all the way to his father's suicide in 1978 when Ansel was just a kid. He found himself spellbound by the accounts of Jimmy Nielson's seventh grade year: a child predator killed two local boys and almost got Jimmy's best friend Biff. The collapse of the Nicollet Dam, however, seemed the most likely explanation of the tunnel. While it certainly could have been a cave that his father drew while in the jungles of Vietnam, it most likely was part of the quarry that flooded, killing Red Dobie, Colin Kirkpatrick, Duncan Samuelson, and Craig Healey when water poured through the dam and into the quarry.

If his father's tunnel was in the quarry, it was now buried under a hundred feet of water.

Now on the bed, Jimmy had several printouts from the microfiche images chronicling the bizarre horrors of the spring of 1962, including how his father and Biff rescued a bus full of kids from a flooded ditch. According to accounts, his father swam after and rescued little Molly Knutson as the raging water threatened to pull her into a culvert. Her little sister Danika was not so fortunate.

Why didn't he just go home after the war?

He was a fucking hero.

Ansel knew the answer to that question. While Jimmy Nielson was a fourth-generation Minnesotan, Aurora Hermann only vacationed at Lake Manitou. Her ugly small town was in Indiana. A summer fling right before boot camp resulted in Ansel's older sister, Tonya. Ansel was born two years after Jimmy's enlistment ended, and the whole family moved to Indiana, where they lived peacefully for three years until a human monster followed Jimmy home from Vietnam.

Shane Lewis returned to New Orleans after the war and then spent a few years in Los Angeles, where he met his wife Cindy. Ansel didn't know if it was childhood trauma, drug abuse, or a mental breakdown during the war, but the hulking man who stood behind Jimmy and Biff in the tattoo parlor preyed upon his entire family.

Before taking his own life, Jimmy Nielson murdered Cindy Lewis and brutally killed his former tank loader with a .357.

With one bullet left in his revolver, Jimmy could have fired it into Shane's face, but Jimmy didn't fire the shot.

He returned home, covered in blood, and then tossed an extension cord into the rafters to hang himself. He could have ended it quicker with that last .357 bullet.

Which Ansel also dreamed of doing.

Ansel slipped the bullet back into the chamber. Back in 1978, Tonya had heard their father return home from the murders. Ansel didn't know if she'd heard the gunshots or the door close, but she'd come rushing into his room for help. Ansel had no problem facing fear, so he walked down the hall, down the stairs, and into the garage, where he found his father hanging.

Why did I do it?

What kind of kid hides a murder weapon?

Ansel had noticed the silver pistol lying in a small pool of blood beneath his father. Even though Ansel had been brave enough to face the horror of the moment, his broken brain didn't let him process his emotions properly, his shrinks later told him. Knowing his father was dead, Ansel cleaned up by taking the pistol, bringing it back to the bedroom, and hiding it inside of one of his stuffed animals for the next seven years.

Now, the mystery of Jimmy Nielson was spread out over his bedspread.

It appears as if I have three choices.

Choice number one was to put the pistol to his own head and take his life. He'd certainly thought about it. Years of counseling hadn't prevented him from becoming the weirdest kid in any class in any school his parents sent him. His obsession with the play *Hamlet* in recent months sent him back to counseling after he viewed Thomas Archibald as King Claudius, his mother as Queen Gertrude, the housekeeper Emily as Polonius, and Tonya as the strung-out, crazy Ophelia. Like Prince Hamlet, Ansel saw himself as the prince mourning the death of his father. In recent months, though, Ansel found himself letting go of his bitterness and instead opening his mind to the mystery of his father.

Choice number two: shoot that damn raven.

While ravens were certainly all over the northeast, there seemed to be one in particular that followed him, haunting him like Edgar Allan Poe. Ansel looked to the roof, wondering if the bird sat upon his roof or in a nearby tree, waiting…watching.

Shooting it would be funny and give him closure, but it wouldn't answer the mystery of why his father had purposefully left one bullet.

Choice number three: Keep it for Lake Manitou.

Just like his inner voice had told him to hide it as a child, now his dreams told him to bring it to Lake Manitou. A literal monster waited in Minnesota. It drove his father away. It killed children. It brought down floods upon communities. But if it could bleed, then perhaps his father kept the last bullet for a reason.

I'll face my father's demons—and then I'll kill them.

CHAPTER THIRTY-SEVEN

Abode of the Dead

Leech Lake, MN
Broken Snowshoe Moon, 1986

Lily Guerin sat in her wheelchair as the medics took away the body of Beth Roulette, who'd been her neighbor for the past eight years.

Beth had been at the supper table the previous evening, but sometime during the night, she'd quietly died.

May your journey be swift, Lily thought as the white sheet rolled down the hallway. She waited until Beth's body turned the corner for the front doors before she rolled back into her room. Her walls were decorated with religious artifacts from the cultures that defined her: Oceti Sakowin, Anishinaabe, and Christian. As a child, she remembered crossing the Blue Knife River to a church that was...what? Methodist? It opened its doors to the Native people. After attending Sacred Heart Indian School, she became Catholic, which is how her future husband Jean Guerin entered her life.

Besides the religious artifacts, she also had numerous pictures of her family. Her only son Louis had died years ago, and of her five grandchildren, only two stayed home. Only Cameron visited her, despite the fact that Nicole had once been closest to her heart. The other girls left home and never looked back.

Lily stopped in front of her calendar, found the marker, and crossed off another day. Her calendar read March, but her Anishinaabe culture taught it was the Broken Snowshoe Moon, when the power of winter ended. Soon, the rivers would be flowing, and like the sucker minnows, she'd also ride the currents.

Her mind traveled to a distant memory eighty-eight years earlier.

Her grandfather Nanakonan sent her looking for fresh willow branches at a place he'd called Manabozho's Lodge—Turtle Island to her. Behind the island, in a crease of land, Jiibay Hollow protected an ancient willow. Lily never reached the willow, but from the shore of the island, she heard an old woman's voice call out: "Granddaughter?"

Having already woken the Tak-Pei and brought down curses upon her life, Lily had nothing to risk and conversed with the voice from the tree.

The old woman promised me a cursed life.

She promised that the Wintermaker would take the one thing most precious to me—my family. Yet a little time remains. I'll fulfill my promise yet give the Wintermaker a surprise in my dying moments.

In less than a month, Easter would arrive in 1986, and the final loop would close. The Tak-Pei chased her away from the willow and the old grandmother, but Lily knew the answer to the old question—*the old woman was me.*

Nine decades ago, she'd seen the future. At the cave where she found the Philosopher's Stone, the young woman had seen her future self alone in a canoe, wearing bright green pants and a broad-brimmed Easter hat. Levi and Joey had also been part of the vision, as well as the disfigured woman who taught her the words to the Song of the Manitou. In just a few more days, Lily's long nightmare would soon be over.

And then Jean and I will be reunited.

In more ways than one, young Lily had played with fire, and the adult Lily paid the painful price. Seventy-six years ago, she'd lost Jean to a car accident, and since then, Lily lost even more—including her memories of his face. *Like Job, once I lose everything, I'll get it all back, too.*

Lily pushed her wheelchair away from the wall and then left her room for her favorite spot—the aviary. Granted, none of the little finches or canaries were Thunderbirds, ravens, or owls, but it still felt spiritual to be in the presence of birds.

She closed her eyes and simply listened to the wings and chirps.

Then another distant memory entered her mind.

An old plan.

"Tell me again about your river theory," the young bride had asked her husband.

Lily had committed many sins, the worst of them involving the Wintermaker, but she'd never committed adultery with Jean. In fact, he'd officially resigned his position as priest years before they officially began courting, even though she loved him almost the first time she'd seen him. Her visions promised her a marriage, and even when Bushy Bill Morrison murdered Jean in cold blood, Lily refused to let go of the forbidden dream she'd seen.

"My river theory?" Jean asked, looking up from whatever dense text he was reading. "The River of Souls?"

"I already know about Jiibay Ziibi," Lily had answered. "I want you to explain to my how you think all these stories overlap."

"The Greeks called it Oceanus. The river carried souls down to the underworld, which is where it divided into five separate parts. Cultures from all over the world view the underworld with water connections. Take the story of Jonah, who, as I interpret it, died by either drowning in the storm or by being swallowed by a fish. While his body was being brought back to dry land, his soul descended to what the Hebrews called Sheol, where the dead were kept. By the time of Christ, Jews viewed it as multi-faceted, just like the Greeks. The righteous dead went to a place called Abraham's bosom, and the unrighteous were separated by a void. Throw in references to the angels being locked in an abyss, and suddenly the concept of a single underworld gets a bit complicated. Christianity has even more abstract ideas with Christ's reference to Paradise and Paul's comment about a Third Heaven."

Jean smiled and shrugged.

"So…" Lily began. His answers were often confusing. "When a person dies, the soul leaves the body and begins a journey on a river."

"Exactly, which is why I loved the Chippewa belief that it is a four day journey."

"Why does that matter?"

"Look at the Lazarus story. When Jesus learns his friend is ill, he waits. He waited on purpose. The Hebrew people, like your Chippewa people, believed that it took three days to travel to the Gates of Sheol. Jesus waited until the fourth day to go to Lazarus, and when he arrived, everyone thought it was too late. Jesus had brought life back to the recently departed, but with Lazarus, his soul had already passed by the Gates of Sheol—so it seemed as if there was no coming back. He showed he was the Son of God by breaking his own rules for the spiritual universe."

"Is that why Jesus was dead for three days?"

"Exactly. The concept of 'Harrowing of the Underworld' explains that Jesus went down to the underworld, to Abraham's Bosom, to gather up all the souls of the righteous dead. Of course, that's one interpretation."

"Does this watery underworld still exist today?"

Jean chuckled. "I've gotten into arguments about this with other priests."

"So, what do you think?"

He moved closer to her, taking hold of her hands. "In the Book of Revelation, chapter twenty, it talks about Judgment Day, when the names found in the Book of Life are read. In that passage, there is a curious verse about 'the Sea giving up the dead.'"

"What's curious about it?"

"By that point in the Book of Revelation, it seems as if all the waters on the earth have been…eliminated by plagues and disaster, which seems to me to indicate that 'Sea' should read 'underworld.' The underworld gave up the dead for judgment. If that is true, even if Christ has allowed for some souls to go directly to Heaven, where we see the souls of the Saints at the altar, it might mean that the old system continued collecting both the righteous and the wicked, or else…what is left to judge?"

Lily missed Jean so much.

For a decade, the two of them spent hours discussing spiritual matters.

When he died outside of Mankato, she pictured his soul drifting into the Minnesota River, then into the Mississippi, and finally into the Gulf of Mexico where it joined Oceanus. She never asked Jean about his literal interpretation of where Jonah's Gates of Sheol were located, but even after burying him beside her family at the Mizheekay Band of Chippewa cemetery, she knew whether he was behind the Gates of Sheol or up at the altar of Heaven, she would be divided from him until the day she died.

After a house fire almost took her life in 1961, she refused to return to Lake Manitou, where the souls of the dead stayed trapped. Her Lakota mother called it Wanagiyata, the Place of Souls, which was considered a haunted place prior to the arrival of the Chippewa.

Even when Jean was alive, she knew the truth about Lake Manitou—the lake of spirits.

A life for a life.

A soul for a soul.

Lily held the sacred Water Drum in her hands.

The Wintermaker held the soul of Jean Guerin.

Fawn was right—I am a vile, selfish woman.

The trade had been worth it.

She had a decade of love.

Jean gave her Louis, a child she loved with all her heart only to have him turn against her as an adult when he learned the family's destiny.

But then came the grandchildren, who again filled her heart with joy.

And sweet, tender Cameron.

He remained loyal to her even after becoming an adult.

And great-grandchildren.

Righteous young Christians—Benjamin, Leah, Reuben, and Daniel.

And Levi.

Bold Levi, who reminded her of her father.

He waited for her in the future for decades, and now in the present, he boldly prepared to help her close the loop.

And sweet Joseph, who she first knew as Clay—Pewabic.

A HAND TOUCHED her arm, and Lily flinched, opening her eyes to find herself still sitting in front of the aviary, with tears on her cheek.

"Let's get you back to your room, Tew," the young Native nurse said, using Lily's birth name.

I was born Tewapa Asibikaashi. The spider who sat upon the water lily, guarding over Lake Manitou. I became Lily Guerin. Will there be a place for me in Sheol or Heaven for the crime I am about to commit?

CHAPTER THIRTY-EIGHT

What's In a Name?

Split Rock, MN
March 15, 1986

Wally Crain stepped out of his truck and stared out at Betsy Luning's front yard. The willow seemed to stare back.

In recent weeks, Wally had become a man on a mission. His sorrow and depression were gone, and he found himself gritting his teeth as he walked to the front door of the mansion.

Back in St. John, everything from the basement in the old house had been brought to his new cottage home, with thirty years of manuscripts and notes now on the dining room table. Nearly everybody in the Isanti Lodge knew all about his theory involving the willow tree, but they were all too preoccupied with the coming ceremony to give it their full attention.

A quick scan of the manuscript revealed an obvious oddity from Nancy: *Ansel!*

Wally knocked on the door and waited for Karson to answer. He'd already revealed to Karson his shocking discovery—his wife had named the central protagonist in her novel *Hamlet's Ghost* in notebooks several years before typing the first few pages. Karson had reacted with awe while Brian reacted with anger, which is why Wally brought his new fact to Karson.

The doors unlocked and Karson appeared in the open doorway. "Kinda early, Wally."

Wally stepped through the doorway and began to unfold the notebook paper he had crumpled in his back pocket. "Get a load of this: I went to the St. John city offices and found the oldest records they had on file. Guess what it is labeled?"

"Can I get you some coffee?" Karson asked, rolling toward the kitchen.

Wally followed. "The drawer was labeled "Mahkahta County."

"Is that supposed to mean something?"

"I think it does. Mahkahta is the Dakota word for blue earth."

"Like the Blue Knife River."

"Exactly. We both know who came to Minnesota looking for blue vitriol."

"Joseph Nicollet," Karson commented.

"And the Order of Eos, most likely the men who killed him. The Mahkahta County drawer was dated 1849, which was a few years before Minnesota officially became a state, and by that time, we had the current names, but at one time, we were in Mahkahta County."

"Any toast or anything?" Karson continued as he poured a little vodka into his orange juice.

"Thanks to Father Guerin, we have his theory that the Philosopher's Stone was once in the Haunted Valley, dug up by Pierre-Charles LeSueur, lost, and then showed up in Chippewa hands here at Lake Manitou. Left alone, the Philosopher's Stone turns anything around it into a strange—"

"Blue earth," Karson interrupted, squinting. "Okay, now I'm listening Wally. What's your point?"

"I left it to Brian to contact Aurora out in New York."

"That Ansel kid. Our missing Isanti Lodge member?"

216 Jason Lee Willis

Wally nodded. "We'll have to see if she can explain how he ended up with the name Ansel, but I couldn't find any way that Nancy could've given it to either Jimmy or Aurora, so I went searching for other explanations on why Nancy or the Nielsons used the name Ansel, and I found it—Ansel Township. It's halfway between Nimrod and Pine River. It's just empty fields. It has a population of under 100 people. I went out there and didn't even see any signs indicating the boundary."

"Another coincidence?"

"Ah, but why was it named Ansel Township? That's how the rabbit hole sent me to the Mahkahta folder in the Hiawatha County records. The county clerk, Nathaniel Iverson, wrote that Ansel Township's name came from and I quote 'the first explorer to Hiawatha County.'"

"Huh," Karson said, swigging down his orange juice. "First explorer, huh? LeSueur and Lahontan came out to the Haunted Valley in the 1680s, and, um, Radisson and Groseilliers found the Dakota on the shores of Lake Superior in the 1650s, so when did this Ansel cat come to Hiawatha County? Who the hell is this Ansel character?"

"And now you've caught up with my morning," Wally said, sitting on a chair at the kitchen table. His head spun, surprised he'd remembered all the details to share. After a moment, he finished his point: "Who the hell is Ansel?"

"I'll speak with Brian, and if he doesn't make any progress on contacting the kid, I'll call Alexandra Nielson. I think she's still living in Granite Falls. Do you remember her married name?"

"Mollitor? Wayne Mollitor."

"Well, now that we've gotten our strange fact of the day, are we all set for our clandestine meeting of the Isanti Lodge on Wednesday?" Karson asked.

"Leonard White Elk arrived on Saturday with his nephew and are staying in Brainerd. Sakima Riel is out at the MBO with Migisi. We rented a big cabin out on Sugar Point, so Lily will only have to make a short drive. Yes, I think we're finally set."

"And Levi?"

"I'm going to visit Gavin and Nicole right after I leave here. To be honest with you, they're both scared shitless. I worry they could do something stupid at the last minute."

"Well, they've got good reason to be scared, don't they?"

Wally nodded and acknowledged the knot in his gut. He'd seen the Tak-Pei back in 1962. "We all have reason to be scared shitless."

CHAPTER THIRTY-NINE

Wendigo Moon

Split Rock, MN
March 21, 1986

The kid is hiding something, Brian Forsberg decided by the time they climbed into his SUV. *Something's just not right.* Parting took longer than anyone had planned, and as they all stepped out of the lodge, dusk had already arrived, and with it, the full moon. Wally Crain took the elbow of Lily as they entered the muddy parking lot and walked toward the old GMC truck. Chuck Luning tended to Karson, Father Mackenzie escorted Migisi, and Leonard White Elk chatted with his nephew Ben LaBiche and Sakima Riel of Turtle Island Jesuit School.

"Drive safely," Wally Crain shouted out after shutting Lily in the passenger seat of his cab.

They'll be safer than anyone realizes, Brian thought as they neared his SUV. Six off-duty deputies earned a Franklin each for sitting in a perimeter around Leech Lake and another hundred dollars for following each vehicle home.

The kid looked over at Forsberg slyly before they parted to walk around the SUV. When Brian sat down, Levi was ready with his question: "You don't believe any of this, do you?"

Brian turned the key in the ignition. "Belief has nothing to do with it."

Levi glanced down for a few seconds, waiting for him to turn the SUV around and begin driving. "Everybody else in the Isanti Lodge has had a brush with the supernatural. The Lunings both have dreams and premonitions; Leonard White Elk and Ben LaBiche have conversed with the spirits of the dead; Father Mackenzie has witnessed exorcisms; Migisi had his soul ripped from his living body and dragged into Lake Manitou; Wally saw GiGi Lily fight the Tak-Pei at Carousel Island—you didn't share a single story before we practiced the ritual."

"What's your point?" Forsberg asked as he turned onto county road 39.

Levi chuckled. "If Lily is right, the future of humanity is on the line here. We've got a once in a generation chance to fight evil, and if we screw up, we could end up dooming the entire world. Everybody else looked terrified for most of the day as we ran through the ritual. Like I admitted, I've checked off most of those boxes: dreams, ghostly encounters, strange omens, and even the Tak-Pei—but you...you just sat there with your arms crossed for most of the day. I worry you're the weakest link that I've seen in all those horror movies. Are you going to our fellowship's Boromir?"

Oh, fuck you! Brian let out an incredulous guffaw instead of unleashing cruelty. Then he counted to ten as he shook his head and tightened his grip on the steering wheel. Everybody talked about the importance of the Omodai in the ritual, yet Levi just sat there like a grinning Cheshire cat during it all, not having a single phrase or verse to add. Sure, Migisi and Lily explained the concept of the Omodai as bait, but Forsberg also noticed how White Elk, LaBiche, and Riel all wrinkled their brows during the explanation. *And the kid singles me out?*

Forsberg pulled off of the winding lake access road and onto the open highway of County Road 8. "I'm going to tell you an old folktale told by your People. I might be white and freckled, but I've spent decades of my life reading legends and lore while you've spent a few months reading about it between Chemistry and Algebra." *Take it easy on him.* He took a deep breath. "There is a creature called the Wendigo."

"The giant cannibals," Levi began but an icy glare from Brian shut him up quickly.

"Yes, the story about the cannibal monster. As you know, the tales of this creature describe some vampire-werewolf-zombie-like creature that prowls the deep woods feasting on the flesh of men, but what they don't focus on is the origin of the Wendigo. The Wendigo began as an ordinary man—a guy with a mom and a dad and sisters and Gigis—just like you and I. Somewhere along the line, this guy crossed a line. Your Ojibwe ancestors talk about the sin being cannibalism—like the shit that purportedly happened on Madeline Island a few centuries ago—but it's not just cannibalism. I've seen the Wendigo dozens of times. I've seen ordinary men transform into monsters. Do you understand me?"

Levi nodded flippantly.

"Do you? I've seen more death than any other member of the Isanti Lodge, and yeah, while I haven't seen the supernatural crap, I've seen real life monsters, and when I've looked in their eyes, I didn't see humans. I've hunted the Wendigo in the pines of Minnesota, the jungles of Vietnam, and the mountains of Nepal. I know monsters, kid."

The wry smile finally left Levi's face, and as they drove south to Lake Manitou, the setting sun hid both of them in the darkness of the SUV cab. It wasn't until they reached Pine River at the northeast corner of Hiawatha County that Brian found a new line of conversation. "I promised your folks to keep you safe, so I don't want any secrets between the two of us. Is that understood?"

"I understand. I know about what happened to Migisi back in 1898, and I know what happened in 1962. I'll keep an eye on Daniel and Joey, too. It's good to know you've got my back. My mom pretty much hates everybody, but she thinks the world of you."

Something's up with the kid. He's holding back.

Brian pictured the old deer stand where he and the other kids gathered to make sense of the strange things happening to them in 1962.

Back then, Nicki Guerin had been open-minded enough to sing the spells given to her by her brother Cameron from Lily. A few days later, when the school bus accident happened, he and Jimmy Nielson dove right into the deadly floodwaters to save all but one kid. Shortly after that, when the Tak-Pei attacked, the same spell protected Nicki, Gavin, and Cameron.

Chris Luning had arrived late to the meeting—and died.

Neither young Biff nor now balding Brian understood what any of the words meant that Nicki had sung in the tree house, but he knew the spell had worked. What he didn't know was the expiration date of the spell.

Today, Lily had talked about the magic of her old spells waning and how the full moon and comet would change the balance in Lake Manitou. He did have belief. He just didn't know if it would be enough.

Levi sat up.

Brian saw it also.

The SUV had just driven through Split Rock and was descending Old Copper Road. At the bottom of the incline, on the platform of the bridge, sat a large black raven.

Brian studied the kid rather than the bird.

He's nervous about a bird?

"Something wrong?"

"That's a big bird," Levi said, trying to hide his interest.

The raven showed no interest in moving, and Brian found his fingers touching the hilt of his pistol. "Is there something you want to tell me?"

"Maybe it's a good omen," Levi said noticing that he had stiffened. "Should I get out?"

Brian pressed on the horn. The big wings extended and held, a sign it wasn't going to back down, but then with a few quick flaps, the bird vanished into the darkness.

Brian lost sight of the bird, but when his eyes returned to the cab, Levi was still looking for it.

So that's what the kid's hiding—it's something about the raven.

CHAPTER FORTY

Mandatum Novum Do Vobis

Indian Head Mountain, British Columbia
March 27, 1986

Leonard White Elk tossed his travel bags and suitcase onto his living room floor and turned right back around to stand on his porch, facing the dark mountain. He'd spent the day traveling, waking before dawn and now arriving home after dusk.

Maundy Thursday—a new mandate.

An hour earlier, he'd dropped off his nephew Ben with a whisper to his brother, "We need to speak. It's important."

So Leonard waited, alone, for his brothers to visit.

He didn't mind living alone, despite the sniggers from his family. Wives and children gave his brothers plenty of drama, and Leonard loved peace and harmony. He could leave his luggage back in the living room for a month and no one would say a word about it. Yes, he'd likely die alone one day—but everyone was going to die. He'd die in harmony.

Reaching into his pocket, he found the gift he'd received from Migisi, his distant cousin. The old Mide and Jessakkid, despite being a man, reminded him of his mother Fawn. He found the big Calabash Pipe, which had come with stories of its original owner, Albert Fisher. At fifty, Leonard began smoking, knowing he was already past the prime of his life. One day in Calgary, he'd found a tobacco shop and picked up a Dublin half-bent pipe with a rusticated exterior. It had been his companion for the past seven years until Migisi traded pipes.

Now, Leonard stuffed some fresh tobacco and lit it as he pondered the many mysteries held in his mind.

His eldest half-brother, Dennis LaBiche, arrived first, followed by his full-brother Russell White Elk and half-brother Clyde LaBiche. Ben's father, Vernon LaBiche, arrived last, even though he called the other three about the meeting.

Clyde broached the subject. "Ben claims everything went well. I take it you didn't see things as optimistically."

Leonard shook his head. He flipped the pipe over, tapping the ashes out on the deck railing. "Our mother was right. We won't be returning to Minnesota for the summer solstice."

"Why not?" Dennis pressed.

"We'll all be dead men by then, or—" Leonard stopped himself, huffing loudly. "I could feel the magic swirling around like a serpent coiled and ready to strike. It's tangled them all up in its grasp and has squeezed them for so many generations that they no longer see clearly."

"Should we intervene?" Russell asked. Like Leonard, Russell was baptized Catholic because of his father PJ White Elk, who had been named after renowned Jesuit missionary Pierre-Jean DeSmet, who'd visited the Blackfoot Lakota. The half-brothers rejected Christianity, seeking instead spiritual enlightenment in Indigenous religions. All four were cultural zealots, ready to rush off to any crisis in any Indigenous community. Even though Leonard had the body of a warrior and they had the bodies of old men, they were far fiercer than he'd ever be.

"If we honor our mother, we will leave them to their insanity," Leonard answered. "They will soon learn all of the promises are lies, and when they do, then they will be ready to listen to us."

"So it will happen *before* the summer solstice?" Vernon LaBiche asked. "What should I tell Ben? He's been studying the Seven Fires prophecies and the sweat lodge rituals for months."

"Ben will still have an important part to play, but he is *not* going to be part of the Isanti Lodge. If Lily is right, then Sakima Riel should not represent the Marten clan. He might have the blood of warriors in him, but Lily set aside the Marten role for the Nielson family, who was not present. If the Isanti Lodge continues with this madness, then the ceremony is doomed to fail and the Wintermaker will rise to victory. I'd rather face death here surrounded by my family than to die in such a cursed place as Lake Manitou."

All five sons of Fawn Chevreuil sat pondering the mysteries for a few minutes. Finally Vernon asked another question. "Did you speak to Riel about…"

The black runestone? Leonard shook his head. Only five people on earth currently knew what he'd found, and he meant to keep it that way for the next few months. "If mother was right, then the purpose of the runestone will be revealed in the era of the Seventh Fire."

"So you're convinced the comet is the harbinger of the Seventh Fire?"

"If I'm wrong, we only have a few weeks before the world comes crashing to a fiery end, but while I was in Minnesota, I met a young man, and when I looked into his eyes, I saw…the eyes of a Trickster."

"How is that encouraging?" Russell scoffed.

"Brother, in the old tales, the Great Spirit sent Manabozho to earth to teach mankind and to trick them. Contrast this with an even older tale of Adam and Eve—they walked with God yet when alone, rejected Him for the promises of Satan. Humans can be shown the truth and the light in all of its glory yet will still choose darkness. Our Anishinaabe brothers believe Manabozho was a Trickster because humans wouldn't listen to the truth unless they were tricked into discovering the truth themselves. Even the Jews of ancient Israel rejected Jesus Christ when he walked the earth with them, yet when they nailed him to the cross, God had the last laugh, didn't he? Perhaps what we need in these final days is someone to trick humanity into choosing the right path."

Russell White Elk nodded.

The three LaBiche brothers nodded.

Leonard reached into his pocket, stuffed fresh tobacco into his new pipe, lit it, and offered it to his brothers.

CHAPTER FORTY-ONE

Good Friday

Old Copper Road
March 28, 1986

Levi flattened the canoe paddle, turning the nose of the canoe to the right to avoid the rock ahead. Joey smiled his approval.

Spring had come early to Hiawatha County, but there was no time to rehearse what Levi now dreamed of doing. Warmth and wind had turned the gray ice of Lake Manitou into drifts of icy shards all along the northern shore, and the creeks and streams along the marshes of northwestern Hiawatha County filled the Blue Knife River with a strong current. All of this Levi noticed during his drive on his first day off for Easter Break.

"We've got another rock," Joey called out again, pointing off the nose of the canoe. The old birch bark canoe did not deny him as he maneuvered it and floated like a leaf on the current. In just a few days, he'd help Gigi Lily launch the canoe. According to her dreams, it had always been just the two boys, whose names were now known—Levi and Joey.

But in her dream, Joey was known as Pewabic.

Sakima Riel had explained to the Isanti Lodge that the word meant something close to clay. "Yes," Lily had said, "blue clay. That is what they must look for during their trip down the river. Clay."

Riel had gone into a long explanation about how in 1836, Chagobay brought Joseph Nicollet up the Blue Knife River after hearing rumors of blue earth along its bank. Fate—a war party of Pillagers—prevented Nicollet from inspecting Chagobay's cave that day, but soon Lily, and then the boys, would complete the loop.

"Turn!" Joey shouted.

A boulder loomed in front of his little brother.

Turning the nose of the canoe only made matters worse, and while he veered right, the side of the canoe crashed into the side of the boulder. For a second, the canoe rode up the boulder but then gravity flipped the passengers back into the current. Levi held onto the edge of the canoe long enough to feel the current upend the interior and then split it in half in the middle.

As Levi's heavier end got shoved up against the boulder, Joey and the nose broke off and drifted downstream.

"Levi!" Joey screamed.

Letting go of the boulder, Levi threw himself into the water, furiously swimming atop the current. His hands reached for his little brother, who slipped below the surface and disappeared.

With a gasp, Levi found himself in his attic bedroom.

A dream.

He hadn't been paddling at all.

It's still night. I'm home. All is well.

THE ALARM CLOCK confirmed it was still Good Friday, and that he'd only been sleeping for an hour. Even so, he threw his legs out from under the blankets and walked down the stairs to Joey's bedroom.

Joey was sound asleep on the bottom bunk.

Both loops would be closed soon. Lily's loop would be closed on Saturday, April 12, the day after Halley's Comet came nearest the earth. Just like she saw in her visions decades ago, an old woman wearing an Easter hat and bright green pants would float down the river, chase away the Tak-Pei following a young, vulnerable Tew, and then use the Song of the Manitou to unlock the magic in windows that opened to 1898 and 1986. Simultaneously, she'd save herself in the past and set up a path for victory in 1986.

Thinking about it hurt Levi's head, and he tossed himself back into bed, pulling the corner of a blanket back over his chest.

Moments later, he was in a dream with Lacy Morrison.

HE STIRRED WHEN he came upon her lying out on an inflatable raft wearing a two-piece bikini. Wearing vintage 1950s sunglasses that made her look like Marylyn Monroe, she turned her head toward him. "Is this what you want? You could have it all if you wanted. Why share me with others?"

Levi didn't know what to say, which prompted her bold laughter.

"Help me with my sunscreen," Lacy crooned, and Levi found his hands massaging the white oils onto her shoulders. "Do you like this?" she teased.

"I...it..."

Lacy laughed even louder this time. "Would it help if I was that redhead from your dreams?" She shook her blonde hair and a flowing mane of red hair came cascading over her shoulders. When she turned, she wasn't wearing the bikini nor was she Lacy Morrison. "If you choose me, imagine the fun we could have together," the redhead told him.

The hands that had just been administering sunscreen found their way to her throat. When he squeezed, she laughed harder than Lacy had laughed. "That's the spirit! Rise, my Jarl; it's time for you to rise."

"Levi! Help me!"

Behind the redhead, Lacy Morrison floated out on Lake Manitou. A horned serpent swam, creating a wake that threatened to capsize her. He tried to let go of the redhead's throat, but she gripped his forearms, keeping him from running to Lacy.

"Levi! Help me! It wants my blood. It knows who I am," Lacy called in a panic, but the Horned Serpent took her foot in its mouth and pulled her leg. She wrapped her arms around the raft, and for a moment, bobbed in the rough waters, but her arms were not strong enough, and soon she vanished beneath the surface.

LEVI WOKE FROM the second dream in a gasp.

Another dream.

It's still night. I'm home. I'll see Lacy at church on Sunday.

The glow of his electronics provided enough residual light for him to see in the dark. He walked over to his stereo cabinet, and there, sitting on the clear plastic of the turntable cover, he found his Ormus CD. From what he'd read in *Circus* magazine, the founder of the British metal band, bass player Dag Bouillon, was dying of cancer. The CD would be the final release from Atlas Records with the original lineup, but their young hotshot manager, Madeline Sinclair, would be holding auditions to replace the bass player so that Bouillon's music and legacy would live on after death.

Levi set the CD down.

His fingers knew the truth.

Red-haired Maddy Sinclair waited for him in the future.

For the third time, Levi settled into bed, this time pulling a pillow over his head in attempts to drown out the world.

When sleep found him, a third dream crept in. In this one, he saw a farmhouse—possibly the old Larson farm—and a boy who had brilliant green eyes sitting cross-legged on the porch.

"Hey, Levi," the boy greeted. "Everyone told me all about you. It's too bad you and I never got to meet."

"Who are you?" Levi asked. The boy had dark copper skin and curly black hair that draped down to his shoulders. He didn't look to be Native American, especially with those green eyes. He had no accent to help place his unique ethnicity.

"I am the Keymaster," he said with a malicious grin, "which I guess makes you the Gatekeeper in this story."

"That's from *Ghostbusters*," Levi muttered.

"Ah, well, I have something to do with a key, and you're...some sort of guardian. Names really don't matter when none of this is going to ever happen."

"Why is that?"

"Because of what you hold in your hand."

Levi looked down and his hand had become a fiery glove. He shook it, but the flames came from a mysterious fuel source. He felt no pain, and then he knew he was in another dream.

So he studied it. "Is this the Philosopher's Stone?"

"Sure hope not," the green-eyed boy teased. "That's my destiny you hold in your hands. Here...I'll show you what I mean."

The boy reached out, transferring the flame from Levi's hand to his own, but unlike Levi's flesh, the boy's flesh turned to ash as the flames crept up his body and soon engulfed the entire house.

Then Levi heard a woman screaming inside the house. "Help me, Levi. Don't let me die!"

Levi took a few steps closer to the burning porch, just enough to see a woman surrounded by fire.

"Don't worry about her," the boy, now just a burning skeleton, said. "She always overreacts. We'll find a different house. Hey, with your other hand, snap your fingers. There's something I want to show you."

Levi snapped his fingers, and the curtain of fire dropped away, leaving only charred wood. Where the boy had sat on the front porch, all that remained of him were his femurs and skull.

The skull whispered, "This is a clue."

LEVI WOKE AGAIN. *None of this is real. It's just the magic from the comet messing with my head.*

It was dark outside, and his alarm clock read 4:30.

Weary and craving true rest, he flopped down face first into the pillow.

"Leeeviiiii," a voice sang out. "Leee...viiiii."

Levi turned his head. The voice came from only a few feet away.

"This is your fourth and final chance," the soft voice called to him. "It's now or never, my sexy rockstar. What will you do?"

Levi stood and found his face pressed against the window. A few feet below, on the roof outside of Joey's bedroom, a dark figure sat on the roof.

"It's me, Fozzie," the figure said, but it was not a raven. The figure was a squatty female wearing black and sporting black hair.

"You're not Fozzie," Levi said but knew the truth to be the opposite.

"Sure I am. I'm so schizophrenic that I can convince myself I'm anything. Am I not convincing you?"

"Why are you here?"

"Your dreams are real, Levi. All of them. They're all real in a way."

"In a way?"

"We need to speak…face to face…and you haven't been listening to any of the clues I've given you, so now, at the last hour, I need you to be a little crazy too. Now, I know you're mister cool, but I need you to take a leap of faith and just go batshit crazy for a day, okay. I don't know how else to convince you but to show you, and there's only one way to do that."

Feeling the magic of the comet growing by the day, Levi entertained the notion. "How is that?"

"Gah, you're such a hottie, but you're really dense sometimes," the figure took a deep breath and almost shouted each syllable at him. "The raven…and…the willow."

"But I found the willow."

"I worried that would confuse you. Albert's willow is an offshoot—a clone, just like Nancy Crain's willow. They are not the original willow. Yeah, they hold some of the old magic, but they're not the old willow." The figure relaxed. "Like Grandmother Willow from *Pocahontas*."

"Huh?"

"Ah, shit, I forgot how old you are. Never mind. Just trust me that there's a really old tree hiding along the shores of Lake Manitou."

"Why should I trust you? For all I know, you're the Wintermaker trying to lure me to my death."

"The redhead you saw…the one who you choke to death…that's Maddy Sinclair, a total fucking villain. She's like some grand archmaster fiend running the Order of Eos, and if you don't come talk to me before Lily's canoe ride, the two of you are going to destroy the world together, one way or another."

"How do you know about Lily's canoe ride?"

The figure fidgeted nervously. "Because she told me all about it when I first met her. Your Gigi Lily is almost as much of a villain as Maddy Sinclair, but luckily, she's much more reasonable dead than alive."

"What?" Levi asked, wondering if something bad had just happened to Lily.

"Do you love your brother Joey?"

"Of course."

"Do you want to save Lacy Morrison from a horrible death?"

"Well, yeah."

"Then you have to trust me. I need you to make that leap of faith."

Suddenly, instead of sitting on the edge of a first story roof, the figure sat on the edge of a steep cliff. She rolled slightly to one side to unsteadily rise to her feet. "My druggie father never brought me to church, but somehow I know the story of how Satan brought Jesus to the edge of a cliff to tempt him to jump."

Am I being tempted by the devil also? "It was the top of the Temple in Jerusalem, and Jesus refused to jump."

"Okay, maybe I should stick to what I know. I'm not good with words. I just need to show you. Follow me."

"Follow you where?"

"Follow me."

"Uh…no."

"Follow me!" the girl shouted and then burst into feathers, a raven soaring away instead of plummeting to death.

LEVI FULLY WOKE to the sound of his mother playing music downstairs on the piano. Goose bumps grew on his arms and the hairs stood up on the back of his neck.

He knew the tune.

It was one of her favorites.

Levi quickly dressed before rushing over to the window.

Fozzie the raven wasn't on the roof, but it waited in a nearby tree.

I'm not dreaming anymore. This is real.

At the bottom of the stairs, Joey's bed was empty, a sign he was watching Saturday morning cartoons. Joey needed to stay safe, so Levi had no plans to let him know about his dream or the raven sighting.

As he walked down the stairs, he heard his mother singing:

"I the Lord of Sea and Sky

I have heard my people cry."

He paused to listen to her sing the rest of the song.

I will go, Lord, if you lead me.

It was a sign, and Levi committed to trusting the raven fully. He slipped on his winter coat and quietly stepped outside.

CHAPTER FORTY-TWO

Sabbath

Jiibay Hollow
March 29, 1986

The raven settled in the leafless branches of a big oak tree, which overlooked the ravine that held the old willow tree. Levi, having walked the entire length of Old Copper Road from his house, past the old Guerin homestead, the Larson homestead, Carousel Park Amusement Park, and up the hill to the old Nielson farm, dropped to the ground in a heap. From there, he'd traveled through woods and fields until he found a crease in the land still filled with snow, which slowed him immensely.

He'd taken the leap of faith and, for most of the morning, followed the raven into almost certain danger, despite the promises he'd given Forsberg and the others in the Isanti Lodge.

Having caught his breath, Levi looked up at the willow.

It was a real monster—with roots that came up from boulders at the bottom of the ravine and branches that reached into the canopy of the forest that surrounded it. Levi guessed the trunk was thick enough that three people would need to link hands to connect around its 20' circumference. Even though it didn't seem tall, its trunk began at the deepest part of the ravine and reached more than seventy feet to its peak. Its canopy filled the entire ravine, preventing any smaller trees from growing on the banks. Even though it had dropped its foliage the previous fall, the branches had already grown green and tender—typical for a willow tree, which bloomed earliest in spring.

The raven didn't move.

Another joined it.

Now Levi was paying attention and as he took assessment of the entire ravine, he saw several silent ravens including a few sitting within the canopy of the willow. Like the willow at the Fisher Mansion, he felt magic—powerful magic—surrounding the area.

He rose and took cautious steps down into the ravine. "Hello?"

A mocking chorus echoed back at him as the ravens attempted to mimic his sound.

"Almost there," the voice from the squatty porch-sitter answered.

There didn't seem to be any place to hide, but Levi felt no fear in that moment. He quickly found himself standing near the trunk of the mighty tree.

He reached out his hand and grazed the trunk with his fingertips, and when he did, he saw a ghostly figure sitting beside the trunk.

"Welcome to my parlor, little fly."

It's the same girl from my dream. "Who are you?" Levi gasped.

"All of you…none of you. My name is Robin."

"Are you a ghost?"

Robin chuckled. "Oh, no. I think I'm the only real one here. If *you* are real, Levi Son of the Parson, then the roots of this old tree are far more powerful than I expected. No, I'm very much alive."

"Why am I here?"

"To be warned. You've been betrayed. All of you. You've all been thrown under the bus driven by your own Gigi Lily. She's set you on a path that will lead to total destruction. You know, the End of the World kinda stuff."

He'd always known there were two paths: the raven or Lily. "How do you know this?"

"At first, I thought it was just some chemical reaction in my brain because of my meds—I, uh, didn't really trust myself with the fine line between dream and reality, but they were persistent and just wouldn't let it go."

"They?"

"The spiders. All three of them reached through the willow to find me. To warn me. The little girl, the disfigured woman, and of course, the old crone."

"Lily?"

"Oh, yes. The saddest thing about Lily is that she doesn't realize she's the villain in the story. Everything she's doing is because of her love for her precious Jean, which is ironic, because if she didn't save him, everything would have been destroyed anyway. She stepped into a lose-lose situation. Now, though, at the end, she would rather submit than fight. She's fattened the cow and will now make her terrible sacrifice so that she can be reunited with her lost love."

Levi didn't feel anger, fear, or even defensiveness. Deep down, he knew it was true. He'd feared it since Albert Fisher's apparition spoke of the Omodai. "Lily is going to sacrifice my life in the ritual."

"Oh no, the ritual is never going to happen. That's all a lie. You're not the one in danger. It's your little brother."

Joey?

No.

Why would she do it?

"The reason I needed to have you come here," Robin continued, "is not just to warn you. I need you to see for yourself. While I've supposedly been crazy for most of my life, I've only been exploring the willow for a short time, so I don't have all the answers yet. What is it? How does it work? Why does it exist? I don't have those answers. But I do know what it does. If you reach up and take hold of a branch, you'll see the future. If you reach down and grab ahold of one of the roots, you'll see the past. This willow has been here for thousands of years from what I can tell. I've given thought to just staying under the tree and hiding from the real world—but I don't have much time left. The spiders are counting on me to fix things. So…here we are, Levi."

"Fix things? How?"

"I can't explain it to you until you see what's waiting in the future, okay. You and I are about to go for a little journey, and when we're done, it'll still be Easter Sabbath for you. I need to show you what Lily's plan will do to you, little Joey, Lacy Morrison, Ansel Nielson, and all of the others who I love so much. For me, they are all in the past. Their story has been written, but for you, the future is not set. After I show you, then we can talk about plans."

Levi felt his heart beating. Either Lily or Robin would lead him to destruction. "This is all some sort of trick, isn't it? You've taken the form of a chubby girl just so you won't freak me out. For all I know, you're the Wintermaker."

"I figured you'd have a hard time trusting me this close to the loop closing and trusting me is really important. You see, if we don't close the loop, we destroy the past and—the Wintermaker wins. If we don't stop Lily, we destroy the future and—the Wintermaker wins. Your poor Gigi Lily really stepped in it. After I show you the future she shapes, I'll let you talk to her. The ghost of Lily is much more reasonable than the desperate, living Lily whom you know. She convinced me; she'll convince you."

Levi shook his head.

"This isn't a trick, Levi," Robin said and made a throat clearing noise. "Shit, Levi, you're the Trickster not me. You're the only one I could find who could pull this off. It needs to be done right at the closing of the loop, right when the power of the comet is at its greatest." Robin reached up and pulled down a branch and held it for Levi. "Trust me, Levi. You have no idea how much I want you to be real."

For Joey.

For Lacy.

For…whoever the hell Ansel is.

Levi took hold of the willow frond.

CHAPTER FORTY-THREE

Divine Intervention

Staten Island, New York
March 30, 1986

Ansel Nielson woke in his bed on Staten Island. It took a few moments to trust the details surrounding him. Until he opened his eyes, he had been dreaming of a previous stay at Mount Sinai Hospital's psych ward. He could still remember the names of the nurses and his primary care giver, Dr. Jacobs, but with one look at his arm, he understood it had all been just a bad dream.

In his dream, his arm looked like a hydrological map, crisscrossed with scars, large and small, like a pink river system. Sitting in his bed, he took a moment to study his unblemished arm while his mind remembered a pain that had never happened.

What a piece of work is man, Ansel mused, and then quickly rolled to look at the details of his night table.

He looked around his room, confirming more of his reality.

Since the raven began haunting him, his life felt like an echo of dream and reality. He flexed his fingers and then alternated the lift on each digit like a wing of a butterfly. He watched the metacarpal bones and tendons fluidly lift at his command. He'd felt so much pain in his dreams that he expected to find a mangled arm. Instead, he used his arm to toss away his blankets.

Ansel's eyes found their way to his legs, which wore flannel pajama bottoms. He stood and walked over to his window, pulling the curtains open to reveal Upper Bay. His second floor bedroom overlooked an expansive yard, which no longer had a blanket of snow upon it and instead already had a tinge of green from the spring sun.

Is tomorrow April already?

I need to make this happen today.

Ansel walked out of his room and jogged downstairs to the adults.

There he saw two women preparing breakfast while his stepfather read the papers. The squatty, dark-haired woman was Emily, the Archibalds' live-in maid. Even though Thomas had minimalized his modest home, he splurged on luxury items, including help for his wife. Growing up, Ansel thought she was an uneducated Mexican immigrant, but Emily turned out to be a highly literate, third-generation Portuguese citizen, capable of giving him intellectual sass rarely given by either of his parents. The other woman was his mother, Aurora Hermann-Nielson-Archibald.

I've only made matters worse by asking all these questions, Ansel realized as he slipped onto a chair at the informal kitchen table. *Every time she looks at me, she must think of my father.*

Emily came sweeping in from the open kitchen to the informal dining room. Without asking, she set a plate full of buttered toast and a glass of orange juice in front of him.

"How would you like your eggs, Ansel?"

Everything seems the same yet still different. "Scrambled, please."

Like my brain. Just ask, you coward.

Ansel reached out for his glass of orange juice but before grabbing it, he flexed and alternated his fingers. His brain could remember the pain of a wound that was not there.

Something had changed his life, and his dreams were only an echo of his former destiny.

A few moments later, his mother carried two plates over, likely so she could force a frosty conversation from him. She set the plate down and slid it across the table.

Aurora was a beautiful woman. She'd given Jimmy Nielson two children by the time she'd reached drinking age, and she treated her body as if it was the canvas of one of her paintings. She meticulously managed her long blonde hair, makeup, slim figure, and her clothing.

I could use my copy of Hamlet now, he mused and then recoiled. *No, that was the old Ansel—the one with the scars on his arm.*

"How are you feeling?" she asked and then stabbed at her own eggs with her fork.

"Are we just staying home today?" Ansel countered. He remembered church as a kid, but since leaving Indiana, Ansel couldn't think of attending a church service, even on Easter or Christmas.

"We are. Is that okay with you?"

Ansel stabbed away at his eggs and nodded in affirmation.

"I've met with your teachers and tutor, and I have work plans for our summer trip to Greece. By the time fall arrives, we'll have you all caught up on your coursework."

Ansel looked up from his plate and out the windows. Spring had arrived, which meant he only had a few weeks before he'd leave for Greece. *Find a way to bring it up.* "Okay. I'll look at it after I take a shower."

This pleased his mother. "You look so healthy," his mom added. "I'm proud of you, Ansel."

Ansel nodded and finished eating his eggs. "Thanks," he said, and quickly got up from the table.

Emily waited in the kitchen to collect his plate, leaving him standing in front of the house desk between the kitchen and living room. The desk held the telephone, calendar, bills, mail, newspapers, keys, flashlights, and other meaningless essentials of life.

In the mail pile, he found the opened envelope of his Easter card with a Minnesota address. *Aunt Faye.* It was postmarked just a few days earlier.

He didn't even know Easter cards were a thing. Instead of lambs, bunnies, or baby chicks, Aunt Faye had sent a crucified Christ on the cover and an empty tomb inside. Aunt Faye had been his godmother, and since he could remember, she sent him reminders of her existence even though he barely knew her.

In handwritten ink, Aunt Faye had written Luke 11:9 *"So I say to you: Ask and it will be given to you; seek and you will find; knock and the door will be opened to you."*

Out on the yard, a black raven landed to inspect something in the grass.

Aunt Faye's card can make it happen, Ansel thought and returned to the kitchen.

Controlling his body language and tone, he cleared his throat and said, "I'd like to visit my family back in Minnesota this summer."

Thomas dropped his newspaper immediately and turned his head to his wife, who looked as if she'd been slapped.

She swallowed hard and said, "That's quite a coincidence. Your Aunt Faye called a few days ago while you were at school and suggested that very idea."

"She did? Why didn't you say anything to me about it?"

"Thomas and I needed a little time to talk about it and to make a few phone calls. Before you got your mind wrapped around the idea, we needed to check the feasibility of the idea."

"And?"

"It's complicated. Your Aunt and Uncle Carpenter have a vacation planned in June, and as you know, we'll be in Greece. But…we did talk to your Grandma Ursula."

The one from Indiana. Hell no. Ansel was shaking his head as he asked, "I wanted to get to understand my dad's side of the family, not your family. I'd rather go to Greece than—"

"We're not sending you to Indiana. Your father and I first met because my folks had a summer cabin on Lake Manitou. My mom's been vacationing at Lake Manitou since I was a little girl. She said you'd be more than welcome to stay with her, and your aunts have all agreed to spend some time with you during the summer. I haven't finalized the details but—"

"Good. I want to do this," Ansel said bluntly. "Please...make this happen."

He turned and walked away before he ruined everything with his big mouth.

One way or another, I'm going to get my answers.

CHAPTER FORTY-FOUR

Closing a Loop

Leech Lake, MN
April 10, 1986

Levi paused for just a moment at the doorway of the nursing home. *This is the point of no return.*

He stepped around to the front of the wheelchair and knelt down in front of his Great-Grandmother Lily. "Are you sure about doing this?"

"The loop must be closed. I have no other choice."

Neither do I. I'm sorry.

He escorted her out the front door and into the parking lot, where the sixteen-foot birch bark canoe rose above the cab of his F-150 truck like a giant shark fin; its tail rested in the open bed of the truck and hung over the dropped tailgate by three feet.

"Hello, old friend," Lily muttered. Levi assumed she spoke to the canoe, but considering the comet had arrived, she could be seeing all manner of apparitions like he'd been seeing.

"Slide over," Levi said as he opened the passenger door.

Joey gasped. "She's coming with?"

Sorry to keep you in the dark, buddy. Tomorrow he'd tell Joey about what happened at the willow, but not until Lily did her part. Despite her age,

Lily was still savvy and Levi didn't want her prying any secrets from a vulnerable Joey.

Lily's splotchy hands flitted for support as Levi gingerly boosted her onto the cloth-covered bench seat.

"Hello, Clay," she said to Joey as Levi buckled her into the seat.

"My name is Joey."

"Joey? Not for much longer—the comet has finally returned."

Joey moved all the way over until he was straddling the gearshift in the middle of the bench. He looked down at his knees, as if ashamed of his youth.

"She's not going to bite, Joey," Levi said as he climbed behind the wheel.

Don't blow it, Joe. Be cool.

In her Easter outfit, Lily stared blankly out the window.

"What are you doing? We can't just take her."

"A nursing home is not a prison," Levi said as he started up the truck and pulled away. "She can come and go as she pleases."

A few minutes down the road, Joey turned to ask Lily, "How old are you?"

GiGi Lily's chins shook as she turned from the window. "I wasn't always old. It seems like yesterday I was fighting the Manitou and now--"

"Don't mind him, Grandma Lily," Levi elbowed Joey as they drove down the wooded road from Onigum back to Walker and the highway home.

"Are you doing this to make Mom mad?" Joey asked.

"I'm doing this because Grandma needs my help."

"Help with what?"

"By the grace of God, I am almost 103 years old," Grandmother Lily interrupted, responding to the earlier question Joey had asked. "But I can remember paddling across Leech Lake to Bear Island." She raised a shaky hand and pointed across Agency Bay. "Can you see the island? My grandfather Sweating Stone lived there."

Levi huffed. "Mom said you're a witch."

"Witch?" Lily cackled as Levi's elbow found Joey's ribcage. "No…no…not a witch. I was a Wabeno, touched by Manabozho from birth."

Levi smirked, shifting so that his brother saw the new talisman around his neck. It was a tiny dream catcher given to him moments ago by Lily.

"Mom's not going to let you wear that in the house," Joey said with certainty.

"Grandma Lily put a mom's cross in its middle," Levi offered. "It's the best of both worlds."

"It will protect your brother after I am gone," Lily said.

Or put a bullseye on me. Levi turned at the little town of Nimrod, crossing the Crow Wing River Bridge. Being with Lily right before she closed the loop made him realize that she had no idea the doom she was about to release. She'd soon be dead and simply didn't care what happened afterwards.

"Where are we going?" Joey asked as they turned away from the road home.

Levi ignored his brother, again, and the truck threw a cloud of dust behind them as they drove down the gravel road. A quarter-mile south of the town, Levi stopped at the Blue Knife River Bridge.

The little tributary was no wider than a ditch, and the bridge spanning it did not have rails, but this was the spot Lily had insisted upon launching the canoe.

Levi backed up and turned off the truck.

"Come on, Joey, I need your help."

As usual, Joey calmly obeyed without question. Together, he and Joey unstrapped the antique canoe and set it beside the truck. Then Levi picked up Lily's heavy suitcase and set it in the nose of the antique watercraft.

Levi opened up the passenger door and helped Lily from her seat. From what he could tell, she could not be more than ninety pounds, but as soon as her feet touched the ground, she immediately began shuffling from the gravel to the grass of the ditch.

"Stay here with Joey for a minute," Levi said then passed her off to his brother and went back to the truck. He returned with a jug of water, his mother's wide-brimmed Easter hat, a lunchbox, and a whistle on a lanyard.

He slipped the whistle around her neck and put the hat on her head. With her green polyester pants and white floral print shirt, the Easter hat made her look more like a bad cartoon character instead of a warrior off to do battle with the dark spirits dwelling in Lake Manitou.

"The hat will keep the sun out of your eyes and keep you cool. I've given you enough food and water to last for two days—that's all you get, okay? If you run into any problems, start blowing that whistle. Somebody is bound to hear you."

"She's going by herself? She'll die!" Joey protested, but Lily's wrinkled hand patted his brother gently on the cheek.

"I should have done this long ago," Lily answered Joey but looked into Levi's eyes, "if the Lord has determined this path for me, who am I to argue?"

Levi handed her the paddle, put his shoulder into the stern of the canoe, and shoved it into the current of the little stream. The nose quickly spun around and ended up parallel to shore.

"Hold it here," Levi told his brother and then escorted Lily down the grassy slope.

Despite sitting in the rear of the canoe, her weight lifted the nose only slightly out of the water. The flow of the current would do most of the work for her. *Before I can do anything, she needs to do her part and close the loop.* "Good luck, Tewapa Asibikaashi," Levi said once she situated herself. "I'll see you on the other side."

The old woman nodded solemnly and began paddling down the Blue Knife River.

"Does she want to die?" Joey asked.

"No, and both of us better pray she doesn't."

"Why"?

"It's complicated," Levi said, feeling the talisman around his neck.

"What did you say to her?"

"I said good luck."

"No, those Indian words. What did they mean?"

"They don't mean anything. It's her name—Tewapa Asibikaashi."

"Does it mean anything cool?"

"Yeah, dummy. It does," Levi said as he turned and headed for the truck. "Tewapa is from her Sioux mother's side. It means Water Lily."

"And the other word?"

"Asibikaashi…it's an Anishinaabeg word from her Ojibwe father. It means Grandmother Spider."

CHAPTER FORTY-FIVE

The River of Souls

Blue Knife River
April 10, 1986

Much of the Blue Knife River looked exactly as it had ninety years earlier. After a few gentle hours of floating on the current, the banks of the river grew taller and taller until the shadows protected her from the summer sun.

Lily knew better than to waste energy paddling, so she simply kept an oar dipped into the water to gently turn the nose left or right. Once a submerged rock spun her canoe in a circle, but the current quickly took hold and sent her off again without any harm.

Forty feet below the top of the wooded ridge, Lily could see only broken drain pipes, a rotten staircase, and an assortment of modern refuse tucked amongst the roots of the trees as if buried by junkyard squirrels. If the three hundred yards of shore were any indication, Turtle Island Jesuit School had not aged as well as she had.

Who ran the school now? Lily wondered as she drifted past another monument to her many failures. *Louis?* No, Louis was her only child who did not die in her womb. Louis had become a farmer. It was Norval, some cousin on her father's side, and his annoying boy who asked so many questions.

By the time Lily remembered Sakima Riel's name, she had drifted past her brother's eighty-acres and into her father Squeak's eighty-acres. The geography remained mostly the same, but all traces of her youth were gone.

Her childhood home, built by her father's hand, had long ago been erased by floodwaters, but her weary soul could imagine the smoke rising through the branches from her mother's prized cast iron stove.

As she passed from her father's eighty acres to her grandfather Nankonan's land, her hardened old heart stopped for a moment.

Our Father in Heaven!

But her eyes were not mistaken.

In the rubble and erosion along the banks of the Blue Knife River, a little trickle of water conspicuously entered the current. A greenish blue stain marked its rocky path down from a small dark chasm in the sandstone.

Hallowed be Thy Name.

Vitriol. Jean had taught her the word so many years ago.

V-I-T-R-I-O-L

"Do you remember what it stands for?"

"Pewabic…clay…ormus…lapidem."

Your kingdom come,

Your will be done…

And now her heart beat as strongly as any drum ever could. She knew exactly what remained in the cave, just where she had left it two decades earlier.

And forgive us our sins

As we forgive those who have sinned against us.

The nose of her canoe brushed against a rock on the shore, spinning her around for a second look at the cave high above her along the sheer rock wall. She stared up at the cave as if staring down a bully from her childhood. The comet had brought powerful magic with it, and the heart within the Philosopher's Stone beat strongly in anticipation, changing the matter around it into the blue ormus that betrayed its location. The next fight would belong to Levi, and she feared how the fight would go.

With the words of Christ as her shield, she lingered in the evil place for a moment, knowing the cave and what waited within did not belong to her destiny.

Am I the hypocrite Christ spoke of? Lily wondered about the passage from Matthew as she looked up at the dark hole that leaked vitriol down onto the rocks.

"Do not speak his name," Lily said aloud. "Do not go into that cave."

Her words sounded weak in the present, but she knew how strongly they would echo to others in both the past and the future.

Finished with her first simple task, she placed her paddle against the rock on the shore and pushed her canoe back into the current.

"And when you pray, do not babble on like pagans."

Perhaps young Joey had it right. *Witch?*

But I cannot go to Heaven, Hell, or the Land of the Midnight Sun without at least trying to atone for my sins.

The river pooled unexpectedly, forcing Lily to paddle for a hundred yards until she saw concrete footings—all that remained of the once mighty Nicollet Dam.

The current hastened as the canoe passed over the submerged stones of the former Nicollet Rapids, before spitting her out into the remaining rapids of her childhood.

A single rock, hit the wrong way, could bring death.

And the river was a minefield of rocks.

Her feeble arms could steer the canoe a bit, but she would not have enough strength if the current sent her into a boulder.

So she set her paddle down for a moment, held onto the canoe's edge as the boulders smashed the soft sides of the birch bark, and prayed to God to deliver her through the channel.

Ha! Lily mocked the Wintermaker, knowing Nicollet Rapids would have been one of two places her life might be claimed. *Now she could close the other loops.*

Picking up her paddle, she dipped it into the current, allowing the river to do the work once again.

A concrete and metal bridge stood above the river spanning the distant river valley like a massive insect.

As she neared the bridge, she smelled smoke drifting down from the wooded ravine to the water. Images of her grandfather Nanakonan's sweat lodge filled her mind, and when she turned to the eastern bank, she thought for a moment she could see the dark mound of bent branches.

No, you fool. Your mind is playing tricks on you. This would have been Thunderface land; Nanakonan's lodge would have been above the Nicollet Rapids.

After passing under the shadow of the bridge, Lily understood the vivid reality of her vision. In the same place where loggers corralled logs from the pineries south of Leech Lake, a state park now stood, filled with tents, campers, and RVs. Dozens of smoldering campfires explained why her mind played tricks on her.

Finally, the Blue Knife River dumped her into Lake Manitou.

Turtle Island, like the rest of Lake Manitou, had been eaten away by modern parasites. Instead of a full canopy of oak trees greeting her, docks, boathouses, and a dozen roofs grew like cancer cells on the flesh of the island.

Yet when she neared it, she could not help but smile when she saw the tallest building, which bore a twenty-foot cross.

Turtle Island had become a Bible camp.

Perhaps there is still power in the Isanti Lodge. Lily set the paddle across her lap and clasped her hands together in triumph, which only lasted a moment. Arrogance had cost her too much in the past, and even though it seemed as if God's grace smiled upon her, she knew better than to take things for granted.

So on she paddled.

With the city of St. John at her back, Lily needed only to use the water tower of little Split Rock to orient her in the middle of the lake. With a northwest wind easing her passage, she cut down the spine of the lake until she reached the far southwestern corner.

The nose of Lily's canoe slid onto the muddy shore. She slipped off her white loafers, and with the support of her paddle, stepped back onto Deadwood Island.

Lily pulled the canoe as far into the tall grass as her frail old arms could manage before retrieving her small suitcase.

And into the woods she vanished to close the final loop.

One soul for another, the voice had once promised after she stepped into the opening of the island. The Tak-Pei feared the Water Drum and stopped their violent assault. Several men died moments prior to her arrival. The future hung in the balance.

Now Lily walked in that future, an old woman. She found the spot where her loved ones had fallen and closed her eyes.

The blood had drained out of Jean's bullet holes; he could offer no advice. Her brother Migisi and cousin Fawn, though alive, waited in an unconscious state.

In that strange silence, the Wintermaker appeared. Neither man nor serpent, his spirit recognized her ability to destroy everything with the white stone she held in her hands. So he offered her a way out.

One soul for another…

Without Jean, the future would've collapsed, so she made the deal and took the Wintermaker's offer. The Wintermaker lived up to his end of the bargain and healed and returned life to Jean's body. The rest she had to figure out on her own.

Now, she had to live up to her end of the bargain. She had to give the Wintermaker an Omodai.

But not without a fight, Lily decided and opened her eyes to the present.

With her eyes fully open, she saw trees growing up through the corpse of the abandoned amusement park, but when she blinked, she saw the souls of the dead that had been marked by the Wintermaker while alive. None of them had ever escaped his web. But now it was Grandmother Spider's turn to spin a web of her own upon the loom that had finally come full circle.

"As you can see," Lily spoke aloud to the Wintermaker during the middle of the beautiful day, "I only have a few breaths of life still in me. When I die, I release you from your slumber, the oath fulfilled."

Only a few leaves shivered in the breeze.

LATER THAT EVENING, with the Serpent Star above them, she sat on Deadwood Island and sang the Song of the Manitou for a final time, using the magic to reach back to her sixteen-year-old self.

The Wintermaker's silence felt like mockery to Lily.

He didn't see any of it as a threat.

THE NEXT MORNING, the Wintermaker did nothing as the frail old woman left Deadwood Island and turned her canoe back toward Split Rock Creek.

CHAPTER FORTY-SIX

The Destroyer of Worlds

Doc Jones Bridge
April 11, 1986

There'd be hell to pay, Levi knew, but seeing his mother's fury didn't concern him after what he'd seen in the willow. He had a purpose—he was the trickster.

First he'd trick Lily, and then he'd trick the Wintermaker.

Dawn was coming.

The trees surrounding the Crow Wing River transformed from shapeless ghouls into pines and oaks, yet a strange fog hung on the air, as if Halley's Comet had let some of its tail sprinkle down to earth.

Seventy-five years from now he'd be in his nineties. *If I leave here right now, there's a chance that I'd*—No.

Levi had taken hold of too many branches and knew his story would tragically end. He believed Robin. He believed the truth of the willow. Levi remembered the cyclopes from Greek mythology and how with their wonderful single eye, they were gifted prophetic skills, but instead of rejoicing in the ability, they fixated on their moments of death. Seeing the end of their lives brought depression and melancholy upon them, tarnishing their entire species.

For Levi, it was worse. He'd seen dozens of deaths, and in most of them, the smiling face of Maddy Sinclair. And then his self-described 'fan-girl' Robin handed him a new branch. "Or you can be a hero," she said and let him see an alternative destiny.

After peering into the future, Levi returned, gasping the name, "Lily."

"I know," Robin grimly answered. "It's a terrible decision she had, isn't it?"

Levi had sighed. "I understand now. I'll do it for Joey. I'll do it for you. I'll do it for all the souls trapped here at Lake Manitou. But what about—?"

"The boy with the green eyes and curly hair? His destiny *must* be severed from ours or a fate worse than death will claim the world—oblivion."

The Keymaster and the Gatekeeper, Levi reflected. "So, I've got just a few weeks to stop Lily, stop the Order of Eos, and stop the kid with green-eyes from coming to Lake Manitou—or the world will come to an end?" He smirked and shrugged under the insane pressure of it all.

"If *we're* right, the world won't end, Levi; there will be a rebirth."

"So, I just need to do my part and the others will do the rest?"

"Everyone must die, Levi," Robin had coldly, "but you…what a unique experience *you'll* have."

"What happens if Lily finds out what I'm about to do?"

"First of all, keep her in the dark. She'll see you as an ally after you help her close the loops. From your work at Fisher Mansion to your assistance getting her in the canoe, she'll trust you to step right into the morbid trap she's set for you and Joey. Play along. Bluff. Trick her. She won't understand right away."

"Fine. You've convinced me. I'll do it."

"Okay, this is happening too fast. I don't know if *I'm* ready," Robin breathed. "Now listen, Levi. It's very, very, very important that you help her to close all the loops. When the Wintermaker learns he's been tricked, he'll go insane. He'll rage. Those witches in the Order of Eos will try to do the same thing I'm doing right now. That's why you need to make sure Lily does her part and you do yours."

"I need to bring Joey to the Wintermaker."

"Right. It's what he's expecting from Lily. He'll take the bait and then we'll close our trap around him. Screw Lily and screw the Isanti Lodge. We're going to blow this whole thing up."

"Let's blow it up."

INSTEAD OF LISTENING to Lily, Levi chose Robin and dropped Joey off back home yesterday and then spent the night waiting on the Doc Jones Bridge. He'd grabbed a couple rocks just in case and sat on the edge of the decking with his feet dangling over the edge.

Where are you, Lily?

For Levi, unlike the rest of the Isanti Lodge, the cat was out of the bag about Lily's plan to trade the soul of Jean Guerin for an Omodai, her great-grandson Joey. In 1898, no one had witnessed the deal she'd made with the Wintermaker, but now, Levi knew.

And he meant to stop it.

The fog intensified as light and warmth came from the rising sun. He squinted as he looked upstream where Split Rock Creek emptied into the Crow Wing River but only saw the mist. He looked to his lap and closed his eyes for just a moment.

A car smashed into the bridge behind him.

The vibration of the metal shook from the southwest post to where Levi sat in the middle of the northern side and almost flung him into the water. His hands hurt from where he'd clutched onto the support cables.

A 1970s Camaro slid to a stop, revealing a body lying in a blanket of shattered glass. The body belonged to a young woman, evident from her short skirt and her bare breasts. For a moment, he thought of Lacy Morrison, but the young woman on the deck of the bridge had long blonde hair, which was covered in flowing blood from a terrible head wound.

The young woman's body twitched and shook for a moment, but then, a strong right hand reached out to grip the wooden planks with its nails. The body turned, revealing a head that had been crushed between the long Camaro passenger door and the side of the bridge.

She was climbing out of the car.

If there had been any beauty, it had been stolen when the upper part of her skull was crushed, leaving displaced eye sockets and an open fissure above the forehead.

The left hand reached out and the figure began to crawl toward Levi.

"Don't…take him…from me," she muttered.

"FUCK!" the driver of the Camaro shouted as he took a couple steps back from the scene of the accident. A second person climbed out from the passenger door.

"Don't…do…it," she implored, reaching out a hand to Levi before it fell limply on the ground.

The two young men rushed forward and then, like the Camaro, evaporated in the mist.

"Don't…" the young woman muttered, her head lying on her cheek on the bridge deck.

It's not real. It's just magic from the comet. Ripples in the waters of time.

It's just an alternate future that won't happen now.

It's the stuff Robin warned me about, Levi told himself as he tried to stay calm.

A moment later, a very real sound came from the east side of Old Copper Road. A young girl on a pink bicycle came gliding down the hill. She put all of her weight onto a pedal of the bike, braking in a long gravel skid, and stared at the same place the accident victim had just lain.

"What did you do?" she asked, wide-eyed.

Levi knew her.

She was a classmate of Joey's—Sommer Chauvin.

The rocks were meant for her.

"Get out of here," Levi shouted, showing her the rock.

"But—"

Robin's right. She's going to fight it if I let her. Levi let loose the rock so that it struck the front of the bridge and skittered toward her. He picked up another rock and doubled the volume of his voice. "Get out of here!"

Sommer went from wide-eyed to angry but took a hint, standing on both pedals to ride back up the hill toward Split Rock.

Good luck dealing with her, Robin.

Gigi Lily emerged from the foggy river.

I am the destroyer of worlds, Levi mused dramatically. *Time to destroy a little more.*

Lily had survived her long night on Deadwood Island, and as promised, pushed off for Split Rock Creek at daybreak. He was supposed to be waiting along the Crow Wing River below the farm, where he and Joey would help her land, put her back in the truck, load up the canoe, and bring her back to Leech Lake.

Instead, Levi waited for her at the Doc Jones Bridge. His F150 was parked in the grass.

He waved at her.

Does she sense it yet?

Levi stood up, brushed off his pants, and then ran across the deck of the bridge. He strode down the grassy slope and out onto the big pink erosion rocks where Sommer Chauvin's body was supposed to be hidden after the accident on the bridge.

Sorry Sommer. Change of plans.

"Why are you here?" Lily's shaky voice called out forty yards upstream from the bridge.

She's blind to the details. The loop only showed her the three locations. Her extraction plan wasn't part of her stolen visions of the future. "There were a bunch of tree branches where you wanted to get picked up. This will be much safer."

"No, I—"

"Did it go well last night?" Levi asked, distracting her.

"Yes, I, yes. I closed the loops. All three of them are closed now."

"Are you feeling okay?"

"I'm tired. I'm so very tired."

Levi stepped out into the water and caught the nose of the canoe as it gently glided to him. "I'm sure you had quite the night. Put your arms around my neck and I'll carry you to the truck."

Lily was indeed too tired to refuse, and in a few minutes, he had her safely in the cab of the truck and the big canoe loaded atop it. When he opened the cab up, Lily flinched as if waking from a dream.

"Now to get you home."

"Yes, I need to sleep."

Sorry old gal, but this is for the good of everyone, including you.

He pulled back onto Old Copper Road, but instead of driving into Split Rock, he turned west. He was past the Forsberg farm before Lily even noticed.

Finally, she noticed and weakly asked, "What are you doing?"

"I'm just going to get you some refreshments real quick before taking you back to Leech Lake."

Lily shook her head. "We need to avoid your mother. You need to take me home. Only the Isanti Lodge can know what I've done. I told you all of this."

"I know, Gigi. I know. I'll be in and out of the house in a jiffy."

When he parked the truck, he took the key and made sure it was in full view of the kitchen window. When he stepped inside, after not coming home at all the previous night, he saw the rage in his mom's eyes.

"Where were you?" she blasted. "We were worried sick!"

"I'm sorry. I'm sorry. Gigi Lily wanted to see that comet last night, so I stayed with her in Leech Lake. I called and left a message with Joey. Didn't he tell you?"

Levi waited for her to take the bait.

"Gigi Lily?"

"Yeah, and now she said she wanted to visit Deadwood Island one last time, so I was going to grab Joey or Daniel to help me launch her old canoe."

It was a lie worthy of being a trickster.

His mom rushed to the window. "You are NOT going to take her to Deadwood Island. She's 100 years old. What's wrong with you?"

"She said it was important," Levi feigned innocence and saw Lily opening the passenger door. Instead of heading to the house, she started shuffling away toward Leech Lake.

His mom was out the door in a heartbeat, giving Levi his first small victory.

CHAPTER FORTY-SEVEN

Memory Care

Golden Shores Nursing Home
April 16, 1986

Karson Luning held his hand over his open mouth in shock. Instead of grabbing the spotlight, he let himself just fade into the background of the nursing home. Veteran nurses swept in from different departments, drawn to the disturbance like moths to the light.

The throng of people transitioned from the window overlooking Lake Manitou to the narrow hallway. When the metal security door closed, the hairs on the back of his neck stood up, and when a hand touched his shoulder, he jumped. Lacy Morrison loomed behind him. "What was that all about?"

"New resident," Karson said without saying the name of Lily Guerin. "I guess she's struggling with her new situation."

"She seemed pretty upset. I could hear her yelling from across the commons."

Karson nodded, replaying the pointed words in her accusations. Karson had transitioned to the role of watchdog after Nicole MacPherson rushed Lily to the hospital on Saturday and then refused to let her go back to the Leech Lake nursing home. Golden Shores, after all, would allow Nicole to keep a closer eye on her confused grandmother.

Despite having visitors, an exhausted Lily slept for most of the day on Sunday and Monday. On Tuesday, she joined others for breakfast and lunch before falling asleep early.

Earlier that day, Karson joined her for breakfast, even though he doubted she'd know who he was. After a private reminder, Lily pressed him about the whereabouts of the old birch bark canoe. All seemed well.

"Is Molly okay?" Lacy asked.

Oh, shit. Molly. "I'll go check. Um, go play something, please. Distract them."

Lacy shifted. "Aye, aye, captain."

By the time Karson left the dining hall, Lacy was pounding out a playful tune on the piano. *Ignorance is bliss, I guess.*

Karson found Molly Chauvin in the kitchen with two of the cooks tending to her. The kitchen was not designed for wheelchairs, so Karson had to steer around some of the racks and equipment to get closer.

"Molly, I hate to be a burden, but some guy from the FDA is here with some questions about a 'mystery meat' that's been recently served to the residents," Karson said as he approached.

"Oh, fuck off," Molly snarled at first and then chuckled realizing he was jesting. "This really hurts." She held up her bandaged hand, which had been impaled by a fork just a few minutes earlier. Molly had only been passing by the table at the window when the chaos began, and in lending a hand, she was wounded by Lily.

"I was just returning to the commons when I saw the commotion. Did you see what upset her?"

"I was ready to go home for the day," Molly said then scoffed. "Some days, Karson. Some days."

"If you're okay, I'll go see how things are with Lily."

Molly rolled her eyes. "Good luck."

The Isanti Lodge would want to know about the situation. When he passed back through the commons, Lacy, oblivious to the drama unfolding, was singing an old love song from the 1920s.

Nicole MacPherson had stolen their Queen Bee from the hive and locked her in the memory care unit, which meant Karson had to be buzzed in before he could enter the hallway. It was an overreaction, as was typical for Nicole. Lily was just tired, Karson assumed. Her cheese was still firmly atop her cracker. Little else was different in the wing except for cameras, locked doors, and secure windows. After conversations, the Isanti Lodge agreed with Nicole's idea of keeping her at Golden Shores since Lily could be watched closely now.

Cameron Guerin was being escorted from the room by a nurse. As a kid, Karson had seen the "Can Man" as a weirdo to be avoided. With his dead eye, ghostly white hair, and nervous twitches, CanMan was not a figure you wanted to meet in an alleyway, but after learning what had happened to him in 1962, Karson now found tenderness for the town outcast. "How is she, Cameron?"

Karson held onto his arm as they passed, forcing the nurse to pause.

"Sh-she's mad. Sh-she keeps s-saying that she's not su-supposed to be here," CanMan stuttered.

"A lot of residents get angry and frustrated at first," the nurse commented. "Your grandmother will just need a few days to adjust to her new home."

Karson didn't let go yet of CanMan's arm. "What were you talking about right before she got angry?"

"We were talking about the comet and how my ancestors called it the Serpent Star because of its long tail. She talked about seeing it back in 1910 and then…then she just went crazy and started talking about her husband Jean."

Jean Guerin died in 1910.

Karson let go. "Don't worry, Cameron. A lot of elderly patients struggle the first few days at a new home. We'll talk more tomorrow."

Shaken, CanMan walked out the front doors. For the past few days, Nicole had been sending a steady stream of family members to visit Lily during the transition. CanMan sat for long stretches like he'd done up at Leech Lake.

Wally Crain stepped out of Lily's doorway just as Karson arrived. Karson could hear Lily muttering inside of the room with a nurse hushing her. A second nurse appeared and stood beside Wally. At seeing Karson, she looked at them both before saying, , "Let's give her some space, gentlemen. She just needs to calm down and rest for the evening."

"Let's talk outside," Wally suggested. Karson and Wally left Lily tucked away with the memory care nurses. They moved past Lacy and stopped under the canopy of the entryway.

Wally avoided the incident. "So Nancy is responding to rehab quite well. Her stroke damaged her ability to speak, and as her brain heals, we just need to find the way back out."

"Four months," Karson repeated what the doctors had said. "Give it another four months and you'll be surprised where she's at."

"Do you think we have four months?" Wally asked with negativity. "I'm just worried about the next few weeks, especially after this curveball with Lily. Are things falling apart right at the end?"

Karson shook his head. "The landing might've been rough, but I think it was all a success. I went over all of our historical notes about the "loop" and I think Lily did everything she needed to do. She helped her younger self by visiting the Blue Knife cave, Turtle Island, and Deadwood Island. For a woman her age to stay all night on an island to witness Halley's Comet, we're lucky she's even alive. Now, we nurse her back to health and prepare for the final battle at the Summer Solstice."

"Do you think the Morrison girl could be a spy?"

Karson recoiled. "What?"

"She's sweet and all, but she's a Morrison, and Morrisons have been part of the Order of Eos since…forever. Is it a coincidence that she's here at the nursing home? She's the blood of our enemy."

Wally suddenly looked ten years older. "She's…she's just a kid, Wally. She's a sweet, confused kid. Father Gary vouched for her."

"Ah, forget I said it. You're right. She's adorable, but we've taken her into our lives. I have her reading to Nancy, and now, Lily's here."

Karson knew Wally was just tired and stressed. "Are you suggesting Molly fire her?"

"No. No, I just—let's focus on Lily for a moment."

"Good. I'd like to get home at some point tonight." Karson gave a recap of Lily's outburst.

"Comet talk?" Wally repeated.

"CanMan said the last thing they were talking about was how the comet came in 1910."

"So her meltdown triggered thoughts about her husband Jean?"

"I think so. Hell, you were in the commons when it happened. What did you see?" Karson asked.

"I was talking to the Morrison girl when I heard Lily start to scream about being tricked. I could tell she was frantic, and that only freaked out Cameron. Lily demanded that we take her back to Leech Lake, and when poor Molly Knutson tried to tell her this was her new home, she slammed that fork into her hand and tried to run for the door."

Chauvin. She married that prick, remember? "I don't want her locked up, but maybe she also just needs to rest. It's two months until the Summer Solstice. After that, we'll get her back to Leech Lake for her last days."

Karson remembered Lily screaming, "I can't die here. Don't let me die here."

He remembered thinking the same thing in the fall of 1972.

Have we made a mistake?

CHAPTER FORTY-EIGHT

Bear Traps

Carousel Island, MN
April 20, 1986

Brian Forsberg connected the AV cables together and picked up his radio. "Twins on yet?"

"Hrbek's looking a little grainy," Ron Spears's voice answered. Of all the men on the Hiawatha County Sheriff's Department staff, Ron Spears was the only one he trusted for such sensitive matters. Granted, Spears was a cold-blooded killer when provoked, but when kept calm, he was loyal and, more importantly, knew how to keep his mouth shut. Even though both of them had served in the Vietnam War, neither of them ever talked about it despite their shared service being the bond that held them together.

Forsberg pushed the two ends of the cable together even tighter. "How about now?"

"I can see the roll of Kent Hrbek's chin," Spears answered stoically with a response full of playfulness.

Forsberg wrapped the "first base" camera cable with waterproof tape and stood up from the mud of the island. Twenty-four years after the collapse of the Nicollet Dam, Carousel Island was covered in the rust and rot of the old amusement park. After the company that owned it filed for bankruptcy, the property fell into legal limbo, which allowed the county to take stewardship of the land. During winter, ice allowed easy access to the island, but with the departure of the ice, the arrival of Halley's Comet, and the coming summer solstice sacred to Eos, Forsberg chose to secure the island.

Inspired by the movie *Scarface,* Forsberg decided to create his own security network like the one Tony Montana employed to protect his cocaine empire. Using state-of-the-art Sanyo cameras, Forsberg deployed wood duck houses and other "blinds" to hide the bulky CCTV cameras and buried the power and optical cables that ran back to a central location.

Forsberg brushed himself off and picked up the last of the equipment. An underwater sleeve ran from the island to the shore, where a fake water intake system ran to his childhood farmhouse. Now, the comings and goings of Deadwood Island and Bleeding Rock could be watched and recorded from the six monitors and VCR system set up in the old garage.

Forsberg returned the old family rowboat to his property, hauled it up onto the bank, and climbed the hill that led to his homestead.

His mother Edna watched from the kitchen window, believing her son and his friend Ron were bringing the old plumbing system up to code. Without his father, Edna became a shut-in, finding joy in cooking, watching television, and gossiping with her friends on the phone. Claiming a spree of burglaries, Forsberg secured the garage with new doors and locks that would keep Edna—and anyone else—from gaining access to the garage.

Ron Spears stood, hands in his front pockets, waiting patiently for Forsberg's final inspection of the system. On the monitors, he could now see the spots where Lily battled the Tak-Pei in 1962, where Adam Thunderface had been shot to death by a local posse, and where Marshal Bushy Bill Morrison and Joseph Little Toad had vanished from the face of the earth after Lily thwarted the plans of the Wintermaker in 1898. He'd waited until after Lily "closed the loop" before finishing his project.

"It's a good system," Spears said over his shoulder. "Need me for anything else?"

Forsberg shook his head and Spears began walking away. "Actually...I'd like to get some dive hours in soon. If you're up for it, swing by the old quarry and figure out a discreet place to deploy."

"Anything we find on the floor of the quarry will be inadmissible evidence."

Forsberg shrugged. "I'd still like to check."

"I'll scope it out then," he answered and then shut the door without needing to say goodbye.

At least I did my part, Forsberg reflected on the quality of their work.

AFTER AN HOUR of observing his creation, Forsberg locked up the garage and walked the few yards to the old farmhouse, where his mother waited for him in the kitchen. "I have some fried chicken warming in the oven," she greeted and Brian sat down at the table like a good son.

He endured her gossip, knowing this was a rare visit. As the sheriff, with access to firsthand accounts of most scandals, it always intrigued him how the stories would come out the other end of the pipe in a much different fashion than reality.

What my mom's friends believe...is true.

After the chicken dinner, Brian almost choked on his cherry pie when his mother mentioned a name. "Slow down, Ma. What did you just say?"

She rewound the conversation three minutes, repeating it all again right up to the point he wanted repeated. "Roland Smith finished working on Ursula Hermann's new porch, but when she asked him about using the pontoon for her grandson, he told her he was planning on selling it since he was moving to an apartment in Brainerd."

"Are you talking about Ansel Nielson?" Forsberg asked.

"Of course. You told me you'd reached out to Faye about him."

"And he's going to visit Ursula?"

"Apparently, he's going to stay at her mobile home for much of the summer, which is why she had Roland Smith fixing up the mobile home before he arrives."

Fuck. I just wanted an opportunity to meet and talk not— "When is he coming?"

"Soon, I think. Ursula is coming the first of May and I think Ansel is coming as soon as school is done, but I think it's a private school, so they finished a few weeks earlier than the kids around here."

"Ansel Nielson is coming to stay with his grandmother?" Brian repeated.

Edna showed no mercy, treating the detail like other bits of gossip, when in fact, the Nielsons were cousins—but through her late husband Glen. Ansel was Brian's second-cousin. "She's just worried about the young man being bored. Maybe you could arrange for Wally Crain to take him fishing."

Brian couldn't decide if this was good or bad news. Either way, he'd need to let the Isanti Lodge know. "Ursula is part of card club with Nancy in St. John, isn't she?"

"For years now. Ursula and her husband used to have a cabin along the western shore, and apparently, Wally Crain was the one who pulled Ursula from the water. After losing the cabin, they bought the mobile home, and she all but lives here now."

Brian finished his cherry pie and stood up. He had too many irons in the fire already. He didn't need to worry about Ansel Nielson, yet the returning of Jimmy's son filled him with more dread than optimism.

CHAPTER FORTY-NINE

Hypothetically Ever After

Split Rock High School
April 21, 1986

Levi Macpherson's double-vision should have kept him home from school, but his mother rousted him from bed and sent him off without so much as a choice.

For most of the morning, he kept his head low and didn't say a word. There were plenty of obnoxious attention-seekers to make up for his low-key silence. In a way, school kept his mind off of the willow for a while.

Until lunch arrived.

99% of the student body was irrelevant, but Lacy Morrison was different. The tarnished senior also wore a mask for her classmates, but hers was a smiling, friendly demeanor. She had no idea what Levi was about to do to her—and what he'd already done. With a hand propping up his head, he studied her out of the corner of his eye.

Spring weather had already changed her wardrobe. She showed off her thighs in a miniskirt and her midriff with a shirt that could only be tucked in if dramatically stretched. When she laughed or walked, she shimmered. From what Robin told him, he knew it had to do with the unseen magic of the comet, but it still disoriented him.

After lunch, he had study hall, and with it, a chance to talk with her.

This time, he was already waiting when she came to the practice room.

"Last week of rehearsal," she purred playfully.

It was the first of many lasts, and after a bit of routine, the wheels came off because of his inability to focus. His strange double-vision problems made him nauseous.

"Are you okay?" she finally asked.

Levi shook his head and chose his words carefully. "It's my great-grandmother."

"Yeah, I got to meet her the other day."

"You did? How's she doing?"

"Um, she's, um, kinda disoriented, but a lot of residents are when they first arrive, so I wouldn't take it personally."

She's figured it out. "Personally?" he pressed.

Lacy nodded. "She's mad at you and your mom. I know it's a private family matter, but she's pretty loud about her displeasure of being brought to Golden Shores."

Rightfully so. Her plan would've given her a happy ending where she got to reunite with her long, lost love, Jean. *I stole that from her. I'd hate me, too. But it had to be done.*

Lacy put a hand on his knee. "It'll be okay. This is good for her. It's all for the best."

"All for the best," Levi repeated. "I've got a hypothetical situation for you."

"Ooh," Lacy took her hand from his knee and enthusiastically rubbed her hands together like she was about to solve a great mystery. "Lay it on me. I love our hypothetical conversations."

Levi thought of Lily, Jean, and Migisi on Deadwood Island back in 1898. Then he thought of his own conundrum. "If you had to choose between true love and family, which one would you pick?"

Lacy raised her eyebrows. "That's a tough one. Is this like a matter of life or death?"

Levi nodded. "You can only pick one—like an episode of Spiderman. On one hand, you've got sexy Mary Jane Watson suspended above a vat of boiling water, and on the other hand, you've got sweet Aunt May above a pool of piranhas."

"Oh, that's awful."

"And he's only got enough webbing to save one. Does he pick true love or family?"

"As tough as it is, I think you've gotta go family. For every Mary Jane, there's a Gwen Stacy right around the corner. Trust me: sweethearts come and go, but family is forever."

Lily chose true love. She saved Jean Guerin and also found a way to bring Migisi's spirit back up from the depths of Lake Manitou. *She still expects to win her fight. If she knows what I've done, will she fight me for the future?*

The hand went back to the knee. "Am I your true love?"

Levi laughed, knowing this was just how she flirted. "Oh, I think you're totally tubular, but as much as you wish it to be true, fate has other plans for the two of us."

"Oh, does it, Spicoli?"

"Hypothetically...I've got another question for you." Levi paused, thinking of one of his strange dreams. "If you had to choose between a guy who was safe, stable, and boring—" *David—that's her husband's name.* "And a fella who's dangerous, dramatic, and incapable of loving you back—" *Ansel. His name is Ansel.* "Which one would you pick?"

"Ooh, a good guy or a bad boy?" Lacy smiled. "Are you this bad boy?"

Levi shook his head, turning Lacy's smile into a playful frown. "I know the right answer of course, but I'm kinda stupid, so knowing me, I'll probably pick the bad boy. How's Def Leppard put it? Better to burn out than fade away. I'd rather have a flash of passion than a lifetime of mediocre."

Levi pulled the lever in his mind, and Lacy's husband David fell into the vat of boiling water, followed moments later by her precious children Paul and Kari. The hypothetical screams made Levi almost sick to his stomach and he leaned forward to almost rest his head between his knees. Lacy began petting his head as if he was a stray dog, helping him through the waves of temporal disturbance he felt rippling from the first of his strategic battles. *I've destroyed your world. How can you show me any tenderness?*

Levi sat up abruptly thinking of Lacy's happy ending built into Lily's happy ending.

Could I fix things if I lost the nerve?

Could Lily reclaim it?

Robin had shown him enough for his resolve to harden. Hopefully, he'd already destroyed the world of David, Paul, and Kari. "Hypothetically...if you knew how you were going to die, would you want to know the details?"

"No," she sassed immediately.

It was so quick that it surprised Levi. "Why not?"

"It's like that Oedipus Rex story. Most people would try to change it, and in doing so, they'd end up making the prophecy happen. Except now, instead of blaming God for their fate, they can only blame themselves for their free will choices. There's no way I'd want to know my future."

Then I guess it's up to me to decide how Lacy Morrison will die. The willow showed him multiple futures, and now that Lily secured the past by closing her loops, he could change the future rather than allowing it to come true. In both scenarios, his loved ones still died, but in only one future did they find a way to defeat the Wintermaker.

Damn you, Robin Berg.

Damn you for making me choose.

CHAPTER FIFTY

Playing with Fire

Leech Lake
April 30, 1986

The fires of Bel, known to the Celts as Beltane, were lit as a sacrifice on the night prior to May Day. One of the traditions was to build a giant wicker man and place a human sacrifice inside of the willow branches before setting it on fire.

Now Lily Guerin prepared to light her own fire.

She knew all about Beltane because of her research into willow and willow trees. Her people revered the willow tree and used its branches for the creation of dreamcatchers, so she spent much of her life trying to understand the magic that flowed in and around Lake Manitou. When she'd accepted Jesus Christ as her Lord and Savior back at the Sacred Heart Mission, she meant it, unlike the other children who were forced to make the profession of faith. She ran away from Grandfather Nanakonan into the arms of Father Jean Guerin to protect her faith, only to have him push her back toward the paganism of the old woods.

Evil was real.

Monsters were real.

Miracles were real.

The Creator was real.

In spending her ten decades of life trying to understand the mysteries of her world, Lily certainly explored other religions despite worrying about lessons learned by Solomon. Solomon's gift from God, wisdom, ultimately corrupted him later in life when he turned away from God and to the gods of his foreign wives. *Am I being punished for having an unfaithful heart? Is God jealous?*

In the first few days after the betrayal, she fought with all her energy to make them understand, but once her weary mind and body got some rest, she understood that Levi willfully destroyed her plans and would continue if she didn't stop him.

So she shut her mouth and kept it shut for almost a month, making small talk only when the doctors and nurses spoke to her.

It worked.

She tricked them all—the nurses, her family, the Isanti Lodge.

Almost three weeks after floating down the Blue Knife River, she floated down the hallway of the Golden Shores Nursing Home for lunch in the commons. They planted her in front of a table with her back to the lake.

I promise…no more outbursts. I understand my situation completely.

She slowly ate what was set in front of her and pondered her situation. The good news was that she closed the loops, locking the events of her youth into the fabric of reality. The bad news was that Levi and Nicole foiled her plans to be reunited with Jean, and even worse, threatened the coming confrontation with the Wintermaker.

Wally Crain loomed over her shoulder before he knelt beside her wheelchair. He placed his hand gently on her hand. "It's good to see you, Lily."

Keep him in the dark. She cleared her throat. "You too, old friend. We now move into the final preparations. We have secured the past but must now prepare the future." Lily carefully prepared her question to determine if Wally remained loyal. "Will I still be moved to Turtle Island during the summer solstice?"

Wally nodded and smiled. "It's good to see the old Lily. Yes, with you looking so much stronger, we'll continue with the plan."

"Good," Lily said, thinking of the Wicker Man burning. *Perhaps this can all still be fixed.* "And the members of the Isanti Lodge…are they well?"

Wally's wrinkled forehead gave her the answer. "Yes, everybody is well. Sheriff Forsberg has done an exceptional job watching over the lake." Finally he got to his concern. "I…um…have a couple of questions for you."

"Go ahead."

"The role of the Wa-bi-zha-shi, the warrior, is filled by Sakima Riel, but in a few weeks, Ed Nielson's grandson is coming to Lake Manitou on his own account. Should we try to include him in the ritual?"

Lily knew what she wanted to say: *it doesn't matter.* As a young Christian, she prayed to be delivered from evil, and for her faith, her precious Jean was returned to her and she was given a decade of joy. Now the price had to be paid in flesh and blood. "Sakima has been properly trained for his duties, so I don't think it is wise to throw a young boy into the mix at such a late hour."

Wally nodded. "Speaking of boys…your granddaughter Nicole is threatening to remove Levi from the ritual. She still doesn't know the truth about your canoe ride, but she has her suspicions. After your hospital visit, you said some strange things about Levi and—"

"I was exhausted," Lily bluffed. *If I keep fighting my confinement here, I'll only make things worse.* "My tired mind played tricks on me, and I got a bit confused."

"So we'll continue with our plans to have Levi at the ritual at Bleeding Rock?"

For her adult life, she'd been prepared to double-cross the Wintermaker at the very end, but now, her great-grandson double-crossed her, making her want to surrender them to their fate. As a young woman, her free will could take down monsters, but now as an old woman, she surrendered to the inevitable: the Wintermaker would rise regardless of what she did.

"Yes, we'll continue with our plans."

Perhaps in the coming days, I'll find a way to reunite with Jean.

SHORTLY AFTER BREAKFAST, another guest visited her—Karson Luning. Although he had the darker pigmentation of his mother, she could still see features of Albert Fisher and Farrell Luning in his face.

The two sat at a small table that faced Lake Manitou.

"I've been thinking of 'The Song of the Manitou,'" Karson declared after making small talk. "What do you think it is?"

"My grandfather Nanakonan said that the Wijigan Clan passed it down from generation to generation, and the words were powerful spells meant to control the Water Drum during the ritual."

"But where did it come from? How old is the Water Drum? The Anishinaabe stories say that it was used in the creation of the world. Do you believe this to be true?"

Lily took several breaths before answering. "I think it is likely, but having held the Philosopher's Stone in my hands, I do not believe it was the force that created the world. There was a malevolent spirit upon it, even though it was not made of flesh. The words given to me were commands that the Stone obeyed, so the Song of the Manitou has likely existed since the creation of the Stone."

"So the days of the Dawn are another way of referencing the Genesis era, at least, the time before the flood, the old world."

Lily nodded, suddenly concerned Karson was trying to trick her. *Does he serve another master also?*

Karson kept pressing. "Your grandfather only gave you bits and pieces of the song during your training?"

Is Levi using him to get the song away from me? "So I would not do what I foolishly ended up doing anyway—waking the evil that slumbered in Lake Manitou."

"And Joseph Little Toad, the heretical Wijigan priest, his ritual didn't work because he had a flawed version of the song, which means that somewhere out there is the original version."

"That is what allowed me to defeat the Wintermaker and cast aside the Tak-Pei," Lily said boldly. "My prayers were answered. I was given the rest of the song by an apparition. The magic within the Stone opened a window in time and I was given enough of the Song to stand against the Wintermaker."

Karson scoffed a little. "What happens if our window doesn't open up during our ritual?"

It no longer matters. "We must put ourselves in the hands of our Creator. We must trust that our way is the light in the darkness."

"Huh," Karson pondered. "Regardless, I'm glad we've got you. We'll get you rested and recharged and ready for June."

THE DAY RUSHED by as Lily remembered the old memories dug up by restless men. She intended to go along with the plan, not letting the others know that Levi had foiled her plan to escape the confrontation.

She wilted in her chair—finally ready to submit after a lifetime of fighting.

Do what you want with me, God.

The Wintermaker is Your problem now.

I can't do this.

And then laughter interrupted her silent prayers.

It was so loud, so youthful, so arrogant, that anger boiled up in her, manifesting itself in pursed lips. Her hands took hold of the wheelchair and she spun herself around.

On the other side of the commons, she saw two young blonde women in the middle of a conversation.

"Who is that?" Lily asked a nearby resident.

"That's the girl who plays the piano. The Morrison girl."

Morrison! The Order of Eos stole her land, killed her family, and murdered Jean Guerin at the hands of Bushy Bill Morrison. "No, the other one."

"That's…the Knutson girl. Molly Chauvin. She's in the office most of the time."

Molly Chauvin. Lily didn't know the name, but she began wheeling closer to them. At fifteen yards, both young women noticed her approaching.

The Morrison girl hustled over. "How was your day, Lily?"

"I don't—"

"I'm Levi's friend, Lacy."

Lily ignored her and reached out a hand to Molly Chauvin, who joined them. "Hello, Lily. Do you need something?"

She lifted her own hand, covering half of the young woman's face. *No, she's the right age but it isn't her. How do I know you?*

Lily closed her eyes and searched her dreams.

"Okay, Lily," Lacy Morrison said. "Let's get you back to your room to rest."

Lily felt her body rolling away.

"You will visit me in the year 1986."

Lily dropped her feet forcing Lacy Morrison to halt. "Lily?"

The Little Spider!

She was supposed to meet the Little Spider on the bridge. The one she saw in the dreamcatcher. The young woman had a disfigured face—the same woman who helped her with the Song of the Manitou. The Little Spider was on a bicycle. She knew her name. She knew Joey. *She's alive and out there somewhere.*

Lacy cleared her throat and spoke again, "Is something wrong Lily?"

I'm not dead yet. Perhaps there is still a chance. "Take me back. I need to speak with Molly."

The Morrison girl covered the length of the commons in just a few heartbeats, allowing Lily to remember the vision she'd had during her darkest hours after the deaths of her mother, father, and grandfather.

She'd taken her newly made dreamcatcher and brought it down to the metal bridge, and inside the windows of the dreamcatcher, she'd communicated with two women from the future.

Levi took them away from me.

The Little Spider was supposed to be waiting at the bridge.

Molly Chauvin saw them returning. "Is something wrong, Lily?"

My great-grandson is meddling in matters he doesn't understand. "You...you have a daughter, don't you?"

Molly looked puzzled. "I do."

"And she likes to ride her bicycle, doesn't she?"

"We just got her that bicycle for her birthday last fall."

"What is her name?"

"Sommer."

Sommer Chauvin—the Little Spider. "She's classmates with my great-grandson Joey, isn't she?"

"Ah, that's how you know her," Molly said with a strange sense of relief.

"I'd very much like it if you could bring her here. I'd like to visit with her."

"I'm sure that can be arranged," Molly said.

You played your tricks, Levi, and now I'll play mine.

CHAPTER FIFTY-ONE

Witenagemot

Kanaranzi Creek
May 12, 1986

The Crow Wing River begins in southern Hubbard County near the town of Akeley and flows southward for 113 miles until it reaches the Mississippi past the town of Pillager. It is considered one of Minnesota's best "wilderness" routes due to its thick forests and consistent depths. The Ojibwe Indians referred to it as Gaagaagiwigwani-ziibi, which loosely translates to "Raven-Feather River." Strangely, the county of Crow Wing has its name despite only sharing a few yards of its mouth. Most of the waterway passes through the heart of Hiawatha County.

Although most of the bridges spanning the Crow Wing River were relatively small, its watershed stretched into nine counties: Becker, Cass, Clearwater, Crow Wing, Hubbard, Morrison, Otter Tail, Todd, and Hiawatha. With 1,653 streams and 627 lakes feeding it, the watershed filled a territory of 1,245,214 acres.

For this reason, Carey "Scat" Jensen sat on Brian Forsberg's porch smoking a joint.

Jensen was a river rat, one that Forsberg had known since kindergarten. Raised by wolves, Jensen dropped out of school in ninth grade and quickly became a cagey criminal, and as a result, he had a decade's head start on understanding the underbelly of society. Rail thin with wiry muscles, Jensen wore a stained tank top, oversized bib overalls, and mud-darkened leather boots. The fingers holding the joint were oily and creased with dirt, which not even steel wool could make clean.

Scat was also Forsberg's oldest surviving friend.

Middle school boys originally nicknamed him Muskrat—one of the staples in Jensen's early trapping days—and modified the name to Skrat and then Scat, when someone pointed out it was another name for animal feces. Scat's sixth-sense interrupted the conversation, and his beady eyes began to blink quicker like the ping of a radar. "You speckin' somebody?"

On County Road 30, a car slowed.

"Probably the priest."

Jensen rolled his eyes, and after a drag from the joint, pinched it with his teeth on the right side of his mouth, allowing him to grab his Old Milwaukee Light can and his leather gloves off the table between them.

Without even saying goodbye, Jensen walked off the porch and scurried down the hill. At the bottom of the ravine, Scat hopped into his twelve-foot long jon boat and sped downriver.

Geri and Freki, Forsberg's German Shepherds, also heard the approaching vehicle, yet it surprised him Father Gary Mackenzie had shown the moxie to locate his house.

As instructed, Big Mack honked his horn three times.

"Stay," Forsberg said when his dogs growled. If not for the horn and command, they would have gone into wolf mode.

His shepherds sat on their haunches of the front porch and watched Big Mack as he stepped through the trees and out onto an open yard. Forsberg wore a white tank top, a pair of blue jeans, and a red and gold silk kimono large enough to fit a sumo wrestler. While the delicate kimono looked out of character, Forsberg still had a shotgun leaning against the faux-log siding of the new log cabin kit home he had personally built. "Morning, Padre, the gal at the Boondocks Cafe must've delivered the message."

"I got the message," Big Mack said.

"To come all the way out here, you must be a man on a mission."

"Actually, I *am* on a mission,"

Forsberg made a clicking noise, and the two dogs rushed from the porch and circled Father Gary as he finished the last stretch of his journey.

"You been talking to my ma again?" Forsberg asked, reaching for his bottle of Lord Calvert whiskey with one hand and two glasses with the other. He set them down on a table between a couple of chairs. "I took her out for Mother's Day, and all she could talk about was at least going to church with her on the holidays."

"Edna did come and talk to me this past Sunday, but it didn't have anything to do with the status of your eternal soul."

"Good." Forsberg gave a hearty chuckle and wiped his mustache with his handkerchief. "I think the woman is convinced I'm going straight to hell for not attending mass. If I'm destined to go to hell, skipping mass is the least of my offenses." Forsberg poured two glasses of whiskey without even asking. He glanced out at his twenty acres of woods. "So what did my ma come talk to you about then?"

"She's worried about how you're dealing with the Nielson boy coming home?"

"I've got more important things to worry about than some weird kid from New York."

Big Mack sighed in frustration. "Your mom is worried about you. I'm not sure how many people around here remember what happened a decade ago with those kids, and it's been twenty years since Jim Nielson even lived in Split Rock, but I know that *you know* what happened."

"And what does any of this have to do with me?"

"Brian, I know that you are holding onto something. I can tell every time I look you in the eyes."

Forsberg looked directly into the eyes of Big Mack. "So is that what this is? You've got some sort of guilt about what happened to Jimmy Nielson and want to make amends with me?" Forsberg listened to Scat's boat motor make a turn in the distance before turning to the priest. "I know what kind of man you are, Padre. You army chaplains just never give up. And I respect that. But you need to just let this one go."

"Now maybe you have everybody else fooled, but you don't have me fooled. I know what you boys went through."

Forsberg simply shook his head at Big Mack's relentlessness. "What can I do for you, Father?"

"Suicides are incredibly difficult to understand, and for most people, it takes years to just push the pain to the backburner. But with Ansel returning, it is an opportunity—"

"Forget it," Forsberg interrupted. *I am not going to throw him into the coming ritual.* "I think I know what you want me to do, and I'm not going to have anything to do with it."

"Could you just stop thinking about yourself for a minute? Don't you owe it to Ansel to at least stop and talk to him about his father?"

Forsberg set his glass down on a railing and stood up. With a nod of his head, he gestured for Big Mack to follow, who obliged in like fashion. Behind the house, the Crow Wing River flowed by from right to left, and the valley was filled with old forest growth. A simple trail led down the slope toward the riverbank, where his small shack and wooden fishing pier had been built.

But Forsberg stopped at the top of the hill and pointed in the distance.

"Do you see that?"

"See what?" Big Mack asked as the German shepherds sniffed around the back of the house.

"Follow the treeline," Pointing with his index finger, Forsberg traced the green horizon where it contrasted with the blue sky until it stopped at a slight dip on the far riverbank. "There. Do you see it?"

Father Gary nodded.

"That is Buffalo Creek, which some farmers named. I could not find a Chippewa name for it, but the Dakota called it Kanaranzi, which translates to *the place where the Kansas died.*"

"Kansas?"

"The Indian tribe, not the state. The Dakota feared Lake Manitou while the Chippewa revered it, and when the Dakota still guarded this territory, they killed anyone who passed by, including a Kansas warrior."

"Kanaranzi...very ominous."

"With the primary outlet of Split Rock Creek, old Kanaranzi Creek doesn't have much flow to it, especially during dry years. The silt likes to catch trees and, with the river grass, plugs up the mouth, making it almost invisible to folks going up or down the Crow Wing River."

"Why are you showing me this?" Big Mack asked, exasperated.

"I just keep going over the history in my head. Halley's Comet arrived a few weeks ago, and not a day has gone by where I don't expect death and mayhem to strike my county. So when I am done with my shift each day as Sheriff, I come here, a watcher on the hill, waiting for the Wintermaker to arrive."

"Luckily for you, summer will be here soon."

"The summer solstice, the longest day of the year, will be here on June 20th, which is when the old druids claimed evil spirits would be at their strongest. So tell Ma that I am fully aware that Jimmy's son has returned home and that I intend to speak with him the first chance I get. Have you been meeting with Migisi?"

Father Gary looked at his shoes, raised his head a bit, and nodded.

"Good. Has he shown you his turtle shield and hatchet?"

Father Gary nodded.

"That hatchet...it's the same one that was used to murder his grandfather Nanakonan. Next time you see him, have him tell you the story of Iyash and the Thunderbird. Put your energy into that. I promise you, when things pass, I'll work on fixing me. You can have as much porch time as you need once this is over."

CHAPTER FIFTY-TWO

The Betrayal of Verðandi

Oak Island, Nova Scotia
May 13, 1986

The private helicopter flew into Mahone Bay from the Atlantic, a tactic Tomas Dobie understood. He'd arrived in Halifax by private jet and taxied to the Sinclair Mansion in a manner that none of the local residents could notice.

Although only a thug for Eos, his bloodline allowed him to keep abreast on the workings of the secret society. He eagerly awaited news from Israel.

Below him, Oak Island came into view. It'd changed quite a bit since his childhood. William Sinclair's three-story stone mansion was exactly the same, but now, a paved road ran from the causeway to the mansion. The greatest change was the most controversial: a visitor's center. Instead of privacy, the new resident embraced legends and lore, proudly sharing tales with visitors of a secret treasure vault with theories connected to the Ark of the Covenant, Captain Kidd's lost treasure, and the lost Templar treasure. In a way, all three prominent rumors had merit, for the Order of Eos had indeed used the island since the 1300s. Even though the Eos elders protested, the visitor center was a clever plan, especially since the vault had been empty since the early 1700s. Now, curicuriosity could be controlled with private tours of the island, which also allowed a reason for private security for the island's sole occupant—Miss Madeline Sinclair.

Aleister Sinclair's vibrant daughter—and heir to his business empire—came out of a side door of the mansion as the helicopter lowered onto the tarmac. As a boy, Tomas remembered sitting around fires as he was taught by another vibrant redhead: Saara Olavintytär. Maddy Sinclair, a youthful twenty-something, certainly was the age to be their daughter.

"Welcome back, Tom," she said, squinting as her hair whipped in her face from the chopper blades.

"How was Israel?" Tom asked.

Maddy scoffed, "We'll talk about Israel once you've had something to drink."

AN HOUR LATER, the two sat in front of a large fireplace in plush chairs angled slightly to face the fire while also allowing conversation. Tom used to have conversations here with the old man.

She hummed. "So tell me about Hvergelmir. How are things in the Land of Roaring Water?"

Fuck Minnesota. What news from Israel? In Norse legend, the World Tree, known to some as Yggdrasil and others as Laerad, had three places where its roots connected to the world: Urðarbrunnr, the Well of Wisdom; Mímisbrunnr, the Primordial gate in the land of the giants; and Hvergelmir, discovered in the realm of ice—Minnesota. The location of Hvergelmir made sense considering for thousands of years, glaciers covered Minnesota, and when they withdrew, left behind 10,000 lakes, including Lake Manitou.

"The Roaring Waters are surprisingly calm," he reported.

"Just wait—the Fossegrim will stir the pot," Maddy said. Despite her youthful beauty, she had the spirit of an old woman behind her eyes—and for good reason.

She won't tell me about Israel until I update her on Minnesota. "We still haven't found the men we lost in February. While it's certainly possible that the Fossegrim turned on them during the sacrifice, in my gut, I think our enemies took them."

"The Periphery?" Maddy asked. Tom shook his head, prompting another quick guess from her. "Surely not the old Jesuit Order."

"I'm convinced there might be local interference. You know the history of Hvergelmir; it's a cursed place for *all* who go there."

Maddy nodded. "Aside from our first offering, the local news coverage has been silent. Only powerful enemies could silence the media."

Offering? The boy's name was Modi. We both knew him well. "When we return for the Summer Solstice, you'll find the spirits will be ready to be commanded. They are well-fed and ready to hear music from the dawn."

"Promise me you won't overreact." Maddy flashed her charm as she made the request.

"What happened in Israel?" Tomas asked coldly.

Maddy blushed—a strange reaction. Her eyes went to her lap, and then up to the ceiling, before finally gazing into the fire to answer without looking at him. "Aron-Miku made contact with one of the Norns."

Tomas swallowed hard. He knew quite well what was in Israel. At the ancient cave of Panaeus, a stream came out of Mount Hermon that once was rumored to be a gateway to the underworld. The bubbling little stream eventually became the River Jordan and emptied far off into the salty Dead Sea, but just a few hundred yards from its headwaters, an ancient willow took root at a place known to Dobie's ancestors as Urðarbrunnr, the Well of Wisdom.

Maddy and Aron-Miku had visited one of the three roots of Laerad.

"Your father warned you about using the tree."

"Urðarbrunnr didn't lie! We still don't know what happened with your uncle, Charani Bessant, and the others, do we? Perhaps the vision was misread, or perhaps something simply went wrong. We have access to one of the greatest wonders of the earth. Why shouldn't we use it?"

Through the years, Tomas had sent dozens of private detectives to both Hiawatha County and also Nepal to find his Uncle Red and the others who vanished in 1962. While rumors of Charani Bessant still persisted, no trace of his Uncle Red or the others were ever found in the dam disaster. "You're young, Maddy. And with youth—"

"I'm not a fucking child, Tom. I know how dangerous Laerad is. Cousin Val and Alphonse will be arriving next week, so I'm not about to get cold feet just because of some voices calling out from a tree, okay? But you *need* to know what the old goat heard."

Heidrun—the goat that lived under the roots of Laerad. She said that on purpose. What is she thinking? "Okay, tell me."

"As you know, the three Norns live within the roots of the World Tree. Urd is the old woman, representing the past; Skuld is the future; and Verdandi is the present."

Tomas seethed, remembering how his Uncle Red had also visited the willow, only to see the Goddess of Death, Hela, waiting for them at the end of the story. He nodded for her to continue.

"We made contact with Verðandi, and in the vision, she tried to warn us about what was happening in Hvergelmir. She said that our plans would fail, and that Fimbulvetr, the triple-winter, would be used to destroy the Order of Eos root and stem, leaving nothing behind for a rebirth of humanity. She said that our enemies have taken hold of the future and know of our plans. She said we are about to be tricked."

Dobie's ancestors believed that the world was caught in a constant battle of fire and ice, where the world was destroyed again and again. When Odin learned of the endless cycle, he did his best to stop it from happening again. Even though Odin died in the last battle, his sacrifice brought a changed world, where mankind survived and replenished the world without the gods. But not all the immortals perished. Four Aesir survived the war only to be buried alive. Surtr the Fire Giant, the sole survivor for the giants, was also buried alive. The Order of Eos existed to make sure the sacrifices of Odin were not in vain, so they searched the world for one of the Aesir before their enemies unearthed Surtr.

In Norse legends, Loki played the role of the Trickster, his loyalties divided between the Aesir of Odin and the evil giants of Surtr. In the previous conflict, he betrayed Odin and helped the giants destroy Asgard. Now, a new Trickster threatened the future.

Only in victory can our world be restored. "We are on the verge of waking a sleeping god, Maddy," Tomas said bitterly. "Generation after generation, the Order of Eos has moved steadily to this moment, and now leadership has passed to us to complete it. The last step is to wake him."

"If Verðandi knows what we are doing, why would she warn us?"

Don't lose your nerve. "What do we know of the Norns?" Tomas asked. "Yes, Odin went to them for answers, but if they were truly allies, shouldn't they have given him better advice? What if they work against us? If we succeed, how does that change their role? We will control our own fate, won't we?"

"Aron-Miku and I discussed this before we agreed to tell you about it. We agree that Verðandi could be guiding us to a future that serves only her interest, which is why we must be ready to shape the World Tree to our liking."

And there it is. "The old goat."

"Aron-Miku reminded me that prophecy is difficult to understand and control, which is why we will act as the old goat Heidrun, who nibbles away at the new growth of the World Tree, preventing it from going in a direction we don't like. Perhaps Delhut is right, and our plan is meant to fail; perhaps my father is right, and we will bring about a rebirth of humanity; or perhaps Verðandi speaks the truth, and the three of us will save the Order of Eos from destruction by being watchful."

Beautiful but brilliant, Tomas Dobie thought, and nodded in agreement. *One day, she will lead the Order of Eos—if we survive the coming days.*

CHAPTER FIFTY-THREE

Repeat After Me

Chippewa Beach
May 16, 1986

Disoriented, Ansel Nielson woke in his bed at Lake Manitou. Screaming thunderbirds, filled with lightning and fury, transformed into the croaking parrots.

Parrots made sense. His Grandma Ursula had two pet parrots, Donald and Daffy, who lived in a cage at the very front of her mobile home.

Above him, he noticed the white ceiling tiles, which had only a few yellow water stains from predictable weathering after being parked at the Chippewa Beach Mobile Home Park for the past twenty years. His bedroom was the opposite side of the mobile home from the parrots, a 10x10 wood-paneled square with three windows, a closet, and the door that led to the only hallway.

Sitting up on his elbows, he was thankful his reality wasn't filled with the spiders and blood splatter from his dreams. Three of his four boxes were still sealed and packed, left against the wall by his grandmother after she received them via mail delivery prior to his arrival. The fourth box, discreetly identified by a small puncture hole he'd made in the bottom left corner, had been sealed exactly as he'd sent it, allowing him to transfer the .357 Magnum from the box to his black backpack, which waited for him like a trusty dog beside his bed.

In the middle of the floor, his suitcase remained wide open. Despite having arrived two days earlier, his mom navigated the transition to his summer home the first few days, but she and Thomas had returned home to leave for their summer trip to Greece. Now Ansel was alone with Grandma Ursula.

Ansel sat up. He wore only boxers since the air conditioning was "on the fritz." Physically, his body was well rested even though his mind was exhausted after playing mental chess for most of the night. With his hands on his knees, Ansel pondered his fragile brain along with his clothing choice.

I have a choice.
I can be the hero that the dream people need me to be.
Just push all that other shit back into the darkness.

His emotions and anxieties boiled just below the surface, and Ansel took a deep calming breath and chose to be the hero instead of the villain...today.

"Good morning," he said after walking down the dark hallway past the bathroom and Ursula's bedroom. The front hall of the mobile home housed an open kitchen with a small dining table, an L-shaped living room with a floor console television, and the parrot cage.

Grandma Ursula was nested in the recliner facing the television, which played "The Price is Right." She lowered her inclined feet and spun the recliner around. "I have some rolls sitting on the counter and some orange juice. Help yourself."

Don't be an asshole. Don't antagonize the people trying to help you. Ansel nodded his head, cleared his throat, and softly said, "Thank you."

She spun around, content.

Ursula Hermann was an obese woman, a heavy smoker, and from all accounts, a terrible mother due to her alcoholism. Yet she'd been the one who lobbied the hardest when the "Minnesota Vacation" plan was being hatched. Jimmy Nielson's suicide fractured both sides of the family. Ursula had lobbied for her daughter to bring the family to Indiana, which is where Jimmy was now buried. In the subsequent years, none of his relatives, maternal or paternal, knew how to deal with him or Tonya. Aside from a few postcards, Ansel knew little about any of them. His mother left both Indiana and Minnesota far behind, rarely traveling any farther west than New Jersey. Several tragedies over a short span in time had taken Ursula's son-in-law, husband, and Jimmy's parents, leaving her a shell of the woman he'd known before Shane and Cindy Lewis came to Indiana. Ansel could see Grandma Ursula did not have much fight left in her, so he was thankful she'd let him come to Lake Manitou.

He sat on the couch and chewed on a roll as he prepared what to say. According to the raven, the future of humanity was on the line, so he couldn't spend all summer watching Bob Barker. After weighing several starting statements, Ansel took a different tactic. "I need your help."

Ursula spun the chair in his direction. "What's the problem?"

"I don't want to be a burden to you all summer," he began. "I know Thomas gave you money to keep me entertained, but that's unfair to you."

He watched Ursula's face begin a false protest that never came because he continued speaking, "He gave me a wad of money for entertainment, and I've thought of all sorts of ways to keep myself busy. What do you think I should do with it?"

"Oh, what a good problem to have," Ursula mocked. "I'm afraid the two of us probably don't have much in common. Your Grandpa's fishing poles are still in the closet. You could try fishing."

Ansel grimaced. While his father was a real life boy scout, he was a city kid. "I don't really know what I'm doing."

"Well, I could give Wally Crain a call. He's a dear friend. He used to take my husband to all the best fishing holes on Lake Manitou."

Wally was a mentor to his father. "Fishing is a good idea," Ansel said even though it kinda repulsed him.

"Your mother said you love music and that you were attending a pretty fancy arts school in New York. If you like music, there's M&M

Music in St. John. They've got records, cassettes, and even CDs and instruments. But no drums."

Ansel looked down at his forearms, which were without scars or even a cast. "I'd like to learn how to play guitar. "I could get headphones and you'd never hear me even playing."

She quietly vetted the suggestion before saying, "There's a good bookstore in Park Rapids. Do you like to read?"

"I do, and all of these are really good ideas," Ansel admitted, "but I feel bad that you're going to have to chauffeur me around everywhere. Back home, I could hop on the ferry or subway and do my own thing, but out here, everything is so spread out."

"Honestly, Ansel, I don't mind bringing you places."

I need to be able to check things out without her watching. Ansel played it out in his mind. Despite her best intentions, her enthusiasm would certainly wane as the summer went along. If he was to play the part of the hero, as the raven offered, he couldn't be limited by Ursula's mood and availability. "I wish I could drive. I've thought about getting a bicycle, but Hiawatha County is so big."

Ansel let the details sit for a few minutes. For things to work, he needed her to arrive at the idea or else the idea would be vetoed.

"I have an idea," she said. "I've seen kids even younger than you driving them. We could look at getting you a three-wheeler."

"A tricycle?" He teased, playing dumb.

Ursula laughed just as heartily as she had in his rehearsed conversation. "No, it's like a motorcycle with big, fat tires. A lot of farm kids have them for farm work, but I've seen more and more just driving down ditches. I don't think you're allowed to take them on roads and highways, but I think a three-wheeler would be perfect for your stay this summer. We'll just sell it before your mother returns in August and she'll be none the wiser. What do you think?"

When Ansel had looked into the black eyes of the raven, he felt as if he could see someone else looking back at him. If he was going to do what the raven wanted him to do, he needed mobility. "Yeah, that's a great idea. It's like you read my mind."

"Tomorrow is Saturday. We'll drive into Brainerd and see what we can find. I think it's a good plan for both of us."

Ansel knew better than to hug her. To pay for the ride to Brainerd, all he needed to do was sit on the couch, watch her television programs, and keep any weird shit out of the conversation.

Once he had his three-wheeler, then he could explore the truth about his father.

CHAPTER FIFTY-FOUR

Bowling with Balboa

Old Copper Road
May 17, 1986

Levi Macpherson watched his younger brother continue to struggle with the climb up the hill. He sat on the tall wooden post of the bullpen, which connected to the barn nearest the woods that led to Lake Manitou.

Joey, dressed in an oversize Def Leppard shirt that Levi had given him, threw his hands up in despair. The heavy object he carried rolled ten yards down the hill until it struck a log that had fallen horizontally against the slope. "It's too heavy."

Levi leaned his black felt hat back onto his head; his hair draped down behind it to his shoulders. "I know, bud. You're way stronger than I was at your age. I need you to show me that you can do this, okay? Show me how strong you are. You almost had it all the way up before you let go."

"I can't do it," Joey protested.

"Yes, you can," Levi insisted. The heels of his snakeskin boots rested on one of the thick boards of the bullpen fence, where his father's prized bull stayed during the winter. "We've gone over this a bunch of times. You agreed. You said you could do it."

"I know, but the rope hurts my hands," Joey whined, standing halfway between the fallen tree and the top of the hill where Levi waited.

The slope of Lake Manitou made his brother look even smaller, which caused Levi to question his impending plan. Then he thought of a solution. "We'll get you some gloves for game day, okay? Show me how strong you are."

After a moment, Joey resolutely nodded and returned to the log. He picked up the rope and took out the slack from the eight-foot length. The knot top on the burlap sack turned to Joey and the heavy object began to move through the leaves and twigs of the woods.

Joey struggled with his balance.

"Hey, I want you to try something, Joey. Turn around and face me."

Joey obliged and pivoted, wrapping himself in rope.

"Now hold the rope in your hands in front of you, but slip the rope onto your shoulder so you drag it rather than pulling it backwards. Hold it like Santa Claus holds his toy bag."

The suggestion worked, and instead of falling down onto his butt with every tug, Joey was now able to reach out his left hand to balance. Soon, the heavy object passed the spot where Joey had previously run out of gas.

"That's awesome. You're almost to the top," Levi called out. He heard a door open and close in the main part of the barn. Across Lake Manitou, he could still see the sun in the western sky, which made it earlier than his father or any of his other brothers normally returned to the barn.

"You are a rock star, little man," Levi said when Joey stepped onto the level ground in front of the fence. "I knew I could count on you."

Joey extended the end of the rope to Levi, who nodded his head. "All the way up to the summit."

The barn door of the empty bullpen opened, and his father stepped out. He wore a short-sleeved buttoned shirt and a pair of pressed slacks, which meant he had not come out to the barn for a forgotten chore. He was even without his faded red International Harvester cap, and thus revealed the deeply-receded hairline and farmer's tan across his brow.

"What's this all about?"

"*Rocky IV* training montage," Levi said with a smirk as Joey doubled his efforts to get back to the top again. "Do you remember the scene where Rocky works out in the Russian barn? Joey's going to be the strongest kid in first grade next fall."

"You don't say," his dad said distantly, standing behind Levi at the fence. For a moment, his father simply gazed at the sun and the glistening waters beyond the trees. "What's in the burlap sack?"

"It's your old bowling ball," Joey said with a hint of glee that Levi might get in trouble.

His dad sighed and shook his head. "I don't know what to do with the two of you."

Levi studied his father for a moment and realized he'd always been a farmer, just like his younger brother Daniel seemed to be born into the life. Joey was odd, which is why Levi wanted to protect him most of all—even from bullies that were supernatural.

"Don't forget about band rehearsal this afternoon. You know how important it is to your mother."

Since betraying Lily by bringing her to the house rather than back to Leech Lake, his mother had become an overly-caffeinated ostrich refusing to remove her head from the sands of St. Marie's Catholic Church. Levi was now starting to understood her trauma. "I'll be there."

His father slowly walked away, paused for a step, and then kept walking.

"So do I get the Metallica shirt?" Joey asked after their father vanished into the barn.

"Yes, but you can't wear it around Mom or she'll take it away or toss it in the garbage. You know how she is."

"Yep," Joey said and slipped right through the boards on the fence. "When do I get to do it for real?"

"Soon, Joe, very soon." Together, they followed their father's path through the main part of the barn and out the front door. Their father was halfway across the yard when a car entered the driveway.

When Lacy Morrison stopped and got out of the car, Levi's heart fluttered a bit, but when she walked up to his father, Levi almost had to steady himself against his little brother.

It was stupid of me to get Lacy involved with Lily.

I'm trying to save her, and instead I put her at risk.

Levi turned to the other person he loved and fought to save. "Handshake," Levi said to his brother. For the past few weeks, Levi had been preparing his little brother for the coming war. The plan had been practiced and their bond strengthened. The handshake had been one of the first steps. *Spock, knuckles, thumbwar, fistbump. He's got it.* "Tell Mom I won't be late."

Joey solemnly nodded and then ran to catch up to his father.

Levi's heart lifted when he saw Lacy's body language and slight skip. She tousled Joey's hair as he walked by. She smiled and then pointed to her cheek, which was bruised. With her other hand, she flashed a piece of yellow paper.

"What's that?"

"A shiner," she said with a light scoff, "courtesy of your Gigi."

"Lily hit you?"

"Slapped me thanks to you and your stupid plan. It was embarrassing. Everyone was looking at me, and she was saying all sorts of stuff about being a Morrison. Wow, that woman can be nasty." She shoved the yellow paper into his chest and stood a step closer.

Lacy's cheek wasn't swollen. He glanced down at the paper and took it from her. "She gave this to you?"

"No, I took it. I've been watching her closely, just like you said to, and last Saturday, I saw her pull Sommer Chauvin aside and give her a package and a few pieces of yellow paper."

"Sommer Chauvin?" Levi repeated to calm his panic.

300   Jason Lee Willis

"She's a kid I babysit from time to time. She's Molly's daughter—the personnel manager at Golden Shores. I'm pretty sure she's in Joey's grade. Apparently, Lily convinced Molly to bring her daughter into work, but I was too busy to find out what Lily said to her. When I got there today, I saw Lily writing more stuff down. What do you think it is?"

Son of a bitch. To most, it would look like gibberish written down by a lunatic, but Levi had been trained by Lily for the past year. Lily had written down the phonetic breakdown of the Song of the Manitou.

"What is it?" Lacy insisted.

Levi quickly folded it up and slipped it into his back pocket. He looked up to the house to see if he could spot his mother. Just like his mom foiled all of Lily's final plans, she could still destroy his plans if he allowed her to rule over him as a parent. He reached into his front pockets for his keys. "Let's go for a little ride. I'll explain it to you."

Lacy put both hands on her hips and reverted back to her flirty self. "Sounds fun. Where are we going?"

I'm moving heaven and earth for you, and you don't have a clue. "Just a short drive."

A FEW MINUTES later, the Mustang was driving down Old Copper Road at such a slow pace that a kid on a bicycle could have passed them. It also allowed Levi to speak with Lacy.

Since his visit to the willow, his heart had fallen for Lacy Morrison. He'd seen the truth about her family history, but he'd also seen her future in the branches of the tree. In each branch, she was not just beautiful but also tragically sweet.

I'm doing this for her, too.

"That's where Lily used to live," Levi said, pointing to the ruins of the abandoned homestead. "That was before the fire and the flood took it all away. Lily was a Firehandler, a type of Anishinaabe sorceress. If the stories about her are true, she apparently used her magic to defeat the Manitou and send it back into the depths. She told me that when she died, her power over the Manitou would be broken."

"I've always heard the whispers about a 'water spirit' in the lake, but I never knew anybody who thought it was true."

Levi pressed on his brakes and turned off the stereo. "I really like you, Lacy."

"I like you too. You're by far the most interesting guy in the whole high school."

Levi sighed and let off the brake. The Mustang moved steadily toward the shadows of the old oak grove. "I'm glad you've been a good friend the past few months because I don't know who else I could've talked to about this stuff. There's so much more I wish I could tell you."

"What's stopping you?"

I killed your husband and kids, that's why this is awkward. "It's complicated. Really complicated."

Lacy shrugged. "I trust you with my life, and I don't trust guys any more. You can trust me, too."

She was a victim in Lily's future and will be a weapon in mine. Levi rolled his eyes. *Welcome to the team, Lacy.* "Two hundred years ago, a war took place right here. My Ojibwe ancestors were invading Minnesota and used an attack at Mille Lacs as a bluff to draw my Dakota ancestors away from Lake Manitou. With all the Dakota warriors away, my Ojibwe ancestors launched a sneak attack on the women and children that lived on Turtle Island. They took a dozen kids as prisoners and brought them up to Bleeding Rock, where they sacrificed each kid to the Manitou."

"Jesus, is that why they called it Bleeding Rock?"

My mom would've slapped her face for taking the Lord's name in vain. Once a Morrison, always a Morrison. Levi nodded as the oak shadows blanketed the car, cooling the air temperature by ten degrees. "It's said that at night or after storms, the spirits of mothers rise from the depths of Lake Manitou to haunt Old Copper Road in search of their murdered children."

"That's horrible."

"Lily told me why our Ojibwe ancestors killed twelve children," Levi said morosely. "There are creatures that guard over Lake Manitou and the evil spirit sleeping in the depths—twelve to be exact. These creatures are half-flesh and half-spirit, and when offered a human sacrifice, they take form. A generation ago, these creatures were all fed and Gigi Lily had to use her magic to put them all back to sleep." Levi hesitated as he drew her into his plan. "Do you remember the Icehouse Murders a few months ago?"

"No way," Lacy said, showing equal parts fear and curiosity.

Levi nodded again. "Somebody tried to wake them up again. I tell you this because I wanted you to know that Lake Manitou is going to be very dangerous in the coming weeks. In the past, there have been a lot of strange accidents. You need to be especially careful of Carousel Island."

"Okay, now I call bullshit because I live across the channel from Carousel Island. You're just trying to mess with me."

Mess with you? I'm destroying your whole world with this conversation.

Levi stepped on the brakes again and put the Mustang into park by the Larson homestead. When he reached out his hand to put it onto her shoulder, there was no trace of flirty Lacy left. She flinched as if he was Ted Bundy sitting across from him.

Levi took his hand away, remembering a dream where he choked the beautiful redhead to death. "There are no coincidences at Lake Manitou. Do you remember what I told you about your ancestor, Bushy Bill Morrison?"

"How could I forget? Lily slapped me because of it."

"We're all puppets on a string," Levi said. "Everyone that came to Lake Manitou has been manipulated into being here, and I'm not just talking about the Dakota and Ojibwe."

Levi pointed to the rusty old mailbox with the faded name Larson written upon it. "Each family along Old Copper Road was selected to be here. A generation ago…a kid that lived in this house fell to his death at Bleeding Rock. There are no coincidences at Lake Manitou."

Lacy nodded to appease him.

"Remember this place," he said and put the Mustang back into gear. A few moments later, they left the shadow of the old oak grove. Levi remained silent about the Nielson farm so that Lacy could make the discovery herself. The increased speed of the Mustang and the light wind filled the silence for the next mile until they reached the stop sign at the top of the hill.

He looked forward for a few moments after they stopped. When he turned, Lacy almost had tears in her eyes as she said, "You're freaking me out a little, Levi? What is all this?"

"If anything happens to me, I want you to know that there are people you can talk to…people who can keep you safe."

"Safe? Safe from the creatures?"

"I think your Morrison blood puts you in danger."

Lacy was speechless.

If you wanted a bad boy, you've got it. "I'm so sorry, Lacy. I've kept this bottled up for…for months now." Levi reached into his back pocket for the yellow paper. "But this means she's fighting it."

"Fighting what?"

"You know all that Indian stuff I've been wearing the past year? That's because of Lily. I've been doing more than just embracing my ancestry: I've been training. There's about to be a big battle between good and evil and I'm going to be center stage, thanks to Lily. This sheet of paper has an ancient language written on it."

And Joey would have been the main course for the Wintermaker.

"This will go one of three ways," he continued. "It'll go badly and the bad guys will win. It'll go Lily's way and the bad guys will win. Or…"

Lacy's body language changed as she figured it out. *My second disciple.*

"Or what?"

My plan works. Levi put his hand back on her shoulder. "I love my little brother more than anyone else in this world, but in second place—I'm doing this for you, Lacy Morrison."

She blushed and looked away to gather her thoughts, then she turned back to rest her cheek against his hand. "That's the sweetest, weirdest shit anyone has ever said to me."

I'm so sorry for ruining your life.

He cleared his throat. "So this is what I need you to do," Levi started and used his dad's "chores" voice to change the mood.

Lacy sat up and nodded.

"This yellow sheet of paper is more dangerous than you understand. You need to keep this safe like it's worth a million dollars. Don't give it to Sommer and don't give it back to Lily. When the time is right, give it to a person you trust most in the world."

"That's you."

"You're an idiot," he said so bluntly that she laughed at him. "I'm putting my life in your hands by giving you this, so take more than five-seconds to think it over."

Lacy nodded, clutching the yellow paper to her chest with both hands. She didn't even know the name of the person she'd give it to—yet. Instead of finding true love, Lacy headed for tragedy.

She's the strongest person on your team. Trust her.

"That's Turtle Island at the bottom of the hill," Levi said.

"The church camp?" Lacy's brow furled in contemplation of the earlier story. "A church camp is built where a bunch of women were killed."

"So very *Poltergeist*, isn't it?" Levi mused.

Good luck getting her to work there now, Father Gary.

Having moved another pawn into position, Levi turned around in the intersection.

Two problems down, one to go.

CHAPTER FIFTY-FIVE

Stained Red

Mizheekay Band of Ojibwe Reservation
May 18, 1986

Father Gary Mackenzie leaned down toward the dashboard of his tiny Chevrolet Chevette for a better angle of the birds circling above the treetops.

Please tell me he's not dead.

Instead of parking at the T-intersection and walking half a mile, Gary kept his small car on the compacted dirt road leading to Migisi Assibikashi's home.

Carrion will circle in the sky if they sense something is dying, Gary thought as he stopped where the dirt road stopped. Brush and downed trees blocked the last few yards. The old hardwood trees had their green buds and a few leaves, but it was still early enough in spring to see the twisted branches, which held large, black specters of death.

Gary found himself hustling around the corner, fearing the worst. He stopped in his tracks when he saw a figure step out of a time machine.

The shack, deck, fire pit, and sweat lodge looked exactly the same as they had the previous trips, but the man standing in the entrance had been changed from a decrepit old grouch into a lean, aggressive warrior.

Migisi brandished a woven spear with a red stone tip, which he held away from his body with his elbows high. He jabbed at invisible enemies, all while his legs were high-stepped like a crane, his knees rising to his waist. As he moved, his whole body shimmered, for around his neck and shoulders were cowry shells, woven onto sinew and string. Along with the woven spear, he held a battle-ax, which sliced the air from time to time. Upon his back, he wore a large snapping turtle shell like armor. His face had been transformed into a mask of vermillion, with three blue stripes, like bear scratches, descending from his left eyebrow to cross his face to his right jaw. Upon his head, he wore a black hat decorated with bird wings.

The fire pit burned the butts of a few logs and was filled with coals. A few yards away, a small trickle of smoke came from the roof of the sweat lodge. A new feature in the yard, a single post as tall as a man, had been sunk into the ground, which kept Migisi in orbit with invisible string.

Migisi danced his way over to the pole, and when he leaned closer, Gary noticed a hole borne through its top. Migisi's gaze followed a line from the pole to the river below. Then pivoting, he stood between the river and pole, using the hole to gaze directly at him, as if noticing him for the first time.

Migisi advanced, and when he came within ten feet, Gary took a step back. When it became apparent Migisi did not plan on using the weapons in hand, he steadied himself as Migisi danced, shook, and hopped.

Suddenly an object flew through the air and struck Father Gary in the chest. The white projectile thumped his sternum and fell onto the ground between them.

Did he just spit at me?

A moment later, another white shell burst from Migisi's mouth toward Father Gary's head, striking his forearm.

"Excuse you!" Gary shouted, but Migisi turned to stomp back toward the pole, where he wilted and transformed back into the wrinkled piece of old leather Gary had grown used to over the past few months.

Migisi set the ax and woven spear against the pole, the hat upon the top, the turtle shell at the base, and lifted the shells off his neck and onto a wooden peg. Despite being relieved of the burdens, he seemed to hunch more. From his mouth, he spit out a dozen more cowry shells into his hands and walked them over to a flat rock adjacent to the fire ring.

"Come," Migisi said, waving his hand for Gary to join him on the deck. Gary picked up the unique shells as Migisi threw himself into a chair, clearly exhausted.

"Did you want these back?" Gary asked, extending a palm that held the two white cowry shells.

"I had to make sure you were real," Migisi said.

"Am I real?"

"Unfortunately yes," Migisi did not smile but Gary could see the old man was pleased with his own humor. The slight smile soon vanished. "The battle has started."

"I thought it started long, long ago."

"The war started long, long ago, but a new battle has begun. I've heard the Song of the Manitou."

"In a dream?"

"No, upon the river. I could feel the Water Drum vibrating beneath my feet and the foul Tak-Pei creeping in the shadows, and I knew the time had come."

Gary swallowed hard. "The *Song of the Manitou?* I thought you said it was hidden away in the Sacred Shell, thousands of miles from here."

"It is, but one from the future stood right over there," Migisi pointed to the bald clearing where exposed stone overlooked the Blue Knife River. "In the future, the Sacred Shell is discovered, allowing the secret verses to be sung. In our foolishness, we can try to change the plans of the Great Spirit, but what is meant to be will always...be."

"I don't understand."

Migisi sighed, closed his eyes, and leaned his head against the exterior wall of his cabin. "I'm not strong enough to fight them. When I was a boy, I fancied I could be Iyash, the boy who rode the Horned Serpent, tricking the great serpent to its doom. The Tak-Pei no longer fear me but laugh at me from the trees. Despite all of my prayers to the Great Spirit, I have failed to fight the Horned Serpent. I know now that I will die without even getting to fight him."

"What about the coming ritual? On the summer solstice, you'll get your chance."

"The Serpent Star brought its magic, but it is being misused. My sister grows weaker by the day, and the Wintermaker grows stronger. I no longer see a path to victory. Bring me my spear," Migisi said, pointing to the pole of relics.

Gary walked over and retrieved the woven spear. He handed it to the time traveling warrior.

"I made this spearhead when I saw the Serpent Star back when I was a young man. There is a place where my Oceti Sakowin relatives make pipes. Some say, the Great Spirit sacrificed the first buffalo to teach humans how to survive."

Gary reconciled the idea with what he knew from scripture: *The LORD made garments of skin for Adam and his wife...*

"Others say," Migisi continued, "the earth became stained red when all the Indian tribes gathered in one place to fight each other."

The LORD saw that the wickedness of man was great on the earth, and that every intention of his heart was only evil continually.

"But I learned that the sacred earth was first used by the Great Spirit to shape the First People, which is why the old pipestone quarry is sacred to all nations."

Then the LORD God formed man of dust from the ground, and breathed into his nostrils the breath of life; and man became a living being: Adam. A Hebrew play on words meaning "to be red."

Migisi snapped the woven wood near the red spearhead, tossing the shaft at his feet. He handed the red mineral to Father Gary. "Have I told you about the Dreamcatcher?"

"Many times."

"Then tell me why the Dreamcatcher was made," Migisi challenged.

"It is a spiritual snare," Gary summarized. "Placed above the crib or bed of a child, the web of the dreamcatcher allows good dreams to slip through the spaces, but bad dreams are caught on the web, like a fly in a spider web, to be burned away in the morning when the sun appears."

"Yes, and the construction of the dreamcatcher?"

"The significance of the feathers?"

"No, tell me about the frame."

"Oh yes, it is constructed of a single willow branch, twisted like a teardrop so the thick and thin ends of the loop cross. The tension of the webbing eventually causes the willow to break, signifying the end of childhood."

"You asked how you can help? I am as brittle as this old wicker staff, and even though I have failed my destiny, the Great Thunderbird will nevertheless answer the call. I need you to gather enough willow to create a new spear. A single piece of wood is easily broken, but fresh willow woven together is almost unbreakable. Fashion a new shaft."

In all practical terms, a ninety-year-old man could pass at any time, yet Gary had just seen how vigorous Migisi remained for his age. "Is there anything in particular I'm supposed to look for?"

"Yes, when I was young, I used to harvest from the ancient tree, hidden in a place known as Jiibay Waanadinaa."

"The tree is in the town of Wadena?"

"No, no. It is on Lake Manitou by the island. Find the willow tree in Ghost Hollow, and bring me fresh strands to fashion a weapon for the thunderbird."

Better tell Forsberg and the others about Migisi's sudden change of heart. Gary took the broken spear. *Whatever happened to just sleeping on my days off?*

CHAPTER FIFTY-SIX

Arson and Old Lace

Kanaranzi Creek
May 30, 1986

In 1865, Sved and Bengta Larson settled in the oak woods along Old Copper Road. The Larsons began by clearing enough trees to make a log cabin, a large chicken coop, and a pigsty. Three decades later, Sved's daughter Dolly had married a wheat farmer and his son Jakob prospered enough to build a modern house beside his father's old log cabin. The third generation to live on the homestead was Neil Larson, who died broken-hearted and alone two years prior at the age of 74. Tragedy had taken his only son and heir, Isaac Larson, when Brian Forsberg was still in junior high.

The Larson family home turned to ash twenty-five years later.

Standing in front of the charred remains of the house, Brian Forsberg found himself thinking of other house fires. Hell, since his law enforcement career began, Brian could think of a dozen house fires, each unique in circumstance, yet two fires prior to him becoming sheriff haunted him still.

Lily Guerin's house fire in 1962 was the first. The other spared Brian Forsberg from having to murder a man. Betzing wrongly labeled that house fire an arson after its owner apparently took his own life, which Forsberg and one other person knew was a lie.

Just before Forsberg got the call about the Larson fire, he'd been dreaming of that person standing in the shadows of the Larson house. Now, he clenched his fists with a sudden and unexpected fury.

Fire Chief Ken Uselman hobbled up to where Brian stood to give him his assessment. Now in his seventies, Uselman showed up to house fires mostly in a managerial capacity.

"We found the gas can, so it's officially a crime scene now. I'll call my people and you can call yours." The last of the flames were getting extinguished. "Kaylee Jones just had the house cleaned top to bottom with hopes of listing it later this summer. Doubt if she's going to get any of that investment back now."

"Who owns the property?" Forsberg asked.

"Not sure. Might've gone back to the state or county. I'll check with Kaylee about that," Uselman said with a shrug. "Don't know about you, but I'm already looking forward to my afternoon nap."

I'll sleep when I'm dead, Forsberg figured with a glance at his watch. It was now a few minutes past five o'clock, but the call had come in at about three o'clock in the morning.

As sheriff, he was used to his days being unexpectedly ruined.

Is it Saturday? It was indeed, making it the first day of summer break. Friday night had been the graduation ceremony at Split Rock High School. None of the kids who graduated would have had a memory of Isaac Larson, and consequently, would see the abandoned house as public property free to vandalize.

While the swarm of first responders went about their duties, Forsberg leaned against the grill of his SUV with his arms crossed, still haunted by the ghost from the 1972 house fire. *Why did that face return to my dreams after so many years?*

"I think we've got something," Deputy Wade Gilchrist called, a slight gleam in his eyes. "I already marked it off, but I found freshly made three-wheeler tracks that went around the whole house. They ran into the gravel of the driveway, but with all the fire trucks, I lost it."

"You don't say," Forsberg began casually but let out a litany of profanity in his mind. *At least no one was hurt. It was an old piece of shit house anyway. The property is still worth twice as much as the old house.* "I want you to go out to Old Copper Road and see if you can find the same tracks going east or west. That'll tell us something."

Ever the puppy dog, Gilchrist went running after the bone his master had thrown him. Forsberg's crew did their duties without question.

Does this mean something?

Does my stupid dream mean something?

A green GMC stopped at the end of the driveway so as not to block in the primary emergency vehicles. Forsberg grimaced. *Is he still listening in on the police scanners?*

Wally Crain, despite having retired from Ulman Oil, had much more pep in his step than his peer Ken Uselman. He paused to speak with his longtime colleague on the Lake Manitou Fire Department and then went over Forsberg.

"I brewed up a thermos of coffee. I figured you were about to have yourself a very long day."

"I shoulda let Harper get his ass out of bed for this one, but…"

"Old Copper Road," Wally finished. "So what are you thinking?"

"Well, the facts so far…the house definitely burned to the ground. Gavin MacPherson called it in around three o'clock, and by that time, the house was fully engulfed, which means it was likely started around two o'clock. High school graduation was last night, but there are no sign of beer cans or even tire tracks on the road. In the grass, we did find tire tracks belonging to a three-wheeler."

"A three-wheeler?" Wally repeated in alarm. "Ursula Hermann just bought—"

"Yeah, I know. I know." *What kind of name is Ansel,* Brian had asked Jimmy Nielson years ago. "Arson," Forsberg muttered.

"You shoulda talked to him two weeks ago when he arrived," Wally chided, thinking the same thing. "I took him and Ursula out in my boat and gave him a tour of the lake. He's curious as heck about his old man."

No shit, Sherlock. "Yeah, I know. Last Saturday, somebody broke into the high school. Kicked in a glass door in the elementary, knocked over a few garbage cans, threw some books off the shelves in the library, and vandalized a bunch of the wrestling pictures that hang outside of the training gym."

"Wrestling pictures?"

To throw off his scent, Ansel had likely shattered several, ripped a dozen or so from the wall, and had taken a single picture from the shattered frame that once belonged to Jimmy Nielson. Forsberg hadn't yet asked about the 1966 Yearbook, but he knew it would probably be missing once the rest of the books were put back on the shelves. "I don't need this shit. We had a plan and now it all seems to be unraveling."

"What are you going to do?"

"Assuming there are no fingerprints on a gas can that was tossed into an inferno, any evidence we find here will be only circumstantial at best. But I'm going to go talk to the kid right now. With all that happened to those kids, I expected him to be messed up, but arson?"

AN HOUR LATER, Brian Forsberg pulled up to the Chippewa Beach Mobile Home Park. With the failure of the Nicollet Dam in 1962, Lake Manitou claimed nearly a dozen cabins along the shore between St. John and Haggard Quarry. Those who got their insurance claims could not rebuild in the same location, and out of necessity, a thriving mobile home park was developed on the other side of the northernmost bay. Only the boat launch and Elmer's bait shop remained the same from his childhood. Now the trees were mature and the mobile homes were beginning to fall apart.

Ursula Hermann had a large deck and two big basswood trees on her lot. Parked behind the deck was a three-wheeler. Brian walked around to the machine, and with a bare hand, he touched the engine block, hoping it would be cold.

It wasn't.

He knocked on the door angrily.

Ursula Hermann, quite rattled, answered. Whereas Aurora Hermann had been a bleached blonde bombshell that had stolen his buddy's heart, Ursula physically manifested her family's tragedies in her appearance. It took a few moments of casual conversation to get her to calm down and stop being so defensive. Finally, he asked the question. "Was Ansel out last night?"

"No," she answered quickly. "He was in his bed by nine o'clock last night. He doesn't know anybody here. Where else would he be?"

If I were him, I'd wait for her to go to bed, sneak out, put the three-wheeler in neutral, push it a hundred yards, and then start it up. "What time did you go to bed?"

She recoiled and crossed her arms. "What is this all about?"

"Can I speak to the boy for a few minutes? I just need to sort out a few things. Nothings going to happen today, I promise. I'll be gone in ten minutes."

The ghost of Jimmy Nielson answered the door. Brian had seen pictures of the kid through the years, including his turbulent middle-school years where he dyed his hair and grew it long, but that was not who answered the door. Instead, Ansel Nielson had shaved his hair down to the scalp, leaving a quarter-inch of blonde stubble that looked like Jimmy during his elementary years or in the early days of boot camp.

"Am I in trouble?" he asked with a sly, curious grin.

Brian didn't answer the question. "You might not know this, but you and I are related. I think the technical term is we're second-cousins. My dad Glen and your Grandma Bonnie were brother and sister. Your pa and I were cousins and best friends."

"A little more than kin and less than kind," Ansel muttered.

"Excuse me?" Forsberg knew it was Shakespeare. The sass pissed him off.

THE TRICKSTER 315

"Sorry, that's a...bad habit of mine," Ansel answered.

"Those engines on three-wheelers are foreign-made pieces of junk, and when you run them hard, they get pretty hot. It takes a few hours for them to cool off. I'm not an idiot. I can be your friend, or we can do this the hard way. What's it going to be?"

Ansel swallowed hard as if he was about to confess but then his eyes narrowed. "I know you from the old polaroids. My dad kept photo albums of his time in Vietnam, so I recognize you. You're fat now but I know your face. I have a couple questions, too. I can also be your friend, or we can do this the hard way. I came here for answers, too. Do you know Latin?"

Jimmy never backed off in a fight. Forsberg shook his head as he pursed his lips.

"There's a phrase in Latin, quid pro quo," Ansel said, showing off. "It means something for something. You ask your question, and then I'll ask mine."

Forsberg wanted to unleash a fist in the kid's smirking face. *The kid's too smart for his own good.* "Did you do it?"

Ansel scoffed. "It? Is that supposed to be sly? Yes, I did *it*." A strange pained look came across the kid's face. "I saw it burning, so I drove up to get a closer look."

Damn, that came easily.

"My turn," Ansel countered. "There's a picture of four soldiers standing outside of a tattoo parlor. I know my dad. I know you. I know the big guy, of course. Who's the fourth guy?"

"The Professor, Jay Campbell, he's my brother-in-law from out in Baltimore."

"He looks familiar. Should I know him?"

"You got your one question. My turn." All of Brian's questions about the arson and school vandalism crumbled away in a wave of inner turmoil. *What the fuck happened to your father's gun?* The moment was right there for the taking, but that was his personal life—he had a job to do. "I found your three-wheeler tracks in the grass around the house. You

316 ⌬ Jason Lee Willis

claim that the house was already burning when you got there. Did you happen to see who started the fire?"

Ansel nodded. "I think so, but I'm not sure if what I saw was real or just…" He waved his fingertips near the side of his head. "I saw a figure go into the trees, heading, um, away. Would you like a description?"

Ansel's description left no doubt who'd burned the house down.

And the identity shook Brian to the core.

CHAPTER FIFTY-SEVEN

In Seventy-Six Years

Old Copper Road
May 31, 1986

Instead of going to Halley's Comet viewing party, Levi stayed home and watched it from the top of the porch roof with Joey, pointing up at the sky to the stranger his ancestors once called the Serpent Star. The rest of the family had gone to a big viewing party where somebody had a telescope, but Levi feigned apathy and volunteered to stay home with his youngest brother.

"How old will I be when it returns?" Joey now asked.

"You'll be an old man," Levi answered. "Eighty-one."

"How old will you be?"

"I'll be dead," Levi answered morosely. "You remember the plan, don't you?"

"You'll only be 'mostly dead,'" Joey smirked. "Why do I have to be the one who grows old?"

"Robin said it was the only way."

"You mean Fozzie."

"Right. Fozzie said it was the only way for this to work," Levi said and pointed to the heavens. Levi pictured Joey as a tall teenager boy with dyed green hair, tattoos, and piercings who wore the same Def Leppard shirt gifted to him a few days earlier. "By the time the comet reaches the coldest, farthest part of its journey, you'll be at your lowest. You'll have a big gray beard and a bald head and tattoos up and down your arms like a pirate. No one will bully you then."

"I like that." Joey smiled. "I like this story."

You better. With Lily's plan, you would've died horribly.

After he put Joey to bed, Levi contemplated the once-in-a-lifetime phenomenon. Sir Isaac Newton had the comet figured out centuries earlier even though his friend Edmond Halley got the naming rights to the comet. Seventy-five years after Newton looked up at it, Levi's ancestor Wiyipisiw looked up at the same comet prior to making a horrible sacrifice at a place called Bleeding Rock.

*Fate...God...the Great Spirit...*Levi's ancestor had a plan too, but Wiyipisiw's plan was destroyed by a coalition of his European and Dakota ancestors who forestalled the day of reckoning for another appearance by the Serpent Star.

In 1835, Levi's ancestor Chagobay looked up from Lake Manitou to the stranger in the stars and, inspired by a dream, went out looking for a man whom he believed was the fulfillment of prophecy. In the Seven Fires Prophecy, a "boy" with a strange light in his eyes would guide not only the Ojibwe but also all of humanity to the right way and avoid a path of doom and destruction. In Chagobay's days, European settlers were on the cusp of flooding his home, and war brewed between the Ojibwe in the north and the angry Dakota to the south. In these apocalyptic times, a stranger from a strange land, a sorcerer who studied the stars, arrived on the continent, bringing compassion, healing, and desire to understand legends and prophecy, so Chagobay and his son Nanakonan loaded their canoe and went down the river in search of the astronomer Jean Nicolas Nicollet.

*Fate...God...the Great Spirit...*Chagobay's plan to bring Nicollet to the cave where the earth bled blue was shattered when his plot was discovered. Nicollet was spared by the local Pillager chieftains, but Chagobay fled to protect his family, who again tried to fulfill the prophecy a generation later. Although Chagobay's great-granddaughter, Tewapa

Asibikaashi, first placed her hands upon the sacred Water Drum in 1898, her plan mirrored the plans of Wiyipisiw 150 years earlier.

*Fate…God…the Great Spirit…*Lily Weber's first attempt to fulfill the prophecy ended with the death of her husband Jean Nicholas Guerin in 1910, and now, thanks to the willful disdain of her great-grandson, her plans were turned to ash again.

Newton better be right about the world ending 2061.

Surrendering to sleep, Levi rubbed his eyes but he still smelled a bit of gasoline upon his hands. Last night, he'd spent twenty minutes in the garage with a bar of Lava trying to get the spilled fuel clean from his skin. His black pants and shirt were stuffed in a burn barrel ready to be incinerated after Mom's Saturday supper filled the kitchen garbage bag. With the burning of the Larson house, he'd done everything Robin asked of him, leaving only a final confrontation with the Wintermaker remaining.

WHEN LEVI WOKE, he had a visitor. Joey slept on the floor beside his bed. "What are you doing, Joe?"

"I was worried about you. I wanted to find out how it went, but you were sleeping."

"You should be watching cartoons. Mom's going to get suspicious."

"I had a bad dream about a fire."

"Don't worry about anything, Joe. We've done everything Fozzie needed us to do, but the next few weeks are going to be very dangerous for us."

"Why?"

"Our enemies might learn something is wrong."

"How? I haven't said anything to anybody."

"I know. I know I can trust you with our big secret, but these creeps have their ways. I'm also worried that Lily might try to stop us."

"Why?"

"She loved Great-Grandfather Jean a lot, and she was really mad that I didn't bring her back to Leech Lake after she closed her loop. We're in danger because we need to close loops also. When she was a girl my age, she saw the two of us on the river. We helped her find the Stone, so if something stops us from doing that, we won't be able to close the loop and—" Levi snapped his fingers. "All over." Joey knew all of this. They'd talked it over in detail since Levi visited the willow.

"When will we go?"

"I don't know the day, but it'll be soon. The Isanti Lodge still thinks we're doing the ritual on the summer Solstice, and I can only pray that doesn't happen."

"Why?"

"Because that means Gigi Lily found a way to stop us, and we can't let that happen, can we?"

Levi reached out a hand and pulled his brother to his feet. He held him by both shoulders. "Okay, now I want you to get your butt downstairs and watch cartoons. I'll come down in a few minutes. We're going to forget all about this Fozzie stuff and enjoy the next few days of being Joey and Levi, right?"

Joey threw his arms around Levi's shoulder and gave him a hug before running downstairs to watch his shows.

Levi sobbed a few minutes, remembering his hands as he wiped tears away.

Okay, Lily. Your turn. What's your next move?

CHAPTER FIFTY-EIGHT

This Mortal Coil

Golden Shores Nursing Home
June 7, 1986

The music angered Lily, who took the humiliation as she listened from a far corner of the commons. Karson, the loud-laughing piano player, was supposed to be her ally in the coming fight, but he sat next to one of their enemies, Lacy Morrison.

Take her children instead of mine. You must recognize her ancient blood.
Why must it be my family?

Lacy Morrison wore a smile, except when she passed by Lily. Now, Karson and Lacy sat together at the piano bench, unintentionally mocking Lily's grand plans.

In the fairy tales, the princess was locked away in a tower waiting for her knight in shining armor to come rescue her. Her handsome knight had died long ago, and now she'd have to face the monsters alone.

She remembered Jean teaching her the word *Avatarati*. The Sanskrit word referred to a vessel to be filled—like her word Omodai—which at first made it seem like a vase in reference to water, but once Jean explained that the Wintermaker waited for a human vessel to enter, the word was ruined.

"Adrianna Sinclair," Jean had repeated the name, inviting her into his discovery.

"Who?"

"The missing heir," he said, pushing away his notebooks on the table to reach for the stack of newspapers. "Do you remember how the Sinclair family worried about foul play involving their sister-in-law? She vanished in 1898, and with the Battle of Sugar Point and all the insanity here at Lake Manitou, the assumption was she was buried in a ditch somewhere."

"The hotel owner," Lily recalled as the three families of Triton Corporation tried to lay legal claim to the properties that once belonged to another Sinclair, their cousin, Adrianna.

"When the private detectives finally found her in Colorado, everyone assumed she left Minnesota to avoid the scandal of having a child out of wedlock."

Jack Morrison.

Years after the Sinclair family lost their male heir, Adrianna had an affair with a local lawman, Bushy Bill Morrison, resulting in the bastard child, Jack Morrison. Even after the "happy ending" in Colorado, the three families severed all legal ties with her and divided up her holdings in Hiawatha County.

Eighty-years later, Lacy Morrison's piano playing annoyed Lily, proving that it was impossible to run from destiny.

But at her living room table with Jean, she still made plans as he explored strange words like Endorheic.

"And what does that word mean?" she had asked.

"Endorheic?" Jean's eyes twinkled. "It is a lake that has no outlets, which is extremely rare. If you were to spill a cup of water anywhere in Hiawatha County, it would eventually end up in the Crow Wing River and then down the Mississippi River. Devil's Lake in North Dakota is one, where it only collects run-off. The Great Salt Lake? That's another."

"And what was your point?"

"Oh, they found Adrianna Sinclair living in Aspen, Colorado. Why Aspen? Well, Aspen is the highest watershed on the continent of North America. If you knew the Wintermaker lived in the waters of Lake Manitou, it is the farthest away from any tributary you could get, and until the snow melts in the summer, it is essentially endorheic."

"Why not live in a desert?" Lily teased.

"The world is made of water; we are made of water. It's hard to find places where the water cannot reach you. Besides, I think Adrianna took her child to Aspen to hide him."

"She worried he would be an Avatarati," Lily said. "Is there anywhere in Minnesota that is endorheic?"

"With our weather, everything floods and spills? Different watersheds spill away from the Mississippi River basin, but—"

"What?"

"The new dam on Leech Lake…when it closes, Leech Lake is cut off from the Mississippi River watershed. It's the closest thing to a stronghold you'd find in the area."

Now, decades later, Lily knew she would die and remain stuck in Lake Manitou. Just as Adrianna Sinclair failed to avoid fate, Lily tasted the same bitterness.

On her bedroom wall were the faces of her family, captured in photographs: her husband Jean, her only son Louis and his wife Hannah, who carried the Curse of the Wijigan to their five children. Three granddaughters managed to leave Hiawatha County, but sweet Cameron and nasty Nicole stayed, aware of the legacy.

Levi had indeed been a Trickster, but not in the way she intended. Decades earlier, she'd bargained with the Wintermaker over the life of her precious Jean. A pact was made with dark magic, and she had lived up to her part, but with treachery in her heart. The Wintermaker first gave her what she wanted, and now, in return, she gave him what he wanted—her descendants—but she secretly armed Levi with a knife capable of killing the ancient Horned Serpent. It was a poisoned promise she'd made.

Instead, the boy plunged the knife into her heart—severing the chance to be reunited with her beloved. *Had the Wintermaker already turned him into a servant? Did he work his dark magic to seduce the boy with promises? Did the foul Tak-Pei turn him into a thrall?*

I have a few tricks up my sleeve also.

Instead of a monster locking her away in a castle, her own beloved friends and family had locked her away. Lily's lies had caught up to her, and now she was trapped by a lie she'd told the Isanti Lodge. They all believed the coming summer solstice—June 20th, the longest day of the year—would be the day she battled the Wintermaker.

With this in mind, they locked her away so she could rest until her big performance. Yet she never planned on singing the song. Her plan had been to join Jean and leave the rest to the will of God. Her great-grandchildren would either win or they'd join their great-grandparents in the hereafter.

In her own way, she'd been a trickster, too.

A battle was coming, but she wouldn't be around to join them.

Karson Luning took the second shift, following Wally Crain, and preceding Cameron's turn after lunch. Others like Father Mackenzie, Captain Chuck, and—once in a blue moon—Brian Forsberg would all take turns to check on her. None of them listened to her. They all treated her like a child and zealously stuck to a plan she'd concocted as a foolish teen. The only one with a clue was Levi, and he served unseen masters.

But she knew she wouldn't live another two weeks.

The strength she used to fight against Levi stole several precious days from her life, and now, as she sat in the main hall, the only strength she could muster was saved for staying awake and upright in her wheelchair.

If tomorrow is my last day, Lily Guerin reflected, *I will not die without a fight.*

Her withered hand reached out and tucked her three utensils—a butter knife, a fork, and a spoon—into the folds of the blankets that rested on her lap.

I will not die at Lake Manitou and be forever separated from my precious Jean.

She began her long journey back to her room, knowing it would be her last.

*Fate...God...the Great Spirit...*Lily welcomed Jesus into her life nine decades ago, but she'd relied upon her own free will to steer her destiny. Tonight would be no different.

Lacy Morrison came jogging up to her from the piano bench. "Would you like help getting back to your room? I'm a friend of Levi's."

"I know who you are," Lily muttered. Bushy Bill Morrison murdered Jean in cold blood. How could she ever forgive or forget that?

Suddenly, from the other shoulder, Molly Chauvin appeared. "I'll take care of Lily."

The piano stopped as Karson listened to the conversation for a moment and then he drew Lacy back to the bench with a new tune.

The happy song annoyed Lily's ears until they reached the hallway, where a buzzer unlocked the door, allowing them into the Memory Care Unit.

In the quiet of the hallway, Lily asked, "Did your daughter like the Dreamcatcher I made for her?"

"Oh, she loved it. It's so beautiful hanging in her window. She enjoyed her visit with you also. You've made quite an impression on her."

Levi left me no other choice.

LATER THAT NIGHT, Lily opened her eyes to the white ceiling of the nursing home. If things had gone according to plan, she would have died looking up at the ceiling of Wanakiwidee Nursing Home at Leech Lake, allowing her soul to drift away on the River of Souls to the watery abode of the dead where she'd be reunited with her Jean. Instead, she looked up at the ceiling of Golden Shores, which was built upon the site where her ancestor Wiyipisiw had been betrayed.

Her door would remain closed until the nurse came to check on her the next morning, but she had other ideas. She found her three utensils in her wheelchair pocket and went over to the window.

One by one, she removed the screws that held her window screen in place. Next, she removed the plate that held the gears of her window latch in place. Her old, wrinkled hands still had strength in them.

After several minutes, she was exhausted and sat back down in front of her bit of deconstruction.

I will not die at the Place of Souls.

Jean existed in one of his theories of Heaven while Winnie, Grandpa Nanak, and so many others lingered in the waters of a haunted lake. Lily didn't plan on joining them. It was too dangerous for her soul to be trapped here.

With the cool June air flooding her room, she felt as if she'd have years left to live instead of days. She grabbed her comforter, not because of the chill, but to cushion the opening of the window. Next, she tossed her pillows and blankets out the window to serve as cushioning if she stumbled on her exit.

Not my best plan, but it's certainly better than waiting to die here.

Finally, she committed to it. Stepping onto a chair, then the counter, and then placing her hands upon the windowsill. She'd drape one leg out first, sitting upon the cushioned sill, and then pivoted her other leg out while she balanced her torso over the opening.

"What do you think you're doing?"

Her room was dark, and the hallway was lit, creating an outline in the doorframe. The voice came from the corner of her room where visitors often sat. "Who are you?"

"Don't you remember me? I visited your home once and you threatened me with a knife."

Charani Bessant.

Impossible.

His face appeared in the darkness, confirming his identity. He wore his white on white suit that he'd worn in 1961. "I've been waiting and watching all of this time. At first, it was only out of curiosity, and then it was out of necessity. Then, just a few days ago, a little summerbird came tweeting in my ear. I saw the little thing in the branches of the tree and almost shoo'd it away, but then it mentioned your name and I remembered all about Lily Guerin and her brother Migisi."

"What do you want?"

"Vengeance," he said softly. "What's the old saying? The enemy of my enemy is my friend. I came to Hiawatha County because of my enemy, the Order of Eos. I spent years gaining their trust and getting closer and closer to their inner circle. When they invited me to Lake Manitou, I wore a mask of friendship. I wanted to know the secrets of this place, and when you greeted me with a knife, you named me *Thief!* How did you know my purpose?"

"I saw your face in my dreams," Lily admitted, her heart pounding irregularly. "And I knew you were the Wintermaker incarnate."

"You are so close to the truth. The Order of Eos wants to resurrect their fallen god, which I will not allow, so I led those in my trust astray. Your Christian prophecies and Ojibwe prophecies both talk about a doom of mankind, which I also will not allow. I am not the Wintermaker, but the original sorcerer you know as the Wintermaker also worked against prophecy. He refused to partake in a prophecy that would allow the doom of mankind to happen, and as his servant, I have become a champion of mankind. I'm here to stop you, Lily Guerin, because if you leave this place, you will doom mankind to certain destruction."

"No," Lily muttered, trying to find her courage. "You are a liar."

"Am I the liar? You're the one lying to herself. You're the one without enough faith or courage to face death."

Something was indeed wrong. Charani Bessant hadn't aged a day, and he wore the exact same outfit he did in 1961 and someone gained access to her room without even opening the door. *He's not real.*

"You sad old woman. Your stubbornness and selfishness became all consuming, despite your best intentions," Bessant continued, turning on the lamp so they could face each other. "How far would you have walked into the darkness?"

"I would have gone east and found the Crow Wing River."

"And tossed yourself in the River of Souls? Oh, Lily, you would have turned your face away from your family in their hour of need. You were so certain your way was the only way that you never thought why your great-grandson betrayed you. And your ploy with the Little Spider? You corrupted her with magic from the Dawn. For what purpose? To once again fight against your family?"

Lily found herself gripping the fork as a weapon against the specter of Charani Bessant. "Are you a Tak-Pei in disguise? A foul demon sent to tempt me?"

Bessant chuckled. "Oh, the real Charani Bessant is out there in the shadows, and so too are the Tak-Pei, but I am neither. I'm only the voice of reason calling out to you from your own head. I'm trying to stop you from your own madness. Put the fork down. Close the window. We'll talk things over, and in the morning, you'll understand why staying in your room is the only way forward."

The apparition was only a figment of her imagination, and in her final moments before death, she began to realize the mistakes that had been made.

Lily tossed the fork against the specter, who only chuckled.

CHAPTER FIFTY-NINE

Up the Water Spout

Split Rock, MN
June 13, 1986

Sommer Chauvin had to confirm that the ghost of the old woman was telling the truth. It would be hard, but it needed to be done. Sommer's parents were both at work, leaving only her sister Penny to watch over her. Luckily, her thirteen-year-old sister would rather listen to cassette tapes and talk on the phone than to pay her six-year-old sister any attention. Sommer turned on PBS in the living room, dropped several dolls on the floor, and then stepped outside to find her bicycle.

Quite terrified to be on her own, Sommer sat her Barbie doll, Becca, into the front basket for proper moral support. With a push of her foot, she shot down the driveway and onto the sidewalk. This part of the route held little terror for her since she'd taken it nearly each day to get to school. For the first few weeks, Penny rode her bike along with her, but as her sister said, it was almost impossible to get lost since her house was on the same street as the school.

Today, she rode past the steep side-street that led to the bicycle corral in front of the school. Once she was past the school, she turned down Central Avenue, which strangely wasn't at the center of town but at the far northern side. She didn't need to cross the eastern Highway 34 that led downtown, but she had to face oncoming traffic as she went down the sidewalk. At the bottom of the hill, she waited for the lights to change so she could cross the intersection to Highway 19, which led north out of town.

She knew better than to tackle the big hill, and instead, hopped off her bike and began walking her faithful steed up the hill. Walking out of the Crow Wing River Valley took her almost half an hour, but soon she stood along the ridgeline that overlooked Lake Manitou. A road sign told her all she needed to know:

Turtle Island State Park 2 Miles
St. John 7 Miles
Sebeka 14 Miles

Sommer only had two miles to go.

The highway was level and the road was smooth, and Sommer's handle tassels whipped in the wind as she pedaled along, but it didn't take her long before doubt brought her to a stop at the corner of County Road 26.

On one side of the road, she saw the entrance to the State Park, and on the other she saw the entrance to the Mizheekay Band of Ojibwe reservation. From her dreams, she knew where to find the cemetery.

The reservation road had been recently tarred and covered in fresh rock, which meant it was too slippery for Sommer's white tires. She took her time approaching and looked for any sign of adults.

It was easy to find Grandmother Spider's grave—it was the only one without any grass. The fresh dirt hadn't even dried yet. The name was written twice.

Tewapa Asibikaashi
Lily Guerin
6/2/1883-6/9/1986

I guess she's telling the truth about being dead, Sommer thought. The old woman who'd given her a dreamcatcher and pieces of a song and had come to her dreams the past few nights with dire warnings, but Sommer's mom insisted that dreams didn't mean anything.

So she ignored what Grandmother Spider said.

Her mom told her that the old lady had gone to Heaven, but that wasn't exactly true.

For two days, the old woman lived near her swimming pool, coming out only at night.

She told Sommer how to find her again, but first Sommer had to make sure the old lady really was dead.

Sommer picked a yellow dandelion and put it on the old woman's grave before turning her bike back around for town. Ten minutes into her return, a truck passed her and stopped a short ways ahead.

Sommer stopped her bike.

An older man opened the truck door, stepped out, but stood at the door. "A girl your age shouldn't be riding by herself on the highway. Are you camping at the State Park with your family?"

She shook her head.

"Are you from Split Rock?"

Sommer nodded.

"I'm Wally Crain. Would you like a ride back into town? I can throw your bike in the back of my truck."

Sommer looked around for authority figures, but finding none, she tentatively nodded her head. *He seems nice enough.*

Wally called her closer with a wag of his index finger, which she obeyed, walking her bike toward the truck. When she stood a few feet in front of him with a broad smile on her face, he reached into his front pocket and found a pack of Big Red chewing gum. He slid one of the tinfoil wrapped sticks an inch from the others and offered it to her. "Gum?"

She sniffled and took it.

"It's got a bit of a cinnamon kick to it, but it keeps my breath fresh," Wally said, continuing on his way. "What's your name?"

Sommer chewed the gum but did not answer.

"Who are your parents then?"

I should be careful. More chewing, this time she answered with an angry scowl.

"Okay, what were you doing all by yourself out on the highway?"

"I wanted to say goodbye."

"Goodbye?"

"To Grandmother Spider"

His smile vanished. "You were at the cemetery?"

Sommer nodded. "She gave me a mirror, like the one in Sleeping Beauty."

"Lily Guerin? She gave you a mirror?"

"She said I can use it to protect my friends."

"Who are you?"

"Sommer."

"Your name is Sommer?"

She nodded. "Sommer Rae Chauvin."

"You're the daughter of Mark and Molly Chauvin. Huh. I was a good friend of Lily Guerin, your Grandmother Spider, and any friend of Lily's is a friend of mine. So you and I are friends, even though we just met. I need you to promise me that you'll be safe from now on. No more biking all over creation, understood?"

Sommer hesitated.

"Understood?"

She nodded. "Promise me that you won't bike outside of town for the rest of the summer. In fact, I want you to promise me that you'll just stay home and play in your backyard. You've got a pool to play in, right?"

"I don't like swimming."

Wally laughed. "Good. You stay away from water, especially the lake. Now I still haven't heard you promise me yet. Now say it: Wally, I promise to stay home."

"I promise to stay home for the rest of the summer."

THE TRICKSTER 333

At the intersection of Highways 34 and 19, Wally turned up the hill toward the newer development along the bluff overlooking the town. He passed the high school, and at the top of the hill, he turned onto 7th Avenue.

"I know your folks live around here, but which house is yours?"

"That one," Sommer said, pointing ahead.

When he stopped in the driveway, Wally turned and said, "Stay put."

Sommer watched him walk up to the front door and ring the doorbell of her house. No one answered. He knocked loudly. Still no answer.

Then Penny came out from behind the pool fence wearing a towel and a bikini.

"Hello," Wally called out. "I believe I've found something that belongs to you."

"Sommer?" Penny said looking at her in the truck cab. "You are in so much trouble."

Wally opened the door for Sommer. "She was riding out on the open road between here and St. John. Are your folks home?"

"Uh, no, they are both at work," Penny said with a face full of wrath.

"Keep a closer eye on her, and I won't say anything to your folks about you losing your little sister. And Sommer? Remember our promise. You'll stay home for the rest of the summer. No going out into the world by yourself."

Sommer nodded. She had still had the Sleeping Beauty mirror, after all, and her Barbie doll named Becca.

CHAPTER SIXTY

Pewabic Means Clay

Blue Knife River
June 14, 1986

For the trick to work, Levi needed to battle the Wintermaker one-on-one. Neither his parents nor the Isanti Lodge knew anything about his plan, and the only one who came with him was the intended sacrificial lamb: his brother Joey. So Levi snuck out of the house early on Saturday morning, transported Lily's canoe in the old truck, and launched onto the Blue Knife River near Nimrod.

"What's that word again?" Joey asked after several prolonged moments of silence.

"What word?" Levi clarified, keeping the old birch bark canoe away from the rocks protruding from the riverbed.

"The word for what I'm supposed to be looking for."

"Vitriol?"

"No, the other word. The word that Grandma Lily used to call me. My Indian name."

"Pewabic."

And Joey repeated it, "Pewapic."

"Pewabic. With a b."

"Pewabic. Pa-wah-bic. Why did she call me that again?"

Win or lose, Joey would be chosen by the Manitou as the *Omodai*. In his little body flowed both Wijigan and Eos blood.

If the Manitou didn't enjoy the plump little morsel set in front of him, it would next turn to Lacey Morrison, whose blood was also ancient and familiar.

Levi grit his teeth, resolute to go close the loop before revealing his trick. "Lily had a dream about you, but Mom wouldn't listen to her, which is why she named you Joseph instead."

"How am I supposed to know what clay looks like?"

"It will be wet and grainy, like sand or mud. Plus it will be strangely colored, either blue or green. Didn't you ever mold things with clay in kindergarten?"

"I used PlayDough."

"Well just keep your eyes open, okay? Gigi Lily said you'd be the only one able to find it."

"What if I don't find it?"

You have to find it, Levi answered silently. *The future is the past, Joey. If you don't find it, then I don't call out to Grandma Lily when she was young, and if I don't call out to Grandma Lily when she was young, then she doesn't find the Water Drum, and if she doesn't find the Water Drum, then she can't save Jean Guerin, our great-grandfather.*

But I am here.

The loop is closing.

"You'll find it, Joey. I guarantee it."

For a few minutes, Joey stayed quiet, allowing Levi to be alone with his thoughts.

Forty feet below the top of the wooded ridge, Levi could see burst drain pipes, a staircase, and an assortment of modern refuse tucked amongst the roots of the trees. He was getting closer.

"Why didn't you go to her funeral if you loved her so much?" Joey finally asked.

Levi didn't answer.

"Why aren't you talking to me? Are you sad that she's dead or something?"

"I suppose I am, Joey, but Gigi Lily lived to be 103 years old, so it's hard to be too sad for someone who lived such a long life. I hope I can live to be that old." *Instead, I'll be dead by this afternoon. Or at least 'mostly' dead.*

"I wouldn't want to be that old. Who was that really old Indian at the funeral?"

"I don't know, Joey. I wasn't there."

"He was really, really old. I don't even know if he could see, and he was all hunched-over and his face was really wrinkled and gross. Really gross."

"That was probably her brother Migisi; he is almost a hundred."

"Do you know him, too?"

"Not really. I don't think he and Grandma Lily spoke much."

"But he still went to her funeral," Joey said.

"Of course…he was her brother."

As Levi looked ahead, he could see the apparition of a boy wading in the river, pulling an angry snapping turtle from the riverbed.

The future and past were crashing together as the Philosopher's Stone prepared to be united with its master.

It wouldn't be much longer now.

"See anything?" Levi asked, closing his eyes to the madness that surrounded him.

"Pa-wah-bic…nope."

The wailing of women filled Levi's ears, growing stronger by the minute. It no longer felt as if they were bawling for their lost children as much as trying to stop him from doing what he intended to do.

I'm sorry for your loss, but this is the only way.

Joey looked at the sky instead of the banks of the river. "It looks like it's going to rain."

"The Wintermaker senses me and is about to have his Tak-Pei make one hell of a storm," Levi said, noticing the black cloudbank building a few miles south. Lacy Morrison was back at Lake Manitou but no longer in harms way on Turtle Island. "I think it suspects something is wrong."

With Lily dead, there would be no one to stop the Wintermaker from rising out of the depths to claim its final victim. Lily's plan to send the Isanti Lodge into battle had been a ruse, and Eos planned for their ceremony to coincide with the Summer Solstice.

Levi had a surprise for the arrogant Wintermaker, even if it meant the unthinkable.

"Clay! There it is. I see it. Clay. Just like you said. Do you see it? Huh, Levi? Do you see it? Right over there in the rocks. It's blue, just like you said. Pewabic."

All around Levi, the spirits swirled, fueling the storm that threatened to reach out all the way from distant Lake Manitou.

"Look, it's dripping out of that hole up there. I think it's a cave."

Levi could see how the sandstone rubble had broken away to reveal a fissure in the harder granite cliff that formed the Blue Knife. He angled the old canoe to the shore.

"Now what?" Joey asked as both of them climbed out of the canoe. Levi reached down and touched the blue vitriol with his fingers. He focused on the grit between his fingers, ignoring how he could see Chagobay just a few feet from him smearing the blue paint on Joseph Nicollet's face in the distant past.

He decided to do the same exact thing to Joey's face, bringing the past and the future into an unending loop of influence.

"Pewabic," Levi repeated. "Let's go climbing."

As the two scrambled up the bluff, Levi noticed the low-flying clouds breaking off the thunderhead building over the lake.

"What if it rains so hard the river floods?" Joey asked as they climbed over the last of the jagged sandstone to break free from the older granite.

"I guess you'll get wet."

"Is that why we're going to this cave? To hide from the storm?"

Levi stopped just below the dark hole.

"What's wrong?" Joey asked. "I'm getting kinda scared, Levi."

"You'll be fine, Clay. This is going to go just like we practiced. You have nothing to worry about."

"You just called me Clay."

"I did, didn't I? Let's keep going."

"Aren't we going to look inside?"

"I already know what's inside, Clay. I need to help somebody first."

"I thought you said you've never been here before."

As the cliff grew steeper, there were fewer and fewer footholds in the rock pile that accumulated from years of erosion. But the granite had enough imperfections and faults for Levi to find a way up the final ten yards.

At the summit, grass and weeds gave him a handhold to help pull Joey up to the top, bringing them into a thicket of dense pine brush.

He stepped off ten yards, waited, and closed his eyes.

First, I must close the loop.

"I know where the Water Drum can be found," Levi said to the past. "I can help you save him. It is over here."

Levi turned, not needing to see Lily standing in the window to the past.

"Save who?" Joey asked.

"Great-grandfather Jean. If I don't show Lily how to find the Water Drum, neither of us can exist and the Wintermaker will win. This is the only way." Levi turned around and led the future and past back to the cave. "In the past, the river was flooded all the way to the top. I need you to lead Lily back down to the cave."

Nervously glancing to the darkening sky, Joey's head frantically looked around him for the invisible reference Levi made.

"I need you to do this, Joey. I need you to go in there first."

"I'm scared, Levi."

"Don't be. I'm doing this to protect you. I'm doing this to protect everybody. I'd never let anything bad happen to you. Now, go down there and crawl into that cave."

Clasping his brother by the hands, Levi helped Joey down to where his feet could grip the granite, and then his brother shuffled back to the dark entrance. "Go ahead, Joey, it will be fine."

Joey disappeared.

The past and future began to crash around Levi, making it impossible to tell what he was seeing.

Faces and voices swirled around him as the wind of the real storm began to build. He felt rain begin to drop from the billowing storm created by the confused Tak-Pei.

"There is something in here," Joey called out.

"I know. Don't touch *anything*."

"I can feel it. It's giving off heat."

"I know!" Levi shouted. "Don't touch it. Remember how we practiced with the bowling ball?"

Joey stopped talking.

Levi opened his eyes to the past, and on one side of the water's edge, he saw Lily Asibikaashi crying as she emerged from the water. On the other side, he saw a woman in her thirties, the side of her head shaved, with a gruesome pink scar above her eye. Where her right eye should have been, he only saw a smooth patch of skin. On her chest, she wore the logo of an NFL football team that did not currently exist.

"I need you to teach her the secrets of the Water Drum," Levi said to the scarred woman. "Sing the missing verses to Lily so she can save him."

Levi took her by the chin and looked her in her remaining eye. "And then I'll play my little trick. Robin told me all about you. We'll fix this together."

Not waiting for an answer, Levi slid off the ledge and climbed down to where Joey had disappeared.

"Okay, Joey, you can come out."

The boy scrambled out like a crab, blinking with wide eyes as the rain continued to intensify. In his hands, he held the end of a rope. "There was someone in there."

"I know."

"Don't go in there, Levi. There's someone…someone hiding in there."

Levi bent down and kissed his brother on the forehead. Then he put the rope in his hands. "Just like we practiced. Do you remember the count?"

"914,000,000 million," Joey teased.

"The short count, Joe."

"A thousand and then I start pulling."

"And don't look back, right?"

"Right." Joey began to cry, and a ripple of lightning in the clouds caused him to flinch. "Don't, Levi."

"Lily made a promise long ago. I am going to fulfill that promise. Now I need you to make another promise. If I don't come out at the count of 914 million, I need you to come get me. Don't leave me in there, Joey, or the Wintermaker will win. This isn't going to make sense now. But it will one day. Can you promise me?"

Joey nodded, and Levi hated himself for what he was doing to the poor boy, but it was better than what Lily would've done to them.

They all shared the same blood.

So he crawled into the little opening of the cave, and the darkness closed in around him. At first, all he could sense was the Wintermaker, but as soon as he heard his ally begin to sing, he knew it'd all be worth it.

CHAPTER SIXTY-ONE

Stormchaser

Chippewa Beach
June 14, 1986

Ansel Nielson knew the storm was unnatural. He stood on the deck to watch the massive thunderhead just sit right over the lake. A great shadow formed from the towering plume of moisture, cooling the air twenty degrees and making the chill that Ansel felt even stronger.

Around the Chippewa Beach Mobile Home Park, other residents stepped outside. Retired know-it-alls shared their meteorological theories that the system had already passed them, but Ansel wasn't so sure.

If not for the stillness of the massive storm cell, Ansel would've thought it was a tornado, but this tornado was frozen in place, and instead of spinning like a top, it funneled energy from the lake and up into the mushrooming thunderhead.

The screen door opened, and Grandma Ursula stepped into the space for a glance up at the ominous sky. Even though it was not yet noon, it'd grown dark as night again, which is what likely drew her from her television programming. "My word," she muttered, and the boards of the deck creaked as she drew closer to watch the storm with him.

Lightning spread through the crown of the mushroom, rippling horizontally rather than crashing down the Hiawatha County. In the illumination of electricity, Ansel saw them.

The oily creatures he'd seen hiding in shadows and hollows ballooned into monsters that swam within the moisture pulled up from the lake. He glanced over at Ursula, who obviously didn't see them. He looked to the onlookers—nothing.

It angered him to be so alone.

But I'm not alone, am I?

The energy of the storm was being fueled by unleashed magic from the dawn of time, and with the cold air that came rushing down from the atmosphere, the curtain that normally covered Lake Manitou was blown off, revealing a boy frantically trying to stay upon some orange raft.

Ansel recognized the boy—*it's me.*

A wave of magic—not real wind—capsized the raft, but when it emerged from the swells, another apparition sat upon it. A wiry farmer wearing a green and yellow DeKalb hat gripped the edges as the small vessel lurched in the waves.

A wave swept him right off the raft. For a few moments, the farmer floundered, searching for the raft and also trying to keep his head above water. Then a ten-foot wave crashed onto his head and buried him under the surface.

A tan, blonde-haired man emerged—*Dad.*

Jimmy Nielson struggled in the wild surf for a few moments, finding breath between being pummeled by waves. He cried out, "Ansel!"

Ansel took a step away from Ursula before remembering that his mind was only playing tricks on him. He gripped the wooden deck railing as he watched the vision from a distance.

Another wave buried Jimmy Nielson under the surf, but this time, instead of his father resurfacing, he saw himself emerge from the water. Right in front of the boat launch, a hand thrust up from the water to grab the metal pole, and when the rest of the body followed, Ansel saw a grievous wound to his own face. His jaw hung limp from his face like a glob of ice cream about to drop from the cone. Blood and teeth fell from the oblong opening that had been his mouth, and then he saw himself collapse on the dock, reaching a hand toward the center of the lake.

A violent, cold gust came up from the beach; this time everybody felt it. Some tried to collect loose items, and others went rushing back inside. Right behind the wind, sheets of rain followed.

Grandma Ursula took him by the elbow and began pulling him back to the mobile home, but he did not go willingly. In the howling of the wind, he heard voices crying out, "Help me!"

"Inside, now," Ursula said as fierce winds ripped through the park. Debris kicked up from the storm, making it truly dangerous.

Ansel relented and followed, rushing to the front of the living room to watch the storm beside the parrots Donald and Daffy. As rain gave into hail, and the real world washed away the world of illusion, a tangible item came out of the storm, crashing onto the beach—an orange raft.

CHAPTER SIXTY-TWO

Shadow and Smoke

Turtle Island Reservation
June 14, 1986

Migisi ignored the screams of terror coming from his grand-nephew Cameron and stepped out into the eye of the storm ready to die a warrior.

The wicker staff that held the sharp piece of pipestone helped steady him as the wind tried to batter him to the ground. His left arm, wrapped in his old turtle shield, shielded his face from the horizontal gusts of wind and his fingers clutched the handle of the old hatchet strapped to the interior of the shield. A pouch at his belt held white cowry shells—the megis shells that had been collected from Minnesota to Montreal.

The pines and birch danced in the violence, but Migisi was steady and soon stood at the center of the storm. He looked up to face his enemy.

The power of the Water Drum had transformed the Tak-Pei from "the little men of the forest" into billowing black monsters that now swam upon the currents of the storm.

"Biboonike! Bagami-ayaa!" Migisi shouted into the clouds above him. *The Wintermaker has arrived!* Granted, it was a week early, and none of the Isanti Lodge were there to support him, but Migisi had prepared his whole life for the moment. He could feel the cold breath of his mortal enemy upon his face.

I shall feign weakness before striking.

So he took a knee in the midst of the mighty storm. He still held onto the wicker spear, and now the turtle shell covered even more of this hunched body as the elements battered him.

"Migisi!" Cameron called from the doorway. "Come inside the cabin."

"Go back and lock the doors," he shouted. "The Tak-Pei have come."

For the past two decades, Migisi had hunted and had been hunted. In the battle at Carousel Island, Lily subdued ten of the twelve creatures, but as two attacked Ed Nielson, they were cast far beyond the island to where Albert Fisher and his grandson Chris were trying to open the floodgates and save Carousel Island from being flooded entirely. Shadow and Smoke, Migisi named them. Like a great bear, Migisi hunted the darkest confines of Lake Manitou for the two weakened predators. Once, he'd almost caught Smoke, only to have it vanish for the past decade. Shadow, however, lingered nearby, waiting for a moment of weakness. Now, with his wolf pack joining him, Shadow returned.

Yet the Tak-Pei, swirling above Migisi's head, took no interest in him.

They are upset. They've been let off their chains and only run in circles.

Who let them off their leash?

The Song of the Manitou filled the air, sung by a chorus of voices. Even after a lifetime, neither he nor Lily discerned the origin of the strange language. Father Jean once believed that the original texts were likely hidden in some sort of container that the Anishinaabe called the Sacred Shell, yet Lily learned the missing verses of the song from an apparition from the future. Now, it seemed, the past, present, and future all sang in harmony.

Even with the chaos of the storm above him, the Song seemed to be coming from a distinct source—near his sweat lodge at the cliff overlooking the river.

His own grandfather had only partially taught him how to build a lodge before his death, so when Migisi was grown, he went to others for their knowledge. As Migisi followed the Song to within a hundred yards of the location, he finally understood that the Tak-Pei had not gathered to fight him but to destroy his lodge.

Why would they attack my lodge?

Torrents of rain knocked him back and almost off his feet. Now, the Tak-Pei descended, sweeping down like great black bats—but not to attack him. One by one, they crashed into the sweat lodge, busting it to pieces, allowing the wind and rain to continue the assault as they circled back.

Now's my chance.

Migisi tossed off his shield, holding the wicker staff with both hands. He advanced slowly, readying his body for a single thrust at the nearest Tak-Pei, even though he hoped it would be Shadow, his old nemesis.

He kept his eyes up and ready, but then an explosion of energy came from the rock foundation of the Blue Knife River channel. He felt his arm and shoulder strike the hard ground.

"Migisi!" Cameron called out, but the sharp pains and spinning made the source of his voice confusing. *Oh, I'm being blown back to the cabin.*

His body stopped rolling when it rested against the supports of his porch. Cameron loomed over him, his busy hands trying to tend to him and get him to safety.

Back at the sweat lodge, blasts of air, water, and magical energy came up out of a hole that had been sealed for years. The Tak-Pei descended into the ravine and into the hole and the storm intensified.

Cameron put his hands under Migisi's armpits and dragged him back into the cabin.

Did I just lose?

CHAPTER SIXTY-THREE

God of Thunder

Brainerd, MN
June 14, 1986

Tomas Dobie sat in the Brainerd Airport when he saw the storm build over Lake Manitou. With two runways and a helicopter pad, the small airport served mostly single-engine planes and a few commercial flights. Triton Corporation had three small planes in the hanger, which allowed businessmen to drop in and out without all the traffic flying into Minneapolis.

Arriving early allowed him to not only witness the storm burst into the heavens but also to allow his nerves to calm a bit in advance of the others' arrival. He had flown in directly from Albany, arriving with the dawn. The extra time allowed him to make sure the white Chevy Suburban suited their needs.

He found a spot near the western glass window, where he could see both the building storm and the white vehicle parked in the lot. At eleven o'clock, a gray blob burst into the upper stratosphere above the town of Brainerd; sunny skies to the east only made circumstances appear darker and more menacing.

From his studies, Dobie knew that the creatures inhabiting Lake Manitou, whether called Pukwudgies or Grim, could manipulate the elements, but he didn't know whether the show warranted celebration or fear. The fireworks weren't supposed to be going off yet.

Finally, one of the two planes arrived. It dropped from the eastern skies like a white paper airplane and then quietly taxied around toward the hanger. Unlike at a large airport, there were no gates connected to the terminal; instead, stairs-on-wheels were pushed out onto the tarmac.

Maddy Sinclair stepped out of the plane door first, her crimson hair unfurling like a flag. She wore khaki shorts with a blouse over a tank top. In her shadow, Trudy. The young girl looked around at the pines surrounding the airport, then at Dobie, and then at the car.

She expects to see her brother Modi, Dobie reflected. She last saw him alive back in December. He put the thoughts of the foul icehouse murder away. "Welcome to Minnesota, ladies. How was your flight?"

"I slept most of the way," Trudy said proudly. "When I woke up, it was the next day."

I wish I could do the same. If only today were already tomorrow. Dobie worried about their bold mission. Delhut wanted caution, but bold Maddy ended up getting her way.

"How are things, Tom?" Maddy asked as she approached the SUV.

"Cousin Val hasn't arrived yet, so we might have to wait for a bit. Do you want to wait in the lobby or in the car?"

"Shouldn't we just wait in the car?" Maddy asked. "How much longer will it be?"

Tom glanced over his shoulder to the storm building in Hiawatha County. A hundred storms like it across the continent could cause delay. "It should be here any minute."

Maddy and Trudy chose to wait in the vehicle.

A few minutes later, another private jet dropped from the sky onto the runway. When the door opened, Alphonse Lavasseur, holding the hand of a six-year-old boy with ginger hair, stepped out of the plane.

The Boy Who Will Be King, Dobie reflected, *the Avatarati.* "Al, good to see you. How was your flight?"

"Quite long."

"Val," Dobie called out to the boy, who looked a bit lethargic. "Are you ready for a grand adventure with all of your other cousins?"

"I guess," the boy said softly and uncertainly.

"Well, the lake is less than an hour away. We'll stop for some lunch and then be on our way."

As the Suburban drove down Highway 10, Maddy introduced the children to each other, acting as if it was the beginning of an important relationship. Dobie knew death or possible possession waited for the two lambs, so he kept his eyes on the storm. At the town of Staples, the temperature dropped ten degrees and large drops of rain began to hit the windshield. By the time the vehicle turned north at Aldrich toward Lake Manitou, the winds and rain beat against the vehicle, forcing a tight grip upon the steering wheel.

Do the evil spirits sense what we're about to do? Has someone woken them already? "Are you seeing this?" Dobie asked softly enough so the kids behind him did not notice.

"Oui, is it a problem?" Lavasseur asked.

Lake Manitou stretched seven miles from corner to corner, yet all of it was blanketed by the darkness of the storm. "I think it's moving east."

Making the final three miles slow, debris and puddles covered the road. At Sterling Junction, a tree covering half of the road forced Dobie to drive into the other lane. Even though the surface of the lake looked like a washing machine on agitation cycle, the windshield wipers managed to keep up, a sign the storm was moving away.

"You can't see it now," Maddy began her lie, "But Modi's school is somewhere on the far side of the lake."

"I'm sure he's fine," Dobie lied about her sacrificed brother as the vehicle passed over the little bridge separating Haggard Bay and Lake Manitou, "but because of the storm, we might not be able to see him until tomorrow." The children accepted the lies, and soon Dobie was driving through the town of St. John.

Sean Stewart lived in a small mansion along the shores of Lake Manitou. The plot of land housed dozens of mature pines and oaks in a field of lush green, over which leaves and branches were now strewn.

Stewart stood on the end of a dock, his hands on his hips, as he watched the storm pass over the distant town of Split Rock. Seeing the suburban, he walked quickly toward them.

"Welcome to Lake Manitou," he called out as the doors began to open, and he acted the part of the gracious host, whisking the children away for indulgence and adventure. *Can't trust a man who doesn't know his place,* Dobie decided. *He wants to elevate his status within both Triton and Eos.* Dobie ignored the handshake.

"Should we be concerned?" Maddy asked in reference to the storm.

"Stay with the kids," Dobie said, knowing other critical matters needed to be set up before the summer solstice events. "I'm going to find Kirkpatrick and see how things are on his end."

"Do you want me to come with you?" Lavasseur asked.

"Of course not. You are to stay with the young prince until this is over, understand?"

Even though Dobie's relatives had lived in Hiawatha County, he'd only been there once before, six months earlier. He'd done the intel, though, and knew the maps and terrain well enough that he instinctively drove east out of town through the gloom of the departing storm.

He turned north at a private driveway of a little house tucked into the pines, but instead of stopping at the house, he drove around the garage and found a simple road that led another mile into the woods. Hidden deep in the woods, he found a small complex of pole barns. Armed guards stepped out of hiding when they saw him exit the vehicle.

Phillip Marquette, once a son-in-law of Scott Sinclair, took the most modest approach to investing his Triton Corporation dowry: he went into the mortuary business. While his brother-in-law Ozias Haggard built a promising stone quarry, and Walter Stewart put his money into local businesses, Marquette Mortuary steadily invested in itself until the family accumulated a small fortune.

Marquette knows his place, Dobie decided.

The Marquette estate, built along the western bank of the Blue Knife River, allowed private recreation and entertainment. The jack pines had been replaced by old forest, and for a mile in all directions, only squirrels watched the house.

Unlike Stewart, the Marquette family stayed in their home, leaving the compound to Dobie and his men. One of the security guards jogged from the barn to arrive at the driver's door before Dobie stepped out.

"You've gotta come quick."

"What is it?"

"I'm not exactly sure."

"What the fuck is this?" Dobie asked, seeing fear in the eyes of all his hired killers. Robert Kirkpatrick stepped out of the barn and also jogged over to where Dobie parked. "So?"

Kirkpatrick stopped in front of him, put his hands on his hips, and shook his head. "There has been an unexpected development."

"The storm?" Dobie asked, seeing it leaving on the eastern side of the lake.

Kirkpatrick's eyes watered as if in pain. "I don't know how to say this."

"Just fucking say it."

"During our preparations, we found, um…."

Dobie didn't know if he should ask what or where, but then knew one question might answer both. "Go on!"

"Down by the river, on the edge of the property. This just happened…a few minutes ago. I didn't know what to do, Tom, but I think I know what it is. You need to see. Maddy needs to see. This changes everything."

"Don't get your panties in a twist, Robbie."

"Trust me, Tom, this changes everything."

CHAPTER SIXTY-FOUR

A Hostile Witness

Old Copper Road
June 14, 1986

*S*heriff Brian Forsberg's suburban slowed to a crawl as he approached the MacPherson farm. Having just been out inspecting storm damage, he understood the strange nature of what he'd just witnessed, so when he got the dispatch to head to the MacPherson farm, he raced as fast as his reflexes would allow. Yet he still hesitated a few hundred yards from the driveway.

What just happened?

It's too early.

The solstice is days away.

He leaned across the leather bench seats for the glove box, ignoring his .357 magnum and instead reaching for the other metallic object, his flask of Lord Calvert Canadian whiskey. He filled his mouth with enough liquid for two gulps, swishing it in his mouth like Listerine before forcing it down his gullet.

He glanced at the ravine leading to the Crow Wing River, now filled with young leaf growth, unable to see the spot that haunted him. From the ash trash, he pulled out a pack of Big Red Gum, and cinnamon and whiskey mixed.

His fears and fury subsided, and once ready, he shifted the SUV into gear and joined a Hiawatha County prowler already parked at the house. The house had a dozen other vehicles parked in front of it, with cousins and uncles from Clan MacPherson ready to do battle with any enemy.

The men gathered around the vehicles knew him as well as Forsberg knew them, and his eyes barked orders that were obeyed. They kept their distance, glancing at the house.

More MacPhersons greeted him inside the coatroom. Most of the elder children and the female in-laws lingered in the kitchen. A few greeted him, but most stepped aside, clearing a path through the kitchen and into the dining room, where deputy Scott "Baby" Gerber sat at the long table with Gavin and Nicole MacPherson.

Gavin stood and shook hands in a fierce grip, but his eyes were filled with sorrow and defeat. *He thinks his son is dead.*

"Oh praise Jesus, you're here," Nicole said from her chair. Instead of rising to greet him, she just hunched over in a ball, hiding her face for a moment in her hands before straightening back out to ask, "What do we do, Biff?"

At one point, Nikki Guerin outranked Marylyn Monroe, Catherine Deneuve, and Elizabeth Taylor as the fantasy girl for seventh-grade boys at Split Rock Schools. Thirty years later, she still dyed her hair blonde, but raising a large family had stolen her youthful figure. Prior to serving a fateful detention, a pubescent Biff looked away every time Nikki walked by, for fear of being aroused, but even after Mrs. Crain united them in common purpose, he still struggled to look her in the eyes. Once, Gavin had drawn his blood, yet Nikki all but castrated him during a melee in the detention room, and three decades later, her eyes still wounded him. Yet Sheriff Forsberg had a job to do.

Forsberg then realized she had her youngest wrapped in a blanket at her feet with her legs serving as pillars of protection. "Whatever it takes, Nikki. Now tell me what happened."

Deputy Gerber repeated the situation previously relayed to him by both phone and radio: Levi MacPherson was missing. Joseph MacPherson, six years old, had been found by Ed Williams, a Split Rock resident, who said the boy was confused and staggering near Split Rock Creek.

In the past few hours, according to Gerber, the boy had not spoken about either his brother or the storm he'd endured. Thanks to the quick detective work of Clan MacPherson, they also knew that Levi had vanished without packing or taking his prized Mustang, pilfering an old farm truck instead. No one knew if Joey had been with Levi or if both had left the house separately prior to the arrival of the storm.

This has got to be the work of Eos. Sweet Jesus, did they snatch up Levi? Did Joey escape alone?

Forsberg felt the whiskey pulsing through the capillaries in his flesh, and the more he learned, the hotter he felt, especially with the eyes of so many relatives around him.

"That was quite the storm, wasn't it little man?" Forsberg asked Joey once Gerber finished. At the lack of response, he looked around the room at all the people looking to him for answers. *If there are too many eyes for me, imagine how the kid feels.* "You've had a long day, little man. Perhaps it's time for bed? Nikki, help me get him upstairs to his bedroom."

"Do you want me to come with?" Gavin asked and Forsberg nodded in affirmation.

With Joey wrapped in a blanket in Nikki's arms, the three adults went up the open stairs that led to the second floor. In a narrow hallway with several doors, Nikki led Forsberg to a small room at the end of the hall, with a bunk bed in the corner. Four feet from the foot of the bunk bed, another staircase led to the third story.

"Whose room is that?" Forsberg asked.

"Levi's," Gavin said, and then he gripped Forsberg by the arm, pulling him aside as Nikki set their youngest down onto the bottom bunk. Gavin struggled for obvious words, and after several false starts that ended in only gasps of air, his grip turned into a full embrace, and the steely farmer crumbled into Forsberg's chest.

Nikki was always stronger, Forsberg realized as he looked at her sitting on the edge of the bed, waiting. *She tried so hard to protect her family from this moment arriving.*

Joey curled into a ball beside his mother, lying sideways, his eyes still open, using the blanket as a shield. Several times in his life, Forsberg had seen traumatized children, including those who'd been snatched from the icy grip of the Manitou.

He's faking, Forsberg thought, but that did not change the reality that something awful had happened. "I'll be right back. Stay here with him."

Then Forsberg walked up the stairs to the third floor, each step creaking under his weight. The attic had been turned into a shrine of adolescence: hard rock posters interspersed with posters of models. Casual chaos without a sign Levi planned on doing anything other than sleeping another night in his own bed.

In the window, a dreamcatcher hung, and Forsberg walked towards it, his boots echoing to the room below.

We thought we had it figured out, also, Forsberg recollected about the study hall gang assembled by Mrs. Crane. *What did this idiot do?*

Forsberg lifted the dreamcatcher to see if anyone looked back at him.

It was empty.

Hoping against a worst-case scenario, Forsberg retreated back downstairs void of any clues.

"Levi told me his plan," Forsberg bluffed to the boy. "He wanted to make sure you were safe. Now, I want to make sure he is safe."

Joey remained frozen, his eyes looking outward, with an occasional blink.

"We haven't been able to get a word out of him since he returned home," Nikki said. "We're not even sure if Levi was with him."

Then I won't ask any questions...for now. "It's been a very long day for Joey, and he should probably get some rest."

"But..." Nikki began. "But Levi."

"Let's just give Joey some time to rest," Forsberg said, patting him on his legs. "Could you get him into a fresh pair of pajamas?"

Nikki seemed to understand the strategy and rose to walk over to the dresser, returning with a pair of pajamas. With a little coaxing, she moved her son into a sitting and then standing position as she had done numerous times before.

Forsberg watched carefully as she lifted his shirt over his head. Once the shirt was off, she handed it to Gavin. "Okay, sweetie, now turn around."

Forsberg scanned for any bruises, abrasions, or scratches on the boy's torso but found nothing amiss. When she lifted his arms to slip on the fresh shirt, she paused. "Your fingernails are filthy."

Still playing the part of zombie-boy, Joey let her twist his palm for inspection before she finished slipping the shirt on. Next, she took off his pants, lifting his knees to step out of them.

There was no soiling of the underwear, nor any marks on his legs either. "Your socks are wet," she said. The boy had been out in the storm, yet after a few hours under the blanket, his clothes had mostly dried.

When Joey was dressed, Forsberg stood up to allow Nikki space to get Joey into bed. Gavin handed him the clothes. It took only a tertiary examination to realize there were sand particles on the shirt, along with some bluish green smudges. On the front of the boy's Star Trek t-shirt, the decal of a furry tribble seemed to have melted a bit.

Turning to the pants, Forsberg noticed how the bottom three inches of the pants were still saturated while the rest of the pants were just lightly damp.

The Blue Knife River.

It was a start.

Forsberg took a few steps away toward the door, and Gavin followed closely. As in the days in the deer stand, both grownup boys waited for the Queen Bee to finish her maternal duties. Nikki pulled the door almost shut to shield their voices as they stood in the hall. Forsberg took another step to peer down the stairs to check for privacy.

"We're going to begin a search of the Blue Knife River. It's most likely the reason why Levi took the truck instead of his Mustang, and from the looks of Joey's socks and cuffs, he's been wading in water. The mud on his shirt means he was either somewhere along the Blue Knife or out at Bleeding Rock."

"Oh dear Lord," Nikki gasped.

Forsberg also thought of what happened to Isaac Larson years earlier. "I don't know where this is going to end."

"It ends with you finding Levi," Nikki snapped.

"All I'm saying is that I'm going to need to call in help, Nikki. The lights are about to get very bright."

"What is that supposed to mean?"

"You've been hiding from it for a long time," Forsberg began and then shifted strategy when he saw her ready to emotionally break. "For all we know, Levi is sitting under a tree with a whiskey bottle, but I'm going to call in a child psychiatrist that specializes in interrogations, and then I'm calling in Ron Spears to begin a search of the Blue Knife, which will most likely end up with a call to the B.C.A. and F.B.I. If Levi is truly missing, the national news will descend upon us. I'll have twenty-four hours before somebody looking for a career case comes with a letter from the governor taking over the investigation. I need any leads so I can act quickly before other investigators show up."

"Lacy Morrison," Nikki quickly offered. "She works at the nursing home, and spent time with both Levi and Lily. You need to talk with her."

"Levi has been spending a lot of time with Joey recently," Gavin offered. "They were, I don't know, working out behind the barn. Something about *Rocky IV* training."

"Levi was training?"

"No, it was for Joey. I think I even remember him saying something about bullying. Perhaps some trouble with kids at school. I don't know."

Gavin and Nicki had tried to distance themselves from the Isanti Lodge, yet they knew what Lily's death meant. Brian let his anger get the better of him. "There is a dreamcatcher hanging in the window upstairs. I've been out patrolling for monsters, all you needed to do was keep your kids home. Was that too much to ask? Why am I just hearing about these issues?"

Gavin put a hand on Forsberg's shoulder, and then also on his wife's shoulder, physically uniting the three of them for a moment. "What do you need from us?"

They're both clueless. "Sit tight for the evening. I'll take this to the next level and get the search started overnight, but by morning, if we haven't found him, there will be a lot of questions asked."

"And?" Gavin asked, finding his resolve again.

"There are three possibilities right now, and the first will come at you fast. The second possibility is that Levi ran away...for a reason. If he did have a reason, then we need to protect your family, don't we? In that case, insist on having myself or Ron Spears with you at all times, or I can even have Lieutenant Harper with you...for oversight. They can watch over you guys if things get intense. The third possibility is abduction. If you remember what happened to Migisi back in the day, you know this can take a few forms. I'm going to have Father Gary and Migisi meet in order to—"

Why didn't I act faster? I coulda hauled his ass to jail for arson and watched over him myself.

"This can't be happening," Nikki said, pulling her shoulder away from Gavin. "Not again. This isn't real. We've...we've..."

Despite her turned back, Gavin wrapped his arms around her, whispering into her ear.

"Use your family," Forsberg said. "Make sure every family member is being watched. Keep them gathered together until I can sort things out."

BY THE TIME Forsberg returned to his SUV, night had arrived. He called dispatch and got the operation rolling, setting up operation centers at Nimrod and Turtle Island Jesuit School. On his way, he'd stop and speak with Migisi, although he feared the answers he'd get.

But as he reached the end of the driveway, he drove down the gravel road only a few yards before stopping. With his big flashlight in hand, he climbed into the grassy ditch and passed by a few old, familiar trees.

The ravine was still damp from the deluge, and the Crow Wing River flowed with a light rumble as it leapt over rock and branch. Looking down, he realized his feet left footprints.

Whatever happened, there will be footprints.

I hope to God there are footprints, Forsberg thought, remembering the tales the others told of Tak-Pei and Manitous. *I can handle footprints.*

His flashlight found a few old boards still clinging to a tree, but the deer stand had rotted away years ago. Levi would not be found huddled inside, but nevertheless, he still scanned the area before the tree for footprints before turning back to begin the hunt for answers.

CHAPTER SIXTY-FIVE

A Change is Gonna Come

St. John, MN
June 15, 1986

Captain Chuck Luning pulled up to the small cottage in his 1985 Ford Bronco II and popped the horn so quickly it sounded like the road runner. He pushed the eject button on the car stereo and Sam Cooke's *20 Greatest Hits* cassette stopped playing.

The garage door opened, revealing an ever-shrinking superhero in leather work boots. Even in retirement, Wally Crain dressed ready for chores. As a boy, Chuck had been part of Boy Scout Pack 88, and his pack leader was the tattooed sailor who reminded everyone of Popeye. Back in 1949, Wally Crain oozed testosterone from his armpits, grit from his brow, and machismo from his mouth. The foul-mouthed World War II vet could flip a switch when around civilized adults, but when he was around eleven-year-old boys, he imparted a crash course on being a man.

When did he get so old?

The garage door opened fully to show Wally holding a metal lunch box, something Chuck didn't even consider bringing. For four decades, Wally hauled fuel oil for Ulman Oil, retired at the age of 58, and lost his house and half of his wife the following year. Wally stepped to the side of the garage and pushed another button to close the garage door behind him.

Wally should be jigging for walleyes in a boat, not dealing with this shit.

"This is a beautiful vehicle," Wally said as soon as he fell into the seat.

"I got the Eddie Bauer edition."

"Who's Eddie Bauer?"

"Damned if I know." Chuck shrugged at his own ignorance and arrogance for bringing it up. He knew his humble family history. Farrell Luning had been a hard-working peasant who worked for lumber baron George Fisher, so he had no problems spending the family inheritance on a nice truck. Chuck's mother Betsy still lived the life of royalty even though Farrell's sawmill and George's lumber mill were both gone. "Any updates from Forsberg?"

Wally shook his head, eyes grim.

"Still think this is a good idea?"

Wally sighed. "It needs to be done. The servants of the Wintermaker come in many forms: spiritual and physical. Back in 1962, our greatest threats came from the human kind."

Chuck backed the Bronco out of the driveway and onto the quiet streets of St. John. Although it was almost eight o'clock, the town still slept on a Sunday morning, with most church services beginning around ten o'clock in Hiawatha County. Back in 1962, Chuck was stationed in Georgia while he was learning how to be a helicopter pilot. He'd heard the stories about the red Thunderbird, the child molester Logan Troost, the terrible winter, and the epic flood that almost destroyed both towns on Lake Manitou, but none of it explained or justified how he'd lost his grandpa and little brother in an accident. Now, Levi MacPherson was missing and Eos still hadn't paid the price for what'd happened decades earlier.

For this reason, Chuck had two loaded shotguns sitting on the backseat of his Bronco.

It was a short drive.

Halfway to the Blue Knife River bridge, Wally spoke softly, "I drove out of town on this very road the day the Stewart boy disappeared. Eos isn't afraid to eat one of its own. Don't forget that."

Time to get in the fight.

Even in the Vietnam War, Chuck had been late to join the fight. When it became obvious that helicopters would be used to fight in the remote jungles of Vietnam, he helped train pilots on all of the new types of helicopters being sent into combat. He'd been flying the new AH-1G gunship when he was shot down in July of 1972 as the U.S. transitioned from a ground war to an air war.

Chuck had less dread when he lost the tail rotor than he did as he stepped on the brake and turned onto the paved Marquette driveway. It had a metal gate closing it off from the world, and even from the truck, Wally could see a lock upon it.

The Marquettes like their privacy.

Chuck put the Bronco into four-wheel drive and drove through a narrow gap in the jack pines. While Forsberg and his deputies had to play by the rules, a couple of well-intentioned local boys would get a free-pass for zealously searching for a missing boy. The Marquettes weren't answering their phone, so a forceful bit of trespassing seemed warranted on a Sunday morning.

The Bronco quickly returned to the paved driveway and slowly approached the estate. When the jack pines opened up to a twenty-acre clearing, a beautifully pristine complex welcomed them.

Several cars and recreational vehicles were parked in the loop in front of the house and in front of the large garage behind the home. Wally reached for his lunchbox as Chuck stepped on the brakes.

The front door was open and a dead dog rested on the ground near the front steps.

Chuck flinched when Wally's hand pulled a revolver from the lunch box. "Father Guerin's pistol."

The hair stood up on Chuck's forearms. After crash landing in Laos, far behind enemy lines, he had to sneak through rivers and jungles to reach Thailand, where a prostitute nursed him back from death's door and helped him find a way home. Four months of hiding from certain death made him wary, so he had no qualms grabbing the shotgun before he opened the doors of the Bronco.

"Hold on one second, Wally," Chuck said as Wally took a few steps toward the open door. Chuck reached back into the Bronco and held the horn down for several seconds and then followed by three quick bursts. "Hello! Is anyone home?"

There wasn't even a dog bark.

"Go around back," Chuck said. "I'll check the house."

"The heck with that. We'll go in together. I don't want you shooting me just because you get jumpy. We'll go in together."

Blood splatter covered the back wall of the entryway, a pair of feet could be seen through an adjacent doorway.

Wally breathed heavily beside him.

"Hello?" Chuck called out again loudly. "Is anyone here?"

Silence answered them.

Chuck could only look at Wally's bewildered face and shake his head.

What are we doing?

"Keep an eye out," he said before stepping closer to check the body. The blood was dark, a sign the murder hadn't happened recently. Marion Marquette had a chunk of her collarbone, neck and jaw missing from the shotgun blast that'd painted the entryway wall. She was quite obviously dead.

The second victim was the phone on the wall, blasted to pieces by the attacker's shotgun.

Chuck looked back to Wally. "Be sure not to touch anything. We don't want to be implicated."

"We need to look to see if there are others," Wally insisted.

Damn it. He's right.

The pool of blood from Marion Marquette had footprints that led deeper into the house. Chuck made sure to steer clear of the boot prints and followed them to the living room where Todd Marquette was lying dead in the shattered pieces of a coffee table. Three bullet holes—likely from a pistol—dotted his chest.

On the far end of the house, Chuck found the old man, Al Marquette lying dead in the hallway.

From there, he found a bedroom where a young woman had been shot three times—Stephanie, if he remembered her name correctly.

"This family was targeted. This wasn't a break-in gone bad," Chuck said aloud. Two shooters entered the house from both sides, one with a shotgun and the other with a pistol. *Didn't Marquette have a young boy? Nate?* Chuck made eye contact with Wally to ask, "What about the boy?"

"Levi! Levi MacPherson? Are you here?" Wally shouted loudly.

Not Levi, Nate. Does he think Levi did this?

Chuck put the timeline together. Levi had vanished less than 24 hours earlier, and from the looks of it, the Marquettes were killed sometime last night. But no, it couldn't have been Levi, even though the Blue Knife River was only a mile away through the jack pines.

It can't be a coincidence.

Eos ate their own to cover something up.

CHAPTER SIXTY-SIX

Caught in the Net

Split Rock, MN
June 15, 1986

Karson Luning threw himself into an old project—assembling a new computer. The rest of the Isanti Lodge were running all over Hiawatha County like chickens with their heads cut off, but Karson could not follow, so he let his own troubled mind fixate on something other than the Levi problem.

His brand new IBM RT PC had arrived in March, but Halley's Comet, astronomy, and the End Times stole his attention. With the new keyboard on his lap, Karson rolled down the hall to his Great-Grandfather Albert's study.

The study held a collection of thousands of books, mostly nonfiction and historical. Thirty-six feet of laminate countertop had been set up in front of the library shelves, allowing Karson the freedom to roll up to his Apple computers, his Apollo, the Sun, or the DEC. The new IBM was faster and more powerful than any of the others—if he could get the stupid keyboard to work.

What a mess.

The packing, box, screwdrivers, cables, tower, monitor, and mouse were still sitting where he'd left them. Now, instead of a missing keyboard, he had a missing person and a murdered family.

The red phone rang, startling him. He pushed away from the countertop and rolled over to his grandfather's desk, where the private, unlisted phone rang for his attention.

"This is Karson," he announced, unsure of who answered the beacon for help.

"Hey, this is Grady out at the Brainerd hanger. I've got some info you might want."

"Same rate as before?"

"Suppose."

"Then whatcha got?" Karson asked, his heart racing.

"Flight departed a few minutes ago headed for MSP."

"The passengers?"

"That smoking hot redhead…she was there. So was the guy and two kids."

"Same four departed together?" Karson clarified, having heard of their staggered arrival after pressing Grady for the information a day prior.

"All together."

"The solo guy in the white Chevy?" Karson asked.

"No sign of him. The other planes are still parked."

"You're the man, Grady, you're the man. Let me know if you see that fella with the goatee come around and I'll double the pay. Keep things on the down low, though."

After hanging up the red phone, Karson could no longer focus on his new computer. He left things where they were and rolled back down the hall to the kitchen for a bite to eat. He was rummaging through the snack cabinet when the wireless wall phone rang.

"Karson speaking," he answered.

"Oh, hey," a woman's voice answered. "I wasn't sure if I'd reach you, and the name in the phonebook was—"

"Yeah, this is my grandma's home. Lacy?"

The sniffle confirmed the young woman had been crying. "Uh-huh. Did you hear about the Marquette murders and Levi McPherson vanishing?"

"I have, Lacy. I know on good authority that a lot of quality people are out looking for him right now," Karson said in reference to Forsberg's A.P.B.

"I've heard that folks think Levi is a suspect."

"Oh, no. Don't rush to judgment. All we know is that he's missing."

"I've got a theory, but, um…"

Is this why she's calling? "Go ahead. You can trust me."

"It's stupid and weird, but…you know Mrs. Crain's manuscript? The one Wally asked me to read to her? Well, in it, she's got a character that seems to be a lot like Levi, and in her story, he decides to run away to get away from his overbearing mother, and one thing leads to another, and he ends up joining his favorite heavy metal band."

Karson also remembered the irony of seeing the Kauffman name used for another character. "What about it?"

"Levi's been acting funny for the past few weeks, and perhaps all of his strange comments were about running away."

"Why would he leave his Mustang at home?" Karson offered. "How did Joey end up north of town all by himself?"

"I don't know, Karson. But I do know the thought of him running away is much better than him getting involved in that mess at the Marquette place. I just can't picture him involved in any of that mess."

"Me either," Karson added and tried to help the Isanti Lodge by asking, "And you haven't spoken to him since…"

"Graduation, I think. I called him after Lily's passing, but he didn't go to the funeral, so I haven't seen him since my open house. I just needed to sort things out in my head, and you're the only one I could talk to about the manuscript. It's so weird. Do you know anybody named Ansel?"

"Yeah, I think I do. What about him?"

"Who is he?"

"Why are you asking?"

"Well, he was all over Mrs. Crain's manuscript also. I mean...I just don't know what to think. It's all kinda *déjà vu* stuff. Do you think Mrs. Crain was psychic?"

Karson let out a long exhalation before he answered. "I don't know what to tell you Lacy. I've known her since I was your age, and there was nothing kooky or strange. To be honest, it's probably just all coincidence. She probably just picked names from her world never expecting folks to read the stories. I'll look into things when I head to work. I'll give you my opinion after I look things over. But just remember, I'm not much of a reader."

"Thanks, Karson. You're the best. I'm going to the Sheriff's Department tomorrow morning to make a statement about my dealings with Levi recently. Should I say anything to them about Mrs. Crain's manuscript?"

"I'm friends with both Wally and Forsberg, so I'll say something to them about it instead. Chin up, kid. Things will work out in the end."

"I hope so. Thanks again, Karson."

Why do I feel as if that's not the last of it with her?

After the conversation ended, Karson returned to the snack cabinet, where he found a can of Pringles. Computers and junk food helped him cope with stress.

He was rolling down the hallway back to the study when he caught a strange image in his reflected image. The sun had set and darkness arrived, making the western windows a mirror, but within the reflection of his own head, he could see through the glass to the yard where the big willow tree loomed. He knew its history as well as its recent events, so when he saw a piece of white fabric move, he skidded to a stop.

What the heck is that?

At first, it looked like a comical Halloween ghost costume, but then he realized it was a white blanket thrown over the shoulders of a small, blonde haired child.

The young girl stopped when she saw him looking out at her from the illuminated hallway.

Karson pivoted and propelled his wheelchair as fast as his arms allowed, but by the time he got to the entryway door, he could only see the girl running across the yard toward the street.

"Hey, wait up. I just want to talk," he called out, but the girl didn't stop running until she reached the end of the driveway and street.

I could hear her footsteps. She wasn't a ghost. That kid was real.

All alone, Karson suddenly realized he had no one to talk to about the strange encounter, and even if he had company, he wasn't sure which of his friends he'd talk to about it.

For a moment, he thought about calling Lacy Morrison back, but instead, he turned to his new computer to forget about everything.

CHAPTER SIXTY-SEVEN

Guardians of the Knife

Turtle Island Reservation
June 15, 1986

Leonard White Elk sat on Migisi's deck and smoked alone. The old man had to be lifted into bed due to the beating he'd taken the previous day, and seeing him in such poor condition made Leonard worry he wasn't going to live long enough to give a proper account of what happened.

This place is indeed evil, Leonard decided as he packed his Calabash pipe with tobacco and lit it with a match. When the flame descended into the tobacco leaves, the light was replaced by the floodlights set up near the river.

It's not my fight, he told himself when he heard voices in the distance. *Just mind your own business for the next few days until the dust settles.*

He'd only taken a few drags from the pipe when the front door opened and closed. His nephew Ben LaBiche joined him at the railing of the porch. Even though they were relatives, Ben carried Anishinaabe and Shuswap DNA whereas Leonard had Anishinaabe and Lakota, making him taller and leaner than his nephew. "Migisi's settled in for the night," Ben declared. "He won't take any medicine and refuses to be taken to a hospital."

"He's a tough old bird," Leonard said with a deep voice that held no humor yet when he turned to Ben, the young man smirked.

"Yes he is. That was quite a story Cameron told us, wasn't it?"

"I'm angry at myself for leaving them in their time of need."

"You thought there was still time to help," Ben reviewed their last-minute trip back to Lake Manitou after the passing of Lily Guerin. "How could you know? So what do you make of the disappearance of the MacPherson boy?"

"Murder creates black magic, and black magic hangs upon the air all around Lake Manitou. If I were to guess, I'd say the murders happened to mask what really happened here."

"And the Memegwesi that attacked Migisi?"

"Demons," Leonard added and then conceded, "evil spirits that haunt this place. Were they serving the will of their master or trying to protect him? That answer is yet to be seen."

"So you think Cameron and Migisi were telling the truth?"

"Migisi is an honest man and Cameron is a simpleton, so yes, I think they were being truthful, but they only saw a small part of what happened. The storm. The murders. Levi. The cave. The child. We might not ever find out what happened here, but we do have one good thing to celebrate."

"Celebrate?" Ben recoiled in near disgust.

"The world did not come to an end today," Leonard reviewed. "We live to fight another day."

For a few minutes, uncle and nephew sat in harmony in the night. Then the angry voices grew louder again and an air horn shattered the peace.

"What's going on?" Ben asked and immediately began walking outside to find out for himself.

Leonard reluctantly followed, knowing already what he'd find.

A hundred paces away, night turned to day under the brightness of the portable floodlights set up on the edge of the river. Across the river and several hundred yards through the woods, the Marquette property drew the attention of the Hiawatha County Sheriff's Department, who not only secured that crime scene but also began a search for the missing Levi MacPherson.

Even though Leonard had grown up in British Columbia, he knew who ran things on the reservation, and within minutes of discovering what had happened to Migisi, he put a contingency plan into place. Now a dozen armed tribal police officers (some real and others just wearing the uniform), stood along the eastern banks of the Blue Knife River.

In the water and on the western bank, HCSD deputies stood with various detectives and investigators. Sheriff Forsberg stood with one foot on a small boulder and another on a jon boat captained by a local river rat. Forsberg still held the air horn in his hand.

Mizheekay Reservation's fiercest men guarded the small opening to the cave—just below where Migisi's sweat lodge had been built.

"Finally," Forsberg muttered when he saw Leonard standing at the top of the ravine. "Can you tell all these fine people that we're allies?"

"Are we?" Leonard asked flatly, bringing grins from the local men. "The MBO might exist within Hiawatha County, within the state of Minnesota, and within the United States of America, but we're a sovereign nation with sovereign rights. The riverbank beneath my feet is beyond your jurisdiction."

"Leonard, I'm just trying to eliminate a few possibilities, and I've got investigators on this side of the river crawling up my ass for answers, and your guys are only making matters worse. By tomorrow afternoon, the FBI will be showing up. Do you want to be dealing with them or me?"

"The FBI only has jurisdiction on sovereign land when a major crime happens against a person living on the reservation. I'm not a lawyer, but neither the Marquette family nor the missing teen belong to the Turtle Island Reservation."

"Neither do you," Forsberg taunted back. "Can you and I talk for a few minutes?"

Little to no privacy remained in the ravine thanks to the four floodlights that illuminated the stretch of river. Forsberg sighed and began climbing to where White Elk stood.

Leonard could hear him muttering profanities with each step he took. He and Forsberg stepped around a corner, using bushes as a shield. He gave Forsberg a moment to catch his breath.

"Any news about the MacPherson boy?" Leonard asked softly.

Forsberg nodded. "We found the birch bark canoe in Lake Manitou this morning, and according to my man down in the jon boat, the truck had been parked up by the Nimrod bridge as recently as Saturday night."

"What about the boy himself?"

Forsberg took one final huff of breath before regaining his composure. "His body could be stuck in that cave."

Leonard shook his head. "I checked it myself—at Migisi's behest."

"You entered a potential crime scene?"

Leonard reached out a hand and clamped it on Forsberg's shoulder. While Forsberg could normally use his size to bully others, Leonard had several inches of height and fifty pounds more muscle than the younger sheriff. While their relationship was limited, Leonard knew Forsberg's role and vice versa. "The White Egg is gone."

Forsberg swallowed and processed the information. "This is all a cover-up, isn't it? Eos stole it and murdered that family for knowing too much. Goddammit. Levi stepped right in the shit, didn't he?"

"Migisi is nursing wounds up at his cabin after what happened in the storm."

"Yeah, I got that much from Cameron when I was interviewing the MacPherson family."

"Migisi claims he and Lily left the Stone hidden in solid rock. It would take dynamite to get it out, yet during the story, the demon Tak-Pei rushed to the cave, and he claimed to have heard the Song of the Manitou on the air."

Jason Lee Willis

Again, Forsberg took a moment to process before he muttered, "The kid was hiding something from us. Could he have taken the Philosopher's Stone and run?"

"It's a better thought than it being in the hands of Eos," Leonard admitted. "The Mizheekay Band of Ojibwe will not allow you, the FBI, or any outsider to take another step toward that cave. You have to understand something very important: generations ago, the Wijigan hid the Water Drum and Ironwood Scrolls in that cave for safekeeping."

"Ironwood Scrolls?" Forsberg queried.

Leonard nodded, finding relief to be speaking to an ally in such matters. "Likely not the *original* Ironwood Scrolls, but they are still a significant historical record for the Ojibwe and the Wijigan Clan. Knowing time was of the essence, I had to alert tribal police, which is why they are so earnestly guarding it and will continue to guard it. You need to take my word that Levi MacPherson is not in the cave."

"The Stone is gone?"

"I believe Migisi when he says they were ambushed, but then again, he never saw Levi during all of it."

"Or Joey."

"Joey?"

"The kid. The little brother. We think the two of them came down the river in the canoe. The boy was found wandering back into town just as the storm was ending."

Now Leonard took his time to process. "The Omodai. All this time, I worried about Lily Guerin betraying us. I hate to say I told you so, but it seems as if her family has somehow secured another generation for humanity."

"Excuse me?"

"My mother Fawn was right; Lily and Jean Guerin were wrong. Halley's Comet was a harbinger for the end of the Sixth Fire and the beginning of the Seventh Fire. All her preparation for fighting the Wintermaker was for naught. The real battle won't happen for another 75 years."

"Okay, but I don't give a shit about that. I'm looking for the boy, the men who killed the Marquette family, and apparently, a missing Stone."

"No one outside the Isanti Lodge can know about the missing Stone. Watch Eos. Their actions will show whether or not they have acquired it. Without the Ironwood Scrolls or…well…let's just say none of their plans can come to fruition unless they have all the pieces of the puzzle."

"Then I need you to do your part and get those relics out of the cave as soon as possible. I'm sure you're familiar with the U.S. Government overstepping treaty rights and with Eos pulling the strings; there might not be much I can do to stop them."

"I understand. We've got some scholars and experts arriving tomorrow."

"Don't let it fall into the wrong hands," Forsberg said and walked back to climb down into the ravine. White Elk followed and nodded in affirmation to Ben. "Okay boys, we're calling it a night. We'll let the Feds sort things here."

He and Ben watched the local agents depart and the jon boat shoot back up the river. When the authorities were gone, Leonard called out, "Well done, gentlemen. Stay vigilant. There's more danger than white men lurking in these woods."

CHAPTER SIXTY-EIGHT

Eye of the Hurricane

St. John, MN
June 16, 1986

Forsberg stepped aside and David Droshe from the B.C.A. stepped to the microphone to explain the procedures they would take to find Levi MacPherson. Like the press conference for the slain Marquettes, this one was packed—the MacPherson clan sat in the front two rows, concerned citizens sat behind, and all the media outlets filled the rear and sides with cameras. Whispers had already begun about a connection between the two cases.

Forsberg felt his tie tighten at his Adam's apple, and his sweat began to soak through his white dress shirt. He listened to the regional superintendent from Bemidji list off all the tools at the B.C.A.'s disposal. He stared at the ashen face of Nikki MacPherson, who listened intently as the B.C.A. promised to expand the net of investigation across Minnesota, which she needed to hear. There had been no sign of the MacPherson family truck anywhere in Hiawatha County.

Nor had they found a body.

Droshe finished his remarks about the case and stepped away from the lectern.

Forsberg stepped back to the microphone, "Again, today is about Levi. Today is about Hope. Levi MacPherson is still missing, and we must share his story if we are to bring him home. If anyone has information involving the whereabouts of Levi MacPherson, they are encouraged to call the Hiawatha County Sheriff's department. We are hopeful that someone will do the right thing, step forward, and help us bring Levi home. I'd like to thank Levi's family for their continued support as well as the county attorney, our county investigators, and the task force from the B.C.A. I'd like to reiterate that we will not give up because we are determined to bring Levi home. Thank you."

For the next twenty minutes, Forsberg's head throbbed with each question thrown at him, but he endured and kept things moving. Soon the wave passed over him. He lingered in the conference room for the casual conversations. Nikki MacPherson tried to give him insight into facts he already knew about Levi; Wally Crain let him know he'd check in on Ansel Nielson; Chuck Luning let him know the MBO agents had access to the cave.

Finally, he walked back to his office for a few moments of solitude. After making the necessary calls, Forsberg pushed his chair away from his desk and walked back out to talk with Mia Donaldson. He handed her a list of items that needed attention and received updates on both investigations. Detective Ray Irvin worked the Marquette case and his least experienced detective, Darlene Van Zanten, worked the MacPherson case. Her experience in robbery investigations would hopefully help. Sitting in Van Zanten's office, Detective Ross Coleman conducted interviews while Van Zanten looked for leads.

Sitting in an interrogation room, Lacy Morrison wiped tears while Coleman jotted down her answers. Coleman had already collected statements from the family, a group of kayakers on the river on Saturday, and several campers at Turtle Island State Park.

As he stood in the hallway, Percy Thorgard caught his eye from the lobby. Forsberg walked over to the lobby. "Not now, Percy."

Percy Thorgard held the press release crafted by the Hiawatha Sheriff's Department two hours earlier. "What's the deal with the truck?"

"Everything we know is written down on that sheet of paper you're holding."

"Oh please, I spoke with the kayakers who found the canoe. It wasn't just any canoe, was it? An antique birch bark canoe? Now you have all these divers looking for a body in Lake Manitou, but the truck is still missing. Who moved the truck from the launch site?"

"For all we know, some shitbird is hiding it in his garage right now, too afraid to step forward."

"So you think the truck was stolen?"

"There is a lot of river to investigate," Forsberg said.

"What do you think the little brother witnessed? At least tell me that."

"Not today, Percy." He walked back into the hallway just as Lacy Morrison stood up from her chair in the interrogation room.

Forsberg opened the door. "Mind if we have a quick talk in my office?"

Both assumed Forsberg was talking to them. "I'll get to you in a bit, Detective. I'd just like a word with Miss Morrison before she leaves."

He took a step back, led her to his office door, and closed his door once she'd found the chair. "This isn't an interrogation, young lady. I just want for us to get to know each other a little" He sat down heavily into his chair. "You're certainly in the eye of the hurricane, aren't you?"

She didn't understand his comment.

You were there with Lily in her final days.

Wally Crain trusts you with his wife's manuscript.

You're friends with Karson.

You work for Molly Chauvin.

You're pals with Levi MacPherson.

And you're a goddamn Morrison to boot.

"Mrs. MacPherson seems to think you know something about her son."

"Levi and I were just friends."

"I'm not disagreeing, but my time in law enforcement has taught me that teens tend to see adults as the enemy and...often hold back in trusting adults with vital information. Now, I'm sure you told Detective Coleman everything you knew about Levi. No one's accusing you of anything. I have a vested interest in keeping the citizens of my county safe and that includes you. What I don't want is to learn something two weeks from now that could've helped our investigation today."

Lacy nodded.

"You're one of, uh, Father Gary's crew, aren't you?"

"Youth group? Yeah. I attend St. Marie's."

"Good. Big Mack and I are old friends, and while you and I have just met, he's likely a person you can trust. Correct?"

"He's like a...we're really close."

"Good. Now, he's got his principles. He's not going to blabber any confession to anyone, including me. Yet he can also see the big picture. He knows a lot more about what's going on than an eighteen-year-old girl would understand, okay? So here's what I'd like you to do: go talk to him. You've had a tough weekend, and he's got pretty broad shoulders to cry on, so go talk to him. Go sort things out. Go tell him what you think he needs to know. If he thinks it's important, he'll steer you in the right direction. Are we clear?"

She nodded again. "Can I go?"

He nodded.

Oh yeah, she knows something.

Perhaps Nikki was right about her.

CHAPTER SIXTY-NINE

Part of the Job

Split Rock, MN
June 19, 1986

Father Gary did his duty even when he no longer believed. In God? Oh yes, he certainly still believed in God. His time in Vietnam as an Army chaplain cured him of any doubt.

Did he still believe in the Isanti Lodge? He had his doubts. Brian Forsberg convinced him fourteen years ago to become an active member in the team, but despite all their research and preparation, their plans fell to ash. The signs of a supernatural battle had been undeniable, but Gary didn't even understand the ramifications.

Did he believe Levi MacPherson was still alive? Unlikely. He sat between Leah MacPherson and Tammy, Benjamin's girlfriend, as both struggled to articulate their grief. With Levi missing for six days, the young women lost their resolve and began to openly mourn Levi, even though no one knew what had happened.

Levi's conservative older brothers, Benjamin and Reuben, immediately became angry, thinking their flakey brother had foolishly run away on an adventure; then they transformed into prayer warriors, expecting God to reveal their brother as if he was a lost set of keys hiding under the couch. Now, they were bitter, throwing up emotional walls to protect what was left of their shattered status quo.

After Monday's press conference, Gavin grew sick with intestinal issues, and with father bedridden, Daniel took to managing the barn duties, where he was able to hide any emotional reaction in hard work.

The extended family—Gavin's uncles and cousins—spent days searching rivers and the lake, fearing an accidental drowning. As farmers, they'd seen tragic deaths plenty of times and came into the house with a somber practicality after chores. With crops and livestock to tend, their support became task oriented, like young Daniel's support.

And Nicole? She worried him the most. After witnessing her slap Sheriff Forsberg during an update, Father Gary observed a performance worthy of an Oscar for Best Actress. She became a frenzied whirlwind of activity around the house—a model hostess instead of a grieving mother. And ever at her side was Joey.

The six-year-old took to sucking his thumb like a toddler and responded to questions in only nods and shakes of his head. After investigators and child psychiatrists had a go at him, Nicole shut the operation down, cradling him in her protective bubble.

A gentle knock at the door turned a dozen heads.

"What's *she* doing here?" Reuben muttered when Lacy Morrison stepped into the doorway of the kitchen.

"Is Father Gary here?" she asked.

Having heard the "Lacy Morrison" theory muttered a dozen times in the past week, Father Gary used the arrival of another visitor to leave the living room filled with adolescents, pass through the dining room filled with adults, and step into the kitchen, which held Lacy, Nicole, and Joey.

Lacy Morrison accepted Nicole's superficial hospitality and dished out equally sweet small talk. Gary paused at the edge of the kitchen to allow fences to be mended.

It'd been Nicole who'd not only opened up the old wound but personally threw salt in it when she offered Lacy Morrison as a person of interest to Sheriff Forsberg. The Lacy Morrison theory involved sex, drugs, and rock and roll. According to the rumor, the wild child of the senior class had latched her claws into Levi in recent months, introducing him to all sorts of hedonism. Whispers of drug dealers and kids from the wrong crowd offered an explanation beyond getting caught in a dangerous crowd.

Gary, privy to countless confessions at St. Marie's and private conversations following youth group in his basement, knew the truth about Lacy Morrison. When the Isanti Lodge met at the Fisher Mansion, he explained this to Forsberg, who agreed with the girl's innocence. Wally's grandson Garrett Johnson, a straight shooter and friend of Levi's from the sophomore class, also defended Lacy as only a friend.

After the pleasantries were dispensed, Lacy crouched down to Joey's level. "Hey Joey, do you remember me? I'm Levi's friend."

Joey looked down to a couple of plastic cows he was playing with.

"I just want to let you know that if you want to be friends, I'm willing to talk about anything you want."

At this, Joey looked up at Lacy. Like so many others, Lacy failed to get Joey to talk. Nicole rolled her eyes and scowled at Gary, who took the hint and began walking across the kitchen to intervene. "Thank you, Lacy. Let's give Joey some space. Let's step out on the porch to talk."

Lacy rose, only to look back to Nicole. "If you've got a moment, I'd—"

Father Gary kept contact with her shoulder, and she acknowledged the hand and the brewing hostility from Mrs. MacPherson. "I'm sorry, I just…"

Now at his side, she retreated through the doorway and into the entryway. Before he could get her outside, she stopped and reached her hand into her back pocket, which crinkled with paper. Father Gary put an arm around her and led her outside.

"Why do they hate me so much?" Lacy said once they had privacy. Tears immediately began to form in her eyes. "Why does *she* hate me so much?"

Because you are a Morrison with roots that go back to Bushy Bill Morrison. It gives me pause, too, even though I know you're innocent. "I don't think any of them understand your friendship with Levi."

"Joey does. He knows, and I also think he knows what happened to Levi."

Father Gary took her by both shoulders. "You're not Nancy Drew. You're not going to interrogate Joey in the MacPherson kitchen."

"But—"

"No buts. Whatever will be will be, but in this crisis, we must remain composed. Now, I meant to say something to you about this a few weeks ago, but life has a way of interrupting. A friend of mine reached out about the need for—"

"My God," Lacy gasped as if she'd seen a ghost. "I mean gosh, oh my gosh. You're…you're talking about working at the Bible Camp, aren't you?"

Gary recoiled. "Yes, did I already say something about it to you in passing? I had this whole spiel worked out in my head about why you should take the job."

Lacy shook her head. "What is happening here? The world's flipped upside down."

"I don't follow. What's got you so frightened?"

She reached into her back pocket to whip out a few pages of yellow paper. "This! Levi! Everything about this place is just…just….nuts."

Gary was almost positive he hadn't said anything to Lacy about it yet, so he proceeded cautiously. "The director at the camp has a job opening that is just perfect for you. I thought—"

"I don't want to play songs at Mizheekay Island while Levi is lost out there somewhere. It'd be all backwards. I'm sorry. I can't. I've gotta go figure something out."

She jogged away from him back to her car, leaving him a bit stunned.

She knew about the job? How?

What has her so upset?

He jogged up to her car as she was backing up. He stood at her window, which she rolled down. "How did you know I was going to ask you about the job?"

"I read about it in *Hamlet's Ghost*," she snapped and let her foot off the break.

At the end of the driveway, she didn't turn back to town. Instead, she turned to Old Copper Road.

CHAPTER SEVENTY

Best Friends Forever (and Never)

Chippewa Beach
June 19, 1986

Ansel's new orange raft turned out to be a 1953 Sunfish sailboat. Wally Crain knew all about it and its former owner, Neil Larson. When it was purchased in the late 1950s, the thirteen-foot fiberglass watercraft had an attachable keel and an aluminum mast that held a multicolored sail. Filled with foam, the little dinghy was virtually unsinkable, claimed Wally, and he hadn't seen the old boat for two decades.

Must've been on Carousel Island and blown into the lake by the storm.

Now, Ansel used a paddle to take him around Lake Manitou. He'd discovered his father's fishing pole in Ursula's closet, and he explored the shores under the guise of catching fish. Today, he explored a curious cove up the rocky shore from Turtle Island, but the shore was just too rocky to anchor.

Tomorrow, I'll take the three-wheeler and explore it by land.

Ursula had told him the news about the murdered family and the boy who'd vanished in the storm, and that morbid bit of news made exploration even more intriguing, especially after recognizing the newspaper images of Levi MacPherson from the scene of the house fire. Part of him wondered if the kid's dead body would come floating up from the deep like in the horror stories. Another part of him imagined the freedom of being out in the world at 16.

If I were an arsonist under investigation, I'd bolt too.

As soon as Ansel came around the corner of Chippewa Point, he could see the mobile home park in the center of the bay. The pieces of the Jimmy Nielson puzzle were coming together nicely, and his encounters with Wally Crain and Brian Forsberg helped him make sense of part of the mess.

But what the hell is this?

Ansel knew the family story. Aurora Hermann, visiting from Indiana during the summer of 1967, used to sunbathe with her mother on the dock. On a final fishing trip before leaving for Basic Training, Jimmy and Wally pulled up to the dock where it was love at first sight between his ill-fated lovebird parents-to-be. Now, like a ripple in time, another blonde waited on the dock.

There was no bikini or sunglasses with this blonde.

In fact, she looked pissed.

She stood with her arms crossed as she looked right at him.

In the distance, he could see Ursula out on the deck, now curiously spying on the situation.

Ansel found a paddling rhythm and let his momentum carry him into the side of the dock.

"Hey," he said, looking up at her.

"I figured it out. This is all your fault."

"Do I know you?" Ansel asked, stalling for time. Of course he knew her—but only from his dreams.

"Sorry, I'm Lacy. Lacy Morrison. I'm sorry to confront you like this, but everything has gone to hell since you showed up. Where is he?"

"The kid in the news?" Ansel shrugged. "How would I know?"

"Levi's not just 'the kid in the news.' He's important. He's a hero. Where were you last Saturday when he disappeared?"

Is she serious? Ansel unstrapped his black bag and set it on the dock and then gathered up his fishing tackle and also set it at her feet. Ansel carefully balanced as he lifted himself up from the boat and onto the dock. "During the storm? I was right up there with my grandmother."

Lacy looked down at the orange vessel. A thick, textured shell had been painted right over the Styrofoam core. Except for a slight depression for a couple of passengers, it wasn't much more than an amped up surfboard. "I read about this. How can it be real? How can you be real? You're Ansel Nielson, aren't you?"

He nodded. *I thought I was supposed to be the crazy one.* Her watery eyes showed she was on the edge of a breakdown. "Are you okay?"

"No, I'm not okay. I'm losing my freaking mind. You know what happened to him. You have to."

"Sorry. I wish I could help you."

"You can help," she said. "No one else will listen to me, but I think you'll know what to do once I tell you. God, I hope you do, or else this is the stupidest thing I've ever done in my life. I need you to make me a promise."

What is this? "I just met you," Ansel scoffed.

"I know, but even so, I want you to promise me that if I blow your mind, you'll help me find Levi."

"Was he your boyfriend or something?"

"No, it wasn't like that. He was just…he was kind when nobody else cared. I think he's in trouble, big trouble, and nobody seems to know how to help him." Lacy reached into her back pocket and produced folded yellow notebook papers—just like those from Ansel's dreams. He'd dreamed of writing songs with her in the rugged old cabin in the woods that he found a few miles away. Now the rest of the dream became reality. "What's that?"

"Levi gave this to me and said it was worth a million dollars. He said that when the time was right, I should give it to a person I trust most in the world."

"Why would you trust me? We just met."

"It's complicated," she said, putting the paper back in her pocket. "Levi seemed to think I was in danger, and he acted like he was trying to protect me. And now he's gone, and you're here." At that, she burst into tears and sat down on the deck in a heap of emotion.

Ansel looked around. He guessed she was a senior, putting her way out of his league as a lowly freshman. He was in the oily early stages of puberty and she was a woman blossomed. He sat down beside her when he didn't know what to say.

"Sorry," she said after a few moments. "I must look like a complete weirdo, huh?"

He nodded and she laughed, wiping away her tears.

"Should we find out if I'm insane?" Lacy asked.

Ansel shrugged. "Rip off the band aid? Folks have thought I was insane most of my life."

"Yeah, I know," Lacy said. "Are you ready for my party trick?"

"I don't know? Am I?"

"Probably not. In order to convince you, I'm going to have to get personal. Are you tough enough for that?"

"Lay it on me."

"You've got a pistol in that black bag, don't you?"

She's not real. I'm hallucinating.

"It's got one bullet in the chamber," she continued, "and your whole life, you've been trying to figure out the purpose of that bullet, so you brought it back to Lake Manitou to find out. You're probably thinking about using it on me, but I'm a victim in all of this, just like you."

She put a hand on top of the bag as if to block him from using it. He reached a hand out and put it on the top loop, ready to jerk it away if needed.

"I'm real, just like you're real, but I've been having dreams, and I read—you've also got your leather-bound journal and the book of poetry your step-father bought. You've got a picture of your sister, and the, uh, magazines, and the velvet bag of coins from all over the world. See? I know you."

This is why the raven came to me. This girl knows my nightmare about the scars. Ansel calmed himself and shook his head. "I got rid of the magazines, and I left the velvet bag of coins back home. That's pretty mind blowing. Cool trick. How'd you do it?"

"I read about us in a book."

Ansel swallowed hard and reflected on all the fragments of the dreams he'd seen. "Us?"

"On the day of the storm, I was supposed to be out on an inflatable raft over at Turtle Island where I worked at the camp. I never got the job, but the storm still came. I was supposed to be rescued by you on that stupid orange raft of yours. We were supposed to find shelter in a boathouse and bam—Stockholm Syndrome…best friends forever."

"I don't follow."

"Something changed, but I still I knew where to find you. I knew your name. She had four or five drafts, but in each one of them, she used the name Ansel."

"Who?"

"Mrs. Crain. She wrote about us, and some of these drafts are from the sixties. She knew twenty years ago that you were coming to Lake Manitou. She wrote that you were possessed by Merak or Gadrel or whatever evil lives in this awful, awful place, but you…you stepped right out of her manuscript and into the real world. Now do you see why I need your help?"

"Okay, now I think I get why the raven sent me here," Ansel muttered.

"Excuse me? A raven? What are you talking about?"

"You're not the only weird one. When I was back in New York, I kept seeing a raven, and it felt as if it was…watching me."

"Levi had a raven crash through his bedroom window and he nursed it back to health."

"When?"

"Last fall."

"I don't think it's the same raven, then."

Lacy went slack jawed and wide eyed. "You both had supernatural encounters with ravens. Does it matter if they're the same bird?"

"No." Ansel shrugged. *This is too much to handle.* "Would you like some fruit punch and rice crispy bars? My grandma is a terrible cook, but she makes really good bars. She's watching us right now, and if we stay down here any longer, she'll call Sheriff Forsberg."

"Rice crispy bars?" Lacy asked angrily and then softened into puzzlement. "Wow, I read about you but sitting right next to you in real life is a trip. I'm sorry for making you uncomfortable."

"Can you do me a favor and just wave at her for a moment?"

"Why?"

"So I can tell if you're real."

"What?"

"I need to confirm that I'm not having a breakdown."

"Yeah, sure. I understand," she said and waved at Grandma Ursula, who waved back.

Okay, I think I'm safe to continue. "Why would you think that I know something about the missing kid?"

"Levi," she harshly spit out his name. "In the manuscripts, you had a chapter with him where the two of you met and talked. That's how I knew about your gun. The two of you turned into enemies who played Russian Roulette, and that was right before he ran away from home to be a musician."

Ansel began shaking his head as he tried to unpack all the insanity that she just gave him. "Cool your jets for just a second. What the hell are you talking about?"

"Mrs. Crain's manuscripts. She's a patient in the nursing home who had a stroke, and to help her recover, her husband, Wally Crain, brought her manuscripts for me to read to her. I think they are some sort of alternate reality. It's like she could see the future, but then something broke, and now it's all been changed."

"And you think I changed it?"

"Yeah, or else, Levi did something."

"What does that mean?"

"That's what I'm trying to figure out. He came to me a few weeks ago acting really weird."

"Did you tell Sheriff Forsberg about this?"

"Kinda. I told him about my encounters with Levi, but I didn't tell him about the yellow papers."

"What's special about the yellow papers?"

"I'm not sure, but he told me they were important and that I should only share them with people I trust. I tried to talk to Sheriff Forsberg and Father Gary about them, but the more I thought about it, the more I realized you were the key to understanding this mess. I think you're the person I'm supposed to give this to."

Lacy reached into her back pocket and handed them to Ansel.

"What am I supposed to do with this?"

"Hell if I know," Lacy laughed and cried simultaneously. "Because of my dreams, Levi, and that stupid manuscript, I just needed to come find you. I think the point of the manuscript is that you and I are destined to be allies in this. I know it's stupid, but I feel like I already know you."

"Obviously," Ansel said, suddenly feeling himself falling into the chaos of his past. "What now? I share my trauma and you'll share yours?"

"If I'm right about this, I already know your trauma, so it's just a matter of whether or not you'll listen to me tell my side of things."

Ansel gripped hold of the yellow sheets firmly, as if trying to hold onto his sanity. "Sure, what the hell? It's what I came here for, right?"

CHAPTER SEVENTY-ONE

Like Pulling Teeth

Grand Rapids, MN
June 20, 1986

Tom Dobie dreamed he was in the scene of *The Exorcist* where the priests tried to hold the girl in place yet she rose into the air and levitated above the mattress. Regan's possessed eyes met his, and suddenly, he was the victim and she was the attacker.

When he woke, Dobie did not even stir. He'd seen enough horrors early in the week to almost laugh off his mind's coping mechanism.

He took assessment of his environment.

The Best Western Hotel in Grand Rapids, MN.

The eve before the Summer Solstice.

Three counties meant three different investigations, so even though it was going to be a challenging day, Dobie calmly kept his eyes closed, hoping it would be the last day he'd have to wake up in Minnesota.

He walked to the bathroom and showered. He'd been taught long ago that cleanliness was an overlooked level of camouflage. Failing to shower was akin to wearing a bright yellow shirt with a smiling face on it—people would notice, especially when things got up close and personal.

Over his fresh boxers and undershirt, Dobie wore nondescript clothing, with enough layers to tuck all the weapons he needed to feel comfortable. He packed the rest of his belongings into a suitcase and stood under the awning outside the front doors.

Unbelievable, Dobie thought as a vehicle came off Highway 2, drove right through the parking lot, and pulled under the awning. Robbie Kirkpatrick sat in the driver's seat, a pair of sunglasses providing little anonymity.

"You couldn't find a mobile hotdog or the Batmobile?" Dobie asked as he tossed his suitcase in the backseat.

"How can you complain?" Kirkpatrick said as Dobie sat beside him in the passenger seat. "This is perfect."

"A cargo van would have been perfect."

"A cargo van wreaks sinister desperation. It makes people ask questions. This is so obvious that folks will shrug and look away."

The light blue 1985 Buick LeSable Hearse pulled out from under the awning and back onto Highway 2, which stretched all the way back to Mackinac Island. Seventy miles and three counties separated the towns of Grand Rapids and Bemidji. Instead of talking business, Dobie focused on the bag of freshly made doughnuts between the seats.

By the time he finished the third, they'd already reached Deer River. Dobie brushed off his hands and glanced in the backseat. Blue carpet lined the floor and walls, and white curtains providing privacy for the windows. Wider than a truck bed, the floor had built-in hardware to secure even the largest coffin.

"How's our young man doing?" Dobie asked, looking through the glass that separated the front seats from the rear.

"Chilling, I hope," Kirkpatrick answered and glanced at the coffin.

After the chaos of the previous week, Dobie was in no mood for humor. "I'll give it to you; this is much better than a cargo van."

The hearse continued its tour of lake country, passing by the town of Bena. To the north of Bena, Lake Winnibigoshish acted as a 56,000 acre backwater of the Mississippi River, which followed the westward route of the highway. Just a few miles south of Bena, Leech Lake filled most of Cass County with its 102,000 acres of deep water.

"Have you personally scouted the cabin we are using?" Dobie asked as he looked south toward Leech Lake.

"I have," Kirkpatrick said. "It's perfect. It has a large garage with doors on both sides. We'll be able to back up the hearse just like a boat, and then the far end opens right onto this channel that leads to the lake. We can have the body stowed away before we even open the door. It's pretty remote also. Even though Leech Lake is a popular recreation lake, it's so big that there are miles of shore still untouched."

"What about Bear Island?"

"It's about four miles from launch to shore. Bear Island is pretty large, with only a few cabins on it. We have all sorts of options that will allow privacy."

"You've done well here in Minnesota."

"Thank you. How are things...elsewhere?"

Eliminating the Marquette family had been the easy part. Forming a plan under such pressure almost gave him an aneurism, but by Saturday night, he was hundreds of miles from Lake Manitou while Kirkpatrick cleaned up the mess. "I'll put in a good word for you after this is all done, especially after you had enough wits to move the truck. Things in Detroit were...a little chaotic. I'm actually glad to be out in the field again. Let them figure out what to do next. Back there, I feel like a fish out of water."

"I can't even imagine."

"No you can't, Robbie," Dobie thought of his unexpected delivery. "No you can't."

The hearse arrived in the town of Bemidji by midmorning. Besides being the "Curling capital of the U.S." and the alleged birthplace of Paul Bunyan, Bemidji was also deemed "The First City on the Mississippi," which flows through Lake Bemidji on its way from the nearby headwaters. The town of Bemidji was located along the western shore of the lake, where Dr. Floyd Ellworth, DDS, lived off of Birchwood Drive.

"Is that him?" Dobie asked as the hearse drove down the road at 30 mph.

"That's him. The past three mornings, he's gone out for a run."

"Perfect. Nice work."

"It's a team effort." Kirkpatrick shrugged off the compliment.

The hearse drove on, finding its way onto Bemidji Avenue, and then several blocks later, it pulled into a back alley behind Lakeside Dental Clinic. Even though most of the town was bustling, the clinic and other nearby businesses were closed on Saturdays, leaving the alley lots empty.

Kirkpatrick backed the hearse up to the rear door and turned off the engine. "Now we just wait for good Dr. Ellsworth to finish his morning run."

Dobie sat staring at the steel door in the brick wall and imagined the Adidas running shoes striking the pavement on the way to the dentist shop. Abduction by gun was a backup plan, and the men hired to follow the doctor were capable of sweeping him off the street in under ten seconds. Letting him step into a trap he designed was the best option, though. "I actually contemplated learning how to drill and fill cavities."

"You don't say, Doctor Dobie."

"Yeah, but this needs to be perfect. It's a shame it has to be like this."

"It is a shame."

"Do you have a plan for the wife and kids? How does this end?"

Kirkpatrick grinned. "Out of all the dentists in the region, Dr. Ellsworth is the most recently divorced. His wife left him and took the kids. I believe his training routine is meant to get him back on the market for the single ladies."

Finally, the door opened, and another killer hired by Kirkpatrick waved both of them in.

Damn fine work, Dobie thought, not wanting to give his former apprentice too much praise. He and Kirkpatrick walked to the back of the hearse, looked around the alley for witnesses, and then opened the rear. Wheels extended below the coffin, allowing the two of them to quickly push it through the backdoor of the dentist office. Ten yards down the hallway, he saw two more men with guns pointed at Dr. Ellsworth.

"Hello, Dr. Ellsworth. As you can see, we are serious men with a serious task. If you listen and do as we say, you'll continue on your way and we'll continue on ours like none of this happened. If you're ready to listen, just nod."

Following the first nod, the explanations were given.

Even when the sixteen-year-old boy's mouth was opened and an audible release of gas from decomposition came from his throat, the good doctor did not complain about the stench of death. Once they transferred the body from the casket to the dentist chair, Dr. Ellsworth looked at the x-ray belonging to Levi MacPherson and began drilling into the proper molars.

Dobie glanced at the dead teen's face just once while the doctor was preparing to fill the cavity. At first, the white flesh almost raised alarm, but having studied the stages of death and composition, Dobie understood the boy's body had gone through *livor mortis*, where the blood collects in the lowest regions affected by gravity. The height, hair color, and age, but not blood, would identify the body. A more thorough examination would add more certainty, but with the heat of summer, and the swampy region in the middle of Bear Island, the decomposition of tissue would provide no clues as to the cause of death.

Dr. Ellsworth tossed his instrument aside, glanced once more at the x-ray, and then stepped away from his patient. He nodded to Dobie, but then said, "There is no way to hide the cracking and chipping of the incisors."

Dobie looked over to Kirkpatrick, who shrugged. "A lot can happen to a kid since his last dental visit. It's better for a crack and chip to appear than to vanish, right doctor?"

Sweating profusely, Dr. Ellsworth nodded, a pistol still pointed at him.

"Then let's load him back into the hearse."

Two of Kirkpatrick's men kept the dentist against the wall while the other two helped load the body back into the casket. Dobie and Kirkpatrick pushed the casket back into the rear of the hearse, and with no witnesses, they drove back out of Bemidji the way they'd come.

"So…" Dobie began once back on Highway Two, "How does the story of Dr. Ellsworth end?"

"Tragically," Kirkpatrick said with little emotion. "After jogging all the way to his office, his heart gave out, leaving him dead in the lobby until Monday morning."

"Ah, explaining any smells of death."

Kirkpatrick nodded. "The dose we gave him, if even detected, is an anti-depression medication, which seemed to fit his profile."

It's a damn shame I'm going to have to get rid of you, too. Delhut and Sinclair rarely agree on anything, but getting rid of loose ends was paramount. When I'm done, will they get rid of me also?

Dobie proudly served Eos, even if he did have to die. "Did you hear the dentist at the end? Why would a fellow bring up the chips and cracks? Talk about a final nail in the coffin. Obviously, we had to kill him then. He'd call every coroner in the Midwest."

"I'm not questioning your plan, Tom, but why are we putting the body-double so close to home—and Bemidji? Why leave him at Leech Lake when we could drop him in some dumpster in Las Vegas and make it seem like he ran away?"

Suicide. Foul play would make people ask questions. Taking his life at his ancestral home ends all questions. "First, no one is going to connect the dentist and the kid. Levi's ancestors lived on Bear Island, so later this summer, when someone finds the body, it will make sense in a symbolic sort of way. It fits the lore, regardless of the cause of death. When they find the body and the truck, I want folks to stop asking questions about Levi MacPherson."

And then the real work begins.

CHAPTER SEVENTY-TWO

My Mind's Eye

Chippewa Beach
June 20, 1986

Ansel Nielson needed a break from Lacy Morrison, so he chose the company of his black bag over the company of his new acquaintance, at least for the evening. Even though she was plenty cute, he rejected her offer for a pontoon ride under the pretense that they could talk under the stars.

A quiet supper with Grandma Ursula and a full belly untied many of the knots that'd formed over the past two days.

"So can I ask about her?" Ursula said as she cleaned up the kitchen.

Ansel sighed as he sifted through all the ways to respond. "Go ahead."

"Who is she?"

"A local girl. Lacy Morrison. She's from Split Rock."

"How did you meet her?"

A manuscript written by some old prophetess English teacher. "I was out on my orange raft when the wind came up. She towed me back to shore on her pontoon. I left a couple things on her pontoon, so she brought them back," he lied for the sake of simplicity.

"You two spent a lot of time talking at the end of the dock. You know, that's how your mom and dad met. Your mom and I were sunbathing on the dock when your father and Wally Crain returned from fishing."

Ansel's head was still swimming and had no room for romantic suggestions. "I think I'm going to go sit on the end of the dock and do some journaling. My doctors said I should do that when sorting through my feelings."

"Can't you do that in your bedroom?"

"It's stuffy in my bedroom. Open up the blinds and watch if you'd like. I'm not trying to pull a fast one on you."

"Journaling is probably a good idea."

A decade of having folks walk on eggshells around him suddenly ended when Lacy Morrison began throwing out all the private details of his life. His inner skeptic had an answer for her knowing about his past. Small town gossip gave Lacy her answer.

His inner optimist?

She knew it all through supernatural means.

Ansel did as he told Grandma Ursula and pulled out his journal and flipped through the filled pages. It amazed him how fractured his brain had been during his middle school years. Even more amazing, he somehow survived it.

He turned around and looked to the trees for any sign of ravens.

No such luck.

It's close, he decided about his quest to understand his father's death. *I think the answers are getting close.*

The longest day of the year allowed him to sit on the dock until almost ten o'clock, which is when Ursula went to bed. He put his memories away, zipped up the bag, and then leaned back and stared up at the stars.

Where are you, Dad?

"Far from danger," a voice answered from the darkness of the lake. "He knew what slept beneath Lake Manitou."

It's not real.

That's neither Jesus nor a real dude.

Ansel could see the figure upon the lake, standing upon the surface of the water. It was no monster; it was a man. He wore heavy clothing, a jacket, and a fur hat with earflaps.

"What sleeps beneath Lake Manitou?" Ansel asked, kicking the water to send a futile ripple toward the figure.

"Nothing. The tomb is now empty, except for those who've been left behind."

"Who are you?" Ansel asked the ghost of an ice fisherman.

"One of many trapped here in the waters of Lake Manitou, but unlike the rest, I'm a little more than kin and less than kind."

That's Shakespeare.

That's fucking Hamlet.

He knows.

"Tell me. I know you, don't I?"

"Your grandfather was my grandson," the specter stated and he closed the distance between the two of them. "In life, I was Martin Nielson. In death, I am trapped here. You have the blood of the cloud champions. My blood. Unlike me, my grandson Edward died away from this cursed place. My son died even farther away. Your father made sure not to die in this evil place, but thankfully, you've returned in this dark hour."

Right. He died in the garage. "How do I know I can trust you?"

"You shouldn't trust me. The evil spirits trapped here can overpower a man and make him do their bidding. They can take the form of a loved one and mimic their voice. This is a dangerous place for you now."

"Should I leave?" Ansel asked.

Martin Nielson shook his head. "You've been led to this place for a reason."

Led by the ravens. "What am I supposed to do?"

"To your eyes, you see a lake, don't you? When I crossed the Atlantic to settle here, I built a farm on a hill because it all looked so lovely, but in reality, this is an evil place. Black magic from old binds the foundations of this place, trapping all spirits—good and evil—in the waters of Lake Manitou. The fate of mankind hangs in the balance. When I was not much older than you, I gathered on Turtle Island with Lily Weber, Father Jean Guerin, Fawn Chevreuil, Migisi Asibikaashi, Bjorn Forsberg, Kermit Crain, and Farrell Luning. We pledged ourselves to defeat the evil spirit that slumbers here. It was a foolish pledge. Now that the Wintermaker has achieved his victory, you must dedicate yourself to a new purpose."

"Whoa, whoa, whoa…victory? What are you talking about? That storm?" *The day Levi disappeared and the Marquettes were murdered.*

"A terrible sacrifice was made, and the Wintermaker, whose name has been lost to time, achieved his great victory and left his tomb. Now that he has left this place, you will need to—"

"Left his tomb? What? What happened? Does this have something to do with that kid Levi?"

"Of course it does. The evil spirits that dwell here have lost their purpose also. For countless generations, they have protected their master, but now, they act only on their own volition. A clock has begun ticking down and—"

"What happened to Levi?"

"He made a terrible but necessary choice, and his sacrifice has given the warriors of light such as yourself an opportunity to defeat the agents of darkness. If you are to honor his sacrifice, you must gather the rest of the Isanti Lodge together and let them know that the final hours are upon them. If you survive the coming days, then you will become a great warrior in this battle against the darkness. When the time is right, you will find your answers in the same place I found my answers."

"I don't understand. What am I supposed to do?"

"I cannot remain here. None of us can remain here. This place is an abomination, and if it is allowed to continue, the ancient prophecies will crumble and Darkness will return to the world. The Wintermaker has attained a victory, but the war is not over. Help me find peace, Ansel.

Help all of these poor souls trapped here. Only then can the world be restored."

"How am I supposed to do that?"

"The raven will guide you. The others in the Isanti Lodge have what you need."

"You know, if I was back in New York, my shrinks would say I'm having a complete breakdown. I'm probably just hallucinating right now. Why would a dead ancestor show up to tell me these things?"

"I died here, and my soul remains trapped."

"Yeah, I got that already. How am I supposed to know if this is real?"

The shadow came first.

Despite the dim light, the reflection appeared on the water in front of the dock. When the impact came, it hit him in the back of his head. The impact almost pushed him in the water, and combined with the flapping of wings, Ansel knew the attacker to be a raven. It almost dropped into the water but managed to get lift and circled back around to land on the end of the dock right beside him.

With one quick peck, Ansel's finger bled. "Ouch, shit."

Hot blood trickled down his neck.

"You can't always trust ravens since you don't know who sent them," Martin Nielson answered. "Nor do you know which tree they came from. If you find the white raven, listen to it. Trust it."

The raven took to wing, and Martin Nielson vanished.

Ansel found himself alone with his wounds.

I guess the blood is real enough.

He stood up and walked back to Ursula's mobile home. Fortunately, she'd already turned in for the night, and he closed and locked the door loudly enough to put her at ease in her bedroom. He grabbed a washrag from the sink to press against his head.

He took hold of the phone and punched in Lacy's phone number.

She picked up the phone on the first ring. "Hello."

"Hey, it's Ansel. I think I'm convinced of what you were saying. We need to talk about what to do next."

CHAPTER SEVENTY-THREE

The Keepers of Secret Knowledge

Mizheekay Band of Ojibwe Reservation
June 20, 1986

Migisi kept a fire in his fireplace even though it was the longest day of summer. He still ached from the attack and sat upon a chair covered in his softest blankets. Cameron Guerin sat on a chair near the deck window, staring off into the night.

There would be no ritual.

There would be no battle between good and evil.

The white men in the Isanti Lodge spent the supper hour with him, but he assured them that without Lily or the Water Drum, there was nothing for them to do. So Sheriff Forsberg, Mayor Luning, Wally Crain, and Karson Luning went back to Split Rock tasting the same defeat Migisi experienced a week earlier.

Cameron flinched, suddenly woken from his thoughts by a sight out the window.

Heavy footsteps announced the return of Leonard White Elk and the others. The deck shook until he, Ben LaBiche, and Sakima Riel reached the door.

"So?" Migisi asked immediately.

Leonard White Elk cautiously watched his head as he walked through the cabin and sat at one of the chairs remaining at the table. "A minor victory."

"The Executive Committee allocated funds for the preservation, protection, and study of the relic," LaBiche added. "It's out of your hands now, but it is at least in the heads of the People."

Despite being one of the smallest sovereign nations within the borders of the United States, MBO was still governed by a five-member Executive Committee. Norval Riel, the former superintendent, served as president and was an ally. Cindy Goodday served as Vice President but did not currently live on the reservation. Kristi Jackson worked at the school and served as treasurer but came from the Fond du Lac reservation near Duluth. Faron LaRoque—a concern— was a malcontent who only looked out for himself and his interests. That left young LeRoy Schrader, a young man shunned by Migisi a decade ago, who viewed himself as a traditionalist yet lived a modern life.

"They supported the resolution?" Migisi asked.

"It passed 3-2," LaBiche added.

"I don't think any of them but my father understood what was found," Riel asserted.

"It was never lost," Migisi corrected. "It's been hidden from the People for generations, but the Wijigan Clan has always known where the Ironwood Scrolls were kept."

"What about the Water Drum?" Leonard White Elk muttered and looked up to cast accusation at Migisi. His antagonism quickly softened with an eye roll.

At least he believes me that I went down fighting. "I cannot believe the Great Spirit allowed it to be kept in the cave for generations only to let our enemies take it," Migisi insisted. "Lily hid it where only she could claim it."

"But she also spent a great deal of time with Levi," White Elk added. At sixty-one, Leonard was still a powerful man whose looming shadow and deep voice provided all the gravitas needed. "He's got the blood of Wijigan also. Could he have taken the Water Drum with him?"

Migisi reflected on Forsberg's update. If the timeline was accurate, the Tak-Pei attack happened about the same time that Levi would have passed by the cave. Forsberg even estimated the amount of time it'd take Joey to walk back into town. "Only a trained Firehandler can command and hold the Stone. I have no reason to believe either of the boys could do such a thing."

The cabin grew silent as they all pondered possibilities.

"But he did have the blood of the Wijigan," White Elk added. "And Lily wasn't trained the first time she used it."

Voices from the future guided her. Is that the Song I heard on the wind?

"I'm not sure I understand the family tree," Ben LaBiche admitted.

Migisi cleared his throat. "Sakima, explain to Benjamin how our families are connected."

"Gladly," Sakima answered. "Our common ancestor was a war chief named Wiyipisiw, who brought his family to Lake Manitou in the 1750s. His son, Makadewaa, had two children: Chagobay and Kishkeedee, the latter married a Frenchman named LaBiche. From Chagobay, we have the paternal Weber family trees."

"Asibikaashi," Migisi muttered.

Sakima shrugged. "Yes, which also now includes the Guerin branch. Going back to Wiyipisiw, he also had a daughter, who I've yet to identify with a name, but her family ended up producing the LeDuc and Saucier branches. My Riel branch joins the LaBiche branch through the sister of Blackfish LaBiche."

Migisi looked at all of the men gathered with him. He knew he'd find death before his bruises could heal. "We're all family, but the war we fight goes beyond family, clan, and tribe. Fawn once tried to tell me that the battle between the Great Thunderbird and the Horned Serpent would not happen until its proper time, and obviously Father Guerin's interpretation of the Seven Fires coinciding with the Serpent Star was wrong."

Leonard uncrossed his arms at the peace offering. "I'm glad to hear you've opened your mind and heart. I wish Lily had been willing to listen to my mother."

"It was a confusing time," Migisi admitted. "The old men in the Wijigan Clan rushed to judgment and wanted only to fulfill their interpretation of the prophecy. Perhaps we can do a better job preparing the next generation."

This seemed to please Leonard. "It is good to witness the three branches of our family coming together. We've entered the first days of the Seventh Fire, and when the Serpent Star returns, we will have learned from our defeats to create victory for the People and all of humanity." Then he added. "But we'll need to begin healing our family by being honest."

Migisi felt his heart sink. "What are you accusing me of?"

"I need to understand what you and your sister have done in the past. If I receive an honest answer and reckoning of what happened to the Water Drum, then you and I will become true allies."

Migisi grunted and groaned as he rose to his feet. "Then let us go. I'll show you where it all began." Cameron rose and offered his arm and elbow to Migisi, and together they began walking out into the darkness. The setting sun still offered a glow to guide their feet, but Migisi knew each step of the path. With the Ironwood Scrolls now safely extracted from the cave, the security team no longer manned the location, leaving it empty and dark.

Migisi stopped at the edge of the ravine and looked down. White Elk, LaBiche, and Riel flanked him. "I didn't find the megis shells—Lily did." He explained how Lily, the discoverer of the megis shell, had been the true Firehandler, but her lack of training brought disaster when she first woke the Tak-Pei and later took hold of the Water Drum to openly confront the evil spirit from myth and legend.

Fawn knew this part of the tale.

So Migisi walked over to a patch of solid stone where a sweat lodge once had been built—the place he captured, tortured, and murdered Red

Dobie. "Lily last used the Water Drum in 1962 when enemies from the Order of Eos sought to wake the Wintermaker and his servants. We learned that just like our three families were fractured, the Order of Eos had division and also an enemy."

"The man in the red Thunderbird," Cameron quickly added.

Leonard White Elk turned to Migisi. "Care to explain."

"Some in the Order of Eos believed as your mother Fawn believed: that the prophecy would be fulfilled in proper time. Yet another faction within Eos worried about an external threat, another secret society looking to steal the prophecy away from Eos."

"Steal the prophecy? Do you think they are responsible for the theft of the Philosopher's Stone," Sakima Riel asked.

Migisi kicked his heel on the hard stone. "For most of my life, I kept the entrance to the cave covered, yet the Stone turned my efforts to dust as solid stone would be transformed to blue vitriol and wash into the river. Knowing this, Lily hid the Water Drum behind a wall of solid stone. The stories describe how the Water Drum had its roots in the creation of life, and perhaps that is true, but when I stood near it, it felt evil and I worry that it worked against us and allowed itself to be found by our enemies."

"So you think the Marquette family massacre is connected to this theft of the Water Drum?" Sakima asked and walked back to the edge of the ravine.

"You're suggesting that the Water Drum dissolved the walls on purpose?" LaBiche asked.

Migisi nodded. "Eos knew to look for the blue earth, it's what drew them here in the first place."

Sakima looked over the edge. "What if the Water Drum hid itself? You told us how Lily's song seemingly brought it to life, and it took on a form like a cloud. What if it just buried itself deeper into the granite?"

"No, it is evil. It was created by the Wintermaker to do his bidding. It wants to be found, which is why it transforms any container into vitriol."

"Yet the Song of the Manitou is what commands it," Leonard countered. "If the Ironwood Scrolls are a poor copy of the original song, what if a better version of the song existed?"

Sakima took a few more steps back toward the group. "I'm just saying that instead of Eos or Levi taking the Stone away from here, what if the stone is still hidden some—" He tripped in the darkness, muttering a profanity as he fell backwards onto his rump. He chuckled at his awkwardness before muttering, "Oh fuck."

A shadow rose up from the stone. In that initial moment, Migisi understood why the legends told of "little people" of the forest. The black form had a hunched back like a raccoon or porcupine. "Get the spear," he whispered.

Cameron bolted toward the cabin.

The Tak-Pei took hold of Sakima Riel in its jaws, shaking and tossing him like an alligator in a death roll. Sakima began to scream, but the black shadow enveloped him.

Without hesitation, White Elk rushed forward, throwing his mighty arms around the assaulting shadow. For a moment, he rolled with Sakima, taking hold of him by a knee. The Tak-Pei was neither solid, gas, nor liquid—but was all three simultaneously.

Ben LaBiche then appeared in the darkness, holding a lantern above the wrestling match. A black arm slapped him away and the lantern shattered against the cabin, erupting in an explosion of flame and light.

Cameron appeared a moment later and froze, terrified by the dark shadow and the flaming wall.

Migisi had to rip the wicker spear away from Cameron's grip. "Fetch my shield."

Far too old to run, Migisi shuffled forward to where the Tak-Pei wrestled all three men. He couldn't tell if it were Smoke or Shadow, his old foes, but he could see the strength and sheer will of Leonard White Elk keeping the two younger men from taking the full brunt of the attack. Like a tornado of black tar, the writhing spirit tried to pull the weaker men to the cliff.

Migisi hesitated for a moment, unsure of where to strike. His reflexes were far too slow to anticipate, so he blindly stabbed at the center.

Sakima Riel grunted at impact.

The blade had not been fashioned to cut or pierce. The sacred mineral used for pipes had been shaped into a spearhead long ago, and even though it struck the flesh of Riel, it did not puncture his ribs. Migisi did not have enough strength to kill any of the men, but when the pipestone spear touched flesh, the black tar of the Tak-Pei congealed at the tip of the weapon.

The wicker staff shook and vibrated, but Migisi held strong and took a step back. As he withdrew, Sakima Riel separated from the black shadow. LaBiche rushed in and took hold of Riel while White Elk rose and joined Migisi. He placed his powerful hands upon the staff and watched as the evil spirit separated from Riel.

Cameron returned, pausing several feet away to call out, "I have it. I have the shield."

"Do not let go," Migisi said to White Elk, who nodded in affirmation.

Migisi transferred the staff and turned to Cameron. Behind him, the flames grew on the wood wall of the cabin because of the spilled oil.

Remember your training.

Migisi calmed himself and took the old snapping turtle shield and placed it upon his left arm. All manners of incantations and imbuements had been rubbed into the shield. Next, he reached for his belt, where he found a bag of megis shells.

Trust.

Don't think.

He poured out the contents of the bag into his mouth then stepped back to take hold of the wicker staff. The hulking ogre cautiously gave the spear back to Migisi.

Migisi lifted the spear, and the black, swarming mass followed. His old feet pivoted carefully until he faced his burning home. Step by step, he drove the angry spirit backwards and then pressed it against the burning wall. Breathing in deeply through his nose, he spit the white shells at the pinned spirit, and immediately, a strange sizzle filled the air as the saliva and shell touched the black spirit.

"Hold him," Migisi commanded and Leonard once again took the wicker staff into his hands, grinding the red mineral against the wood of the cabin.

Migisi worried he'd fall dead. His heart pounded loudly enough to be heard and his breathing labored in the smoky air. Yet he had waited his whole life for this fight, and although it was not the Wintermaker, he delighted in battle.

The flame tortured the Tak-Pei as the magic of the megis shells bound the spirit in place. A cabin could be rebuilt, but a chance to interrogate an enemy was worth giving his life, so Migisi regrouped and stood beside White Elk.

"Where is your master?" Migisi asked. "Tell me and I will cast you into the river. Fight me, and I will send your spirit into the Land of the Midnight Sun."

The Tak-Pei answered.

CHAPTER SEVENTY-FOUR

The Long Game

Split Rock, MN
June 21, 1986

Father Gary Mackenzie understood the long game being played and trusted God to move the right pieces into the right places at the right time. Today, he listened to his colleague Father Tom deliver a homily on "optimism" to the congregation. Fifteen years earlier—right about the time God brought Ansel Nielson onto the great chess board—Gary learned he'd been assigned to St. Marie's Catholic Church in Split Rock, Minnesota.

Why?

The long game.

The surface answer had been that the Catholic Church wanted an active missionary presence in the region to serve and heal residual distrust between Indian populations and the Church, so who better than a Vietnam veteran and army chaplain? From time to time, Father Gary would deliver his own homily to his home congregation, but most of the time was spent leading the youth groups, visiting hospitals, and delivering outreach to several reservations in the area.

But it was all a facade.

Today, he sat in the chancel chair and looked out at the congregation. The entire MacPherson family sat in three rows near the organ, but Nicole stepped aside to let another play the music today. Edna Forsberg sat with two other widows. The surprise came when he spotted Lacy Morrison sitting in the balcony with Ansel Nielson.

Why?

The long game.

A day earlier, he'd sat with the rest of the Isanti Lodge as they despaired about the failed plans for the summer solstice. With the key players, Levi and Lily, missing, the only optimistic thought they could muster was the fact that the world didn't come to an end.

But it's coming.

Back in seminary school, he'd sat in a backyard drinking some fine wine with friends when they shared End Times theories. None of them, of course, knew anything about the Seven Fires Prophecies of the Anishinaabe, but four theories came to light:

Y2K—two thousand years since the birth of Christ.

2012—a strange Mayan prophecy with a countdown to doomsday.

2030—A modified version of the Y2K theory yet built upon the premise of Christ's death rather than birth.

2061—Apparently, the smartest man on the planet, Sir Isaac Newton, calculated the end of the world.

So as Gary listened to Leonard White Elk tell the group they were living in the first days of the Seventh Fire and the Great Battle wouldn't come for another 75 years, he suddenly realized that he'd become an adherent of the 2061 theory. While the Bible didn't come out and say it, Gary knew that one of the triggers for the End Times would be the "falling away," or Apostasy as it was called in school.

Although the MacPherson family held tightly to their faith in times of trouble, the rest of the pews in St. Marie's Church were mostly empty. His faith had been strongest in the jungles of Vietnam, but along the shores of Lake Manitou, his confidence in the institution eroded with each historical and supernatural discovery. One look into the balcony gave him his motivation.

Ansel and Lacy represented the long game.

They'd be key players in the final fight.

WHEN MASS ENDED, Gary took his place at the rear doors, shaking the hands of his parish as they departed. When a congregant leaned in to disclose a personal trauma, Father Tom would keep the line moving, or visa versa. Today, Lacy Morrison stepped in to say, "Do you have time to talk with us?"

He wanted to give them his undivided attention and nodded solemnly. "If you can stick around for about an hour, I'll meet you inside."

They slipped away without another word.

He pushed it from his mind for the better part of an hour, but as he was hanging his robes in his office closet, he heard piano music coming from the sanctuary. He found Ansel and Lacy sitting on the piano bench together. She kept playing as he approached and stood on the back side of the piano.

"Sorry for getting weird the other day," Lacy said once the song finished. "I shouldn't have come to talk to you at the MacPherson farm. That was stupid."

"Everyone is concerned about Levi."

Lacy's eyes tightened as she winced in emotional pain. "Can I tell you something strange?"

Gary looked around to ensure their privacy. "There's no better place to share."

"Levi sabotaged me."

"What do you mean by that?"

Lacy looked at Ansel, who nodded to continue. "He was looking out for me, I think. Somehow, he knew that you were going to offer me that job, but he sabotaged it by warning me about it. It's one of the last conversations I had with him. He took me to the hill overlooking the camp and all but warned me about it, so when you brought it up, it kinda freaked me out."

"I see," Gary offered to keep her talking.

"Ansel had something similar happen to him. He was out on his three-wheeler when he came across the Larson house on fire. He's pretty sure he saw Levi leaving the scene of the crime."

Ansel nodded silently.

"Does Sheriff Forsberg know about this?"

"It happened a few weeks before Levi vanished," Ansel said as he nodded. "But there are other things that I haven't told Sheriff Forsberg."

"About Levi?"

Lacy interrupted. "About his father."

This took the wind out of his sails. Gary walked around the piano and sat on the nearest pew. "I served with your father in Vietnam."

"We assumed," Lacy quickly added.

"Assumed?"

"This is where it gets weird," Lacy warned. "I read about it. At least...I read about a version of it."

"Say that again."

Ansel and Lacy exchanged worried glances before she continued. "Here's what we think happened. Levi had a vision of the future, and when he learned what was going to happen, he did everything he could to change it. Mrs. Crain also saw that future, and years ago, she wrote it down as if she'd just dreamt it all up, but she knew things. She knew about Ansel and his father and the gun and me and the raft and—"

"What gun?" Gary asked, feeling chills on the back of his neck.

Ansel reached into his black backpack and took out an old Polaroid. "What do you know about this picture?"

Gary covered his mouth with his hand, exhaling through his fingers. "I was the field chaplain for the 11th Armored Cavalry Regiment, which had a few thousand men in it. Your father served in J-Company, which was always out in the field, so I honestly didn't know those men as well as those who served from the base camp in Xuan Loc. The tank companies saw action on an almost daily basis, so they were not only difficult to track down, but they were also hardened men."

"I read about the Blackhorse Regiment," Ansel offered in unspoken understanding. "What do you know about the men in this picture?"

"They called him the Professor," Gary said, pointing to the dark-haired tank commander. "That's Jay Campbell, he married Julia Forsberg. They live in Baltimore. The two in the middle are Brian and Jimmy, your father, and, um…" Ansel's eyes locked his as he shamefully hesitated. "The big guy was Shane Lewis, the loader."

"And you know what happened to him?" Ansel asked.

Gary nodded as if he bore the shame. "When I heard what happened in Indiana, I went to your grandparents to counsel them through their grief."

"Did you hear what my father did to Shane?"

Gary nodded. "Is that why you asked me about the pistol?"

Ansel shook his head. "No, I wanted to understand why my father didn't use the last bullet to take his life."

"I don't understand what you mean?"

Ansel lifted the black bag and shook it to reveal the weight inside of it. "I can't trust my brain to know if I imagined things or not, but I think he wanted me to have this pistol for a reason. That's why he brought it back with him after he killed the Lewises." Ansel set the bag down and coldly stared at him. "Do you know why he brought it back to the garage?"

"It was just a passing moment," Gary began. "There was a break in the fighting after the battle at the Michelin plantation. J-Company was in tatters and waiting to be refitted. When I found your father, he was still suffering from the trauma of seeing all the men in his tank taken away by helicopter. The rest of J-Company was worried about him. I tried to get him to talk about it, but he refused. He even pulled the pistol on me before handing it to me. He said, "Evil is hunting me, Father. Bless these bullets so I can defend myself."

Lacy nodded and whispered, "Told you so."

Ansel took a breath as if he'd just broken the surface of the water. He grit his teeth and grimaced before relaxing. "Yeah, that's what we thought."

"You've had the pistol all this time?"

"I kept it hidden so they wouldn't take it away from me."

"We need your help," Lacy began. "Ansel needs to talk to Sheriff Forsberg about the pistol and…other things. If we can make sense of Ansel's situation, we might understand how to find Levi and figure out where he went and why he left."

"You think this has something to do with Levi?"

"In a roundabout way," Lacy continued. "Like I said, it's like Levi changed everyone's futures including his own. We need to talk to Sheriff Forsberg so we can sort through some of this."

I've been trying to sort through things with him for fifteen years.

Why not?

"I know he's really busy right now, but I also believe both of you; this is important! I'll call him this evening and set up a meeting for Wednesday. Will that work?"

Lacy nodded. "As long as it happens before August 2nd."

She looked over to Ansel and took his hand. "Something bad is supposed to happen to Ansel, and we think we'll need Sheriff Forsberg's help to stop it."

What am I supposed to make of this?

Yet in his heart, he knew his business with Jimmy Nielson was far from over.

CHAPTER SEVENTY-FIVE

Like a Canary

St. John, MN
June 25, 1986

Duty left Brian Forsberg shackled to his desk. Since becoming Hiawatha County Sheriff, he did less and less investigative work and more stamping reports and paraphrasing the work of others. His five detectives normally operated under Lieutenant Griff Harper, but with the Marquette murders and the missing person case, he expected direct updates.

So Detective Ray Irvin took the opportunity to show off for his boss. Part of the reason for Irvin's thoroughness was to remind Forsberg that he worked for Hiawatha County Sheriff's Department while Biff was still in high school. Another reason for Irvin's lengthy explanations centered on budget requests and staffing.

"A team?" Forsberg repeated after the briefing concluded.

"Two shooters with a third supervising from a distance. The storm softened the ground and made it fairly easy to note the spot where he stood watch. If the Marquette boy had fled from the house, I think he would've been another victim."

"And the times of death?"

"The coroner reports put it several hours after the storm," Irvin anticipated and then clarified, "Likely at dusk."

"So young Nathan Marquette should've been in bed when the attack came," Forsberg noted. "Care to explain how he survived."

"He was already hiding."

"Did he tell you that?"

"Lots of raised voices, apparently. Shouting. Anger. Men he didn't know had been to the house earlier, prompting him to find a secure place before the shootings even happened."

Even though Forsberg feared the real answer, he nevertheless asked, "What do you think Marquette got mixed up in?"

"I've got Kent Bollman looking into the drug angle, but we didn't find a stitch of evidence to support that theory. We found evidence in the old man's office to indicate he expected guests that day, so we're going to search the phone logs to see if we can determine who he might've been meeting. The kid said his folks insisted that everyone stayed inside, which upset him since he wanted to ride his BMX out in the woods."

"But the woods were off limits," Forsberg surmised. "And these killers were likely hired?"

"Aside from the kid, everyone was killed efficiently. No malice. No anger."

"No witnesses," Forsberg added. "Do we need to worry about the kid's life?"

"The beef likely involved the father or grandfather, and both are dead now, but it's hard to say. An aunt on the mother's side took him away a couple days ago, but other than hearing the chaos in the background, the boy didn't see anything."

"Where does this aunt live?"

"Albany, New York."

Of course. "Thanks for the briefing."

"Looks like your runaway had nothing to do with this."

I wish I knew that to be true.

THE TRICKSTER   419

He stood and walked Detective Irving to the door and lingered until Mia Donaldson stuck her head around the hallway. A moment later, she led Father Gary, Ansel Nielson, and Lacy Morrison back to his office. He pulled a spare chair to his desk.

"Have a seat," Forsberg said and walked around the desk to sit down.

Play nice, he reminded himself. Big Mack knew about all the shit going down, so he hoped it would be worth the time he was giving up. Along with Detective Irvin's update, Karson Luning called to let him know that not only had Migisi's cabin burned to the ground, but they also strongly believed Levi had confronted the Wintermaker on his own—during the storm. "So...what's going on?"

Lacy Morrison began. "I think this is important." She set folded sheets of yellow paper upon his desk.

"What is this?"

"It's a song I think. The words aren't gibberish they're—"

"Phonetic," Forsberg finished. "I've seen something just like this before, and even though it's been quite a while, I'd been willing to guess who made this: Lily Guerin."

Lacy gasped and the boy recoiled. Even Big Mack seemed startled. "Tell me how you ended up with this," he added.

While she explained things, Brian tried to remain calm. The theft of the Philosopher's Stone was predicated on the ability to access it, and if Lily was making written copies of the Song of the Manitou prior to her death, it certainly explained things. "So Levi had access to this?"

"Yes," she snapped. "He's the one who gave it to me. He said it was...important."

"And you've been holding onto this for over a month now?"

"I didn't know what to think of it, but after talking things over with Ansel and Father Gary, I wanted to be sure you knew about it. Trust, right?"

"I'm glad you finally realize I'm your ally in all of this," he said. "What else do you need to share?"

Big Mack began to summarize how Ansel and Lacy met, but as he talked, Brian realized that the office door hadn't closed all the way, and as a result, he could hear Ray Irvin and Detective Van Zanten talking right outside of his door. "One second, Gary."

Brian rose and walked to the door. Before he could close it, Darlene spotted him and excitedly declared, "They found the truck parked up at Leech Lake. I'm heading up there right now."

Son of a bitch!

Forsberg grimaced as Lacy Morrison gasped; she understood that the truck belonged to Levi.

CHAPTER SEVENTY-SIX

Clay Means Vitriol

Old Copper Road
June 27, 1986

Joey nodded, but he knew his brother couldn't be dead. *He told me the plan. I know where he's at. I'm supposed to go back when I finish counting.*

Yet seeing the family fall into absolute despair could not shield his heart from the same emotions.

For the first time in weeks, he allowed his vibranium shield to come down and all his pent up feelings to empty onto his mother's shoulder. He could feel her also crying, and her arms wrapped around him as if she could squeeze Levi back to life. His father stood with his fists on the counter and head leaning against the cupboards. Leah wrapped both Reuben and Daniel in her arms, modeling her mother's response, using the shoulders of both of her brothers to wipe away her own tears. Tammy held Benjamin's hand as they both hunched over in chairs, weeping at the news. Sheriff Forsberg remained in the doorway to the entryway.

He's a liar, Joey reminded himself. *Nothing he said was true.*

Half an hour earlier, Joey had been playing with his Masters of the Universe action figures when he heard his mother's unexpected wail fill the kitchen, prompting him to sit on the third stair and listen from the protection of the narrow space.

Authorities had found a body.

Same age.

Same snakeskin boots.

Same dental records.

The talk about teeth really sickened Joey, as he learned that the body had badly decomposed in the summer heat, leaving teeth as the absolute proof of identity.

And the truck.

The truck had been found in an old shed on the shore across from Bear Island, leading the sheriff of Cass County to believe Levi had taken his own life, which brought an even louder outburst from his mother.

Joey tried to compare the new facts with what he knew to be true, but they quickly overwhelmed him and he curled up in the corner of the stairs, until Tammy found him and lifted him into her arms and then over to his mother, who now continued to squeeze him.

"I'm going to get a deputy to come over," Forsberg finally interrupted, allowing Joey to slide off his mother's lap. "There is a lot of information coming in, and I will need to prepare for a press conference. The media is going to want your reactions, so my guy will keep them away. I'll get Father Gary over here, and I will stop by later in the day."

No one even acknowledged the sheriff as he left, but as promised, an hour or so later, a silver Chevette appeared. Dad stepped away from the counter and walked over to the doorway where Forsberg had been. "It's Father Gary."

Relief and even greater sorrows flooded the kitchen as the MacPherson family continued to grieve the loss of Levi.

"OKAY, BUD," LEVI had said several weeks ago, "Tell me again what is going to happen with Fozzie's plan *after* we go to the river and you take care of business."

"You are going to disappear," Joey had said for the umpteenth time.

"Right, and if you manage to keep your mouth shut, then what?"

"They are going to say you are dead," Joey answered.

At this, Levi took him by both shoulders and with a stare that still burned in his memory, asked, "But what's the truth?"

"You're going to be fighting a monster," Joey said, understanding both the coming events and distant events that formulated their plan. "I have a question, though."

"Go ahead, bud."

"Why do they call me Clay?"

"Oh, like I said, when we go down the river, we'll be looking for the copper vitriol. Gigi Lily said it is called *pewabic*. In her vision, she somehow knows you are the one who finds it."

"I know that, but Fozzie and the others, they don't call me by my real name. They all call me Clay instead of Joey. Why do they do that?"

For the first time, Levi seemed puzzled by the question. "I don't understand most of this raven and willow stuff, but it means you're going to be a new you. A different you. You can either be a dead boy named Joey, or you can grow up and become a hero named Clay. Do you want to be a hero?"

Joey nodded.

"Me too. What other choice do I have? What other choice do you have? We practiced, and now we're going to make it all happen. You've got this, Joey."

SEVERAL WEEKS LATER, Father Gary entered and wrapped his arms around Dad, and the whole family crumbled in misery, including Joey.

I don't want to be Joey any more, so when do I become Clay?

CHAPTER SEVENTY-SEVEN

Evidence Discovery

Split Rock, MN
July 11, 1986

With his Colt Python strapped to the side of his chest, Brian Forsberg paused in his truck, aware he was walking into an ambush.

He walked up the front steps, where he could see through the screen door and into the small kitchen. He knocked loudly on the aluminum frame.

Big Mack came up the stairs from the basement to appear in the kitchen. His gait paused before he continued to the doorway. "I'm glad you're here."

I'm not sure if I agree.

"Have a seat at the table. The kids are downstairs. I'll go get Ansel."

He could hear crying in the basement—Lacy.

He'd spent the past few days in the center of the emotional tornado that ripped through the community, yet even after the funeral, the matter didn't seem settled yet.

At least the girl seems to believe Levi's dead. Can't have a crazy woman stirring the pot.

Ansel came up the stairs by himself but with the black backpack.

The coward stayed downstairs, Forsberg fumed, hoping to have Big Mack's talents during the conversation.

"Have a seat, kid," he told Ansel, and as the boy sat, Forsberg reached into his shirt to pull the pistol out of his holster. He set it on the table. "I'll show you mine if you show me yours."

What the fuck did I say that for? Think!

Ansel took it in stride and placed the backpack on the table, unzipped it, and then slid out the matching mother-of-pearl Colt Python .357 Magnum.

Jimmy's gun.

"Your father's suicide has festered in my mind almost on a daily basis for all these years. So let me be blunt with you: I fucked up. I failed him. I failed him as a best friend. I failed him as a cousin. I failed him as a veteran. Hell, I failed him as a member of the Isanti Lodge."

"He's the one who chose to run away," Ansel added.

The statement made Brian want to backhand Ansel, but deep down inside, he knew the kid was right. So Brian stuck to the facts. "The detectives in Whitley County assumed they understand the situation. After finding the bodies of Shane and Cindy Lewis, they found all the child pornography, um, material down in the basement. Hell, they got all excited about chasing down the entire distribution ring while your mother dealt with all the sudden trauma in her life. They shrugged off the ballistics. Do you know what that means?"

"Bullets."

"That's right. They found Shane Lewis's ivory-handled .357, knew it was empty, and assumed your father hung himself after the murders because he ran out of bullets. The dumbasses couldn't figure out that Shane likely had his own pistol at home. Your dad finished him off with Shane's own gun. Did you know your dad cut off Shane's forearm that had the Black Horse tattoo?"

Ansel froze. "I guess that explains all the blood."

"You ain't kidding. I've seen the crime scene photos of the Lewis house. Your dad might've been smaller than me, but in a fight, he was badass. Don't forget that."

Ansel quietly took in the compliment, but then his forehead wrinkled in thought. "Did Levi really commit suicide?"

"What makes you ask that?"

"The Whitley County Sheriff's department."

Brian chuckled morosely. He went back to old business instead. "None of us knew what was happening to you kids. Hell, I didn't even know Shane Lewis had reconnected with your dad and moved into the neighborhood. Hell, I shoulda been the one who put a bullet in that sick pig's head. If I'd been a better friend to your dad, he would've asked me for help. Worse than that, I feel like I turned my back on you. My own shame for failing him made it hard to pick up the phone to call, and when your mom moved out to New York, I let the distance be an excuse. So, once again, I fucked up."

"Why did my dad run away from home?"

"Well, we enlisted together."

Ansel shook his head. "No, he ran away from home. Enlisting let him do it. I just want to hear you say it."

Fuck it. "Your dad…ugh…well, there was an incident in the quarry, gah, and to make a long story short, he believed he came into contact with an evil spirit. The manitou of Lake Manitou. The Wintermaker, as Migisi and Lily put it. He believed he could see the spirits of the dead in the waters of Lake Manitou. Since we're crossing this line, you might want to talk to Wally Crain about the shit that went down at Carousel Island."

"Okay. Again, it's weird, and I can't tell if it's real, a dream, or just delusion, but I feel as if my father left that final bullet for the Wintermaker." Ansel withdrew for a few moments as he sorted through his childhood trauma. "I wish he'd just gone to prison. He shoulda just called the cops and sat on the front steps. But as Father Gary said, my

THE TRICKSTER 427

dad believed he was being hunted and haunted by you-know-who. He tagged out and I tagged in, I guess."

"As an officer of the law, it makes me a bit nervous knowing you're walking around with that cannon in your bag. So can I get you some gun training in the days to come? Get that fucker registered in your name?"

Ansel nodded in agreement and slipped the pistol back in the bag and slowly zipped it up. Then he coldly looked up at Forsberg with unflinching purpose. "So?"

"So what?"

"You dodged the question about Levi."

"Undetermined," Forsberg muttered disdainfully. "I'm doing my job kid, but you'll only make matters worse if you push this narrative with Lacy. Once I have all the evidence, I'll sort through it. It's what I do. I knew about your dad's pistol from the evidence, didn't I?"

"Only because I brought it to you. Lacy believes that this manuscript is some sort of psychic prophecy guideline to the future, and she's convinced something bad is going to happen to me on August 2nd. How specific is that? It kinda freaks me out. Even though she went to Levi's funeral, she still believes he ran away like my dad did and is in trouble with some secret society. How crazy is she?"

"You're young. You're both young. So…the adults have been worried about how much to tell you, but the same shit happened when I was a kid, and it almost killed us kids. So we're going to get you up to speed over the next month until your folks return to take you away. Then you'll have to decide what to do from there. We need you to be part of the Isanti Lodge, kid."

"Isanti Lodge."

Forsberg nodded. "I've heard it means 'Guardians of the Frontier' or 'Guardians of the Knife.'"

"The Blue Knife River?"

"Sure, but I think it goes back to Wally's father. Again, you should talk to him about it."

"I think we definitely need to go visit Wally," Ansel said and stood up. "But first, you need to come down to the basement and tell Lacy and Father Gary everything you just told me."

Leonard White Elk is right. We're just gearing up for the real fight.

This time, the Isanti Lodge will be ready.

CHAPTER SEVENTY-EIGHT

Manu Scriptus

St. John, MN
July 12, 1986

Wally Crain stood in the garage door opening as all four visitors stepped out of the SUV. Father Gary led, followed by Lacy Morrison, a sheepish Ansel Nielson, and finally, by a reluctant Brian Forsberg.

How did they manage to get Forsberg committed to this idea?

I tried and failed for decades.

"Thanks for doing this," Father Gary said with a firm handshake.

"No bother at all," Wally admitted. "It took me a while to find them in all of this clutter," he said in reference to all the other unpacked boxes. "Obviously, we lost the manuscript she'd been working on. It's what she used to start the fire in the first place, but she kept the others in her hope chest in the bedroom closet, which was on the far end of the house. Luckily, the chest prevented any water damage."

"That's a lot of paper," Ansel said as he peeked into the filled chest.

"Her first complete manuscript is at the nursing home, but there are at least four more in here. She bound the completed manuscripts together, but from what I can tell, she'd come back to them and write a completely different version a year or two later."

"And she never had any of these published?" Father Gary asked.

Wally shook his head. "Between teaching and raising the girls, she never got around to it. To be honest, I'm surprised how much it ended up being. She was always clanking around on that typewriter when the girls and I weren't around, but I honestly didn't realize how much material she ended up producing."

"We need to get them to Karson. He'll be able to organize them and keep track of things with those computers of his," Forsberg added suddenly. He stood behind everyone else with his arms crossed.

"So what do you think we've got here?"

All eyes turned to Lacy Morrison, who gave a crooked grin before explaining, "We think Mrs. Crain saw visions of the future. *Hamlet's Ghost* was based on the Shakespeare play and how young Prince Hamlet mourned the death of his mighty father and struggled with his sanity as he unraveled a murder plot involving his mother and stepfather. That's Ansel! From what I've read, she saw versions of me, Ansel, and even Levi, but she used fake names when she wrote them."

"Pseudonyms," Ansel offered quietly.

"Right, pseudonyms," Lacy responded with a smile. "These pseudonyms were usually names from mythology or Shakespeare. I found pen marks where she'd crossed out names and changed them. That's how I found the name Ansel."

She was close friends with Ed and Bonnie Nielson, Wally reminded himself. *She knew of Ansel.*

"Tell Wally about the pistol," Father Gary steered.

"Right. So both Ansel and Sheriff Forsberg have been carrying around their own secrets about the pistol. Ansel hid the pistol so nobody knew it even existed, and Sheriff Forsberg had evidence from the crime scene in Indiana that only he understood. Mrs. Crain put that right in her book. She knew. Somehow, she knew."

Ansel caught her eye and he added, "Don't forget about the storm and what's coming in August."

"Right! She had the same crazy-ass storm on the same day that Levi went missing. Now her version of the story only included the Lacy and Ansel characters, and even though they seemed to be copies of us, they did different things. Book Ansel has a mangled arm and is possessed by a demon, but real Ansel's arm is totally fine. I was supposed to go work at the Bible Camp on Turtle Island, but Levi purposely steered me in a different direction. How'd he know to do that?"

"And the arson?" Ansel added.

"Right. We think Levi burned down the old Larson house to put us all on a different path. It's like an alternate reality of ourselves that began when Ansel first saw the raven. Nancy's version is what coulda happened."

Wally looked to the two adults for their reactions. "Raven?"

Forsberg shifted his arms. "A raven is a messenger of the gods."

"In both mythology and even in the Bible," Gary built on the concept.

Am I the voice of reason suddenly? "What about Ansel's raven?"

"We think that was when things changed. Just like in *Hamlet's Ghost*, Ansel came to Lake Manitou, but this time, the raven guided him to a different destiny," Lacy finished with wide-eyed enthusiasm.

"Huh," Wally muttered when no one else spoke. "I always thought she drew her inspiration from real life. I used to pray to God to give me guidance, and all this time, she was in the other room giving me the answers. It's like that parable about the man standing on his roof praying to God to see him through. God sent me his help and I was too blind to see it."

"In *Hamlet's Ghost,* Levi was just a minor character, but towards the end of the story, Mrs. Crain described how he ended up running away from home, so perhaps there is something in the text that says what really happened to Levi. Maybe it's all just some cover-up and he's actually—"

"Hold your horses, missy," Forsberg interrupted. "Dial things back a bit."

Wally could see the grief and mourning in her eyes.

Father Gary interceded quickly. "Wally, we know you've seen some strange supernatural things in the past and also had encountered some tangible villains as well, so we're just hoping we can glean some ideas from what Nancy wrote."

"I think I understand," Wally added. "You're welcome to them."

Forsberg stepped forward and took one handle of the chest. "Gary, can you lend a hand."

The two men lifted the chest and carried it to the rear of the big SUV.

Lacy stood at his side. "If Nancy's drafts are a prediction of events, there's something quite serious about to happen in a few weeks"

"Something quite serious has already happened," Forsberg muttered from a distance.

Lacy ignored Forsberg. "Could we go fetch the draft of *Hamlet's Ghost* from the nursing home?"

"It's a bit late in the day," Wally said after a glance at his watch.

"I know, but that way we can do it without drawing attention," Lacy explained. "We want to see if she can answer some of our questions."

Wally waited for the men to return. "What do you fellas think?"

"I'm going along with the little lady on this," Forsberg said and gave Lacy a nod of respect. "I've got real villains to catch, and if any of Nancy's visions could give us clues, I'll gladly chase them down. Why don't Gary and I will bring this over to Karson's place and you babysit the Mystery, Inc. kids. Go grab that manuscript, and all of us can sort through it."

So Ansel and Lacy climbed into the cab of Wally's truck as Forsberg headed off for Split Rock. Wally reached into his front pocket for two sticks of Big Red gum. It didn't take long for Lacy to start talking again. "Sorry for bothering you like this. Ansel and I have been sorting through this for a week, but I only got Bs in school, so it's probably important for us to look over the manuscript again rather than relying on my memories of it."

"Along with those chapters on demonic possession," Ansel began, "there's stuff about me getting attacked with a baseball bat."

"A baseball bat?" Wally repeated.

Ansel sighed and shook his head, gave Lacy a look, and then turned to Wally. "My sister is supposed to visit, and some crack head boyfriend of hers tracks her down and attacks the whole family."

"Real life villains," Wally repeated what Forsberg said earlier. "I see why we're interested in the manuscript."

"His jaw is broken and he gets a gnarly scar from it," Lacy added. "It's why he grows a beard as an adult."

"Huh," Wally added, unsure of what to even say.

"It's the alternate version of me," Ansel added. "I don't think we need to worry."

Wally passed by the narrows where cabins had once existed. Ahead, he could see Golden Shores Nursing Home built where his father had stabbed the Manitou in the belly. Who was he to judge reality?

Lacy kept explaining. "If Levi *is* alive, it means that he's become some sort of living monster or he's been abducted for some sinister purpose that even I couldn't wrap my brain around. I don't know if there's a happy ending to this story, but perhaps Mrs. Crain will remember. Levi tried to tell me but he…we owe it to him to try, don't we? Granted, we're not the same as the two kids in Mrs. Crain's manuscript, but it's still close enough to blow my mind. It reminds me of that story *Othello* where the harder he tries to change his fate, the more he makes it happen."

"*Oedipus Rex?*" Ansel corrected.

"Oh, yeah, sorry. I get those two names mixed up," Lacy said, finding humor in her mistake. "My point is that despite everything that happened, or didn't happen, we still ended up together. We're destined to be together."

"In the play, Oedipus ended up accidentally sleeping with his own mother because he couldn't let things go. It ends in incest," Ansel coldly added.

Wally choked on the brazenness shown by the young man.

"I'm sorry," Lacy offered, showing she knew about Ansel's traumatic past.

The truck pulled into the parking lot in silence.

"Well, let's go find out," Wally offered and led the way.

The attendant at the front desk only nodded when the trio walked past. The dining hall was empty with nary a soul around. Most of the doors were closed, a sign the nurses had tucked the residents in for the night. Nancy's door was also closed.

God, just give her back to me, please. I feel so alone.

Wally gently opened the door to see his wife sleeping soundly. He stepped aside for the two to enter. Lacy went directly to the desk drawer, where she pulled out the bound manuscript. Ansel stood in the corner, so Wally gently closed the door and slid a chair to Ansel, who sat.

Lacy sat down at the small desk chair and immediately began flipping through pages.

"The doctors think she had a stroke right before the fire," Wally explained, "and her brain malfunctioned and led her to start the fire. About the time help arrived, she lost consciousness and hasn't really come back from it yet."

Nancy awoke and huffed, getting a bit of a rattle from her throat. Wally dabbed at the drool from the corner of her mouth as she concentrated on forming a single word, "help."

Wally looked to the others to see how they interpreted the word.

"We want to help," Lacy replied, turning from the manuscript. "And it seems you were trying to help us from the very beginning, Mrs. Crain. Ansel wanted to know what inspired you to write these stories in the first place."

"How did you know so much about me?" Ansel asked but Nancy's eyes flustered and closed.

So Wally answered for her. "Even though your mother took you to Indiana and then New York, you and your sister were always in our thoughts and prayers. The Nielsons and Crains have been family friends for generations. Your father was like the son I never had."

"I'm beginning to understand why he left, though. He knew about the darkness that sleeps here, didn't he?"

"We want you to be part of the Isanti Lodge. Lily thought a fight was coming with the return of Halley's Comet, but she was wrong, and this obviously isn't the end of this story."

"Trick," Nancy blurted and her body began to rock with tremors.

"You knew something about it, didn't you?" Wally said to her. "We're going to have to untie this tangled knot together as a team—not on our own," he said, directing that to the kids.

"Exactly," Ansel added. "We want Nancy's help."

"Help…me," Nancy muttered and she extended a hand toward Ansel. It shook until she let it rest on the table.

Ansel stared at it like it was a dead kitten placed in front of him.

"Tell us more about the writing of her manuscripts," Lacy asked Wally. "Tell us about her writing process."

"It's no big secret. Wednesday's were writing days. We'd hear the bell of that typewriter on school days, and then she'd come hurrying out of the dining room and jump in the car."

"So she wrote in the dining room?" Lacy asked.

"Yes, well, she typed in the dining room, but she had her notebooks where she'd doodle. By the time Wednesdays rolled around she had the chapters pretty much written."

"But we only saw the manuscripts."

"Those were kept in the garage. The house fire obviously claimed all the handwritten journals. She'd sit under our willow tree filling those notebooks all summer long."

"A willow tree?" Ansel asked and swallowed a lump in his throat.

Wally nodded. "My father planted it right outside the living room window. It hosted picnics with the girls, held a hammock for a while, and during the summer, it was a writing retreat where Nancy would write under that curtain of green."

"Help me," Nancy said a second time; her resting hand lurched forward to grab Ansel by the wrist.

Despite her wide eyes, Ansel left his hand on the table.

The tremor in Nancy's hand spread up her arm and her torso. Her grip kept her from falling over, but her eyes fluttered and then rolled back.

"Nancy?" Lacy gasped.

Then a violent spasm shook her and the whole table. Alarmed, Lacy jumped up from the table, knocking over the chair beside her. Wally put his hands on her back and left arm to steady her, but a shockingly strong elbow caught him in the chest.

Ansel rose to his feet, but his forearm was caught in the vice of her grip.

"I think she's having a seizure," Wally said, holding her in a tight hug as she convulsed.

"Jesus!" Ansel's eyes looked to his arm; the nails dragged across his arm created dark grooves. Instead of blood appearing, a strange black liquid shimmered. Ansel jerked his arm free, but strands of the black substance extended from his forearm to Nancy's hand. He tried to sever the strings, only to have them stick to his other hand.

Nancy went limp.

Oh, shit... Wally then knew what he saw—a Tak-Pei.

The shadow grew as it passed from Nancy to Ansel, who lost control of his legs and stumbled backwards to the ground. His back arched as his muscles flexed involuntarily.

"I'll call 911," Lacy gasped.

"No!"

Wally almost passed out when he heard the crisp, strong syllable come from Nancy's mouth in the same manner she'd once scolded children. Nancy turned her head, and his wife's eyes met his gaze to say, "He needs to go to the willow tree."

CHAPTER SEVENTY-NINE

A Strong Man's House

Split Rock, MN
July 13, 1986

When Gary Mackenzie dropped out of the graduate program at St. John's Seminary School in Camarillo, California, there wasn't a raven nearby to influence his decision—but that choice surely changed his life. While Gary certainly disappointed Bishop Santiago, he pleased Father Thuan, who ran an underground railroad helping Vietnamese Catholics flee to South Vietnam.

Gary'd first met Father Thuan as an undergraduate in the early 60's, and after a lecture trying to drum up support for the communist oppression of Catholic citizens, which included harrowing tales of beheadings, Gary's career path began to narrow. Hours after the lecture, at a dinner party hosted by Dr. Lee off campus, Father Thuan's storytelling skills took a strange turn to the macabre.

Father Thuan had assisted in an exorcism.

A young woman from Tri Tam exhibited strange ailments and even stranger behaviors until she was brought to the local priest at the Basilique Ste. Madeleine, who immediately called his superiors for spiritual guidance. On a whim, Father Thuan had offered to assist the exorcism of the young woman, and for his part, all he'd done was hold the girl's ankles to keep her from harming herself.

"That was the day I learned demons were not just undiagnosed medical ailments," Father Thuan had declared to the group of men in Dr. Lee's backyard. Thuan's face was placid but his eyes twinkled. "From that day, I no longer needed faith—I knew."

Now I also know.

Following Father Thuan's storytelling, Gary hit the library to read everything he could on exorcism. From the Catholic Exorcism Rite to the ancient Solomonic rituals used prior to Jesus, Gary read everything he could get his hands on, including those from other cultures. Demons and exorcists were global, and even though Father Thuan witnessed a successful exorcism, other cultures from Africa to America told of success also, making Gary question the nature of demons.

Now, Father Gary Mackenzie found himself holding Ansel Nielson's ankle during an even stranger exorcism at the Fisher Mansion. When Wally frantically brought the boy to them, it seemed an overreaction as Ansel's only affliction manifested itself like intoxication. But within minutes, something other than Ansel began to take control of the boy's body.

Beside him, Captain Chuck Luning applied pressure on the boy's shoulder and elbow, with Brian Forsberg now on the opposite arm and shoulder. Both stocky men needed their strength and weight to keep the hundred-twenty pound freshman down. On the opposite leg, Leonard White Elk held firm yet avoided all eye contact towards Ansel.

I am here for this moment. This is why God sent me.

Almost twenty hours into the ordeal, Ansel was kept inside of a simple camping tent in the middle of the main living room. The makeshift sweat lodge allowed Migisi to perform a ritual he'd learned before the turn of the century. With Ben LaBiche at his side, Migisi continued singing in syllables unfamiliar to Gary but recognizable as Anishinaabemowin.

The demon fears him and he's not even a Christian.

The demon attacking Ansel had not so much possessed him as attached itself to him. Like one of those poor ducklings covered in oil, Ansel was covered by the living liquid that swirled on and into his skin.

Migisi stopped.

For a moment, Gary worried about Migisi's heart, but Migisi cleared his throat and called out, "Ben, prepare more stone and water. We almost drew it out."

Ansel's voice also returned to that of a normal sixteen year old, "I think it's helping." His eyes closed and he turned his head in exhaustion as the black oil slowly congealed.

"Stay strong, Ansel," Father Gary added.

When the zipper opened, an exchange of air flowed from the tent.

Gary heard voices near the living room: Betsy, Lacy, and Karson talked. Wally guarded the door to the room.

Shortly after Gary and Sheriff Forsberg brought him to the Fisher Mansion, Ansel's demonic rage seemed to fixate on Lacy, so she and Betsy Luning were banished from the wing of the house, but now, it seemed, the storm grew outside.

Karson explained to Wally at the doorway, "There's a thunderstorm heading right for us, and for the sake of precaution, I'm going to get some flashlights and candles in case the power goes out."

"Keep Lacy out of here," Wally insisted.

"She's going down to the library. She'll be safe there with Grandma Betsy. Elmer's going to keep an eye out on the property."

Elmer Johnson's here? Too many people are witness to the strangeness.

Brian Forsberg stared over at Father Gary and rolled his eyes.

The new heated stones were set in a baking pan to create a new cloud of steam that was trapped by the waterproof tent. Gary knew Migisi's training included the traditional Anishinaabe Midewiwin ways along with the more exotic Jessakkid. Although Migisi was not a Firehandler like his sister, the Wijigan elders that tested him did believe in his innate skills as a Jessakkid, so as a teenager, he was trained as a seer, necromancer, and exorcist.

This time, when Migisi began to sing, he sang something beside his native tongue.

The Song of the Manitou.

Between the tutelage of Nanakonan, and their abilities to speak with ghosts and prophets, the Weber children knew enough of the ancient magic to not need the Ironwood Scrolls. Now, as Migisi sang, a strange echo seemed to follow each syllable.

The demon recognized it also, and Ansel's body lurched and bucked with renewed strength.

Four grown men struggled to keep him steady.

"Ben! Ready yourself. It is time," Migisi shouted. He took the cup next to his thigh and poured it into his mouth. His cheeks puffed out like a wrinkled chipmunk, and then he leaned forward, crawling on hands and knees until he hovered over Ansel.

And then he vomited a mixture of liquid and cowry shells onto the face and chest of Ansel.

Sacred megis shells, Gary observed. The old Jewish exorcists did something similar. Instead of the Song of the Manitou, they had a replica of King Solomon's ring, which they held to the nostril of the possessed.

Migisi withdrew for a moment while the demon almost fully separated itself from Ansel. The pool of black now almost covered all of his face and torso.

Gary watched his hands to make sure the black slime didn't touch him.

Migisi returned with a long stick, but it actually was a straw. He sucked on one end, and with the other, placed it over the face of Ansel. With each breath Migisi took, Ansel screamed louder.

Like siphoning water from a hose, Migisi plugged the tube with his thumb after each breath. He withdrew toward the tent flap and repeated a phrase three times, first in the ancient tongue, second in Anishinaabemowin, and finally in English, "I draw you out."

A flash of lightning appeared at the same time as a violent clap of thunder, shaking through the bricks and into the tent.

Whether the power of electricity or the suddenness of its timing, Migisi lost focus and balance, tripping as he fell near the door. The wooden straw clattered to the ground, and like a genie released from a bottle, the shadow came billowing out.

"Get that thing away from me," Ansel muttered and wrenched his leg free, kicking the shadow before it could return. The dense cloud of swirling black burst through the tent, sending poles and branches flying outward and into the room.

Suddenly they were all exposed, and so was the demon. It swirled above them like a lion searching for the weakest wildebeest until it congealed and threw itself at Leonard White Elk, tossing the man like a bowling ball into Wally Crain and Ben LaBiche. Bolstered by Ansel's recovery, Gary grabbed the wooden straw and held it out for Migisi, who was frozen in puzzlement.

A solitary figure stood against the Tak-Pei. In his hands, the wicker staff of willow and the red pipestone spearhead.

"You son of a bitch," Ansel muttered, hands spread wide upon the spear like a pole-vaulter at the ready. No longer under the influence of the demon, Ansel's anger remained. With bared teeth and a barbaric yawp, he thrust at the black cloud, which stuck to the red blade. He drove the demon across the room, pinning it against the brickwork of the fireplace.

Ben LaBiche helped White Elk to his feet and both advanced to where Ansel stood. Father Gary aided them, muttered what Latin phrases he remembered from the Catholic exorcism rites.

"Where are you going, huh?" Ansel taunted the black apparition. "I got you. I got you."

Ben LaBiche took the straw from Migisi, who was supported by the strong arms of Leonard White Elk and Brian Forsberg. As Migisi repeated the words, Ben LaBiche mimicked the ritual, sucking the black vapors into the tube as the brick shook with such fury that soot and ash extinguished the flames.

When the tip of the pipestone spearhead grated against brick, Ben LaBiche stopped and placed his thumb over the tube.

"Now expel it into the teapot," Migisi said, pointing to the improvised copper vessel used for the climax of the exorcism. "We can't let it escape."

Captain Chuck opened the whistle cap and Ben stuck the straw into it, blowing the evil spirit into the contained waters. The Solomon exorcists used a tray of water in the same manner; likewise, the Gerasene demons Jesus encountered outside of Lake Galilee were thrown into a watery abyss.

As soon as Ben finished, Captain Chuck capped the teapot with duct tape before wrapping strands of willow around it. The pot rested on longer branches, which were quickly tied around Betsy Luning's decorative pot, which previously held an ivy plant.

The sound of breathing filled the living room and all the men transitioned from terror to triumph. Captain Chuck broke the silence with a chuckle and muttered, "Hot damn."

Ansel followed with a bitter, "Bastard."

Forsberg wrapped his arms around the boy. "Are you okay?"

Ansel nodded.

In the doorway, wide-eyed Karson Luning appeared. "Everything good?"

The men nodded yet kept an eye on the teapot.

"That lightning strike hit a pine tree, and a second later, this little girl goes bolting across the yard. It's not the first time I've seen here messing around with the tree, either."

"Sommer Chauvin," Wally answered.

"Molly's daughter?" Karson clarified.

Migisi groaned, drawing the attention of the men.

Ansel began to shiver, prompting Forsberg to toss a blanket over his shoulders.

THE TRICKSTER 443

Ben LaBiche hooked the teapot with the willow spear.

"So what now?" Captain Chuck asked.

With Migisi and Ben LaBiche exhausted, Gary felt eyes turn to him. "In the Bible, Jesus insinuated that a cast out demon would come back to the host again and again and again, and when he encountered a demon, the demon feared being cast into the watery abyss. I say we get this cursed thing as far away from Lake Manitou as we can and then throw it into the ocean."

It was an ad-lib, but deep in his gut, it felt like the right course of action.

CHAPTER EIGHTY

A New Era

Split Rock, MN
July 14, 1986

Migisi didn't lift a finger to help. The hairs that stood on the back of his neck were not triggered by the Horned Serpent, another Tak-Pei, or a servant of the Wintermaker—old age was coming for him soon.

How much time do I have left? He no longer counted time in years and knew his life could be ticking down to days and hours. His body would never recover from the beating it'd taken over the last few weeks, but at least his mind was clear.

He smiled, knowing he'd finally gotten the fight he'd wanted when he was a ten-year-old boy.

I helped destroy a Tak-Pei.

Everything returned to normal by noon, and Migisi found enough energy to turn his head to watch Betsy Luning and Lacy Morrison putting furniture back in place—all except that big recliner that cradled him in its arms.

Albert Fisher built a spectacular watchtower atop the hill, Migisi observed now that the chaos was over.

Migisi had an important decision to make: where to die? *This certainly wouldn't be a bad place to die.* Yet the recliner sat on the far side of the Crow Wing River and beyond the spiritual barrier created by foul sorcery so long ago. If he died on the "good" side of the barrier, his soul would be free to travel its intended path—be that the Christian Heaven or the Ojibwe River of Souls. If he died along the shores of Lake Manitou, his spirit would be trapped, but it would be trapped with others. In that regard, he could find comfort in the arms of his mother, grandfather, and sister, but that thought also meant villains like Adam Thunderface, Joseph Little Toad, and Bushy Bill Morrison also lingered there. Death at Lake Manitou meant the potential for Heaven and Hell.

"Chuckie is picking up lunch at the Crow Bar," Betsy Luning said to him in purposely-slow syllables. "What should we order for you?"

Migisi had spent most of his life disdaining American culture, but today… "A cheeseburger." He watched as Betsy darted back to the kitchen to add his request to the order. Looking around the living room now, it was hard to imagine that an exorcism and demonic battle had occurred just twelve-hours earlier. The tent had been removed, the floor cleaned, and the furniture returned. Now the air was filled with the smells of Pledge, Lysol, and vanilla sprays.

Outside the big living room windows, the pine tree still smoldered from the lightning strike. If Migisi were to guess, he assumed the spiteful Tak-Pei deliberately summoned the last of its magical ability to strike after Ansel separated it from the rest of the pack. Luckily, the house and willow tree were missed.

Now I know where Smoke hid these past several months.

When dawn came, the Isanti Lodge scattered. Sheriff Brian Forsberg, visibility shaken, returned to the real world with a soft mumble and a promise to return for supper. Wally Crain had been reborn overnight and, like a lad on a first date, enthusiastically departed for Golden Shores Nursing Home to see Nancy. Father Gary, Leonard White Elk, and Benjamin LaBiche took the wrapped copper pot below the dam at Little Falls and released it into the flowing waters of the Mississippi.

Except for Sheriff Forsberg, Chuck Luning, and Wally Crain, they all gathered in the kitchen, unsure of what to do next.

"Fetch the boy," Migisi finally found his voice after all the chaos had ended. He said it to the dutiful young girl who'd spent most of the morning setting things right. Almost a century ago, her great-grandfather Bushy Bill Morrison almost murdered him on Deadwood Island and now Lacy gave her all to help the team. *A very unexpected ally.*

"Ansel? I'll get him."

"And Cameron," Migisi added. "Cameron's here, isn't he?"

"He came while you were napping," Lacy said and backed her way to the kitchen.

A moment later, Ansel walked toward him with Cameron and Lacy lingering behind. "You wanted to see me?"

Migisi nodded. "My sister was not wrong…but she was not right. She began a chain of events that led us to this moment. Her selfishness was driven by her love of Jean Guerin, but if she'd had her way, the Wintermaker would have risen to power and restored his kingdom. Lily would have been in the arms of her beloved Jean, and the world would have suffered the consequences. I worry that Levi paid for her sins."

"What do you think happened to him?" Lacy asked from the doorway of the kitchen, surrounded by the others who listened to what Migisi said.

"From what Shadow told me," he said in reference to the Tak-Pei he'd briefly trapped a week earlier, "I think Levi won the battle that will allow us to win the war. If he truly died at Leech Lake, then his sacrifice allowed us to pass through the storm created by my sister. If he lives, then this battle is not yet over," Migisi added. He took a break to swallow to rest his hoarse throat.

The Tak-Pei worry for their Master and rage against Levi.

What could he have done to upset them so?

His focus shifted back to Ansel. "When I was a boy, my Grandfather Nanakonan told me that the Horned Serpent would be defeated by a great warrior. My mother named me Migisi after the majestic eagle, and in my grandfather's tales, it was the Thunderbird that swept down to destroy the Horned Serpent. Yet it was my sister who discovered the Megis shells—not me. And it was my sister who was born with the abilities of the Wabeno—not me. The blood of the Wijigan gave me the power of a Jessikkid, and thus I began my training and a journey that led me to this point. Your blood has obviously given you gifts as well. With Cameron's help, I'd like to train you in the ways of the Jessikkid."

"Train me? What does that mean?"

"When Lily summoned the Isanti Lodge, your forefather came and filled the role of warrior, the Wa-bi-zha-shi, but it seems to me now that I was never destined to defeat the Horned Serpent, but after what I saw last night, I believe you might be the one to fulfill the prophecy. Cameron, tell him what you saw from Ed Nielson on the night the Tak-Pei attacked you at Carousel Park."

Cameron still bore the scars from the fight and he began to twitch nervously. "I saw Mr. Nielson throw two of them to the far shore of the lake."

Shadow and Smoke. Migisi nodded. *Now only eleven remain.* "You might not have the blood of the Dakota or the Chippewa flowing in your veins; nevertheless, the Great Spirit blessed your lineage. I'll train Ben to take my place in the Isanti Lodge; he'll represent the Midewiwin priesthood just as Father Mackenzie will represent the Jesuit priesthood, but you…you will be the tip of our spear." He lifted a shaky hand to point at the gouge on the fireplace brick.

"I'm supposed to go back to New York in a few weeks," Ansel protested. "I don't even know how I'm going to explain what happened to me."

"Let the adults worry about the adults," Migisi said. "I don't even know if I have a few weeks left to train you, but I'll make use of the time I've been given."

"Will this give us answers about Levi?" Lacy asked.

"If Ansel has been blessed with the powers of a Jessakkid, then he'll be able to speak with the dead and find all the answers he needs," Migisi answered and looked into the boy's eyes. "When you picked up that wicker spear, you began a path that will lead to the final battle."

"I take it this wasn't the final battle?" Karson Luning asked.

"Leonard White Elk is correct: we've just entered the era of the Seventh Fire and the days are already counting down to the return of the Serpent Star. Even though we've taken great losses, we will regroup and learn from our mistakes."

"We live to fight another day," Karson asked, only to look down in shame for those who didn't survive the recent appearance of the Serpent Star.

"The fight will be fought by the next generation," Migisi agreed, "and for my part, I will fight to my last breath."

"But first," Betsy Luning interrupted. "you need to eat your cheeseburger or you won't have any strength for anything. Chucky's back with the lunch, everybody."

CHAPTER EIGHTY-ONE

The Hour of Doom

Chippewa Beach Mobile Home Park
August 2nd, 1986

As the tow truck hauled away the white 1968 Camaro, Brian Forsberg looked down at his hands and discovered they were shaking uncontrollably. Sitting alone in his SUV, he slowly released a breath to slow his heart rate and breathing. He rolled down the windows so the slight fogging could dissipate into the cool night air.

Bring down your spikes, you fool.

Nothing even happened.

Now that he was alone, the emotions of it all took over, and he became a blubbering mess. He gave himself three good sobs before angrily wiping his eyes.

Starting his vehicle, he drove all the way into the mobile home park where Ansel Nielson and his grandmother slept blissfully unaware of the carnage and chaos they'd just missed. Forsberg waited until 3:30 just to make sure fate didn't throw a Hail Mary at them.

Finally content, Forsberg drove back to St. John.

When he arrived, he could see the old Camaro and tow truck parked inside the impoundment lot, already being processed. Deputy Santino Cruz finished gathering any trace evidence to help the case.

No one greeted him when he stepped into the main office, which was good. While he didn't pick the three o'clock hour for the arrest, he knew it'd be all but forgotten by midmorning.

He stepped into the dispatch center.

Staffed 24-7-365, the dispatch center was always running but he nevertheless requested Katie Lopez to be on staff, and seeing her at her desk, he nodded his appreciation for her taking the shift. He continued through the building until he reached the county jail.

"You're either very early for work or you've had a very long day," the door attendant noted.

"A long day," Forsberg answered. "Is Tavares finished booking?"

"Should be almost done."

Forsberg continued, and with crossed arms, he watched Detective Jared Tavares processing the man they'd just arrested.

He didn't need to read anything that the young detective gathered; Mrs. Crain already provided him with most of the details. Even though Tavares hadn't read the chapter in *Hamlet's Ghost*, Forsberg soon learned all about the devious past of the man destined to attack Ansel Nielson with a baseball bat.

Fuck you, Johnny Greer, Forsberg thought as he looked at the lowlife criminal out of Chicago. After booking, Greer would be sent to Illinois for more serious charges. *And fuck fate while we're at it.*

Forsberg rapped his knuckles on the glass and nodded his appreciation to Detective Tavares before returning to his office. Thankfully, the ambush had gone down without a hitch. The first step had been to prevent Tonya Nielson from adding fuel to the fire, so two days earlier, he had an APB on a 1973 Mercury Cougar registered to Johnny Greer, which Mrs. Crain had accurately described. Instead of sending Tonya to jail for theft, he transferred her to a private drug treatment facility near Ely. He'd let Aurora and Thomas Archibald III deal with Tonya's mess in a few weeks, and with her out of the way, he fixated on the second half of the prophecy.

While the fates of Hiawatha County spun wildly in new destinies since the winter solstice, the rest of the world had not caught up yet, and the lives of Tonya Nielson and Johnny Greer had continued unchanged. Instead of the family receiving violent retribution for the theft of Johnny's car and drug money, Johnny Greer drove right into a trap set by Forsberg. Three Sheriff vehicles converged as he slowed to find Calico Lane, and with guns drawn, they arrested him for possession, weapons, and an outstanding warrant. He never got to lay a hand on either Tonya or Ansel.

Now back in his office, Forsberg placed his finger upon the manuscript paragraph where Ursula Hermann killed Greer while defending her two grandchildren.

Sorry for stealing your glory, but I owed it to the kids.

He tidied up the pages and reverently put the manuscript into a cabinet drawer. For several minutes, he held his hand to his forehead as he tried to make sense of the night's events. While this had nothing to do with either Eos or the Wintermaker, it still shook him to his core.

Lacy Morrison had only seen the tip of the iceberg with Nancy Crain's *Hamlet's Ghost*. Karson Luning scanned the other pages and reported how the other manuscripts developed. From running away in *Hamlet's Ghost*, Levi took on a starring role in *Pan's Apprentice*, where his part in a heavy metal band led him into a secret society that symbolically matched the Order of Eos

Having spent his adult life researching this nefarious secret society, Forsberg knew Mrs. Crain had tapped into some dark conduit into the future.

Did Levi see this future also?

Forsberg opened another drawer, and right behind the folder for James Edward Nielson, he found a new file for Levi MacPherson.

Detective Darlene Van Zanten's work only established a timeline. Although young Joey MacPherson still hadn't corroborated the story, Van Zanten established the brothers picked up the canoe and then brought it upriver to the Nimrod canoe landing. While not in the report,

Carey Jensen's unofficial testimony agreed with her findings about where the truck had been parked.

Next, he turned to the Cass County Sheriff's Department reports. The truck had been found across from channel from where the body had been found.

The body.

The decomposition rates accelerated during the hot summer days, leaving the coroner to confirm gender, age, and height. Dental records almost exactly matched those of Levi MacPherson.

Teeth fall from the jaw after two weeks of decomposition, which is why the Cass County coroner only noted the placement of the filings. Levi's dental records from Brainerd were a year old yet five teeth seemed different from the images from the coroner.

So Brian privately sought a second opinion.

Not wanting to ruffle any feathers with his neighbors in Cass County, Forsberg looked for a dentist in adjacent Beltrami County, only to discover the suicide of a local dentist.

"Bohica," Forsberg muttered aloud as he looked at the two similar images. Wally Crain taught him the colorful World War Two era profanity: Bend over, here it comes again.

Eos is fucking with us.

Knowing that the secret society existed for thousands of years reminded Forsberg that they'd go to any length to accomplish even a simple task.

What happened?

That question suddenly seemed irrelevant. Something *had* happened, and the actions of Eos now seemed clear. A doppelganger had to be acquired, brought to Cass County, and left at Bear Island on Leech Lake. To be truly convincing, the doppelganger's dental work needed to match Levi, so…

They matched the dental work and killed the dentist. Holy fuck.

Meanwhile, a team of killers took out the Marquette family. Why? Witnesses. They likely saw something that Eos never wanted to be known. Considering the cave was less than a mile from the Marquette property, it seemed the most logical next step for a cold-blooded killer. Despite ties to Eos, the Marquette family was collateral damage.

Forsberg returned to his previous question: *What happened?*

He had three good answers. The most radical thought involved the Wintermaker rising from a tomb deep under Lake Manitou and walking onto the Marquette property. Preposterous. The next thought involved agents of Eos using stolen magic to wake and discover the Philosopher's Stone. This theory did not require the murder of the Marquettes or the use of a doppelganger.

If Levi walked onto the Marquette property holding the Philosopher's Stone, they could've just killed Levi, dumped his body, and taken the stone.

Why would Eos want the world to think Levi MacPherson killed himself?

He put the file away and poured himself a drink, which would help him sleep. He'd sleep in his office, attend the morning meetings, and then go home to get hammered. Any surviving brain cells that still knew the answer to his question could then try to figure out how to explain this to the Isanti Lodge.

CHAPTER EIGHTY-TWO

The Face of Brotherhood

Split Rock, MN
August 4, 1986

The entire Isanti Lodge met for the first time since 1898 in the big kitchen of the Fisher Mansion, and as they ate Betsy Luning's homemade lasagna, Leonard White Elk knew he still needed to be cautious. With the sudden boldness from Brian Forsberg, the group seemed ready to charge across a battlefield to face an unknown enemy, but with their secret weapon suddenly missing, he knew he might be the only one alive who had the instruction manual on how to use it.

That's why they failed.

The Song of the Manitou is incomplete.

"Would you like any dessert?" Betsy Luning asked, but he shook his head no after seeing Brian Forsberg rise to go into the office on the far side of the building.

Captain Chuck Luning also turned down dessert to kiss his mother on the head before following Forsberg.

"Members only?" Lacy Morrison asked playfully. Since Forsberg's nefarious accusations against the Order of Eos, she seemed unburdened from her grief. There were several other "non-members" with them:

Chuck's wife Helen, the groundskeeper Elmer Johnson, and the special guest of honor, Nancy Crain, who'd been released after her quick recovery. Together with Lacy and Betsy, they all understood how they served in a support role to the Isanti Lodge.

Father Gary nodded to Lacy and also rose.

"Wish me luck," Ansel said to her as he left the table and walked beside the priest down the long hallway.

Migisi slowly ate his dessert with Ben LaBiche patiently waiting.

Karson joined Leonard as they followed the long entourage heading to Albert Fisher's old study.

"I checked into the Chauvin girl's genealogy," Karson said along the way. "She's as Caucasian as Caucasian gets. The Chauvins are an old French family. They're Cajuns from Louisiana."

"Is that a tribe?"

"No, they're swamp people. The Chauvins have been living in Louisiana since the first colonies. Mark's Grandpa Bones still lives down there. They are only two-generations of living in Minnesota, so I don't think there's any chance they have any Wijigan blood in them."

"And the mother?"

"Molly? Um, no, she's as Nordic as it gets. Her family comes from Norway, and from what she knows, that bloodline is pretty pure also," Karson added to their private conversation. "I'll admit that it's pretty weird for that girl to be trespassing to play in my front yard, but kids are kinda odd. She just lives a few blocks down the road. Molly promised to keep a better eye on her."

"It doesn't solve our problem, does it?"

"What problem's that?"

"We've lost our Firehandler," Leonard added, "and can't start dropping hot rocks into open hands."

"And it's not something that can be taught?"

"According to Migisi, it's a gift given. When he was a boy, he tried and failed the test. The only true way to test a subject is if we still had the Stone."

"I'd bet my bottom dollar that the youngest MacPherson boy turns out to be our new Firehandler. He's got the bloodline, and from what we know, he was in the vicinity of the last known location of the Stone when it vanished."

"Regardless of what Forsberg privately confesses, Nicole MacPherson believes her son took his own life, and I don't think there's anyway she'll let us near the boy."

"So what do we do? Wait until he turns eighteen?"

"My mother firmly believed that we needed to trust the prophecy, and that by forcing the prophecy, we'd only delay it from arriving. When we trust our Creator, then our destiny will present itself to us."

"Well, neither of us will be alive when Halley's Comet returns in 75 years. Guess I'm not going to find out."

"The war might be over by the time the Serpent Star returns."

"What do you mean?"

"It's possible our enemies have woken the Wintermaker and possess the sacred Water Drum. If this is true, they might soon figure out how to bring their version of the story to life."

But not until they know the full Song of the Manitou. Am I a fool for guarding my secret so closely?

HALF AN HOUR later, Migisi and Ben LaBiche joined them in the office. Migisi chose to sit right beside Leonard, and as he sat, he placed his hand upon his knee and then patted it for good measure.

The schism in the family between Lily and Fawn had finally healed.

Wally Crain cleared his throat. "Beginning with Pearl Harbor and continuing to the Philippines, Japan defeated the United States in several crushing battles. Yet in these losses, America kept regrouping, coming back stronger and stronger and stronger against an unbreakable enemy. Eventually, we dropped the bomb, broke our enemy, and won the war. I was there when the USS South Dakota dropped anchor in Tokyo Bay, and in the words of General Douglas McArthur, 'I shall return to fight another day.'

"Like in the days following Pearl Harbor, our plans for the war have turned to ash. We must recruit new members to replace old men like me. We must begin to think of an offensive strategy rather than just remaining at Lake Manitou like sitting ducks. With your permission, I'd like to begin training my grandson Garrett to fill my role. God willing, he'll be an old man by the time the Serpent Star returns."

I'm 61 and childless. Who will replace me? Leonard looked over to Migisi, who seemed at peace with his impending death.

"It is a wise plan," Migisi agreed. "I will spend my final days preparing young Ansel to play the role of warrior and also to teach Ben the ways of the Midewiwin and Wijigan priesthoods. We've all seen the face of evil, and the Isanti Lodge should have the counsel of both religions in the days to come."

Father Gary nodded in affirmation. "For my part, I will learn all I can from the Catholic exorcists and any others who will teach me their ways. We've cast out only one of the twelve demon Tak-Pei, and if it is true that they no longer have a master here to serve, they will feed their own selfish appetites."

Captain Chuck patted Gary on the shoulder. "There's only so much I can offer as the mayor of Split Rock, which is why I've decided to run for the Minnesota House of Representatives. We need to do everything we can to protect the reservation and its people in the days to come, and having a politician on the inside can only help matters."

Karson followed his father. "From what Sheriff Forsberg has told us, the Order of Eos is international. While my first priority it to scan all of Mrs. Crain's manuscripts so we can search for other clues, I'll make it my next priority to give the Isanti Lodge the edge with computers. I'll be the eyes and ears for the lodge."

The group looked next to Leonard and Sheriff Forsberg.

"Obviously, my investigation into what happened to the Marquette family as well as Levi MacPherson is just beginning, and I'll continue to use all the resources of my office to figure it all out. I agree with Wally. We can't win by playing defense, which is what we've been doing since the days of the Nicollet Dam. We need to come up with an offensive plan. If my investigation leads to anything (and I'm pretty damn sure it will), we need to be ready to act—with violent force if necessary. A bunch of old men and kids can't be counted on to measure out justice."

Captain Chuck scoffed. "What are you suggesting? A private militia?"

"The Second Amendment is as American as Mom's apple pie, and yes, I'd make sure there would be no infringement, they'd be well-armed and well-regulated too."

"Jeez, Biff, really?" Wally added.

Migisi cleared his throat. "Three times in my life our enemies have descended upon Lake Manitou and left a slough of bodies. They strike from the clouds and vanish. The fate of humanity rests in our ability to stop these dark creatures. I agree with the Bear's plan."

Leonard knew he had not contributed to the plan, so he gathered himself. In the old ways, the Wa-wa-shesh-she were the poets within Anishinaabe society, so he took his time to gather his philosophy.

"It is good that we can all speak openly like this, but let us remember the old prophecy," he began. "At the end of the Seventh Fire, the boy-with-strange-eyes will be the one who makes a decision that will either save or doom humanity. We do not yet know who that figure will be. In the Oceti Sakowin prophecies, the Wishwee will battle the ancient shape shifter known as No Soul. While we know where No Soul slumbered, we do not know if he is still here, nor do we know the identity of Wishwee. In the Wijigan prophecies, we learn of another young boy, Iyash, who tricks the evil Horned Serpent into a state of false security only to lure it to its doom by a mighty Thunderbird. Again, we do not yet know the identity of the Thunderbird, but to defeat our ancient enemy, we need to arm our warrior with the ancient weapon, which can only be wielded by a powerful Firehandler. For us to attain victory, our top priority must be recovering and protecting the Stone."

"When Migisi is working with Ansel," Ben LaBiche answered, "I will organize efforts to search the ravine and surrounding property for any signs of it. I'll make it my purpose to learn all I can about the lore surrounding the White Egg, the Philosopher's Stone, and the original Water Drum."

Good. If I am to pass on what I know about the Song of the Manitou, it is best to work with a close relative. If I let the world know what I've found too soon, then I put the whole world in jeopardy. Better to die with my secrets than to risk the knowledge falling into the wrong hands.

Migisi looked over to Leonard in silent contemplation. "If we are to overcome this foe, we must learn from the mistakes made in the past. It is the only way we can give those in the future what they need to defeat our enemy."

CHAPTER EIGHTY-THREE

Farewell, Sweet Prince

Chippewa Beach
August 16, 1986

Ansel Nielson peeked out the back window of the mobile home when he heard another well-wisher join his going away party. "Who is it?" Lacy Morrison asked from the edge of his bed.

"Wally and Nancy," Ansel answered, seeing his grandma wrapped around Mrs. Crain. They joined Father Gary, Sheriff Forsberg, and his parents, who were there to take him back to New York. "I'll give them a few minutes to sort things out. Maybe they'll find a way to let me stay longer."

"There's something I've been meaning to give you," Lacy said. "I just couldn't figure out how to begin the conversation."

Ansel turned around and saw that she'd spread several pieces of yellow paper onto the bare bed. "This again?" Ansel asked, sitting on the edge of the bed. "What do you think it is?"

"It's a promise," she said.

"How so?"

"Levi gave it to me like it really meant something. These were made by Lily Guerin, and when I looked at them she pretty much assaulted me. When I showed them to Levi, he...he almost told me what he was going to do. You know I still believe he's alive."

Ansel nodded. *She's in love with a memory now.*

"Right before Levi disappeared, he told me that things would go one of three ways. In two situations, the bad guys would win. In the other, he'd manage to find a way to save me and his little brother Joey. Whatever happened to him, he did it to protect us."

"He's quite the hero," Ansel said with too much bitterness.

"What's your deal?"

Ansel shrugged. "If he did something to save humanity, he sure left everybody in the dark. I guess time will tell."

"He didn't leave everybody in the dark. He left me with this," she said and gestured to the papers.

Ansel picked up and looked at one of the papers closely. It was broken down into syllables without any coherence. "I don't get it."

"I thought you were supposed to be so smart."

"Okay, so it's some sort of song, but the lyrics aren't in English. You're saying Lily Guerin, the Firehandler, gave this to you. Please tell me you didn't sing this aloud and awaken some monster by accident."

"No. When Levi saw this, he told me it was dangerous. He said I should keep it safe like it's worth a million dollars."

"Well, you're not doing a very good job protecting your million dollars."

"Levi also told me that when the time was right, I should give it to the person I trust most in the world. Now obviously, I don't feel the same way about you that Book Lacy felt for her Ansel, right? You might still be an idiot, but you're special. Who else would I give this to? I want you to take these with you to New York. Figure out what they're for. Figure out why Levi said this was important. It's our promise. Regardless of what happens, I'm giving them to you because I trust you completely. Okay?"

Ansel didn't know what to say.

She began to collect them, and when he reached out, she handed them to him. He folded them back into the square she'd made and put them in his front pocket.

"Then I've got something for you, too." He reached down and pulled his black backpack on his bed. "I want you to keep this until we meet again."

"You want me to keep your dad's pistol?"

"I can't bring it onto a plane. You just need to keep it until I fly out again for Thanksgiving break. Then I can figure out what to do with it."

"Show me the bullet," Lacy said.

Ansel took the pistol out, opened the chamber, and produced the .357 bullet. "That's my promise to you. We're in this together, aren't we?"

"We are."

Ansel looked around the empty room and sighed. "Well, should we go out onto the deck? I need an ally to endure the conversation we're about to have."

"I'll be right beside you the whole time."

Lacy slipped the backpack onto her shoulders and the two walked out onto the deck together.

It had been agreed that no one would utter any "spooky supernatural shit" outside of the Fisher Mansion. Out on the deck, Sheriff Forsberg stood in a short-sleeved plaid shirt watching them like a crazy gym teacher administering a fitness test. For almost an hour, he nodded as Ansel and Lacy faked their way through a generic summer romance that never occurred.

His mother ate it up. Ursula, too, refrained from alarming Ansel's parents, sugar coating the summer's events as best as she could.

Nancy Crain, however, did not play by the agreed-upon rules.

After playing along for the better part of the hour and accepting Ursula's hospitality with smiles, Nancy lost focus, staring off into the distance for long stretches.

Ansel noticed, even while the others kept yapping.

When Nancy rose, they all shut up.

"You need to go," she said without looking at him.

But Ansel knew she was talking to him.

"Maybe we should get you home," Wally said, and in an instant, Father Mack and Forsberg were swooping in for the assist.

"No, no," Nancy protested. "He can't leave yet. He needs to go to the willow tree."

"Your willow tree is gone, Nancy," Wally referenced the fire. The willow tree at the Fisher mansion had provided no answers either.

"He needs to go to the Old Willow," she said, pointing to the trees beyond the mobile home park. "Jiibay Hollow."

"What's this all about?" Ansel's stepfather asked in a moment of hesitation from the others.

Nancy held up her hands like a shield. "Stop it. I'm not crazy. I know what I'm talking about. I should have listened to my instincts earlier. Do you see it?"

All eyes went to the distant tree where a single black raven perched.

"I see it," Ansel said. He felt shivers up his spine.

"Follow it. It'll lead you to the Old Willow. Don't leave here until you find out what needs to be done."

"I don't understand what she's talking about," his mother added, but the members of the Isanti Lodge nodded in unspoken affirmation.

"Follow it?" Ansel asked Nancy.

"Yes, and take her with you," Nancy Crain said pointing to Lacy.

JIIBAY HOLLOW EXISTED in a crease of land a mile away from Chippewa Beach. Geologists certainly would have noted the high rise of land around the shores of Lake Manitou, an indication of an ice age that first carved out the lakebed and then left a large ice block that formed the shores of the lake. The high sedimentary banks filled in around the glacier, leaving an uneven deposit of soil around it.

Sorcerers, on the other hand, would have noted that even farther below the surface, a barrier built by blood magic prior to the ice age made

Lake Manitou an anomaly on the earth. The colliding geological masses and later ice fields moved around the protective barrier, leaving moraine above and around the barrier like a treasure chest buried on a sandy beach.

With eleven hungry Tak-Pei still lurking inside of the magical barrier, Ansel approached Jiibay Hollow cautiously, making sure neither the black shadows nor the nearby neighbors took note as he cut across a marshy field to find the origins of the hollow.

"Is this it?" Lacy asked once the three-wheeler quieted to a purr.

He pointed beyond the swampy marsh. "Do you see that roof just beyond the hill? That's where my great-great grandfather Martin Nielson built a barn. Why there? It's like he knew or something."

"Knew what?"

"Knew what was here."

Ansel turned from the large field of marshy lowland that collected water from an area almost a square mile to the defined shore of Lake Manitou. From where the three-wheeler parked, the shoreline was higher in elevation, yet there was a gap that allowed the marsh to drain into the lake.

That's where I'll find it.

He led the three-wheeler to the gap on the northern horizon until the wetland produced a narrow creek. He parked the three-wheeler there and shut it off. "We'll start walking here. We don't want to miss it."

"Willows are the ones with long droopy branches, right?"

Ansel nodded. Migisi had already explained to him how dreamcatchers were made from willow trees because of their sacred, mystical qualities. Karson Luning found information on his computer network that willow trees were essentially immortal since they could produce shoots that were genetic clones, and while the old trunk rotted away, the new growth was the same tree with a new lease on life. The Isanti Lodge openly discussed the strange phenomenon of both the Fisher Mansion willow and the Sterling Junction willow, with Migisi pointing out that both trees were cuttings from an even older willow that grew at Jiibay Hollow.

It took considerable effort for Ansel and Lacy to stay near the creek, with brush, bushes, and trees choking the steep banks of the ravine. Branches in their faces soon became a canopy above their heads as the floor of the hollow dropped to meet the distant shore.

A ridge of rock thirty yards wide spread the creek out, creating a slight dam that forced the water into a waterfall, even though it was only a drop of about seven feet.

A single green canopy filled the area in front of this rocky ridge.

That's it.

Ansel studied the tree for a moment, seeing nothing but fronds. He looked around to see if there was an ambush, but he didn't even see the raven anymore. "We need to walk around the side. Keep your eyes on it while we climb down the ridge. If Migisi is right, it has magic that makes it blend in and disappear.

They walked around to the right, where the fronds of the willow touched stone. Pushing the branches aside, they crawled backwards down some of the boulders until they could look back at the ridge and the water trickling over the field of rocks.

There was a reason why he couldn't see the trunk. The willow tree was rooted another thirty yards downstream from the rocky ridge at a spot where the creek reformed. Its canopy covered an area larger than a normal house and nothing else grew under its majestic arms. Roots thick as a leg wrapped round shattered rock allowing a thick trunk to rise up into the space of the ravine. If Lacy stood on one side and Ansel on the other, they wouldn't have come close to being able to link their arms together. The air was still and humid under the willow, but the trickling water kept it fresh and cool.

Ansel felt Lacy's hand grab his as they recognized eyes were now watching them. His heart fluttered at the sight of two-dozen silent ravens perched in the shadowy branches of the willow. One creature, though, was different than the others. It sat near the lowest branches where the trunk divided. Almost twice the size of the other ravens, it filled the space between the divided branches with its dull, white feathers. At first, Ansel thought it might be an albino raven, but its black beak was as dark as its eyes.

"I'm glad you came," a voice said, but it was not the white raven that spoke.

Lacy now held tight to Ansel's left arm.

It took Ansel a moment to locate the origin of the voice. At the place where the willow canopy touched stone, a flat rock rested beside the trickling stream that continued to Lake Manitou. A shadowy figure sat upon the rock.

"Who are you?" Ansel asked, walking the fine line between terror and intrigue.

"Nope. We can't do that. One of you could get caught and tortured and you'd spill the beans about me. I can't tell you my name or even when this is happening. I'm sitting here in the future looking back upon the events of 1986. To me, you're just ghosts from the past. I sent the ravens to get your attention. Aren't they beautiful? Some of them are as old as time."

"You sent the raven to Levi?" Lacy asked.

"I had to warn him. I had to warn all of you."

"About what?" Ansel asked.

"The end of the world is coming. I'm close enough to the end to see it coming. I had nightmares about all the horrible ways the world was going to end until one day, a raven visited me, too."

"I don't see anyone else here," Ansel said. "Who sent you the raven?"

"I can't tell you that either, but I can tell you why she sent it: we lost. The world was destroyed by our enemies, and as our last ally slowly died, she crawled up to the willow tree to send me a raven with her last breath. Because of her, I'm sitting here with you today. I had to both help Lily and stop Lily. Do you know how hard that was? Once I got her to close the last loops, I got Levi to help with the rest."

"Is Levi alive?" Lacy asked.

"Does it matter? He made his sacrifice because of the love for his little brother Joey and the feelings he had for you. I thought it was uber-Romantic."

Uber? The figure doesn't speak like some dark deity from ancient times.

"I don't understand," Lacy continued. "Is he alive or not?"

"To me, you're all dead. None of you survive."

Ansel got it. Levi had gone under the willow tree also. "So Levi knew what he was doing because he came and visited you under here?"

"Bingo. It's so awesome meeting you Ansel. I like Mrs. Crain's version of Ansel, too, but in my version, you remind me of Hiccup from *How to Train Your Dragon*. Right now, you're this Viking warrior on the cusp of greatness."

"What do you mean by Mrs. Crain's version of things?" Ansel pressed.

"I already told you. If I didn't interfere and change things, the world would have slowly unraveled. Mrs. Crain dreamed it just like I used to dream it. Her visions that she wrote down were warnings about the world ending badly. Luckily, you listened to your raven, and so did Levi. I got you both to change the path. We won all the important battles of 1986. We had to give our enemies a couple of victories, but in the end, it will help us win the war. The two of you are going to have very important roles to play in coming years."

"What if I don't want to help you?" Ansel asked coolly.

"Sassy! I figured you'd say that. You're about to head back to New York, which scares me a little bit considering that's what you did in the Mrs. Crain's version of things. We'll take a short break for a few months—to let the dust settle a bit—and then we'll begin the next phase of this war. Come a little closer and I'll show you both what you have to fight for."

Ansel took hold of Lacy's arm. "I don't know..."

"Come on, Ansel. I'm not a Tak-Pei luring you in to rip you to shreds. I'm going to show you a glimpse into the future. I'll give you some motivation to continue the fight. You too, Lacy."

"How do you know the future?" she asked.

"I don't know the future. I know the past. The willow tree is like an island in the river of time. It's been here since the beginning and it lasts until the end. But when I take hold of the willow branches, I can see what happened around it. It's time travel without going anywhere. You two have been my private YouTube Channel. Come here. I'll show you."

Migisi, Leonard White Elk, and Ben LaBiche were grooming him for leadership, and acquiring knowledge would give him a weapon in the coming fight. He pulled Lacy with him, and the air grew darker as he neared the shadow.

My ancestors want me to do this.

The figure sitting upon the stone did not appear as clear as Lacy and had a strange transparency like a ghost. But now just a foot away, Ansel could see the figure better. With short hair and a fat face, the figure was androgynous, wearing a black hoodie.

Who is this?

"Lacy, I want you to go first," the hooded figure said. "I felt badly about changing your life so much, so this branch here will give you something worth fighting for."

"What do I do?" Lacy asked nervously.

"Just take hold of it and close your eyes. You'll see what the willow tree sees. Like it was for Nancy, it'll appear as a dream. I found this branch just for you."

"Should I?" Lacy asked him.

Ansel shrugged.

She took hold of the branch.

Nothing happened to her, and as Ansel watched her, he realized how beautiful Lacy really was. In Nancy Crain's version of his life, Lacy went on to find a husband who gave her children. She had a happy ending—at least until the end of the world came.

Lacy returned with a gasp. "He's alive. Ansel, Levi is alive. Eos has him. Holy shit. Is this real?"

The shadow's head shook. "It can all be taken away just as easily as I changed the narrative. I can sense someone else trying to use the memories of the willow tree. Someone is trying to undo everything I've done. Eos is about to join the fight, but so will other enemies. The shit's going to hit the fan, so to speak."

"I saw him," Lacy continued. "He's older, but I saw him. I saw Levi in my future."

The hooded figure continued, "For this reason, I can't have you go to St. Cloud State in a few weeks. You can't become some music director at some church somewhere. You're part of this now, Lacy Morrison. I need you to come back here in November and we'll finish the fight together."

Lacy nodded enthusiastically albeit wide-eyed and terrified.

"It's your turn, Ansel," the hooded figure said. The shadow took hold of another branch and handed it to Ansel. "Close your eyes and I'll show you why you need to come back in November."

Ansel closed his eyes.

When he opened them, he not only knew how he'd die, but he also knew who he'd give up his life to save.

"Do you trust me now?" the shadow asked.

Ansel nodded. "That's some gnarly stuff waiting for me." The twisted knot that'd been in his belly for the past decade suddenly released upon seeing his death.

CHAPTER EIGHTY-FOUR

Burying Joey

Old Copper Road
October 17, 1986

Joey MacPherson followed on the heels of Uncle Cameron, his volunteer guardian angel.

I made a pinky swear. Don't say anything.

Joey found himself studying Can Man's dead, white eye as the two did the household chores on the list for Friday. Today, it was dusting. Joey got to spray with the can of Pledge and Uncle Can Man followed with the rag. It took over an hour to dust the whole house, beginning with Levi's restored room, the second floor bedrooms—mostly the hallway and stairs—and then downstairs into the living room, dining room, and finally the big finish in the kitchen, where Great-Uncle Donnie sat with a box of donuts.

"So what do you boys got planned for the day?" Donnie asked as they put the Pledge back in the closet.

Can Man looked down at the list. "Air the comforters and blankets on the clothes lines."

"Well, I hate to tell you this, but you won't be able to do that with the drizzle we're getting today. You might want to just put them in the dryer. Ma used to drape them on the dining room chairs back in the day."

Uncle Can Man's face scrunched up as he contemplated the change in plans.

"Angie made you some sandwiches for lunch since I'm going to Fargo to check out that bull I told you about yesterday. David and his family are going to be bringing pizza and chicken tonight, so if you run out of things to do, just watch television with Joey until they show up at 5:00 PM. Got it?"

Can Man nodded as Donnie stood up.

Donnie extended his calloused palm to Joey, who gave him what he wanted with a hard slap. "Do I get a good bye?"

Joey shook his head no.

Levi had been gone for four months now, and during that time, Joey had effectively been a prisoner. His mother decided to home-school him, and she decided to take a long break for MEA just like the public schools. He liked working with Uncle Cameron more than being taught by his mom.

They were on their second comforter when a knock came at the front door. Joey listened from the safety of the dining room while Cameron answered the door.

"I found the note on your door, Cameron. Did you still want a ride to the reservation?" a man's voice asked.

The reservation!

This could be my chance.

"Oh no. It's Friday, isn't it? I'm supposed to empty cans on Friday. Oh no. Nicki asked me to watch Joey but I forgot all about collecting cans. It's Friday?"

Unlike all the other adults, Uncle Can Man never asked him any questions, which was refreshing. The sheriff, the priest, and the doctor all peppered him with questions during the summer. Uncle Cameron seemed to understand and never pressed him about his silence or what happened earlier in the summer. Now Joey empathized for the anxiety felt by his uncle.

"I can still bring you to the reservation," the man said. "I know how important your routine is to you."

"I'm supposed to watch Joey," Cameron insisted.

"Joey," the stranger began, looking at him. "My name is Ben LaBiche. I'm a friend of the family, and somewhere in the distant past, we connect to the same family tree. I have an idea of what you've been through, which is why I moved from the Rocky Mountains to Minnesota. Do you know the Rocky Mountains?"

Of course. Just because I don't speak doesn't mean I'm an idiot.

"What do you say, little man? Care to get out of the house for a while?"

This is a trap. They're trying to get me to talk. But Joey nodded for his own reasons.

"Supper is at five o'clock," Can Man insisted.

"We'll have you both back in time for supper. I promise."

JOEY HAD PROMISED also, which is why he remained wary for a trap. As they drove to the reservation, Joey revisited the harrowing events of the storm, including his lonely walk home from the cemetery. Today, the weather was much nicer and everything seemed a lot smaller and closer together than it had been in June.

They're going to try to trick you, he kept reminding himself.

But a trick never came.

Ten minutes after arriving, Ben LaBiche left them with the wagon full of cans.

"And now we crush them so they are easier to bring home," Cameron said. "Normally, I have my bicycle, but Mr. LaBiche said we can use his trunk. I like to step on the cans."

Joey liked stepping on the cans too.

They dumped out a bag of cans, and one by one, he smooshed them into little disks.

"I'm going to go fetch some more," Can Man said. "Keep stomping."

And that was the window of opportunity Joey hoped to get.

THE TRICKSTER ☬ 473

He crushed several more cans, but as Can Man continued down the road to another building, Joey paused.

Then he was running.

It wasn't hard to find his way.

He and Levi had floated down the river all morning until they came upon Turtle Island Jesuit School. Shortly after that, Joey spotted the blue clay.

Clay, Joey repeated. *That'll be my name when I start talking again. No more Joey. I'm Clay.*

But what was the other word?

Joey didn't even bother being sneaky this time: he darted right down the road instead of through the trees. This time, he saw Migisi's home was just charred remains.

Standing above the Blue Knife River, he took a moment to assess the situation. In his mind, he heard *Rocky IV* music playing and his arms ached, but even this bitter memory brought him a little joy. There were no villains or monsters lurking, so he descended the rocks.

Instead of looking for the blue clay weaving around boulders from the bank, a big post with a no trespassing sign marked the entrance of the cave.

Someone is always watching, Joey remembered, knowing the eyes could be human, monster, or electronic.

But he didn't care.

He just wanted to talk.

Pewabic!

That was the word Gigi Lily used.

The word for Clay.

Without the massive storm billowing overhead, entering the cave was much easier. He crouched as he entered and then sat on his haunches. No monsters came crawling out of the cracks nor did demons circle above his head. The cave was dark, without magical fire to light it, but it was also cold and quiet.

Joey now moved on his hands and knees, ascending the steep sidewall of the cave to a cavity that only allowed investigators an opportunity to send cameras into the space. Joey flattened and wiggled up into the crevice. The ceiling of the cave scraped against his back, but when he reached the top, the ground underneath sloped back down.

He descended the slope headfirst until his feet cleared the narrow passage, and then he spun around, hearing his own breathing in the small space.

"What are you doing here, bud?"

See, Levi is alive. Joey swallowed hard. "I had to make sure."

"We talked about this. You can't come back until it's time. You should still be counting. If you love me, you'd stick to the plan."

Joey couldn't figure out where the voice was coming from. It felt like his ears were hearing the words but it also felt as if it was only in his mind. "I do love you, but everyone thinks you're dead."

"I told you what would happen. You're risking everything by coming back here, though. For our plan to work, you've got to forget all about me. You can come back when the time is right. You remember what to look for?"

Joey remembered. "I'm sorry. Does it hurt?"

"I'm fine, Joey. I don't feel a thing. Remember, our big trick is making people think I'm dead, but after, we've got an even bigger trick don't we?"

The magic trick.

"Mom really misses you."

"I know, but I'm doing this for her, for Dad, for everybody. Once you graduate from high school, you can tell Sheriff Forsberg what I've done, but you need to keep our secret until then. Now...go back and don't tell anybody about me or the cave, okay?"

Joey nodded. "Okay."

He pivoted and crawled back up into the crevice, pausing before fully withdrawing to ask a perplexing question, "Levi...what happened to your body?"

CHAPTER EIGHTY-FIVE

Operation: Red Thunderbird

Madeira, Portugal
September 15, 1988

Madeira is a mountainous island located three hundred nautical miles off the western coast of Africa. Although the Portuguese island was settled in the 1400s, archeological evidence suggests the Vikings may have visited it as early as 900 A.D. While isolated from the world, the city of Funchal receives daily correspondence via a seaport and airport. A few miles up the volcanic slopes from Funchal, a state-of-the-art military facility also allows telecommunication to the rest of the world through its radar and satellites.

Tomas Dobie knew better than to get swept up into the grandeur of the island's beauty, but each morning as he sat on the edge of the porch overlooking the southern shore of the island, it still took his breath away. The cities and sewers of the world flowed and filled, but the accounts of the world seemed as inconsequential as the exploits of Bugs Bunny. The world was just a rumor.

Even so, Dobie stayed abreast. With a small bunch of bananas and a cigar for breakfast, he flipped through the local newspaper dated September 15, 1988. Although the news of the island was quaint, the world news were paraphrases of things that had happened in the past week, most with little impact on island life.

By the time he tossed his banana peels into the abyss of the deep valley below the porch, the real news was being brought to him on 8 ½ x 11" sheets of paper. Terry, one of the younger employees working for Triton at the complex, walked across the concrete porch, handed him the papers, and then lingered for a bit as if to bait Dobie into a conversation, which he didn't oblige.

Dobie quickly flipped through the printouts until he found a digital summary of the events at Alice Springs, Australia. Although September 15th was just a few hours old, on the other side of the world, it was still yesterday, and the news beamed into space and back down again carried news from the previous day, September 13th. In Hiawatha County, it was still the middle of Wednesday night. In Australia, where the news printout originated, the sun was setting on unexpected violence deep in the outback.

Dobie read with gripped fascination how park rangers had to disperse a strange gathering of New Age cultists who wanted to link hands around Ayers Rock to bring about some "harmonic convergence" that would usher in a new era for humanity. A few miles from the strange scene, a car accident claimed the lives of three tourists, Dr. Ramanuju Anwar and Dr. Mira Beckett, both genetic engineers from Mount Shasta, California. Their unnamed son had also died in the car accident.

Along with the car accident, a house fire claimed the lives of two local aboriginals, an elderly woman and her son, a disabled park ranger.

An eventful day for the news staff in Alice Springs.

"Son of a bitch," Dobie muttered to himself and crushed his cigar butt against the concrete. *It worked. We did it. We stopped that prophecy dead in its tracks. Take that, Charani Bessant!*

The Madeira complex appeared to be three separate facilities from the outside. The communications building, built by Triton and given to the municipal government, sat atop one of the tallest peaks overlooking the island. The large porch where Dobie smoked doubled as a helipad if necessary. While most of the telecommunication equipment sat squarely on the hill, Dobie entered a small building near the ravine. Even though isolated geographically from all the other interests of Triton, the powerful satellites connected him to the rubber tree plantations in Vietnam, the steel mills in Michigan, the studios in the U.K., his home in Albany, the Sinclair mansion on Oak Island, and even the surviving relatives in Hiawatha County.

Two subterranean tunnels led in opposite directions. One tunnel led down the slope toward the city of Funchal. The tunnel was a series of stairs that ran for about a thousand yards, emerging downslope at the older mansion complex. Usually, guests would be escorted via car to the mansion, but when the communication complex was built atop the peak to avoid unseemliness, the tunnel was built to protect from the elements.

The second tunnel led to the school with only one pupil.

When Dobie descended the stairs, he planned on staying for at least a day since it was almost a mile of poured concrete to the other side of the tunnel. The school complex had only been built a decade earlier, and many of the workers flown in to oversee construction believed they were building a prison, and, in a way, they were correct. From the porch where he read the news and smoked each morning, Dobie could see the roof, leaving him to only imagine what took place each day.

It doesn't concern me, Dobie had told himself repeatedly, but today, he read something that needed to be shared.

He emerged from the tunnel into the darkness of night. It had only taken him a few minutes to descend the stairs, but hidden behind a steep ridge that separated the center of the island from its coast, the school complex only saw sunlight for a few hours during lunch.

A security guard met him at the end of the stairs, and another nodded as he ventured into the rear entry of the three-story facility. He went right to the security room, where a team of four guards watched the monitors.

They acknowledged him with staggered glances and continued their surveillance of a figure sleeping on a bed that jutted out from the solid, padded walls.

An assistant entered the room with a cup of coffee and handed it to Dobie. "Miss Sinclair will be here in just a moment. Is there anything you need?"

"This should do it," Dobie said, sending the smiling assistant out of the room.

Maddy Sinclair held papers in her hands as she walked down the hallway from her living quarters to the security room. Dobie's eyes followed her passage in the monitors, but then his eyes wandered to another of the living quarters, where an old woman sat on the edge of her bed yawning.

Arin Michu? Machu Pichu? Aron-Miku. Yes, the old witch is named Aron-Miku.

A buzzer sounded and the door was opened for Maddy Sinclair.

"Good morning, Tom. Are you going to sort all of this out for me?" she asked, showing him her faxed documents.

"Operation Red Thunderbird was a success."

"I could tell from the twinkle in your eye, but what does that mean?"

After cleaning up the mess with the Marquette family and then giving Levi MacPherson a plausible death, he turned his attention to other enemies: Charani Bessant and Vendita. "Surely you know why we named it Red Thunderbird."

"Of course. The legend speaks of the thunderbirds hiding in the clouds, and when the boy with strange eyes lures the Horned Serpent into the shallow waters, the thunderbird descends to destroy his enemy. I am just confused by our ever-shifting metaphors."

"This time, we played the part of thunderbird, and when our enemy came out of the depths, we struck decisively. We won, Maddy. We've woken the ancient one and crushed our enemies. Everything that was taken from us back in 1962 has been put back in place. We killed Charani Bessant's bastard and crushed his prophet before the egg could hatch."

Despite his bluster about stopping Charani Bessant, he knew Maddy was struggling with her mission. "You'll figure out what's wrong with him. It's only been two years. Think of how long he's been sleeping. He's still a toddler learning how to control his new body."

"I appreciate your optimism, Tom, but something has gone terribly wrong."

The news from Australia still buoyed his spirits. "And now we have one less thing to worry about from the traitor Bessant. The little girl in the tree told the truth about the boy in Australia. All of Bessant's plans have been finished. Now, we hold the keys to the future."

Maddy put a hand to the side of his face, held it there for a tender moment, yet then with condescension, patted his cheek while shaking her head. "No we don't, Tom. The Alpha is angry, and from what Aron-Miku has been able to discover, it has something to do with a key. You don't happen to know anything about a missing key, do you, Tom?"

The key is lost.

The Water Drum has not been found.

But...but...we didn't need it. We won without magic and sorcery.

The old Finnish woman arrived at her spot on the other side of the security glass and gently tapped on the glass. The ancient god in the body of an eighteen-year-old stirred.

Dammit all, Dobie thought to himself. *Why do I know this conversation is going to end with me taking a plane back to Minnesota?*

EPILUDE

Right Beside Her

Cass County, MN
July 2029

Robin stayed off paved roads, darting across a few highways for the safety of quiet gravel roads. Driving a car, especially a stolen one, wasn't as hard as she'd seen in the movies, but she kept it around 20 miles per hour to be safe. When she approached Highway 64, which ran north to south, she no longer felt lost.

She paused at the intersection to gather her thoughts and look for her feathery friend.

Where are you?

The black raven glided over the car and perched in a tree across the road.

Robin smiled.

She waited until not a single car could be seen in either direction and then crossed. The raven took to wing and headed down the road toward the Crow Wing River. In both worlds, the river existed. In both worlds, Minnesota existed. Somewhere back in time, the Order of Eos or Charani Bessant's Team #WTF had altered history.

But Robin knew where Lake Manitou was supposed to be found.

Regardless of the gravel road, if she drove west, she'd run into the Crow Wing River as it also flowed from north to south. Just like with Hiawatha County, there were only a couple bridges that crossed the Crow Wing River, and if she found—

"Oh shit," Robin exclaimed as the right tire caught in the thick gravel along the edge of the road and began to pull the car toward the ditch. She jerked the steering wheel hard in the other direction, but as soon as the wheel came free from the deep gravel, her car was propelled to the other ditch.

For a moment, the tall grass seemed like it would be a soft landing, but a singular birch tree on the other side of a fence leapt into the grill of her car and Robin's head smashed into the steering wheel.

WHEN CONSCIOUSNESS RETURNED, a blonde girl sat upon the hood of her car, giggling. "They sent *you* to stop me? I can't even tell if you're a boy or a girl. You're so ugly."

Sommer Rae Chauvin.

Robin knew the little girl from her dreams. She'd seen her several times. When was it? Sommer was in the same grade as Joey MacPherson. She was always riding around Split Rock on her bicycle. Levi threw a rock at her. Wally Crain saw her riding her bike on the highway—after Lily Guerin's funeral. And she was hiding under the Fisher willow when the lightning struck.

Sommer's not real. I've been knocked unconscious.

Unlike the ghosts in her dreams, the apparition of Sommer filled Robin with fear. She honked the horn and flipped her off. "Get off my hood, you little brat."

"You're the one who got Levi to ruin everything, aren't you? It was you," Sommer said. Despite her angelic face, her eyes simmered with hatred.

"I'm fixing everything," Robin insisted.

"No, you left Lily to die at Lake Manitou. She came to me in my dreams and told me what you and Levi were doing. How could you keep her from Jean? How could you take Jude away from me?"

"Jude? I don't know anyone named Jude."

"You told Levi to burn down the Larson house knowing that Jude was supposed to move there. He was supposed to be the love of my life. He was the only thing that mattered to me and you TOOK HIM away from me. Now I'm going to destroy everything you love."

Even though she only saw a young girl, Sommer spoke like an angry teenager. "Good luck with that," Robin muttered. "I hate this world."

"Yes, but you love Hiawatha County, don't you?" Sommer's nose began to bleed and she wiped the blood off onto the top of her hand. It left a bloody smear across her face, making the first grader look even more sinister.

Why is this happening?

The answer filtered into her mind. Levi changed the story. He tricked Lily, Eos, and the Wintermaker in order to do what was needed to save the world from doom and destruction, but Lily didn't go down without a fight. In her final days, she reached out to Sommer Chauvin through her mother Molly. Lacy Morrison had even intercepted a few of those messages.

"What do you want?"

"I'm going to stop you," Sommer muttered.

Robin had been bullied her whole life, but she wasn't about to be bullied by an apparition from her imaginary world.

Wait...I know what's missing. The doll!

The good Sommer has a doll. This is the bad Sommer. "Where's your friend? Becca? Is that what you named her? Why isn't she with you anymore?"

Now Sommer all but snarled. She leaned forward, crawling on all four to the windshield. Drops of blood fell from her nose as she leaned forward. "She won't talk to me any more. Did you do that, too? Did you steal her from me?"

"No, I didn't steal her. She came to me. Lily came to me also, when she realized what a mistake she'd made. Both of them like me more than they like you. Becca, Lily, and I…we're not going to let you stop us from fixing this."

A black raven fell from the sky, landing on the young girl's back, pecking furiously until the apparition vanished with banshee screams, leaving only the raven.

Robin felt her own nose begin to throb, and when she touched it, blood began to flow.

She was conscious.

She was stuck in a ditch somewhere between Cass and Wadena County. The birch tree had been knocked over at the car bumper, and aside from the crumpled grill, the car was still running.

Robin shifted the car into reverse and stomped onto the accelerator.

The car responded and went bouncing out of the ditch with such suddenness that she almost rolled across the road and into the other ditch, but she stepped on the brakes and slid to a stop.

She inspected her bloody nose in the rear-view mirror and her bloody shirt.

There's no hiding this. I might as well make the best of it.

Robin put the car in drive and began rolling toward Hiawatha County.

If it's a fight you want, little girl, it's a fight you're going to get. I'm not going to let you undo all of my hard work. I'm not going to let you take Hiawatha County from me.

THE END

The Dreamcatcher Chronicles
will continue with Book Four:
THE SUMMERBIRD

Robin Berg's Dream Journal
"Who's Who in Hiawatha County"
#1986 People

<u>Those who Live on Old Copper Road (Starting at Split Rock)</u>
The Forsberg Family: #bearclan #guardians
    BIFF-the sulking hero. #gingershavenosoul!
    Edna-a <u>Haggard</u>, his mother.
    Julia, his younger sister. #livinginbaltimore

The MacPherson Family: #sonoftheparson
    GAVIN-now balding. #stoicfather
    NICOLE-now impossible. #overbearingmom
    Benjamin-oldest son
    Leah-oldest daughter
    Reuben-brother
    Levi-the one from Lily's dreams. #trickster
    Daniel-wants to be a farmer
    Joey-also from the loop. #clay
    Donnie MacPherson-Gavin's Uncle
    Angie MacPherson-Gavin's Aunt

The Guerin Family: #skullclan #ravenclan
    LILY GUERIN-Tewapa Tew Asibikaashi. Now super old. Mixed heritage. Maternal line=Lakota. Paternal line=Anishinaabe. Married Jean Nicholas Guerin (d. 1910). #thefirehandler #thespider #heroandvillain
    Louis-her angry son. Kinda messed up.
    Hannah Guerin, Levi's grandmother.
    Charlotte, Levi's old maid aunt. #siouxfalls
    Cameron Guerin, Levi's Uncle. #odd. #oneeye

The Nielson Family: #martenclan #warrior #cloudchampions
    Ansel-freshman from New York. #sonofjimmy
    Aurora Archibald-his mother
    Thomas Archibald-his step-father
    Ursula Hermann-his maternal grandmother
    Tonya-Jimmy's oldest child. #crackheadfromchicago
    Faye Carpenter, Ansel's aunt. #southdakota
    Alexandra Mollitor, his aunt. #granitefalls

The Berg Family: #poorwhitetrash #sirnotappearinginthisfilm

The Crain Family: #craneclan #leaders
    WALLY CRAIN, a retired oil deliveryman.
    Nancy, his wife. An English teacher and writer.
    Cindy, Margaret, Janet- his daughters.
    Garrett Johnson-Wally's Grandson

<u>The Order of Eos: #menofthedawn #badguys</u>
THE DELHUT FAMILY: #American branch #Detroit
    ROSS DELHUT-Powerful head of the Order.
    #northstarsteel #tritoncorp

THE SINCLAIR FAMILY: the English branch of Eos.
    Aleister Sinclair-old school. #musicmogul
    Maddy Sinclair-the heir
    Aron-Miku-a Finnish witch
    Aamu Huuhtanen-a Finnish witch.
    Shamar Tietaja-a Finnish shaman.
    Tom Dobie-family enforcer
    Robert Kirkpatrick-henchman

THE TERRONT FAMILY: the French branch of Eos. #rubber
    plantions
    Alphonse Lavasseur-family enforcer
    Cousin Val-the intended Avatarati #luckytobealive

THE LOCAL GUYS: #tritoncorporation
    Haggards—just Edna?
    Sean Stewart—business partner of Triton
    Myles Stewart—his surviving son. #someonetoremember
    Al Marquette—owner of Marquette mortuary.
    Todd Marquette—his son.
    Marion Marquette—his daughter-in-law
    Stephanie and Nate—his grandchildren

TEAM: WTF?: #enemyofmyenemy
    CHARANI BESSANT—the guy in the red thunderbird.
    #betrayedEos. #vendita? #wheredidhego?

Those Along the Blue Knife River:
    MIGISI ASIBIKAASHI—a Mizheekay Reservation elder. Son of Big Squeak and Winnie Weber. Trained as a Midewiwin. Not a Wabeno. Possible Jessikkid.
    Norval Riel—former superintendent of the Turtle Island Jesuit School. MBO president.
    Sakima Riel—Norval's son. School Principal.
    Cindy Goodday—MBO Board
    Kristi Jackson—MBO Board
    Faron LaRoque—MBO Board
    LeRoy Schrader—MBO Board

Those who Live in British Columbia
    Leonard White Elk—Son of Fawn Chevreuil
    Russell White Elk—his brother
    Dennis LaBiche—his elder half-brother
    Clyde LaBiche—his half-brother
    Vernon LaBiche—his half-brother
    Ben LaBiche—Son of Dennis

<u>Those Who Live in Split Rock</u>
The Fisher Family: #Fishclan #intellectuals
    Betsy Luning-his only child. Married Marlin Luning.
    Elmer Johnson-the groundskeeper and bait shop owner.

The Luning Family: #Loonclan #leaders
    Chuck Luning-Former combat pilot. #mayor
    Helen Luning- Sister of Minnesota Viking Ellis Redding.
    Karson Luning-their disabled son.

The Chauvin Family: #ragingcajuns
    Mark Chauvin-recent arrival to Minnesota
    Molly (Knutson) Chauvin-works at nursing home. Survived the bus accident in 1962. #deadsister
    Penelope Chauvin-dark-haired oldest daughter
    Sommer Chauvin-blonde-haired youngest daughter.
    Gary Mackenzie-Jesuit priest #Bigmack

Hiawatha County Sheriff's Department
    Brian Forsberg-Sheriff
    Geri and Freki-His guard dogs
    Ron Spears-Emergency Management Director
    Dave Ribbar-Chief Deputy
    Griff Harper-Lieutenant
    Ray Irvin-Detective
    Darlene Van Zanten-Detective
    Mia Donaldson-Secretary
    Charlene Dunn-Dispatch
    Katie Lopez-Dispatch
    Scott Gerber-Deputy
    Jared Tavares-Deputy

Everybody Else:
  Lacy Morrison-Senior at Split Rock High School
  Sherry Lucas-Waitress at the Boondocks Café
  Percy Thorgard-Reporter with North Star News
  Andrew Ross-BCA Investigator
  David Droshe-BCA Investigator
  Roland Smith-a local carpenter
  Carey "Scat" Jensen-a river rat
  Ken Uselman-Chief of the Fire Department.
  Grady-a airplane mechanic

ABOUT THE AUTHOR

Imagine the love child of Rambo and Ma Ingalls. That's Jason Lee Willis. Overly nurtured by his Vietnam War veteran father and Lutheran church secretary mother, he grew up in the fantasy realm of South Dakota before his exodus brought him to mysterious Minnesota for college.

His love of mythology and storytelling led him to a career as a high school English teacher, where he guided his students in writing poetry, short stories, and even screenplays. As a professional storyteller, he's done historical lectures, book talks, radio segments, podcasts, and a video channel on YouTube, The Minnesota Alchemist.

Willis currently lives in Minnesota, where he lives the life of a hobbit by gardening, writing, walking around barefoot, wearing vests, fishing, and going on adventures with his wife, Julie.

YouTube: https://youtube.com/@mnalchemist
Facebook: https://www.facebook.com/jasonwillisnovels/
Website: https://jasonleewillis.wixsite.com/novels
Instagram: https://www.instagram.com/minnesota_alchemist/

Milton Keynes UK
Ingram Content Group UK Ltd.
UKHW021934281024
450365UK00017B/1076